Checked and Balanced

Aurora Steinhart

CHECKED AND BALANCED

AURORA STEINHART

PLAYLIST

I LISTEN TO SO MUCH DAMN MUSIC WHEN I WRITE. UNFORTUNATELY, I'M NOT ABLE TO CATALOGUE IT ALL HERE. IT WOULD JUST BE SO MANY PAGES. SO NOW I HAVE RESORTED TO QR CODES FOR SUCH THINGS.
ANYWAY.
ENJOY THIS HORRIFICALLY CHAOTIC PLAYLIST FOR CHECKED AND BALANCED. IT'S A MESS. JUST LIKE ME AND JUST LIKE THIS BOOK. BUT I THINK WE KNOW BY NOW THAT AURORA DOESN'T DO ORGANIZED. IT'S ALWAYS A MESS OVER HERE AND THAT'S HOW WE LIKE IT. DON'T WE, GIRLS? 😉

CHIRP CHIRP
IT'S A PUCKING GLOSSARY

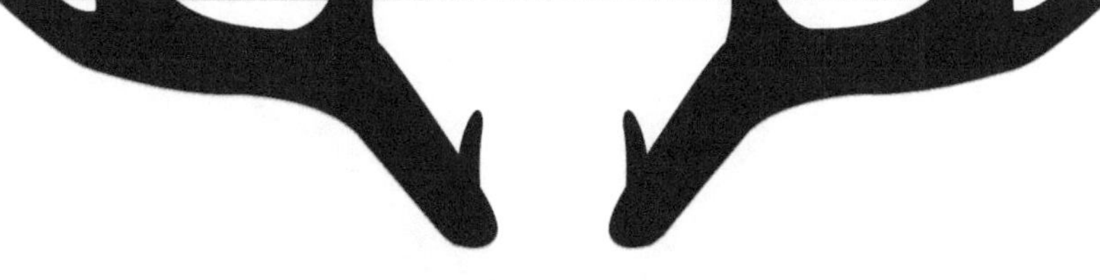

Hockey is its own world. And with a world of its own comes a language you may not understand.

If you watch Letterkenny or Shoresy, these characters are heavily inspired by that.

If you don't, you're going to be very confused, as this is not your normal hockey romance.

And if you've never watched a hockey game, I implore you, just go take a gander at one and come back to me.

Shit's fucking great.

Anyway, without any further ado, I give you some hockey lingo.

• Beaut – a player loved not only for their skills but their personality. Just an all-around solid human.

• dangle – the act of stick-handling

• flow – long hair, typical amongst hockey players

• celly – a celebration, especially after a goal

• dirty/filthy – great, amazing, fantastic

• bender – a new skater, one who bends their knees in while they learn to skate

• tendy – goaltender

• players calling out numbers (two-two, three-three) – just a condensed version of their jersey numbers. So instead of Thirty-Three. Sometimes it's three-three.

PLAY BY PLAY
THE SPICY CHAPTER LIST

If this is your first time reading one of my books, this here is a staple in all of them.

They go by different names.

"Table of Cuntents" in **Elevated Ambitions**
"Cock Docket" in **Hunted by Fate**
(shameless self-rec, this is my book I can do those things here)

It's a little list of all the spicy chapters in this book. That way you can either go read them, because you're a horny degenerate like me.

Or you can skip them.

But I reckon if you're picking up this book, I doubt you're here to skip the spicy scenes.

So without further ado, here are all the smutty little scenes your heart desires in one neat little package.

- Chapter 12

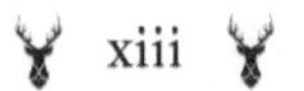

DISCLAIMER
I FUCKED AROUND
AND FOUND OUT

This is an experiment. This whole book.

It's just for fun. I'm an author. I like to just write and have fun with it when I can.

Granted, this book had its boot on my throat and beat me senseless for like nine whole months.

Crazy, right? This book tortured me because, apparently, I am incapable of writing without a plot. Go fuckin' figure I guess, shit.

I wanted to write a hockey romance on a whim. I wanted to write a book where I didn't advertise it much. I didn't send out ARCs. ((Edited to add, I did in fact send out ARCs. Everyone clap.))

I didn't get an editor for this book. And that will more than likely be apparent.

But I can not stress enough how little plot this has. I need you to understand that this is just a vibey, horny little read. It's character-driven. Like, if you're looking for something that is gonna blow your mind, you won't find it here. THIS BOOK

IS JUST HORNY. SO HORNY. THE WHOLE THING. IT'S PROBABLY UNREALISTIC, IT PROBABLY DOESN'T MAKE SENSE, BUT IT HAS LIKE... I DON'T KNOW PROBABLY REALLY GOOD SMUT??? You be the judge.

This is not a literary masterpiece; this is not something that is gonna change your life. We're talking a fuckin' 75/25 smut to plot ratio here, people. It's not rocket science, it's just smut.

This is JUST SMUT. I NEED YOU TO REMEMBER THAT. I JUST WANTED TO WRITE UNHINGED SPICE FOR THE FUCK OF IT, OKAY? <u>PLEASE UNDERSTAND.</u>

<u>I'm JUST A HORNY LITTLE SMUT AUTHOR WHO WANTS TO WRITE UNNECESSARY SMUT.</u>

I wanted to try out some character personas and tropes I'd never done before.

Therefore, there is a breeding kink in this book. **<u>A BREEDING KINK.</u>**

HE TELLS HER HE WANTS TO GET HER **<u>PREGNANT.</u>** SO IF YOU DON'T FUCK WITH **<u>BREEDING KINKS</u>** PLEASE JUST BACK OUT NOW I BEG OF YOU.

YES, **<u>A BREEDING KINK</u>** OKAY. I'VE ALWAYS WANTED TO WRITE ONE SO WE'RE TRIALING IT HERE FRIENDS, WE'RE DOING THE DAMN THING.

And like look, here's the thing. Your girl has a breeding kink (shocking!!! wow!!!). Whoops cats out of the bag, too late to grab it.

Anyway, uhhhhhh, I was terrified to write it because in my little pea brain, I said, "Okay so maybe the girlies like a breeding kink. But they're going to think the dialogue is weird/gross/hot. They're not as lost in the sauce as my horny little degenerate ass brain is. I'm dumb, why am I doing this? Fuck! FUCK!"

SO. Gunnar is in fact me in a certain... chapter because uh. I don't know, how the fuck do you write about a breeding kink you've never written before even if you... love it??

Because like. Shit, this is vulnerable work here. I'm telling you people I have a breeding kink and then explaining, in detail, how I like it. That's just a wild concept if you think about it, ya know? SO it was a tad nerve wracking.

I don't write stuff that I personally don't like in books.

So I'm not giving my characters like a latex gimp suit fetish situation. (No shame if you do, but it's just not your girl's thing.)

Either WAY! IT WAS HARD FOR ME TO WRITE OKAY. ONLY BECAUSE IT SCARED ME AND I DON'T KNOW IF THE GIRLIES LIKE A BREEDING KINK HOW I DO. AND MAYBE YOU DO AND THAT'S FUCKING SLAY BUT LIKE I WAS SCARED OKAYYY.

It's just a silly, horny time. There are so many smut scenes because Gunnar is so hot; I needed as many chapters of these two as I could write. He's probably my favorite MMC to date.

If you accept that, then maybe you'll like it.

Your local neighborhood smut peddler,
Aurora Steinhart

P.S. Please do not misinterpret the caps lock for condescension. It's more like desperation because I tried to warn y'all and I don't wanna hear fuck all about how I didn't warn you.

"Oh Aurora, there's a breeding kink in here! He wants to get her pregnant! This book sucks!"

YES.

I KNOW.

I WARNED YOU.

This is probably like a 3-star book at best, okay?

And if you dooooo like this book, and think it is better than that, that doesn't
SO... NOW THAT THAT'S OUT OF THE WAY...

I give you "Checked and Balanced"
A hockey romance experiment by Aurora Steinhart

Chapter Eight

Art by: Olivia a.k.a
@liverosess on
Instagram

CHAPTER ONE
GUNNAR HAYZE

The crash of a hard body slams into the ice. But holy *fuck*, I'm sure glad it isn't mine.

"Oh shit, didn't see ya there. Sorry bud," I tell the opposing player as I offer a hand to him.

The asshole glares at it for a moment before he grabs it and I yank him to a stand. He's probably about a buck fifty soaking wet, so he jerks a bit as I pull him up a little too hard. As I smile, I feel it morph. The grin on my cheeks turns devious before I check him again, slamming him into the boards.

"Get fucked two-two!" I call out as I skate away.

There is no better feeling than pummeling a piece of shit who's had his eye on me for the entire game. Over and over, that dumb motherfucker came for me.

A check here, a nudge there. He's not even half my size, but he tries — and fails — to check me. The idiot wants to run into a wall. I'll give him a fucking wall to run into.

Plus, what better way to secure my position on this new team than to wreck this pretentious lil' bender?

The crowd around us loses their minds as I skate back into

the game, looking for the puck. When a body slams into me again. I turn around to see the same dumbass floundering on his back against the ice.

"Comin' back for round two, eh? Yeah, they usually do." I laugh as I glide away, zeroing in on where our captain has the puck.

I get lost watching the puck until I see that stupid twenty-two again. This time, he's going for my center. I beeline straight for him, barreling my shoulder into his body with a hard check into the boards.

The stands go wild again with cheers because they love a good check. And I am always ready to cash 'em.

I press my body hard against his, holding him against the glass so my captain has a second to get past me with the puck.

"Hear that? They love watching me fuck you," I say as I shove him one more time. The glass rattles as he slams into it again, and I glide backwards on the ice.

And wouldn't you know it?

I reckon he enjoys being fucked.

He turns around, glaring at me, before he shoves his stick to the ice and whips his hands out like he thinks he's Wolverine. Instead of claws, however, he merely rids himself of his gloves.

I mirror him, tossing my stick away and throwing my gloves off.

"Fuck, d'ja bring protection this time, two-two?! I don't think you could handle three rounds, bud!" I call out with a laugh.

A hard press of my skate sends my body careening into his, where I grasp the collar of his ugly green and white jersey before bringing his face into my fist. His helmet skews on his head and he fights to keep his eyesight.

He lands a nasty right hook on my cheek, and *fuck*, does it sting. But I know how to take a punch.

My lip splits under his hit, and I slide my tongue across it, dragging the blood along my teeth. A feral, bloodied grin is my only response as I land another solid punch right into his mouth. He sends one into my jaw, and I laugh to throw him off.

"Harder! I like it rough!" I call over the raucous cheering around us.

His face contorts in a startled grimace, and my next punch lands on the underside of his jaw. The clacking of his teeth results in a pained grunt from him as the crowd's cheers drown out everything around us. Which includes the yelling of the referees. His helmet falls off his head to hit the ice with a loud clatter, and I'm gripped by the hands of a ref.

I spit blood onto the ice as I lock eyes with my new friend and blow him a kiss. His eyes are rabid with confusion as the ref pulls him away.

"The fuck's your issue thirty-three!?" he yells as he fights the hold the ref has on him.

He's bold, I'll give him that. If he had the balls to challenge me like this, he should use them to get his team a goal. His once clean face is now marred with blueish-purple bruising around his cheeks and a bloody set of teeth.

"I've gotten better hits from a bong!" I yell back as I push back against the ref that's pulling me from the fight.

"Fuck you!" he calls back.

"Your fuckin' coach know you're out here?! I bet they're looking for you!" I laugh.

The ref attempting to haul me to my side of the rink is struggling with containing me, considering he's several inches shorter than me.

Unfortunately for him, I have the advantage of always seeing my opponents.

"Shove it, thirty-three!" one of the other team's players yells as they skate past the ref and me.

"Did your mom tell you to say that?" I call back to them.

I swipe my tongue across my lip to rid it of the blood as the ref snatches my shoulder to turn me to face him.

"Get your shit together Hayze, or you're going to the box," he grits through his teeth. He shoves me away, and I give him a playful smile.

"Aw, come on, you know you love a good tussle!" I pant in response as I lean down to grab my stick and gloves.

"His helmet fell off, you know the fucking rules," he calls as he rolls his eyes and skates away from me.

"But all the best fun is illegal!" I hold my stick between my legs as I press my gloves back on, when I feel the heat of someone's annoying stare on me.

I look up to see twenty-two glaring at me with contempt.

He turns away, but not before I slap the ice with my stick to grab his attention again. A sly smirk forms on my lips as I place my twig between my legs to stroke it at him.

His only response is a headshake before he skates away.

A loud whistle sounds in the arena, along with the deafening sound of the buzzer. I look at the ref as he straightens his spine and turns to the crowd.

"TWO-MINUTE MINOR PENALTY! SEATTLE STAGS, NUMBER THIRTY-THREE, GUNNAR HAYZE. UNSPORTSMANLIKE CONDUCT." The ref's voice blares through the speakers, echoing in the arena as his arm comes out to point at me.

And with it comes the loud boos of Seattle Stags fans and angry rings of cowbells.

I throw my hands up at the ref before he points a finger at

the box. With a gentle push of my skate, I float to the edge of the rink, step onto the box's ledge, and kick the slush off my blades before I take a seat on the bench. The referee shakes his head in annoyance as he closes the door.

The fans continue to hoot and holler around me, and I take a moment to wave at them.

My new teammates continue to chirp at the opposing team as they skate and miss another shot at our goalie.

"Come on, forty-five, your mom handles a stick better than you do!" Leroy shouts from the bench.

"If it had a set of balls, I bet you'd know what to do with it, eighty-two!" Banks–our captain—chirps.

As I wait for my penalty to be over, I continue watching the game, still dumbfounded to be sitting here.

I never thought I'd make it to the pros. I've been playing minor league for years. Some D1 hockey in college, with Banks, actually. But I've been playing hockey since I could walk. Somehow, the Seattle Stags noticed me and scooped me up. I still remember getting the call that they had picked me up. Part of me has to owe it to Banks because I know he had something to do with it.

It's hard for me to believe I'm playing for a team I've idolized my entire life. Even if I'm in the box right now, I don't care.

I'm livin' my fuckin' dream.

"The fuck is your issue, Hayze?! Your first game and you get boxed?!" Coach Bubbles yells from the middle of the now damp and musty locker room.

We won the game, of course. I wouldn't have accepted this

team if we weren't good. But Coach is mad about the scrap. Which is insane because fights in hockey are just part of the culture.

Someone disrespects your teammate. You get a scrap.

Someone steps to you in a shitty way. Tussle.

Regardless, fights are just a way of life on the ice.

But Bubbles here didn't want me to be a goon in my first game.

That's fair. But *I'm a goon*. That's just what we *do*.

We call him Coach Bubbles because his last name is Dawn. It seems to rile him up.

I've come to learn that on this team, they like to play jokes on the admin. And they seem to be good sports about it.

"He wanted to ride my ass, so I gave him something to ride." I shrug before I lean down to unlace my skates.

The other members of the Seattle Stags don't look nearly as mad as Coach. Some aren't even listening as they remove their gear, shoving it into the big personalized cubbies we sit in front of.

"I brought you to this team because you're a solid fucking defender. And you know I don't mind a good fight, but give it a game or two first, Jesus." Coach sighs as he grips the meat between his eyebrows in frustration.

I roll my eyes and cross my arms over my bare chest as I dip my chin. Flicking my tongue out, I catch the silver chain with a stag pendant on it. It's a good luck charm of sorts, so I'm rarely ever caught without it.

I honestly can't even remember the last time I removed it.

While it functions as a good luck charm, it comes in handy as a thing to fiddle with. Which means I'm constantly chewing on it.

I grab the chain between my teeth; sliding my tongue back

and forth mindlessly against it as Coach's words play in the background of my thoughts.

The group of us have stripped out of our jerseys, leaving us all bare chested. As they do, I'm reminded that I happen to be the biggest motherfucker on this team. Six-six and built out of pure muscle and grit, the rest wouldn't stand a chance if I had to throw them against the ice. Luckily, they don't have to worry about that.

Coach's voice finally breaks through my thoughts, and I catch the last of his spiel.

"If you can't get a handle on your shit, I'm benching you next game."

I throw my hands up in surrender. "Take me to dinner before you fuck me, Bubbles," I murmur against the chain in my teeth.

He rolls his eyes. "Anyway, be decent. My daughters have to come in."

Daughters, you say?

Curiosity gets the better of me, causing my eyebrow to raise as I clasp my hands in front of me. Leaning over, I rest my elbows on my knees, waiting with rapt attention. The chain is a solid grounding force for me as I slide my tongue against it.

Coach whistles to the door, where two females enter. One is wearing a massive Seattle Stags jersey, who grins and titters with glee. I recognize her from earlier. When she was giving me my gear, she said she's the equipment and social media manager.

The other is in a tight black and white pinstriped pencil skirt and suit jacket. She looks all business and is not even the slightest bit excited to be here. I don't know if I'd met her yet, but boy, would I like to.

"The rest of you guys know Tiana and Charlotte. But

Hayze here hasn't had the chance to meet both of them properly," Coach says with an annoyed sigh.

"Hi! I'm Charlotte! You guys played an amazing game today!" she praises as she giggles uncontrollably. She has her tight brown curls pulled into a ponytail at the back of her head, and it seems as if both of them have bright green eyes.

They're stunning, to be honest, but the other one... the business one...

She's *radiant*.

Her curls are perfectly wound little coils. Brown ringlets that have little streaks of gold in them. Black square glasses sit on her sharp pointed nose, and she presses them up as they fall slightly down the bridge. While her nails are a pretty nude-pink shade and tapered to a long, rounded point.

I don't even hear what else Coach is saying as I stare unabashedly at the business one. I reckon that's Tiana.

She doesn't pay us any mind. If anything, her plump, full lip almost curls in disgust.

Don't care. She's a fuckin' treat and I'm trying to lick my fingers clean.

"Hayze, if you stare any harder, your fuckin' eyes will pop out of that skull." Coach's voice breaks through my stare.

I clear my throat and shake my head as I throw my hands behind my head and lean back against my cubby. "Sorry Coach, I thought I saw an angel," I say through the chain gripped between my teeth.

A sly grin pulls at my lips as I look up and down Little Miss Business. Her stony demeanor pulls me in like a moth to a flame, and I admire every bit of her before Coach's voice brings me back again.

"Touch her and you'll have to pee through a straw."

I give him a small salute. "Aye, aye, captain."

"My name is Tiana. I'm the legal liaison for the Seattle

Stags. My purpose here is to get your asses out of trouble if you maim a player on the ice and they sue you. I also provide legal counsel for whatever bullshit you may have gotten yourselves into." Her voice is sweet, like honey, but hard as a rock.

Shit, just like I am. Thank fuck for these thick pants.

She has a perfectly tapered, tight waist and slender, yet rounded hips. Her suit jacket strains where her generous breasts press against it, and I try to breathe through the hypnotizing effect she's got on me.

"Ti...an...uhhh..." I say out loud as my eyes roam the ceiling in thought.

The way her name rolls off my tongue. It's a damn sin. I wrap the chain around my tongue with a flick as my arms come back to my chest and I lean my head back to watch her.

Tiana side eyes me with a grimace, her eyes trailing my body up and down before she turns back to the rest of my teammates.

"You all know the drill. Don't bother me unless you have legal troubles. It's the first game of the season, so please, just try to behave for a few more months. I don't want to do any more paperwork than I need to. My office is down the hall, and I swear to God if any of you knock for anything other than a traffic violation, I'll sue you myself."

A feisty one. I like it. A lot more than I think I should.

I rarely go for the business types. But she's got some fire to her that drives me nuts.

"Banks, you were a fuckin' beaut out there today. Tremendous goals," Coach says as he turns his attention back to us.

Adrian Banks.

He really is a thing of beauty, that man. We went to college and played on the same team together for a bit. But when he got picked up by the Stags, we lost contact for a while. I always cheered him on from my couch when I could, though.

He's a big boy, thanks to growing up on a farm, but nimble. Quick on his skates and fast with a stick. From my understanding, his family owns a ranch wrangling cattle somewhere over yonder, so he's got that down-home country boy strength. Surely has given him an advantage on the ice.

He gives Coach a humble nod before he continues to tug off his socks.

Coach keeps giving kudos where kudos are due, and eventually his voice drowns out in the back of my skull as I lock my gaze on the beaut next to him.

She's watching him speak, and I can't hear a damn thing he's yammering about. Every inch of her is beautifully sculpted, as if she was made by Michaelangelo. Right down to the scowl on her face.

I haven't had a lady in quite some time. With D1 hockey, the draft, and trying to get to the pros, I never had time for a commitment like that. I had too much to grind for. Maybe some hook-ups here and there, but nothing solid.

In all honesty, I didn't want anything, and neither did they. It was just a little fun when I had time. I'm a massive, attractive guy who plays hockey. Puck-bunnies just seem to love me.

But I also don't want a puck-bunny. Not when they have such a thirst for sticks.

If you get my drift.

But this little lady looks like she couldn't care less about the room of meat she's currently in.

Something about that gives me a little rush. Plus, she looks like she would be fun to mess with. I enjoy poking people and she would be a treat to poke at.

Something is hiding under the surface of that little broody expression, though. And *I'm* going to get to the bottom of it.

CHAPTER TWO
TIANA DAWN

I never enjoy coming into the locker room after a game. The humidity of the melting ice, the combined scent of said ice and sweaty man. Not to mention, that many bodies in one area? Hate it. Can't stand it.

Who in the hell wants to walk into a room with a bunch of giant men drenched in their nasty sweat?

Not fucking me.

But here I am. Out of legal obligation to meet a client I hadn't had the chance to formally meet. My father said he signed a new defender, and I was too busy with other obligations to meet him when he was signed. Of course, he had to bring me in after their first game.

I pay little attention to the games or the players; I'm just the one who tries to keep them out of trouble. I wouldn't even be here for the game today if my dad hadn't asked me to come. Charlotte is the one who's always been obsessed with all the ins and outs of the game.

I've always taken more of my mother's route. She's the owner and head attorney for a large sports firm here in Seattle.

So, she's usually busy dealing with some of the bigger names in sports. I'm just the go-between for the big firm and our team. If there is something that requires more heavy lifting, she's the one who handles it. Signing players isn't in my wheelhouse. But I'm usually there for signings so that I can meet them and give them my end of the deal when it comes to my job in the arena.

One of the heavy-liftings under my mother's jurisdiction was this brute.

Even currently, I try to ignore him, as he won't stop ogling me from his spot on the bench. But I can't get the pressure of his stare off of me. It's intense, like a heated brand.

As much as I hate the staring, it's also strange to be noticed this way. I haven't really been interested in men for a long while. I have been more than happy running my life without a needy thing clinging to me every second.

Men are annoying. A nuisance. You're too much or too little. Too loud or too quiet. It never seems to be quite good enough for them. And don't get me started on how most men find a lawyer intimidating, because most men don't enjoy being told what to do.

That's fine. Fewer men for me to deal with in the future. Which I don't have the time for. Not to mention, he's a client.

Forbidden.

Which makes my aversion to him that much higher.

Although, even I can appreciate a set of muscles. I have eyes, even if I'm not interested, and this guy is packed with them. He may be the biggest guy on the team. I don't think I've ever seen a man this... large?

Despite that, his little quips irk me. He's already hit on me twice in the three seconds I've been in the room, along with his unabashed, shameless gawking.

I sincerely hope I don't have to deal with him much in the future. The fact he got boxed in the first game sets alarm bells off in my head. He doesn't seem like the type to give a shit about legalities. And if I have to deal with his bullshit, I'm making dad get rid of him.

A liability is a liability, no matter how much of a *"beaut"* they are.

Eventually, my dad's little pep talk ends. First-season rundowns are always the longest, and I am sincerely grateful to not have to listen to another one of these until next year.

As soon as I hear his telltale ending, I all but sprint out of that humid locker room.

The strange tinge of ice, hockey gear, and man sweat. All of it is a sensory nightmare. Not to mention the sounds of everyone removing their gear, or the scrape of their skates and the small murmurs of conversation that goes in and out of focus.

I abhor it in every sense of the word.

The tip-tapping of my heels helps settle some of the overwhelming sensations as I beeline straight for my office. The back halls of the arena aren't open to any of the patrons visiting the game, so I can walk there without intrusion. All the while, I fantasize about the hot shower I'll take when I get home. God, and the feel of my heated blanket as I cuddle up on my couch with a good book.

I haven't been able to relax in months, with the season starting. Which makes the week before the first game a nightmare, and I'm glad this part is over, so it can start getting back to normal.

My office is far away from any prying eyes. It's one reason I agreed to this position. I wanted a small little cave all my own, where no one could bother me.

Entering the little room, my desk sits front and center. Right in front of the back wall. On that back wall, right behind my office chair, is a corkboard with various pinned notes and reminders. Along the right wall when you enter are a few metal filing cabinets, with a plain back corner.

It's extremely... male... but it's mine.

That's all that matters to me. Aesthetics be damned.

I round my desk, grabbing my black tote from under it to place on the large calendar covering the surface. Going through my desktop computer one last time, I make sure there aren't any files I need to bring with me, as well as close everything down. When I have the proper files on my laptop, I unplug it and shove it in my bag, taking a few folders as well. Taking one last look around to make sure I don't miss anything, my mind starts going over my work for tomorrow, when I'm suddenly interrupted by a knock on the open door jamb.

Startled, my gaze snaps up, and I feel an annoyed droop pull at my features as I look at the intrusion.

The big fucking brute himself.

Not an ounce of self-control.

This guy is going to be trouble, and I'm already thinking about the amount of paperwork I'm going to have to do to get him out of it.

I look back down at my task with disdain. "Office hours are closed," I mumble as I shove my Seattle Stags notebook into my tote.

His enormous arms brace against the door frame on either side, and my eyes widen against my will when I glance up and watch his muscles flex. He wears a tight, black Seattle Stags shirt that clings to every bit of his toned, muscular frame and a pair of black sweatpants that hang low on his hips. The carved muscles along his hip bones are prominent in a sharp V, which highlights the line of hair running down the center of his stomach. Which continues down until it hides under the band of his pants.

However, even in thick, black sweatpants, they leave almost

nothing to the imagination as my gaze follows that line of hair like a trail of unwanted desire.

Heat swallows my face as I realize what I've seen, and I clear my throat before zipping my bag shut.

Fuck, why did he have to be attractive? I don't find men attractive. They're a problem.

Glancing up, I watch as he leans back to look around the door, his eyes connecting to the wall outside of it. Then, he leans in to study the front of my door.

My face contorts in a look of pure confusion as I no longer glance and just watch the strange creature.

His eyes connect with mine, a stunning combination of browns and greens that I accidentally get lost in, causing the heat that swallows my face to engulf my entire body. It doesn't help when he offers a playful smirk that shows his pretty teeth.

"I don't see a sign anywhere."

Pushing away the physical attraction, I remind myself this is all just attention I haven't felt in a while, and roll my eyes as I sling my bag over my shoulder. Grabbing the handle of my Stanley water cup—a well-intentioned pun–I round my desk to shove past him.

Unfortunately, it's like pushing past a pine-scented wall of meat.

A pine-scented wall of meat that, when I collide with, sends strange jolts of electricity through my skin and limbs.

The sensation catches me off guard, causing my steps to pick up. I hurriedly walk through the back halls, making my way toward the exit. The sound of my heels clacking against the finished cement floors helps push away some of the over-whelming heat of this unnecessary interaction.

The thud of his steps closes in as he catches up, apparently eating up my hurried escape in only a few long strides.

"Wait, I..." he calls out.

My brow quirks in mild curiosity as I stop and turn around to glance at him.

I didn't realize how close he got to me. Or how taller he really is. I'm only five-three, and he towers miles above me. I don't even think I'm looking at his chest. Taking a step back, I cross my arms over my chest as I glare daggers into him.

"I got off on the wrong foot in the locker room. I'm Gunnar. Gunnar Hayze." He extends one of his hands to me in greeting, and I eye it suspiciously before I track my gaze up to his face.

A shy, boyish smile plasters his face, while tufts of dark brown hair fall over his brow as he looks down at me. A taper fade decorates the sides of his head, with more length on the top and at the back. The length in the back has some semblance of wave to it.

A fucking hockey flow. He would.

He has strong cheekbones and a well-defined jaw that seems to be free of any stubble.

I watch him for a moment, analyzing him, while also not accepting his greeting.

A lawyer has to be able to read body language. And while I can tell he's nervous, I'm not exactly sure of the reason why.

He pulls his hand back, his lips quirking in a hesitant half smile at me as he shoves his hands into his pockets. Rocking back onto his heels, he sways his hips back and forth.

"You're fuckin' gorgeous."

My eyebrows tense wildly in shock as I look at him. "Is that what you came here to tell me?" I ask with a grimace.

"Well, that, and I'd like to take you on a date."

Now my jaw drops, because he gets one look at me and wants to take me on a date? I barely even know him. Of course, I'm not going on a fucking date with this stranger.

Not to mention, I'm his *lawyer.*

"I don't know you. Why would I go on a date with you? And I'm your lawyer. I can't exactly 'go on a date' with you," I remind him with a set of air quotes.

One of his brows rises, almost in challenge. "Alright, what if I rephrased it? Not a date. A 'dinner' to discuss business."

I roll my eyes boringly. "Fine. I'll bite. What kind of business?"

"I'm sure I can think of something," he says confidently, with a large cheeky grin plastered on his face.

My eyes narrow on him. "Did the boys put you up to this? Are you all playing a prank on me?"

His brow furrows, as if he can't believe such a thing. "Why would they need to put me up to this?"

"Because no one has ever tried to ask me out in the past."

That is mostly the truth. They rarely try to fuck with me because they know I don't have time for their shit. There are times they all try to mess with me as a team, but none of them have individually gone after me.

Not until this one.

Gunnar laughs. "Most hockey players don't go for the coach's daughter."

He leans down, coming within inches of my face to lock gazes with me. Those wild hazel eyes twinkle with devious intent. "I'm not most hockey players," he whispers with a Cheshire grin.

Fuck this unnaturally attractive goon my father drafted. I will have words with him later.

I shove at his chest, and he rises to his full height, caressing the space I pushed like a prize.

"I'm not going on a date with you," I tell him as I turn back and continue my path down the back halls.

"Well, at least let me walk you out to your car! It's bad manners to let a lady walk alone at night." His voice echoes through the corridor, bouncing off the concrete walls, and I stop.

I stay facing forward, not wanting him to see the face of defeat I make.

I don't want to admit he's right, but he is. I'm usually fine walking to my car at night. But it was the first big game of the season with a new player, and there can be straggling fans with bad intentions.

I groan and throw my head back before I continue walking. "Fine!" I call back to him.

A quiet ruffle of fabric and the sound of a jump is heard behind me. As well as a quiet celebration, before he speeds up to walk beside me.

That piney scent swallows me as he gets closer, and it brings about a strange sense of calm. Almost like the forest at night. A fond smell, with fond memories. One I would not like to associate with him.

As we approach the doors, he races ahead of me to hold it open, and I don't glance at him as I walk past. With the woods that surround the arena and his scent, they almost blend into one as we walk into the night air. It's fall, which means it's cooling down and the leaves are changing.

One of my favorite seasons, to be fair.

As we make our way through the parking lot, I see some of the other hockey players climbing into their expensive sports cars, giving a wave to Gunnar before they drive off. All the while, I search for my car, becoming viscerally confused when I notice an ancient truck sitting right next to it. My vehicle is a BMW M4, so the truck looks starkly out of place amongst that and the other expensive ones in the lot.

"Which one is yours?" Gunnar asks as we step through the brisk Seattle air. It's so wonderfully cool. Not like the strange mechanical chill produced by a hockey arena.

"The BMW," I murmur.

"Oh, looks like we parked next to each other," he says. I can practically hear the grin in his voice.

I look at him in confusion. "You have the truck?"

"Sure do," he says as we approach the two vehicles.

"Why didn't you buy a newer car? Most hockey players go buck wild with their new salaries," I say as I open the passenger door and place my things inside. With my arms free, I close the door and fold my arms over my chest as I lean back against the passenger door. My eyes stay locked on his face, observing him.

He seems to watch me with the same amount of curiosity. Though I imagine his version is admiration. Whereas mine is scrutiny.

There is zero reason for this man to be so hellbent on me like this. It's bizarre.

But there is the smallest... *teeniest, tiniest* fraction of me that is enjoying the attention.

I shove that fraction as far down as physically possible.

After a long moment of staring, he finally speaks, "Sugar, I told you. I'm not most hockey players," he says with a gruff chuckle.

The way he says it makes my heart pound. I've never had... a pet name before. I suppose that's what that sort of thing would be.

"Sugar?" I ask, to deflect the way my heart is trying to burst from my chest.

"'Cause you're sweet as sin," he says with a devious grin.

My eyes widen as my throat constricts.

I am not enjoying the way this name makes me feel.

I will also not be acknowledging the way it makes me feel.

To shift gears, I look back at his vehicle again. He notices, following my gaze, before he pats the hood once, and he turns to me.

"This was my Pa's. He's the reason my family skates," he says. His smile is reminiscent as he looks over it, as if his thoughts are elsewhere, but he quickly comes back to the present and smiles at me.

My eyes gaze over the truck again. It's a degraded light blue, with chips of paint missing, and it seems to be held together by rust. As my eyes roam the truck, they eventually come back to study him. He beams with pride for this old machine. Like a little boy with his favorite toy.

"Very touching," I say deadpan.

Gunnar props an elbow on the hood, leaning against it as he rests his other hand on the dangling wrist before his eyes flick down to my chest. They linger there for a moment before they go back up to my eyes.

"I sure would like to be," he says, low and sweet.

Barf.

I roll my eyes before I round the front of my vehicle to throw the driver's door open. Placing my foot inside, I look at him over the roof of my car.

"This was an absolute nightmare, but thank you for walking me to my vehicle. Goodnight, Gunnar," I say as I climb into my seat.

Gunnar pushes from his truck and takes a step toward my car. When I press the ignition, he bends over to swirl his finger in front of the passenger window, indicating for me to roll it down.

I breathe a heavy sigh as I open it. "What?" I ask with an annoyed glare.

He presses his massive shoulders through the opening, and my car tilts with the weight of him. He barely fits inside it, but he doesn't care.

I'm sure he wouldn't.

"When will I see you again?" he asks with a hopeful smile.

"Probably in your dreams."

Gunnar laughs before he lets out a soft sigh. "One can only hope."

God, this guy lays it on thick.

I roll my eyes again, and I feel like I'm going to get a headache from the spinning of it all. He pulls himself from the window and stands before he pats the hood of my car.

"Get home safe, sugar," he says as he walks over to his truck to unlock the door.

I quickly roll up the window and take that as my cue to get the absolute hell out of this godforsaken parking lot.

CHAPTER THREE

GUNNAR

She really wanted to get home.

I don't blame her. It's nighttime and there's a massive stud here.

I may be dumb, but at least I'm self aware. Little Miss Business is a tougher nut to crack than I thought. Then again, I can probably see why. I was a bit... aggressive in my approach. And she doesn't know me. So it's valid.

But fuck, I'm a GOON. THAT'S IN MY JOB DESCRIPTION.

I don't know nice and easy.

Even if I wasn't a goon, there is a magnetism here I can't deny. I think even if I tried to stay away from her, I couldn't. Which is crazy in itself. I just met her.

But... I *want* her. I wanna see what she's about.

Of course, it'll take time. If no one else has shot their shot at her, then she's maybe not used to this. Especially if she was so shocked to be hit on by a hockey player.

She's so withdrawn, and I wonder why. Especially if she has

to represent a team this way. Her dad doesn't seem withdrawn, neither does Charlotte nor Mrs. Tamisha.

But she exudes a distinct energy that differs from the rest of them entirely.

I smirk at the thought with a shake of my head as I climb into my Pa's 1973 Chevrolet Silverado. It was his pride and joy, and honestly, he took good care of it, all things considered. When he died, he left it to me and I'd be a fool to let it sit in a garage somewhere. Plus, there wasn't any kind of vehicle I wanted more.

I love this one.

I turn the key in the ignition and the old engine sputters to life with a metallic shake. Driving out of my parking spot, I head toward my new apartment in the city.

When I got my sign-on bonus, my mind didn't really go to the things I wanted to buy. I'm not very materialistic. So, I gave some of the money to my mamaw, who has been struggling since Pa died. I also gave some to my mom and dad to help pay for more of my brother's hockey dreams.

Then I used some to move into an apartment, then I put the rest into savings. Since I'd been living with my parents, all I really thought about blowing money on was a place of my own.

Luckily for me, the apartment I wanted was relatively close to the arena.

But, I didn't go pro for the money or the fame. I just love the game. Plus, the rink is available to us whenever we want to use it. Sometimes I just want to have a fuck about on the ice.

The street lights are a kind companion as my old beast moves down some of the tighter streets of downtown Seattle. I love a pleasant drive, and the comedown from a first of the season game is always more draining than it needs to be. Taking my time on the roads gives me just a slight chance at relaxation.

Eventually, I pull into the parking garage of my apartment

complex and mosey my way to my designated parking spot. Taking a deep sigh, I let my head crash against the headrest before I work up the energy to climb out of the truck. I pull my backpack out of the passenger seat, wrapping it around my shoulder before I get out and head to the elevator in the back of the garage. The sound of the button for the elevator car echoes through the quiet stoned structure as I wait for it to retrieve me.

As the door beeps open and I walk in, I lean against the mirrored wall of the car, letting the shake of the it rock me.

I'm excited to relax. Since Coach wanted to make sure we were good to go for the first game, the past few weeks have honestly been some of the most stressful I've had in a while. Which means I've barely been able to spend any time here with practices. My parents basically moved all my stuff in.

The car brings me to the lobby, which is pretty nice itself. Nicer than any place I've ever been. High, vaulted ceilings, with a massive chandelier that hangs in the middle. The front of the complex is made of giant glass panes and when you walk in from the street side, you basically approach the front desk some feet in.

When you head straight to the back, there's a long hallway that leads to a bunch of elevators. A hall on each side for each wing of the complex.

My apartment elevator is on the left side when you come in from the lobby.

When I get to my elevator hall, I take another car, waiting for it to bring me to my floor before I'm able to walk down the hall to my apartment.

When I pull out my keys to unlock the door, I already hear the excited barks from my friend within. As I open it, I drop my backpack by the entry and am immediately greeted by my best buddy, Tucker. His long, black tail wags in excitement as he nuzzles up to my legs in 'Hello.' A black lab of only about five years old, he's been my best friend since I got him as a pup.

My apartment is a three-bedroom space, with a pretty pleasant kitchen to the left when you walk in. A large kitchen island in the middle, with the counters along the wall surrounding it for the sink, stove, and the large stainless steel fridge at the end. Dead ahead from the front door is the living room, with a big glass wall the looks out at the street below. To the left of the kitchen and the living room is a corridor that holds two bedrooms. However, on the left side of the front door, when you walk in, there is a small alcove space with a bathroom that shares a wall with a separate corridor that leads to the main bedroom. My bedroom.

I actually spent a lot of money on new furniture and some decor. Since I do like to have a nice space, I hired an interior designer while I was at practice to make sure it didn't look like a single bachelor lived here.

I obviously intend to bring a girl back at some point, and I know a man's hovel can be a make or break for some women. As for my trophies, I've secluded them all to a separate room. When you've been grinding for as long as I have, you're going to have a bunch of little trinkets to go along with it. Plus, I didn't really want to display them around my residence unless the lady asked to see them.

Tucker begins to jump and bark at me as I reach down and scratch at his ears.

"Hey, Tucktuck. Walk time?" I laugh in question. He barks excitedly as he spins in a circle, ready to go out for the night.

"Alright, alright! So impatient!" I laugh again as I reach for his leash.

Of course, it's a Seattle Stags merchandised leash. They're my favorite team, even before I was picked to play for them. So,

I have all sorts of random Stag memorabilia all over the house. Blankets, mugs, hoodies, shirts.

Not to mention the amount of apparel I received when I got drafted.

I clip his leash to his collar as he moves to the door with a pant and a few jumps of excitement. And when I open the door, nothing can stop this little guy from tugging with all his might against the leash to get me out of here.

There isn't much going on at this hour. It's already about ten pm, because, of course, game days are always long.

In all honesty, I need to lie down because I'm spent, but duty calls.

Duty just so happens to be named Tucker.

We make our way to the outside of the complex and to the small dog park attached to it. A little fenced in portion of land for dogs to do their business and run around in. When I was looking at apartments, it was important to me he had a place to run.

I unclip his leash and he sprints around the park like a bat out of hell. A small laugh bubbles out of me at his energy, and I take a seat on the wooden bench inside the space.

Inhaling the fall Seattle air, I stretch back, letting my arms splay against the back of the bench. My head cranes and I look up at the stars, relishing in the thought of the weekend ahead. I feel like I haven't had a calm one in ages.

Somehow, as I sit and watch the stars, I'm reminded I'm actually on my own again. It's nice to have my own space. And while I miss my brothers and parents, it really is great to have an entire place to myself. It should have happened sooner, but I wanted to stick around and help my brothers with their own hockey careers.

I'm the oldest. My middle brother, Gretzky, is a D1 hockey player, and it'd be nice to see him in the pros one day. My youngest brother, Brooks, is a senior in highschool and plays varsity for their hockey team. Of course, he's being scouted by some big houses around the country. I reckon probably even more, since I got drafted. But we're all pretty similar looking and a family of pretty large men. Growing up in an all male household leads to a lot of scraps and our house was no exception.

After a few minutes, Tucker finally decides he's ready to go in. Trotting up to me, he lays in the grass at my feet with heavy pants while he gazes out at the park. His hot breaths steam and swirl in the night air as they huff out of his maw.

I stand and take another big stretch before bending down to attach his leash, leading him out of the little dog park.

As I walk toward the entrance, a familiar swath of brown, curly hair, with its little streaks of golden highlights, walks through the large glass doors of the lobby.

Tiana's tote is slung over her shoulder and she's focused on her phone.

Does Little Miss Business live in the same apartment complex as me?

It feels like my heart does a little celly in my chest and a grin tugs against my cheeks. Yanking open the doors a bit more enthusiastically than I should, I speed the hell up to catch her. Tucker runs with me as I jog to meet her halfway.

"Well hey there, sweetness!" I call out.

My voice echoes in the spacious lobby of the complex, and she startles as she looks up at me.

Her shocked face turns into one of disdain as her head leans back in angst.

"So, we're stalking our lawyers now?" she murmurs as she shakes her head and continues to walk to the elevator hall.

A laugh bubbles in my chest as I let Tucker walk me to the hall.

"I wish I could say that's what I was doing. But I do live here."

Tiana's head turns to me quickly, as if she can't understand me. "Excuse me?" she responds.

"I live here," I repeat.

"No. You do not," she says. Rather confidently, I might add.

I tilt my head as I look at her. "I do, in fact. Apartment 444."

Her face almost pales as she looks at me.

"You're fucking with me. You have to be. This has to be some kind of weird set up by you and the boys," she murmurs as she walks to the elevator doors and presses the button.

The elevator beeps slowly as it descends. As we wait, Tucker sits next to my feet, panting happily at Tiana. She seems to pay my friend no mind as she taps her shiny black heel against the tile and shakes her head with her arms crossed against her chest in annoyance.

"Would it be so bad to share a space with me?" I tease with a grin.

"I do believe that would probably be my worst nightmare, yes. But, because the boys know where I live, I'm chalking this up to some sort of sick joke."

I laugh at that, because I reckon it surely would be a sick joke.

If it were one.

"Sure, I'll play along. The boys sent me here to terrorize you."

Tiana stays stone faced as she looks up at the descending elevator numbers until the soft ding rings through the little hallway and she storms into the metal car.

Tucker quickly pulls me in behind her and nuzzles her hand in excitement. Her eyes slide down to glance at him with an odd expression before she taps his nose softly with one of her long nude-pink nails. Tucker takes that as a sign of some sort and sniffs down her legs, all the way to her feet. In the process, he circles around her, then around *me*. His leash wraps around our ankles, forcing us closer together with awkward little steps.

Well, this was not supposed to happen.

"Ah, fuck, I'm so sorry. Tucker stop!" I try to reprimand.

Her feet pull together and she wobbles as she lets out a small, breathy gasp. He continues to circle us until she's pressed up against me and I attempt to unravel it, but it fails, leaving us flush against eachother in this little metal box.

I look down at her nervously and her eyes widen as her head cranes up at me.

I would like to offer her an apologetic smile. I really, really would. But I don't think I can with how incredible she feels against me.

Tucker may be the best wingman on the planet.

Her body fits against mine so, *so* well. So tiny, but her form is rigid. Not only from her shock, but from her muscles. She has some strength to her, and it turns me the fuck on.

Her green eyes are brilliant—even through their shock and her glasses—in the harsh lighting of the elevator, and her face is splattered in a plethora of faint freckles across her nose and cheekbones. I wasn't close enough to see them when we were in her office. But I'm glad I get the chance to see them now. She looks like an absolutely ethereal little goddess and smells like a beach. Coconut, sea salt and some kind of floral thing. It's intoxicating and delicious.

With her held against me, this close and the sensory overload of every bit of her, I would drop to my knees right now just to worship her. Fuck, what I wouldn't do for a taste of her. I could throw her around with such ease. And I realize the longer she's against me, the more my thoughts run, causing my blood to rush through my veins faster than I could have ever expected.

All of my veins.

Tucker finally unravels from around us as the elevator dings and the doors slide open. Tiana turns with an unparalleled quickness as she pries herself off of me, shoving hard to get away from me before she exits the elevator. I wasn't sure someone could walk that fast in heels. Good for her.

Unfortunately, I do have to follow her because my apartment is in the same direction.

"Will you please, for the love of God and everything holy, stop following me?!" she groans loudly.

I halt my steps and Tucker is yanked back as he continues walking against this leash.

Lesson number one of being a gentleman. If a lady asks you to stop, you do.

That's just common decency.

She doesn't look back at me as she slips her key into the door directly beside mine and rushes inside.

So, Miss Business *is* my neighbor.

How fortuitous for me.

Maybe not so much for her, but that's fine. I can't help it if I happened to be placed next to her.

But, I imagine in order to make her feel as if I'm not messing with her, I may have to show her my apartment. It probably is strange to have a giant follow you around so soon after being put on your team. Well... and hitting on you. And... being pressed against you in the elevator of your apartment complex by an unknown dog.

If anything, I don't want her to be uncomfortable. Especially since she knows we work together now.

Though part of me feels as if that ship may have sailed and I need to go into some sort of problem-solving mode.

Even if she doesn't take me up on my date offer, she at least deserves to feel safe in my presence.

I'll work on that plan later. For now, I have to get Tucker inside. Making sure I'm extra quiet, I enter my home and remove Tucker's leash. He runs to his little bed next to the large window at the back wall to chew on a Seattle Stags plushie I gave him.

I hang his leash and take a deep breath before heading to the kitchen to make myself a protein shake.

As I prepare my little dinner, my mind drifts to Little Miss Business. I can't believe the way she's gotten into my brain like this. I just met her and I would do anything to spend just a few more moments picking her brain. It's out of character for me as I don't get attached easily. But there's something about her... something that pushes me to chase her.

I don't think I've ever chased someone like this.

Maybe it's the fact she's so damn gorgeous, but she's also a lawyer. Do you know how hard it is to become a lawyer? Especially for a large sports firm?

The work ethic that goes into something like that is insane and *so* fucking sexy. I love a good work ethic, and it's even better when it comes wrapped in a black pencil skirt.

I release a thick groan as I shove my hardened cock down with my wrist. It begins to ache after being held against her in the elevator. I reallllllly hope she didn't feel it. Coupled with the fact I can't get her out of my skull. With another groan of annoyance, I shake my head clear of the thoughts and finish my protein shake.

Eventually, I shower again, washing away the day before I change into some boxers to curl up in my bed.

I inhale a deep breath as Tucker excitedly comes to rest with me. And with that pretty little lawyer stuck on my brain, I drift off to sleep.

CHAPTER FOUR

TIANA

The sound of my Keurig, and the scent of fresh coffee, bubbles through my apartment as I ready for my weekend. Games are usually on Fridays, which means I have the entire weekend to do absolutely *nothing* after dealing with mountains of paperwork and insane hockey players all week.

Honestly, our team isn't too bad. They're pretty good boys for the most part.

But there are things that my mom has me do for other teams. While my main job is at the arena, I'm also technically my mother's right hand. So alot of her work gets put on me as well.

The amount of bullshit divorce contracts, or just unnecessary paperwork some of these sports stars need done, has my head pounding on a regular. So, I *always* take the weekend for myself. My space and free time are incredibly important to me.

I'm not a partier, or even a people person. So any chance I get to hide away from the world, I take it.

That usually entails some kind of self care; reading or

picking up groceries. Which is what I have to do today. My day-to-day needs structure, and it's something that gives me a small bit of ease. If I know how the day is going to go, things are much better for me to handle mentally.

My routine is something I've crafted in my years alone, and I take pride in it. I take the same routes to work, get dressed and do everything the same way every day. The second that is off kilter, the entire ship goes down.

I just don't have time to let the ship go down. I'm the captain, and if I can't control it, we're sinking.

As I sip my coffee, I rattle off a mental list of the things I need to grab from the store. Usually I order my groceries for pickup, but I feel like it's a nice day to get some sun. So I'm making sure I plan out my route perfectly so that I'm not wasting time backtracking. I always go through this step so that I'm not wandering the store aimlessly and know exactly what I need.

But against my carefully laid plans, small snippets of that damn hockey player dance around them. Distracting me from what I'm supposed to be focusing on.

Perhaps it's the insanity of it all that has me obsessing over it.

First, he follows me to my house and then I'm forced against him in the elevator by, I guess, a decoy dog?? I've never known the players to go to these lengths to plan these kinds of pranks, but I guess anything is possible with them.

They like to mess with me because they know I'm just a hardass. And sometimes I don't even really realize they're playing a prank, so I never really get the joke.

They rarely do it to Charlotte. I imagine it's because it wouldn't be as fun. She would just enjoy it too much. Most of them see me as an annoying older sister that has to keep them out of trouble.

I'm *also* annoyed at the way it felt to be against him. His giant body seemed to swallow me whole, and I would be a dirty liar if I said it didn't make my stomach flutter. I really don't like the way my body reacted to his. It's confusing and utterly disappointing.

I thought my vagina and I were on the same page, but we clearly weren't. It gets one second of male contact and now the bastard can't get out of my head.

Mental, I'm telling you. Absolutely mental.

Shaking my head of the unnecessary thoughts of last night, I make my way to my room to finish getting ready for the day.

Even though I have my business attire to wear during the week, I much rather enjoy my comfort. So the weekend calls for yoga pants and a large black Seattle Stags hoodie that swallows my entire body. There's something about a massive hoodie in the fall that feels like it sets everything right in the world.

I throw my curls into a messy bun on the top of my head before I head to my front door to grab my Dior backpack. As I adjust the straps and grab my keys, I make for the door, opening it to be greeted by an enragingly familiar, piney scent.

My eyes lock on the black fabric of a Seattle Stags jersey before trailing my eyes up to the behemoth it's draped on.

God. Fucking. Damnit.

What in the hell is this brute doing here again?! Now, he's on my *doorstep* at ten in the morning on a Saturday! I'll have to have a talk with the team on Monday because this is getting out of hand. They know how precious my weekends are to me.

I was already shocked to find him here yesterday. And it's not that I don't like him. I don't fucking know him! I haven't had the chance to even form an opinion!

I know how most hockey players are. I know what they do; I know how they go about their lives. As far as sportsmen, they're not the worst.

They're just not my type.

ESPECIALLY not a massive defender with a fucking death wish.

Gunnar gives me a kind smile as he looks down at me.

My gaze sweeps over him again.

Seattle Stags jersey... pulled... on top of hoodie? With the hood pulled out. Strange? But okay. Jeans also, sure. But he also happens to be... barefoot?

The fuck?

"Hey there. Mind if I borrow a cup of sugar?" he asks playfully.

My face twists in confusion as I look at him. "Why are you here? Didn't I tell you to leave me alone?"

His hand comes up to scratch at the back of his neck nervously before he gives a soft chuckle. "I know it's kinda weird for me to be here. But I wanted to make sure you knew I wasn't following you. I didn't know you lived here until last night. I just moved in and I've been so busy with prep for the first game that I haven't been here often. So, I wanted to make sure you knew you weren't being followed."

My brow furrows as I look at him and his face softens in sincerity. I watch him for a long moment, his hand slipping into his pocket as he waits for my answer.

"How am I supposed to believe you?" I ask as I cross my arms over my chest.

Gunnar takes a step back to glance down the hall, toward the elevators, before he looks back at me. "I brought my keys, and I locked my door. I could show you that I do, in fact, live there. If it will help you be more comfortable."

Heat crawls along my cheeks and nose as I listen to him, but I nod. Because at this point, I still don't fully believe him. And if the boys are playing a prank, I'm squashing it now.

Gunnar smiles and nods to the door beside mine, waiting for me to move.

I take a few tentative steps out of my apartment and close the door behind me, while he walks ahead to lead me to the apartment right beside mine.

Apartment 444; the one he mentioned last night.

Coming up a few feet from his door, he looks at me as he fishes his keys from his pants and holds it up for me to see. He all but displays it for me before he slips the key into the lock.

It turns with ease and the door flings open. As it does, I'm greeted by the black dog that forced us against each other last night, and I scratch his head as he pants up at me in excitement.

I peek my head inside the door and look around.

It is surprisingly clean, and honestly, nicely decorated. There's a lit candle on the island in his kitchen, making the whole place smell like warm vanilla. If I didn't know better, it would feel like a woman lived here.

"Ha! Hilarious. There's no way you live alone, and the place is this nice. You're a hockey player," I say as I cross my arms and stand defiantly outside of his door.

He gives me an amused smile. "Sweetness, one day you'll understand that I'm not every other hockey player. But I reckon today's not that day. I can show you my trophies if you still don't believe me."

He nods to the inside of his home, as if coaxing me to take a peek at these "trophies."

I roll my eyes and try to ignore the way "sweetness" sounds coming out of his mouth. My foot taps against the hallway floor as I glare at him for a few moments longer.

"Why is it so nicely decorated? Don't you live alone?" I ask to give myself some more time.

His brow raises with a small smirk. "My parents moved most of my stuff in while I was getting ready for the first game.

And then I hired an interior designer to make it nice for me," he says with a shrug as he presses his hands into his pockets.

"And you just expect me to believe that? That you, a single hockey player, decided to hire an interior designer for your house?"

He laughs. And the sound is rich. Warming in all the worst ways. "No, I don't. I probably wouldn't believe it myself. But it's my first place on my own and I expected to have a lady in here one day. I didn't want to give off the impression that I'm a degen."

My brow furrows as I look at him. What a fucking bizarre vocabulary.

"What in the ever living fuck is a degen?" I ask.

"A degenerate. I like to present as a gentleman," he says with a grin.

I eye him with an incredulous look.

"For the most part," he adds nervously.

My foot tapping increases, furiously beating before I groan as I finally cave. "Fine," I say in annoyance.

Gunnar steps to the side to let me in first and I take a few tentative steps inside the door. Looking around the space, I try to see if there are any other hockey players in here.

There is no way this isn't some sort of sick joke. It has to be. I don't know what I would do if I actually had to live next to this man.

I throw a glance over my shoulder, where he follows close behind, but leaves the door open.

The decoy dog comes up to sniff at my hand, like he had last night, and Gunnar takes a quick step forward.

"Tuck, stay. No go," he tells the furry friend. The dog trots back to a small bed by the window, curling up and laying down to watch me from its post.

Gazing around the interior, I take slow steps around. I

check in any of the hidden corners or behind furniture to see if there are any men. To my dismay, none of the players are here. But it really is impeccably clean. There are even throw pillows on the massive black couch.

"Wow, you guys went through a lot of trouble for this. Impressive," I tell him. Though rather unconvincingly.

The longer I look around, the more it does seem like this may not be a trick. But I think if I tell myself out loud it's a prank, I'll believe it.

Gunnar whistles to get my attention and I look over at him. He stands with a smile, his hands in his pockets as he nods to the back corridor.

"For what?" I ask.

"I have some more proof if you don't believe me," he says.

Rolling my eyes, I let an annoyed sigh go.

And reluctantly, I follow.

Is it dumb to follow an enormous, strange man down the hall of possibly someone else's house?

Yes.

But he doesn't feel like a threat and I want so badly for the players to be in this back room. I would really enjoy for this nightmare to be over.

He leads me to a door with a Seattle Stags parking sign on it and sends a smile over his shoulder as he opens it. Covered in various trophies are a plethora of mounted shelves. In any of the empty wall space are medals or plaques. There is even a Seattle Stags rug on the carpeted floor.

My brow tenses as I step into the room, getting closer to all the little trinkets and knickknacks placed everywhere.

Sure enough, *every single one* has his name carved or etched into it.

Gunnar Hayze, MVP. Gunnar Hayze, Player of the Year.

Gunnar Hayze is on *all of them.*

I turn to him in disbelief and he watches me with a pleased smile. "I have to admit, I thought I had some time before I got you into my house, but I guess this works just fine," he says with a shrug and a laugh.

"So... you really weren't following me last night... and this isn't some sort of sick prank..." I say, almost to myself, as my gaze drifts to the floor and blanks out.

The realization of this seeps into me, and I fight the urge to scream.

The world is out to get me. I'm sure of it at this point.

This is madness. This is just a sick joke from the beyond.

His voice is soft as it breaks through my internal mental breakdown. "'Fraid not, sweetness. I just happen to be your neighbor. Maybe one of these days I'll be able to grab that cup of sugar from you," he says.

My gaze tracks back up to him and he gives me a cheeky grin.

"You are insufferable, you know that?" I murmur.

"Only for pretty ladies like yourself." His eyes almost sparkle as he realizes it's finally clicked for me.

I roll my eyes as I push past him to get the hell out of this room. Walking from the back corridor, I make straight for the exit.

His thick steps quickly follow behind and before I make it to the front door, his strong hand wraps around my wrist.

I turn to look at it in surprise before my eyes trail up his arm to connect to his face. The shock of his touch is unnecessarily electrifying. It sends heat throughout all of me. The same way it felt when I was against him in the elevator and when I pushed past him in my office. But I tamp the feeling as far down as physically, emotionally, and mentally possible.

A sad expression pulls at his handsome features before he lets go of my hand.

"I hope this helped. I really didn't want you to feel like the new guy is following you. I understand it can be a bit scary for a lady like you to have a stalker. But scout's honor, I wasn't." He holds up three fingers in promise.

I watch him for a long moment, resisting the urge to admire his boyish features and the sincere smile that has spread across his face.

I rub the wrist he grabbed softly. "Thanks," I murmur.

"Of course. I never want to make it seem like you're in danger. You'll never be in danger around me, sugar. That's a promise."

Heat swallows my face at the sincerity in his voice, and all I can do is nod. Turning to the front door, I all but sprint to my apartment and slam the door behind me.

I press my back against it and stare, wide eyed, at the rest of my home. All the while inhaling deep, *deep* breaths.

What the fuck was all of that? What is even happening right now?

This crazy defenseman, who is obsessed with me, is my *neighbor? We share a fucking wall!? What the...*

I shake my head before I walk to the living room and collapse on the couch, groaning loudly into the cushions in an attempt to dispel the insanity of it all.

It did not work. And I did not go to get groceries.

CHAPTER FIVE
GUNNAR

The weekend goes by in a blur.

Along with finally being able to relax for once, I spent it watching highlight reels and some of the recent game. Just to see where I can progress.

Some would call it egotistical. But I am more self deprecating than anything and I watched it to find things I could fix or do better.

When Monday comes around, I've donned my hockey gear and am welcomed by the glorious smell of cool ice.

Ice scrapes against my kneepads as I stretch out on the rink, leaning onto my elbows to deepen the stretch on my inner thighs. The team is spread out all around the ice, doing the same. Coach Bubbles takes leisurely slides around the ice, weaving in and out of us.

"Hayze," Bubbles murmurs.

I look up at him, placing my hands on the ice to come up on all fours. He skids to a stop before me, spraying me with slush.

"I heard you're my daughter's neighbor," he says.

I give him a nervous smile as I sit back on my skates, wiping the slush from my face. "That was not planned Coach, I swear."

"She sure seems to think it was." Coach laughs. "Don't worry, I don't think you planned it. Tiana is just weird about her space."

I give a hesitant chuckle in response and go back to stretching.

"Yeah Hayze, quit bugging the lawyer!" Crowder says from in front of me. He's one of the older members of the team, another big boy and a solid one to boot.

"I didn't do it on purpose! I didn't even know she lived there!" Groaning, I lean back over on the ice.

The rest of them laugh, coming up to press their leg in front of them for a good hammy stretch.

"She's crazy weird about her space. One time we showed up at her apartment with gifts for Valentines Day and she slammed the door in our faces," Crowder adds.

"She's also very specific about her schedule. Doesn't really like her times impeded on. She is so insanely rigid, it's almost impossible to get her out for a celly or drinks. As soon as five p.m. comes around, she's out of here. She's a skittish girl, that one," Balder says as he presses deeper into his stretch.

Bubbles shrugs. "She's always been like that. She has other priorities, I guess."

I roll my eyes as I stand, skating over to the wall to grab my stick and helmet. Shoving it on my head, I weave in and out around the players still stretching. "Are we gonna run our mouths or are we gonna fuckin skate, boys?"

Soon, we've started practice and everyone has shut their gobs about my potential stalking.

I try most of my time to focus.

Keyword here is, try. But honestly, my brain is stuck on

that cute lawyer. The one that I know is *just* down the hall in that gorgeous little black pencil skirt of hers.

I saw her BMW in the parking lot today. And while I so badly wanted to park next to her, I parked as far away as physically possible. I don't need her thinking I'm following her. Especially if I am trying to chirp at her eventually.

After seeing the way she reacted to me living next to her, I reckon it's really going to be an undertaking getting on Miss Tiana's good side.

And fuck, I *really* wanna be on Miss Tiana's good side.

It was a long shot trying to convince her, but I wasn't gonna have her think I was following her. It was a necessary evil.

If I was her—and a woman—I'd probably react the same way. Especially if you are particular about your space. I just accidentally happened to be impeding it.

If I had known she was my neighbor, maybe I wouldn't have laid it on so thick that first night I saw her. But what's done is done and I gotta ride the wave.

"Hayze! Get your fuckin' tits out if you're gonna fuck us!" Banks yells at me as I miss a pass he slaps my way.

I groan as I shake my head. "How'd you know what I told your mom last night? She was supposed to keep that to herself!"

Banks slides past me with a mean hip check and slams me into the boards. "Eyes on the prize, Hayze. Come on."

Eventually, I throw the little lawyer out of my head and get the lead out.

Practice comes and goes, leaving me worn the hell out. With my Seattle Stags backpack over my shoulder, I mosey out of the locker room and down the hall. There is an absolute battle raging inside of me to turn around and go see if Tiana is still in her office, but I resist.

I don't know why I want to see her face so damn bad. But I really, *really* want to. Her curls and her face are just so... visually satisfying. *She* is visually satisfying.

In *so* many ways.

There's also this air around her. Like she knows what she's about, even if others don't. She lives in her own world, and she's perfectly fine having the walls around that world. I don't know if that is the truth. It's just what I feel like I'm picking up from her in the few moments I have spent with her. It's like she doesn't have time for the things she's not interested in.

If that is her deal, there is a level of attractiveness in that. She knows how precious her energy is and isn't going to waste it for the sake of others.

Gotta love a woman that protects her peace.

But I still wanna break through that tough shell and see the gooey center I know she's got.

Ugh, a terrible choice of phrasing.

I shake my head of the internal faux pas, focusing on getting out of the arena without her seeing me.

However, as I continue my path through the back halls and toward the exit of the arena, I spot the wispy curls of that gorgeous woman.

She's preoccupied with something on her phone. Her brow scrunched in focus as she presses her glasses up onto her head to look closer at the screen. She seems to be in her own little world right now.

Of course, I hadn't planned for this, but Tiana will surely think I did.

If I didn't plan on doing this anyway, I could have a little fun with her. I truly wasn't following her. I just happened to run into her. It's not my fault the Gods decided to bless me with an angel.

"Gosh, I didn't think I'd get to be waited on like this. I'd have come quicker if that was the case."

Tiana's head jolts up from her phone in confusion, pulling her glasses down over her eyes to find the new voice. Her head swivels, trying to spot the source. When she realizes it's me, she rolls her eyes.

"Is there a way I can get you to stop following me?" she grumbles as she turns back to her phone.

I move in her direction, and as I get closer, the smell of her intense beachy perfume overrides all my sense of self worth. It takes everything in my power not to throw myself to the ground in front of her.

"Take me on a date and I'll consider it," I say with a teasing grin.

Her brow contorts as her nostrils flare in disgust. "So, you admit you were following me?"

"Forgot you were a lawyer. Does that mean anything I say or do will be held against me?"

She sighs in annoyance. "I'm a lawyer, not a judge."

"Tiana. Tiana. Tiana. Tiana. Tiana," I say rapidly.

She does not find that joke funny and merely blinks as she stares boredly at me.

"Come on... one date. I'll make it worth your while," I say with a pleading grin.

Tiana's green eyes glance over my entire body as she takes a step back, scrutinizing every inch of me.

I find the slow sweep of it to be incredibly sexy.

"Why should I go on a date with you?" she asks.

"Because I'll be so fucking good to you," I tell her as I take a step into her perfumed little bubble to close the distance between us.

To my surprise, she doesn't flinch. Her head merely cranes back to keep her eyes on my face.

Such a little woman, but not afraid of the big, annoying hockey player.

Hot.

Tiana laughs a sarcastic chuckle. "You're a hockey player. *You* don't interest me."

"No?" I lift the sleeve of my jersey to flex my bicep. I may not be a normal hockey player, but I'm still a man. "How about now?" I ask with a grin.

Her eyes look over my arms in boredom and her head tilts. "Is that really all you've got?"

I release my sleeve and scratch at my neck. "What if... I planned a really elaborate date? You didn't have to plan anything. I would just tell you what to wear and when to wear it?"

"Again, is there any other reason that I *should* go on a date with you? Why should I spend any of my very little free time with you?" she asks.

My mind works over her words, and I realize she's legitimately asking for me to give her reason. Not just a turn of phrase.

What a tough fuckin' nut to crack.

I imagine... a lawyer... she loves the truth. At least, that's the best I got right now.

"Because you're an absolute beauty," I say. I soften my gaze and my voice before I give her a sincere smile.

Her face attempts to stay stony, but I see the way a pink tint creeps across her cheeks.

"You make my heart pitter patter like rain on a Chevy hood

and I'm trying to get lost in the storm." I lean down, leveling my gaze on hers.

As I search those perfect green little pools, there's nothing I want more than to dive the fuck in.

Her eyes widen and the pink tint increases as I challenge her with my heated gaze. Her teeth catch her full bottom lip and she shies away at the intensity of it. It feels as if lightning dances in the small bit of space between us, heating and lighting the air with a vibrant static cling to draw us closer.

And damn it if the way she bites that lip of hers doesn't get me hard as a fuckin' puck to the skull. I rise to my full height, looking down at her with a sweet smile.

Her eyes nervously glance up at me through her long, black lashes and she takes a deep breath. "Fine. I'll go on a date with you. But if I hate it, you never follow me again."

A wide grin spreads across my face and I press a hand out to her.

Her face shifts in surprise as she startles. She looks at it in confusion before she glances back up at me and takes it with a confused tilt of her head.

"It's a deal. I hope you've got a lot of outfits, sweetness." I shake her hand before releasing it. Giving her a triumphant smile and a small pat on the head, I walk past her.

With that, and a lil' pep in my step, I make my way to the parking lot to climb in my truck and head home.

CHAPTER SIX

TIANA

Accusing Gunnar of following me was dumb.

He fucking works here.

Of course he's going to *be* here. Not only was I trying to squash away the weird butterflies in my stomach from seeing him, I also wanted to make him feel like he was bothering me. And he was, until he hit me with that sly compliment of his.

I can't remember the last time someone complimented me because they were interested in me. Hell, I can't even remember the last time someone *was* actually interested in me. I've never really made myself available. Even now, I'm not technically making myself available. My assumption is that I'll go on this date with Gunnar, I'll hate it, and then he'll never talk to me again unless he actually needs me. That's a simple enough plan.

I hate to admit that... it felt *really* good to be complimented by him.

I don't know why Gunnar's words are the ones that have

landed their mark after so long. Maybe it's the pestering finally getting to me.

Granted, I had asked him to tell me. I just wasn't expecting anything he said.

I haven't dated or hooked up with anyone, probably since I got into law school, too much work to do. Though, college was a good time. I had my fun and my *"hoe phase"* where I needed it.

Once I got to law school, though, I had to buckle down. I didn't have the time or need to look at men. There were much more pressing matters to attend to, and men were not one of them. Plus, most of the men I had come in contact with complained constantly.

"Your schedule is too rigid."

"You're boring. Why don't we go anywhere?"

"What do you mean, I can't come over? I haven't seen you in days and you just want to hang out on your own."

Wah, wah, wah, bunch of bitches unable to handle boundaries. And they call women the emotional ones.

I really felt as if I was doing fine without compliments. They aren't anything I missed or even thought about. I have more than enough self-confidence in myself.

But then Gunnar had to fuck the *whole* thing up.

I could feel the heat crawl through my skin in a violent urge to be released when he looked into my eyes. The way the hazel glimmered with challenge. I couldn't believe the bullshit reaction my body had to it. The way I felt that telltale pulse low in my core.

Aside from the physical reaction, I don't think I've ever had a guy pine after me this hard. Usually men take the hint, but Gunnar doesn't seem to let up. He is a defenseman after all. I guess that is in his job description.

For whatever reason, the next day, I have to resist the urge to go out to the rink and watch the hockey players practice.

It's stupid. I've never cared in the past, but I tell myself that maybe I just want to see my dad some more. Which is the dumbest lie I've ever told myself. I see my dad all day, every day.

I curse my stupid thoughts as I walk from my office to the ice rink, murmuring almost inaudibly to myself about how I should turn around and go do some actual work. But it's like my feet have a mind of their own and continue to carry me to the fucking rink.

When I go to sit next to Charlotte on the bench, she almost jumps out of her skin at the excitement of seeing me here.

"Titi! You're here!" she giggles as she jumps up and down. She pauses, realizing I *am* actually here in the stands. "Wait. You never come out here," she says as she tilts her head and places one of the squeezable water bottles on the edge of the bench wall.

I release a heavy sigh. "Yeah, well. I was done with my work early, I guess."

Another lie.

I'm drowning in paperwork, but I couldn't get any of it done because Gunnar was on my mind.

Asinine. Absolutely asinine that this little goon got through my fortress so easily. It took many years for me to craft that damn thing.

"That's awesome! Well, the boys are having a great practice today," she says cheerfully.

Charlotte has always loved hockey. She used to play once upon a time. But when Dad became the coach for the Seattle Stags, she decided she wanted to help. So, he placed her on the sidelines. She didn't mind at all because she still gets to enjoy the sport she loves, even if it's from a distance.

My eyes roam the rink, trying to spot the wild defender I came to see.

Until I do.

Inches taller than even our previously larger players, he's easy to spot.

"HAYZE" is emblazoned in white lettering against the stark black fabric, with the number "33" in bright white under it. My heart pounds in my throat as I catch sight of him.

He moves with so much grace, it makes it hard to breathe. With his size, it's especially hard to believe he can move like that. But the way he handles a puck or checks someone into the boards makes my heart flutter uncontrollably.

God, this type of reaction to a hockey player. Tiana from three days ago would beat my ass.

I cross my arms against my chest as I watch the rink.

"Gunnar asked me on a date," I murmur to Charlotte absently. It feels impossible to look away from Gunnar as he skates around the rink. He's completely oblivious to me here, and it shows me a candid side to him I feel like I haven't been able to see. One where he's focused on his job. Zeroed in on his duties.

Damn my stupid woman's brain for being attracted to a man doing his job.

Charlotte takes a heaving gasp. "Oh my god, really?! What did you say?" she asks excitedly as she turns to me.

She grips my shoulders, shaking me back and forth. My body goes limp as I let her shake me and my head rolls to the side with a groan.

"Which time?" I ask with a sigh.

Charlotte releases my shoulders with a confused tilt of her head. "What do you mean 'which time?' Did he ask more than once?"

I roll my eyes with an annoyed nod before I lean back against the wall, crossing one leg over the other.

"He asked me the first time, literally right after the first game, after we met them in the locker room. I said no then," I explain.

Charlotte's face contorts as she listens, trying to put together the chain of events in her head. "Okay... And the next?"

"Yesterday he asked me out again. When I asked him why I should, he complimented me and I caved and said yes."

Charlotte claps her hands in glee. "You have to let me dress you! Do you know where you're going? Do you know what you're doing? Oh my god, when is it? Can I come with?!"

All of her questions rock into my skull and I have to hold a hand up to stop her. "Whoa, let's calm down. Give me a second."

She nods again, though with as much restraint as she can muster, and jumps onto the edge of the box that faces the rink. She waits patiently with a nip at her lip in excitement as she kicks her feet back and forth against the wall. Her hands grip the edge so hard that her knuckles begin to pale.

I let out a heavy breath as I go through each one of her questions in my head before answering.

"I have no idea where we're going. I have no idea what we're doing. I don't know when it is and no, you can not come with. You can dress me, only because I don't want to think about it. But you can't tell Mom and Dad about it. I'm not even technically supposed to be seeing him for anything other than business. It could get us both in trouble."

Charlotte kicks her feet excitedly and damn near shakes with excitement. "Ah! This is so great! We all took bets on when you were gonna go on a date again! But don't worry! I won't tell a soul!" she says with a proud nod.

My brow tenses as I make sense of her words and look at her. "What are you talking about?"

"Mom, Dad and I took bets to see when you'd finally cave and go on a date. I won!"

My palms rocks into my forehead as I take a deep breath. "You all are absolutely insufferable."

Soon, the sound of a harsh skid on ice brings my attention back to the rink.

Gunnar takes his helmet off to wave his hair back. It's damp with sweat, while his face is pink and flush from his exertion, but god *damnit* if he isn't a beautiful man.

Taking deep, steadying breaths as he grips his hockey stick between his legs, he waves his hair back before he presses his helmet back on.

He grabs his hockey stick from where his thighs grip it, to lean over and press against his knees. As his gaze swivels around the rink, watching the players, he bends over. His tongue swipes across his lower lip, and he seems to breathe heavy through his mouth, using this moment to take a beat. His eyes continue to swirl around the rink until it finds me and locks in on it. It's almost as if he could sense me.

As our gazes lock, I feel my eyes widen and my heart begins to pound relentlessly in my chest. It doesn't help that he is calculatedly smooth in his reaction. There are no twitches of the face as he rises from his bent over position to lean his head back. Merely a heated gaze as his eyes swipe up and down over me, as he bites his tongue between his teeth and his lower lip flips under it. A sly wink is all he gives me before he turns his focus back on practice.

There's a war raging inside of me. A war that I am losing.

I can't take it any longer. I've never, *ever*, reacted to a hockey player like this. Now, all of a sudden, this pretty goon says a few words to me and it's like he's playing chicken with my lady bits; constantly setting every inch of my skin on fire. Even through the chill of the arena.

I *have* to get out of here.

"I just remembered, I have some stuff that needs to get done. I'll see you later," I tell Charlotte quickly as I stand and damn near run out of the box.

"Oh, uh. Okay! Let me know what happens!" she calls after me.

I send a wave over my shoulder, as I speed walk as fast as my heels will allow me. Down the tunnel, back toward the hallway that leads to the back offices and locker rooms. I take a right outside of the tunnel and straight to my office. My heels clack furiously against the cement as I speed up even more, almost bending over to rip them off.

When I reach my office, I bolt inside, slamming the door shut behind me and locking it like a fucking murderer is on my tail.

My back hits the door and I pant as I slowly slide down it.

The chilled air of the arena cools me down just enough for me to regain control of myself and my thoughts.

"This is insanity. This is absurd," I whisper to myself as I catch my breath.

After a moment that feels as if it lasts far too long, I finally push the overwhelming feelings away and come to a stand. Swiping my damp hands down my skirt, I smooth out the non-existent wrinkles before I adjust my shoulders with a shake and a deep breath. But it does nothing as I slump down in my office chair and grip my hair in frustration.

In order to stave off the thought of that feral goon, the one that skates on the ice *just* down the hall; I attempt to bury myself deep into my actual job.

It doesn't work.

None of it does.

CHAPTER SEVEN
GUNNAR

Man, were the boys surprised to see Tiana at the rink today.

It filled me with a strong air of confidence. One I obviously couldn't explain to them.

They said she never comes to watch the games of her own volition. So, for her to even show up at practice was unheard of.

Of course, I tried not to let it get to my head. But how could I when I caught her watching me?

Today, she was sans her suit jacket. Which was absolutely insane to witness because her tight black blouse hugged every dip and curve on her body.

I was so damn hard. The only way I was going to be able to hide it was to bend over. The sight of her tits against those blouse buttons almost sent me into a coma.

But when you're on the ice, you gotta stay alert.

I took my chance where I could and turned on the smoke show as soon as I saw her watching. It was spectacular to see that little lawyer tremble under my gaze. I'm trying to make that happen in a few other ways, too.

And I'm nothing but a man of my word.

One down and several to go.

Seeing the blush sweep across her face was everything I could have asked for.

Didn't realize Santa took requests in the fall, but I ain't complaining.

When practice ends, I'm riding on the high of a great practice and knowing that Tiana came to see me. Even if I know she would never admit that, I'll take what I can get from her.

As we move off the ice, I decide I want to at least talk to her. I want to see what she has to say about being in the rink today.

We break to the locker room, where I make quick work of my gear and then shower. You don't show up to a pretty lady smelling like ball sweat, that's bad manners.

My teammates look at me like I'm on fire with the speed I'm moving at. But I don't care. I'm trying to catch Tiana before she leaves.

I throw my backpack over my shoulder and make it out of the locker room, where I'm stopped by Coach Bubbles. Like a bucket of ice water, my mood is dampened and squelched right before my eyes as he approaches me.

Please, Bubbles, I beg. It's right there, right in my line of sight.

"Hayze, great fuckin' dangles out there today, bud. You really are a thing of beauty. I gotta hand it to you," he says as he claps a hand on my shoulder.

My eyes roam over his head, locking onto Tiana's door. "Yeah, thanks Bubbles, now if you'll ex-"

"I wanted to talk to you about something, you got a minute?" he asks.

I fight back the urge to release a groan, and I reluctantly nod. Do I want to say, "no?" Of course, but this is my fucking Coach, I can't exactly tell him to fuck right off.

He takes me by the shoulder, turning me in the opposite direction as he continues to ramble about something, some other bullshit. I don't even hear him.

I look back over my shoulder to see Tiana, her phone in her hand with her head down as she locks up her office before absentmindedly trotting down the hall. With not a single care in the world, her pretty heels clack against the floor as she struts away to the exit.

That minute took three hours.
Three fucking hours.
Coach wanted to give me a spiel on my plays from last Friday and show me the things he saw I need to work on. Some of them were things I already noted for myself when I rewatched the game.

After hour one, I just gave up and listened.

I knew at that point I would not see Tiana. Nor was I going to see her when I got to the complex.

It ends up being ten by the time I get home and Tucker is *not* pleased. So, I quickly take him out for his little playtime, then come back inside.

When I'm finally able to relax, I feel like the only thing I can do is to plan out my date with Tiana.

Cozying up on my couch; I throw my feet on the coffee table in front of me before grabbing my laptop and opening the internet browser.

Unfortunately, I stare at that screen for a long moment.

I've never had to actually plan a date like this before. It has to be down to the T. But I also have to appeal to her likes.

Which I know absolutely nothing about.

She's not a hockey player and I don't want to make it seem like I'm forcing her to do what I want to do. So ice skating, or going to see a different hockey team play is out of the question.

I should have asked her what she likes before I started this. I feel like I'm going to fail before I even start, but an idea comes to mind and I type "Fun things to do in Seattle" in the search bar.

Closing my eyes, I scroll. Moving the mouse mindlessly across the screen, I click something at random and open my eyes.

Chihuly Glass Garden.

I look around at some of the pictures. It's basically what it says it is.

A glass garden. Sculptures of glass, I guess created by a local artist, configured inside and outside. There is a garden we can walk through to see some works, as well as a large glass almost atrium with intricate works of glass art along the ceiling.

I can work with that. I could... I could rent it out for the night, so there are no distractions or other people. Something tells me she doesn't like people.

It's at this moment that I'm incredibly grateful I didn't blow my draft money on a stupid car. I could rent the garden out and have dinner served in one of the large rooms.

Yes... yes, that's perfect! Gunnar Hayze, you absolute fucking unit, bud. Great fuckin' job.

I fight the urge to pat myself on the back and begin making the arrangements for the wonderful day. Though I know nothing of Tiana's schedule. So I spend a good portion of the night texting Charlotte any information on Tiana that she has.

What she would eat, if she would like something like this,

her schedules and times. Any free days Charlotte might know that Tiana has, in order to make it work with her times as much as I can.

All the while, I'm writing down the information Charlotte gives me, and looking up the proper channels to get this squared away as soon as I can.

I'm going to take the unbendable Tiana Dawn on a date. And she's going to love every fucking second of it.

The next morning, I try to wake bright and early so I can get to the arena before Tiana. But I have to make a few calls first.

Groggily, I reach for my phone on my nightstand, looking over the time. I still have a bit before the garden opens up for me to call them, so I decide to get up and get ready for the day.

I shower, brush my teeth, ruffle my hair, before I pick out my sweats and jersey. By the time I finish, I'm able to call the garden. Going to my kitchen, I lean against the island with the paper set in front of me, and quickly dial the number I procured last night.

It rings a few times before someone answers.

"Chihuly Glass Garden, how can I help you?" a woman on the other end of the line asks.

"Hi, yeah. I would like to rent out your entire area for just one night, please," I tell the lady quickly.

There is a long pause on the other end of the line. "Did you have a date in mind?" she asks.

I quickly scan over the paper, looking at any of the dates that would work best for Tiana. At least, according to Charlotte.

"I have any Saturday nights available for the next several weeks," I respond.

There is clicking on the other end, as well as another long pause. "We have an opening in about two weeks. From about six pm to ten pm."

I give a silent air pump in excitement before I take deep breaths to steady my racing heart. "Perfect, and would I be able to have someone cater in that big glass atrium thing? I would like to have dinner in there with my date," I ask.

I can't believe I'm fucking doing this. Part of me is surprised that I've never gone to these lengths before. This is an incredible feeling.

"We can provide those accommodations here, sir," she responds.

"Ma'am, you just made my day," I tell her as a large grin plasters on my face.

We go through a few more of the details before I quickly call the restaurant that I think she would like to have. Charlotte said Tiana is a simple girl. Meat and potatoes.

That's easy enough for me.

After a few calls, I've squared away all the arrangements, writing all the concrete details down on a piece of paper. And by the time I have finished, I look over my little sheet of detail with pride.

Soon, I rush out of the complex in a blur of black and red, heading straight for the stadium. And when I pull up, I take note of the cars and notice it's still sans Tiana. Coach's truck is here, but he is usually in his office before practice.

I take a deep breath and steel myself as I stare at the front of the stadium. Looking over the paper again, I make sure I have all the bits and pieces properly in place. Going over the plan repeatedly in my head, while trying to remember everything Charlotte told me.

From everything I've gathered, Tiana is very structured and I want to do it her way as best as I possibly can. I listed specific times, what we would eat, and what we would be doing.

I've honestly never actually *courted* a woman before. It was usually hook ups at an after party. But I can't remember the last time I tried this hard.

It's kinda sexy that she's making me work for it.

I love this process a bit more than I thought I would.

Grabbing my backpack; I hop out of my truck and make my way to the arena. It's eerily quiet because not a lot of players have come in yet. I skip the locker room entirely and go stand by Tiana's office to wait for her.

As I do, more tired men come down the hall to suit up for practice.

Eventually, Little Miss Business walks down the hall to her office with a cup of coffee in one hand, her phone in the other and her Stanley cup in the crook of her elbow as she tiredly scrolls through something.

My goodness, she's always on that thing, isn't she?

Tiana's wearing a shin length puffer jacket. I imagine because it's getting colder outside, and it doesn't get any better when you walk in the arena.

As she approaches the door, I clear my throat to grab her attention. "Good morning, sweetness," I muse playfully.

She pulls her attention away from her phone slowly to look up at me. Her eyes roll and she shoves me to the side to unlock her office door. Because her hands are full, she fumbles with her keys and I pluck her water cup from the crook of her arm to help her.

As the door clicks open, her gaze snaps to me in annoyance, glaring sleepily at me. She snatches the cup from my hand before she enters her office, rounding her desk to put her things on it, and I follow close behind.

"Is there a reason you're standing outside of my door this early?" she murmurs.

"Other than to get a glimpse of your gorgeous face? Yes, indeed," I say with an enormous grin.

Her tired eyes glance up at me with disdain. "Do you recall the words I said on the first day in the locker room?" she asks as she unzips her puffer jacket. Shrugging it off of her shoulders, she catches it behind her back to throw on her chair.

I go to speak, but the words snag in my throat as I catch sight of her. She's straightened her hair today and the flowing brown and gold strands drape across her shoulders. It's much longer than I expected it to be. Considering it's always curly when I've seen her, I really didn't think she straightened it.

Her black blouse and suit jacket strain against her breasts and my bottom lip inadvertently catches between my teeth as I drink her in.

A fucking beaut is an understatement.

She's wearing another one of those black pencil skirts and it doesn't matter that it seems like she wears the same damn thing every time I see her. It hasn't gotten old yet.

"I don't believe I do. Why don't you refresh my memory, sugar?" I ask slyly.

Tiana crosses her arms as she brings a hand up to grip between her eyebrows.

"I said, and I quote, 'Don't bother me unless it's for a traffic violation.' So, what? Did you get a ticket?" she sighs as she uncrosses her arms. She clasps her hands in front of her before she places her elbows on the back of her chair to glare at me.

"If the traffic violation was driving over the limit to see your gorgeous face, then I suppose I'm guilty of that, yes. Though, I didn't get caught. 'Spose I'll have to make sure a cop sees me so I can give you a trophy of my affections." I laugh.

She makes a sound of annoyance before she leans up from her chair to turn it around. Sitting down, she turns it to her desk and scoots up close to it so she can begin pulling things from her bag.

"I actually came to give you this," I say as I step forward. I pull the paper from behind my back and gently place it in front of her.

Her eyebrow raises as she looks at me, then peers down at the paper. She takes it in her hands and scans over it hesitantly.

"What is this?" she asks as she looks up at me.

"It's the plans for our date. I know you're pretty rigid with schedules and stuff, so I talked to Charlotte and asked for as much of your schedule as she knew. So you wouldn't have the excuse to chicken out." I give her a triumphant grin as she glares daggers at me.

Tiana's eyes scan the paper once more and she sighs as she looks over at her desktop computer.

"Fine. I'm a woman of my word," she mutters as she places the paper on the desk. Sitting back in her office chair, she runs her hands over her face before she slumps deeper into it.

A pang of hurt runs through me at her obvious disdain for this.

"Is it really that bad to go on a date with me? We don't have to if you don't want to," I remind her with a kind smile.

Maybe I moved too hard, too fast. Such is the way of the goon. It's just so hard to control myself around her. Part of me doesn't know why, and the other part doesn't question it.

I want her. To that part of me, that's all there is to it.

But I definitely don't want to make her uncomfortable.

Her face softens, and she groans as she throws her head back. Moving her office chair side to side slowly, her head tilts and her gaze dips to her desk.

"It's not you. I just... haven't gone on a date in a really long time. No one has been interested in me for a long time. So this is a little... daunting, if you will," she explains.

Wasn't expecting that sort of admission, but I'll take it.

"I'll take such good care of you, sweetness. Scout's honor," I tell her with a kind smile as I hold up three fingers.

Tiana looks at me with a small smirk. One she tries so hard to fight off and she sighs.

"Go get ready for practice. I'm not ready to handle my dad this early in the morning," she says with a wave of her hand. That small smirk stays a little longer as she shakes her shoulders and takes a deep breath.

I give her a smile and step toward the door, holding onto the door frame as I leave.

"I'll see you after practice, sugar," I tell her sweetly.

She rolls her eyes and glares at me with a "go away, please" look before she types away at her computer.

I swear the grin that pulls at my face as I walk to the locker room damn near gets stuck there.

CHAPTER EIGHT

TIANA

I'm unable to believe the work that went into planning this date. He actually took the time to find out my schedule and work around it. Whatever chirping is going on around the team appears to be too accurate for my liking. The idea of going on a date with this man is terrifying. Only because I haven't been on a date in ages.

I don't date. Let alone *hockey players*.

But he seems so excited to take me.

The glass garden isn't a bad idea either. I've never been, but I have heard about it. I just hate having to be around people.

The paper he gave me says he rented it out so there won't be any people there, and he arranged for dinner to be served there.

I hate to say how endearing I find it. A little date through a work of art with no people and dinner served?

It's probably the best date I've ever had, just by mere planning alone.

He also left the outfit choice up to me. And I am genuinely thankful that Charlotte offered to help dress me because most of my wardrobe is athletic, casual or just business. Not much of an in between, as I'm a homebody that enjoys my time and space.

I shake my head as I continue working on the shit I have to get done for the day. Gunnar doesn't come in between practices and I don't see him until I'm packing up my bag for the end of the day. He's dressed in the same outfit I saw him in this morning, but his hair is damp.

As his large frame crouches into the door, his fresh, piney scent fills the office. It's become a familiar smell. One that causes my heart to race against my will.

But, I continue to tamp down the way it makes me feel. Though it feels as if it gets harder to push it away completely.

"Can I walk you to your car, sweetness?" he asks with his usual playful grin.

"Is there a way I can get you to call me anything other than that?" I groan as I come to a stand. Bending over to log out and close a few things on my computer, I make sure I have everything I need before I start packing my things away.

The nickname is abhorrent. I don't understand why he insists on calling me that.

"I could call you Suds, if that works?" he asks.

I roll my eyes as I shove my laptop into my bag and sigh. "Fine. Sweetness it is, I guess."

"Bitchin'," Gunnar says with a confident smile.

I reach for my things, but Gunnar notices and quickly jolts forward, yanking the tote from my desk and snatching my Stanley.

"Hey! That's my stuff!" I groan.

"A gentleman doesn't let a lady carry her bags." Gunnar nods as he turns to walk out of the door. The way he has to bend down to come in and out of my office is hotter than it needs to be and stuns me for only a moment before I remember he took my shit!

He doesn't even wait for me as I quickly round my desk and trot out to the hallway, where his long strides have already made it halfway down the back halls. I try to catch up, but the little click-clack of my heels reminds me of how slow I'll be.

God damnit, fuck these heels!

With an annoyed growl, I press my hand against the wall beside me to steady myself and lean down to tug my heels off, leaving me in my little stocking half-socks. Hooking my heels on my fingers, I basically skate down the hall to catch him, as running wouldn't work in these stupid, slippery socks.

"Gunnar! You asshole! Bring my things back!" I yell as I chase after him.

I don't realize how fast I am without my heels, because he stops in his tracks and turns around.

I slam into his hard body like a giant flesh wall, subsequently swallowed by that piney scent as I'm about to fall. But a large arm wraps securely around my back.

My spine bows from the impact and I'm stuck looking up at his handsome face with my heels clutched to my chest.

A playful smile tugs across his beautiful lips, and the long bits of his damp hair fall over his brow. Hazel eyes swirl with mischief and I feel his fingers splay wide against my lower back. My blood is like lava as it rushes through me at rocket speed and my breath hitches in my throat.

Time feels as if it stalls, and the world slows to a halt in this bubble he has inadvertently created.

With the way his hand and body feel pressed against me, it causes my thoughts to vacate in their entirety. Right now, it's only Gunnar and me in this tiny pocket of space.

"If you wanted a hug, sweetness, all you had to do was ask," he says in a low, sultry tone.

My eyes widen and suddenly everything around me is too hot. Too hot, too hot, too HOT!

I feel like I can't breathe.

Righting myself, I shove my heels against his chest to pry myself from his grip. "I didn't want a hug. I want my things," I murmur in annoyance.

He looks at my cup in his arm and at my tote that he's slung on his shoulder. He's hooked it there like it belongs to him. Slowly, curiously, his eyes sweep up and down me. They linger on my stockinged feet and my hands that hold my heels, before his head tilts in observation.

"Well, this surely won't do," he seems to murmur to himself as he squats deeply in front of me.

I watch him in confusion as he gently presses a shoulder into my stomach. "Hey! What the f-" My words are cut off when he jolts forward and scoops me over his shoulder to carry me. Soon, I'm bobbing against his body as he walks to the exit.

"Put me *down*, you big fucking oaf! I am perfectly capable of walking!" I yell as I slam my heels against his back in retaliation.

"Can't really walk outside with no shoes on, sugar," he responds cooly. His arm wraps around my legs to hold me in place and eventually I give up when we reach the cold outside air.

"I could have put them on at the door!"

"Yeaaaaaah, you could have. But I got you first. Might wanna be quicker to the puck next time."

A growl rumbles out of me as I give in to my demise. I realize now he's not only carrying his backpack, he's also carrying me, my Stanley, and my tote.

And all I can really do is groan, "You did not have to do this."

"I surely didn't, but I'm certainly not complaining," he says.

Gunnar continues walking until he reaches my car. Where he then turns away so I can face the driver's side door and squats.

"What are you doing?" I ask in confusion.

"Open your car so I can put you in."

I'm sorry? Put me in?

My brow furrows in confusion before it all clicks and my eyes float to the top of my head in annoyance.

I'm really wishing at this moment that I had keys instead of a key fob.

I groan as I grip the car handle and press the button that unlocks it. He hears the mechanism click and stands. Turning around, he opens the car door and then tugs me off his shoulder to cradle me in his arms, gently placing me in the driver's seat.

Staring blankly out the windshield, I try to grasp what the actual fuck is happening right now.

I don't think I've ever heard of a man doing this, and now it's happening to me. I haven't even asked for any of this!

I hate the way my heart beats wildly and butterflies flutter uncontrollably in my stomach at this level of pampering. It's not in my DNA to like this kind of thing. I'm independent. I can do everything I want to do on my *own*! Just the way *I* want to do it!

But I'd be a damn liar if I said I wasn't enjoying this even a little.

He closes my door, with my things still in his arms, and goes around to the other side of my vehicle to open the passenger door. Gingerly, he places my tote in the seat and my Stanley in the cup holder before he crawls out and shuts the door.

I'm still in awe at what is happening and I roll the window down to gawk at him.

"Why the hell did you do that?" I ask as I stare, dumbfounded at him.

Gunnar gives me a sweet smile as he leans into the window, the car leaning with him.

"I told you, I'd be so fuckin' good to you, sugar. Just gotta let me show you." His grin is wide as he looks at me.

"Thank you," I murmur as I continue to look at him in disbelief. My eyes roam over all of him, trying to grasp some level of sanity through all the madness.

Gunnar's eyes watch me with a giddy amusement. As if he's happy he finally got me off my guard.

"Get home safe," he says sincerely. His eyes twinkle before he rises from the window to pat the hood of my car.

I roll up the window and shift into gear before I speed out of the parking lot.

My mind is swirling with weird feelings and thoughts. I don't need to date anyone. I don't *want* to. I like my space, I like my time to myself.

But fuck! He's showing me a side of things I never thought could even happen. The man fucking carried my things *and* me out to my damn car... then shoved me in it!

I can't even wrap my head around this. It's unheard of. I haven't even read it in a plethora of the books I own. And I read a lot of romances.

Go figure, right?

He really is slowly proving he isn't like most hockey players. Hell, he doesn't even appear to be like most men.

And I sit with that thought. All the way back to my apartment.

CHAPTER NINE

GUNNAR

Am I being a tad overbearing this morning?

Probably, but I can't stop the feeling I had when I felt her heart pound as I carried her out to her car last night. Whatever I'm doing is working. I surely don't intend to let up now.

So, EARLY this morning, I get up and run down to a cafe to get her a coffee before she leaves the complex. Does that require a random call to Charlotte to find out her favorite coffee and coffee shop?

Yes, yes, it does.

Charlotte, for whatever reason, seems more than happy to oblige. She gushes about how long they have wanted Tiana to have a boyfriend or at least someone to help take the strain off of her life.

Tiana will have choice words for me, but I don't care. If there is a way I'm weaseling my way into her little heart, I'll just weasel in a *liiiiittle* bit more.

I come back up the elevator with her coffee in hand and

wait outside of her door. As Charlotte predicted, six-o'clock on the dot, Tiana's front door opens and she steps out.

She looks immaculate with her large puffer jacket thrown over her arm, her tight little business woman get up, her Stanley in hand, and her tote slung over her shoulder for a day on the job.

Tiana halts when she finds the shadow of my body in the harsh lights of the hallway and looks at me with a furrowed brow.

"Good lord, don't you have somewhere to be?" she groans as she walks past me. She doesn't even see the coffee in my hand as she walks down the hall to the elevators.

I make to follow her but get distracted when I see the way her hips sway with her strides.

A *real* fucking beaut. In every sense of the word.

I shake my head at the distraction before I run to catch up with her, coming to walk smoothly by her side.

"Sugar, anywhere you are is where I need to be," I tease.

She doesn't even glance in my direction as she presses the button for the elevator and watches the numbers slowly descend.

I clear my throat and hold the coffee out for her. "I got you some coffee," I say sweetly.

She looks me in the face before her eyes catch the plastic drink cup in my hand. Her eyes snap from my face, back to the cup, before she attempts to read the little white sticky label pressed to the outside. Leaning in, she lifts her glasses to get a closer look and her eyes narrow on me as she comes to a stand.

"Sugar?" she sighs with a tilt of her head as she replaces her glasses.

"Well, the coffee obviously isn't for me. So, I had to make sure you knew who it belonged to," I say as a grin tugs at my lips.

She hesitantly takes the coffee from my hand. The feel of her fingertips barely touching mine sends fiery sparks of electricity between us and I press it deeper into her palm, just for a few more seconds of her touch.

Her eyes connect with mine for the briefest of moments, and a blush crawls along her cheeks, lighting up the freckles across her nose.

"Thank you," she mumbles. She quickly pulls back and takes a sip of the coffee with a soft, contented sigh. "How do you know what my order is?" she mumbles.

"Your sister is a keen accomplice," I respond.

The elevator dings and the doors slide open. Rolling her eyes, she quickly steps in, pressing the button for the lobby before shoving herself in the elevator's corner.

"I reckon you're not gonna let me take your things this time, are you?" I ask with a teasing smile.

"Absolutely not," she responds, taking another sip of her coffee.

Tiana watches the descending numbers, attempting to portray her displeasure at the situation. But the way the heat inside of this little metal box climbs tells me otherwise. Especially when I know it's pumping directly off of her.

I watch her with a small grin and she completely ignores me, waiting for the elevator to open. When it does, she makes her way through the lobby, beelining straight to the elevator for the parking garage.

I'm impressed by this little woman's speed in those heels. Though I don't know why she's damn near running. She knows we have to go to the same place, and even if she says she doesn't like me, I don't think she would leave me high and dry without an elevator.

We take the second elevator to the parking garage, and

when it opens, she rushes out to head straight for her vehicle at the far end of the structure.

"See you at work, sweetness!" I call out.

Tiana doesn't so much as look back when I call to her. She merely sends a middle finger over her shoulder.

I chuckle a loud laugh and it echoes through the garage as I make my way to my truck. As I get in and start it up, the engine turns over... and over... and over...

My truck isn't starting.

Fuck.

I try again, cursing myself for a few more seconds, before I see Tiana's car heading for the exit.

She's gonna fucking hate me for this. But Coach will hate me more.

I quickly eject from my truck and run as fast as I can to her stop her before she can get too far. Throwing myself in front of it, I shove my hands out and she stomps hard on the break. She's jolted forward from the stop and her face deepens in annoyance as her head falls against her steering wheel.

I come to the passenger door and she rolls down the window without so much as lifting her head.

"Gunnar, we are literally going to the same place. Can't this wait?" she groans.

"Yeah, see... about that... Um... My truck won't start," I say nervously as I lean into the window.

Her head lifts from the steering wheel to swing toward me as her face slacks in bored annoyance, glaring daggers into my soul. She groans another noise before her gaze blanks off and her head falls back against the headrest.

She inhales a deep breath. "Fine, get in," she grumbles as she unlocks the doors.

I really can't help the way I titter with absolute glee as I climb into the front seat.

Or attempt to. I don't realize how small her car is and I have to get out to adjust the seat before I can climb in comfortably.

Because her car is a coupe, there are no backdoors on it so I have to get in and throw my stuff to the back.

Pulling my seatbelt on, I wiggle my self in her seat before I slap my hands against my thighs and I look at her with a nervous smile.

"I wouldn't be asking this of you if I didn't have to," I remind her innocently.

"Somehow, I do not believe that," she says with a sigh as she shifts into gear and continues out of the exit.

I forgot how nice newer cars are. The engine purrs like a designer kitty-cat and it actually is making me consider a new vehicle. If I can't get Pa's truck to work, I may not have a choice.

I could also ask Tiana to come with me. She's a lawyer. I'm sure she knows how to negotiate the shit out of a car note.

"That's fair," I respond as I look out the window.

She weaves and speeds through traffic as we make our way to the arena, and I am humbly surprised at the lead foot and agility she has on the road. I also realize that her car is not an automatic. She has opted for a manual transmission and she shifts the gears with ease as she speeds through the streets.

"Where did you learn how to drive like this?" I ask her as I watch her shift down.

Tiana is silent for a long moment before she speaks, "I like to watch F1."

Now, *that* is something.

"Formula One?" I ask.

"Mhmmm," she confirms.

"Why?"

"Well, because my dad watches it. And I like the way their cars move on the track."

Shit. This woman just keeps getting hotter and hotter. I adjust in my seat as my cock hardens and I'm sincerely appreciative in this moment that she couldn't give less of a fuck about me.

I close my eyes and start mentally naming some teams that have held the Stanley Cup in order to get the bastard to retreat until eventually I'm free. When I open my eyes, I realize we've parked and we're already at the arena.

"That was fast," I murmur as I look around.

"I have shit to do," she responds as she reaches down to the floor of the passenger seat.

She leans over the center console and the only thing I can imagine is her leaning over this way to give me head in her fucking car.

God fucking damnit.

My dick hardens again at the thought, and I swear she nudges it with her elbow as she pulls her bag from the floor.

Her arm yanks her bag, and she clutches it against her chest.

"What the fuck was that?" she asks as her face contorts in rabid confusion.

My eyes widen as I look at her. "What was what?" I ask with a clueless expression.

Which is difficult as shit to do, considering she *definitely* just felt my hard cock.

"I just bumped something in your pants. Do you have a fucking boner right now?" she asks.

My mind works for a long moment, and I decide to feign ignorance.

"A boner? Right now? What kind of man do you take me for?" I ask.

"A horny one," she states with a bored look on her face.

Well.

"It's just my rock hard thighs. I am a hockey player. Gotta get to the puck somehow," I tell her with a convincing smile.

Her eyes trail down my body, and luckily, the distraction of her questions rid me of my boner, so there is but a mere print through my black sweatpants.

Thank God for black fucking sweatpants.

"All you gotta do is ask. I'll be more than happy to show you," I say with a playful grin.

She groans with an annoyed roll of her eyes as she grabs her coffee, her tumbler, and her tote to leave the car with a loud slam of her door.

Tiana waits for me to grab my backpack before she locks her car and quickly trots up to the arena. I make a note of running in front of her to get to the door so she doesn't have to open it.

She glares at me as she enters and rushes toward her office

"Can you give me a ride home today, sweetness?!" I call after her.

I hear her make another loud groan in response as she turns into her office and she throws the door shut behind her.

A laugh makes its way out of me as I walk to the locker rooms and ready myself for practice.

CHAPTER TEN

TIANA

I swear to God, if this fucking man doesn't stop with his weird advances, I'm going to like it and that is the absolute last thing that I want.

Or need.

After Gunnar asked me on the date, I took the chance to look over some rules for interpersonal relationships between lawyers and players.

Turns out, this is extremely risky.

It's against code to date players. It's a liability and a conflict of interest if I were to represent him in court.

Unfortunately, I can't just hand off all his issues onto my mother. Not only would she be infuriated with me, she'd be disappointed. And that's another strife added to the list of things I don't want to happen.

I've had to make sure I keep Charlotte's mouth shut and told her if she wants me to see this through, mom and dad cannot know about it.

I couldn't believe he showed up to my fucking door with coffee this morning. Charlotte is about two seconds away from getting a cease and desist because I want to be annoyed, and I really *want* to hate these sweet things.

But I can't! And I hate that I can't! *Men* confuse me. Relationships *irritate* me. It feels like too much work and too much bullshit for very little payoff. Always want to be in your space, always upset when you want to just recharge. It's always been annoying to tell a grown ass man to go play.

Gunnar has made nothing difficult, aside from his constant nagging. And he's... worked with my schedule, instead of against it. It's something that is much more endearing than I imagined.

He's slowly breaking my walls down bit by bit, and I have no control over it.

I was even a little excited to drive him to work this morning. Even though the entire way there, I told myself that I hated it and it was stupid, and he needs to get a new car.

Hell, I'll even go with him to help if it'll get him out of my presence.

Jesus Christ, what am I even saying? I'm going as far as suggesting I spend more time with him than I need to?

I just need to not think about him until our date. That should be easy. That should be fine. I have gone so many years without the thought of a man by my side. If I could do it then, who is to say I can't do it now?

I drop my things on my desk and groan as I sit in my office chair, rolling up to my desk and getting straight to work.

The thought arises that I actually have to drive him back home today... and we have to walk to the same hallway.

I want to be upset. I want to tell him to fuck off and find someone else to get him home.

But all the reasoning for it makes sense. I don't want it to make sense. But it does.

As I continue working on everything for the rest of the day, my heart starts to 'pitter patter' when I think about seeing Gunnar at the end of practice.

I don't know why I start anticipating the piney, clean scent of him when the clock ticks down to five p.m. But I do.

When the soft knock raps at the open door frame of my office at five and I get a glimpse at him, butterflies go wild in my stomach. It takes everything in me to tamp them down and don a face of boredom.

Gunnar crouches down to linger in the doorway with a wide grin and his damp hair.

"Is there a reason that you have to shower here?" The words blurt out of me before I even think about them. As they fall out of my mouth, I realize how absolutely dumb of a question that is. I shake my head and he gives me a questioning look.

"Well, I have a little gentleman code I go by. And if I'm about to be in the presence of a pretty lady, I don't exactly like smelling like hockey gear and ball sack." He laughs.

My face slacks in disdain at his verbiage and he gives me a shrug.

"You asked. I just gave you the truth."

I roll my eyes as I put everything in my tote to leave, glancing up at Gunnar every so often.

He watches me closely, like a curious little critter, and I feel my temperature rise. As I take one more glance at him, I see his body tighten, waiting for me.

"Am I moving too slowly for you?" I tease.

"Not at all. You could move a bit slower if you'd like," he says with a smile.

"Then why are you so tense?"

Gunnar bites his lower lip as his eyes glance down at my things on the desk and then back up to my face.

Curiosity clashes against the heat inside of me. The way his teeth tug at his lip sends a pulse fluttering low in my belly, and I feel as if I'm really losing the strength—or the care—to tamp it down entirely. But as I mull over the small action, I realize what he's asking.

"You really wanna carry my things, don't you?" I ask with a faint smile.

Gunnar's eyes lighten and he gives me a quick nod.

A laugh bubbles out of me I'm not able to control, and I shake my head. "What is it with you and my things?"

Now the pink begins to rise against his cheeks, and he gives me a nervous smile as he brings a hand up to scratch at his neck.

"It's just part of my code. And they smell like you."

My eyes widen, and his smile turns mischievous as he realizes his words hit their mark.

Damn him.

"And what exactly do I smell like?" I ask.

"Like the beach. A fun summer day. Coconuts and sunscreen. The good kind," he says. His voice turns silky, as if he's imagining the scent and getting lost in it.

A gulp tugs at my throat as I realize that's basically my perfume. As well as my lotions and body wash.

I switch gears, trying to ignore his attention to detail. "You can carry my things, only so I don't have to bend over in front of you again." I wave him off as I finish putting my things away and step back from the desk to cross my arms against my chest.

Gunnar's smile is so wide his face might break, and he comes deeper into my office. He grabs my tote and cup from my desk, his eyes lingering on me.

"For the record, I would be more than happy to have you bend over in front of me," he says with a sly smirk.

Fucking hell, it's so goddamned hot in this building. I can't be in here.

"You wish," I mumble as I snatch my puffer jacket off the back of my office chair and round my desk.

Throwing it over my arm, my steps quicken as I make to get ahead of him. But his large strides keep pace right behind me.

"Every night, I surely do," I hear him say.

The flutters and heat swirling in me cause me to stop in my tracks, and I turn to face him. "Why are you so attracted to me?" I blurt out.

His face turns to one of surprise as he looks down at me. His gaze from this angle is achingly seductive, and more sparks pop and skitter across my skin.

"Just fuckin' look at you," he says with a low purr. His lips tug into a teasing smile as his eyes glimmer.

"It can't be just that," I remark as I challenge his heated gaze with a steely one of my own.

All these feelings are overwhelming me, and there is a war raging in my head.

I hate this. I hate that he's teasing me and making me sweat... but it also feels... fun?

To play this game with him. I never would have liked it in the past. But there's something here I can't deny, even if I want to. Even if I *need* to, I *can't*.

He bends over, his face inches from mine, before he leans in closer, right next to my ear. His fresh, woody scent invades every corner of me, and I want to melt just at the mere proximity.

A gentle graze of his breath swipes across my neck as he speaks, low and soft. "Because there have been too many nights where I've imagined you stuffed with my cock. And the faster I warm you up, the quicker that happens," he whispers.

Gunnar leans back, just enough to see my face, and he tilts his head as he watches me. He pins me with a desired glare so deep that it takes everything in me not to crash to my knees in front of him. All I can do is stare at him in shock.

"Got a question for you, sugar," he whispers.

My brow arches in response. It's the only thing I can muster because I have no words for this interaction. It's... stimulating. It's exciting. And I don't. Know. Why.

The willpower to keep my gaze cold is fraying more and more. The general air surrounding us sparking exponentially.

"I've been wondering... how is it you like to be fucked?"

My breath catches, my eyes widening as I gulp. I rarely enjoy eye contact. But it's impossible to look away in this moment.

His eyes flick down to catch the action before they come back up to meet my face.

"Hard? Soft? Deep? Shallow? Whatever it is, I can provide... but you look like you can take a good fucking, can't you?"

The words sink into me, spearing straight to my center to settle there with a vicious pulse.

I'd be a fool to say his silky words didn't put a vibrant image in my head that I'm incapable of pushing out.

"You're insane," I murmur through my shock.

"Only for you, sugar," he whispers. His teeth sink into his bottom lip as his eyes flick to my lips. His lids lower, just a bit, before he grins against where his teeth grip his lip. He lingers there for a moment before he stands and continues to walk past me toward the exit of the arena.

I feel like I can't move. No one–and I mean, *no one*—has ever been bold enough to outright say anything like that to me. My only reaction is to stare blankly ahead of me.

I want to be disgusted and appalled at the crass question and admission.

But I can't. It was too fucking hot to be appalled with.

And the reality of that is jarring. I've never had a man affect me like this. I would have vomited if a man said this to me in the past.

But that teeny tiny part of me that enjoys his teasing becomes bigger with every second I spend near him. It threatens to swallow me whole.

"I don't have all day, sweetness! Tucker awaits!" I hear Gunnar's voice echo against the concrete walls.

The reverberation of his voice pulls me from the shock, and I shake my head as I mindlessly turn around to follow behind him.

CHAPTER ELEVEN
GUNNAR

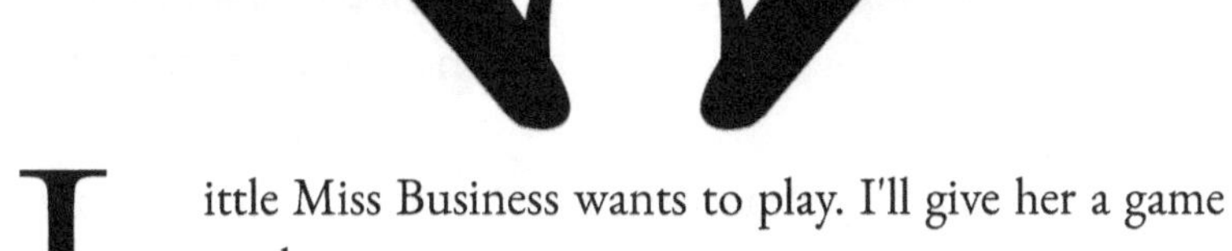

Little Miss Business wants to play. I'll give her a game to play.

I saw the way her body moved when I came to her office. I saw the slight twinkle in her eye when she got wind of me.

I'm slowly breaking through her little walls, and I'm going to take my chance where I can get it.

Was what I said insane? Absolutely. Was it fun? Hell fucking yeah.

The way her cheeks heated under my gaze. I'd say all of those things ten more times to get a reaction like that out of her.

I hear the furious clicking of her heels when she catches up to me and I hold open the door for her as she rounds the corner. She catches sight of me holding the door and her gaze shies away as she slows toward me.

She walks through it, taking care not to get within inches of me.

As I follow her to her car, all I can watch is the way her hips move. The way they swing when she walks in those little red bottom heels of hers is intoxicating and I nearly slam into her as we approach her car.

Luckily for me, I have quick reflexes and I stop myself before I do.

As she unlocks her car, I open the door to place her things in the back with my backpack. She throws herself into the vehicle and grips the ever loving shit out of her steering wheel as she waits for me to get in.

I take my time, because I'm enjoying making her so nervous. She's almost sweating.

As I buckle myself in, I expand myself into the seat, placing my hands on my thighs as I swing my head toward her with a cheshire grin.

"Am I making you nervous, sweetness?" I ask. I try to press a smokey hint of seduction into my voice. Watching her crumble under my taunts is the best shit I've done in a while.

"Would you like the honest answer?" she murmurs as she starts her car and peels out of the parking space.

The tires damn near burn against the pavement with the intensity she stomps on the gas, and I grip the "oh-shit" handle as she whips a sharp turn to the streets and throws me around.

My grin widens as I watch her handle this machine with the ease of a race car driver, even through her nerves.

"Always."

She doesn't spare me a glance, but she takes a heavy breath. "No one has ever said anything like that to me before."

I grin even wider. "Do you like it?"

"I... don't..." she trails off as she grips the steering wheel so hard her knuckles pale against it.

"You don't what, sweetness? Use your words."

Her brow furrows as she glances at me. "Or what?"

"I'll make you use them," I tell her smoothly.

She rolls her eyes as she looks back at the road. "Is that a threat?"

"It's a promise, sugar. And I always keep my promises."

I swear I see a bead of sweat roll down that bronzy chest of hers as her body tenses.

She's flustered beyond belief and I have to admit, making the hard-ass fall apart is sexy as hell.

I adjust the fabric of my pants as my dick hardens and I stretch my arms back to wrap around the headrest.

"Do you want me to stop?" I ask.

Sure, I'm having fun. But if she's not, then I'm not.

"I'm not your handler," she murmurs. She grips the steering wheel so hard, the tendons in the top of her hands become more apparent.

"Do you... want me... to stop?" I ask again. "If you want me to stop, I will."

She doesn't respond. I imagine she doesn't want to admit that she doesn't want me to stop. That would admit defeat in her eyes.

Tiana doesn't seem like the type to admit defeat.

Either way, I'll stop for the time being. It's not a direct yes or no. And I've had my fun so far, anyway.

Her gaze stays focused on the road ahead as she eventually makes her way into the parking garage. She parks next to my truck and takes a deep breath as she turns her vehicle off.

"When do you plan on getting your truck fixed?" she murmurs as her head collapses against the steering wheel.

I take a moment, my gaze floating to the ceiling of the vehicle in thought.

"I may just go get a new one and fix the ol' blue bastard at a later date. Care to accompany me on such an endeavor?" I ask slyly.

Tiana breathes again. "Will it get you out of my car faster?"

"If I find the right car, it surely will."

"Thank God," she murmurs as she finally presses the car door open.

Remembering her things, I spring into action. Leaning into the back seat, I try and gather as much of her things as my arms will allow me before I hop out of the car, snatching her water cup on the way out.

Tiana groans as she realizes I've beaten her to the punch and she begins to lead the way to the parking garage elevators.

I follow close behind, waiting quietly and patiently behind her.

As we make our way through the elevators to our floor, I decide not to tempt her any further. This is her safe place, in a sense. And the last thing I want to do is make her uncomfortable in her own home.

The arena is free game, level ice.

Soon, we make it up to our doors and she turns to me with boredom. She stretches her hands out to claim her things, and I gently hang her bag on her wrist before I hand over her Stanley cup.

I smile as I bring my hands to the straps of my backpack to look down at her.

"Goodnight, Gunnar," she grumbles as she turns on her heels to her apartment.

I watch as she walks to her apartment. "Goodnight, sweetness," I call softly.

She doesn't look back at me as she enters and the door clicks shut behind her.

CHAPTER TWELVE
TIANA

A deep, steeling breath moves through my body as I shut the door to my apartment and press my back flush against it. A shaky hand comes to grip the center of my chest as I bring all of my emotions back down to center.

The way this man is making me feel is causing my head to spin. Violently.

My tote slides from my wrist, along with my jacket, to crash to the floor in a sound of chaotic jingles as I clamber over to the kitchen island to slam my cup down on it.

My body slumps against it and a loud groan leaves me to echo through my apartment.

"What the fuck is wrong with me?" I whisper.

There is a pulsing ache in between my legs. Incessant, if I could call it anything.

I tried so hard to be disgusted with him and the way he spoke to me. But I could only think about the way his body would move on top of mine. I had to at least put on a face of disdain for it all, otherwise he would think I was enjoying it. I can't possibly let him think that. He'll only taunt me more.

God and the idea of actually being stuffed with him.

Who the fuck says stuffed? And who the fuck has that much on them to be *stuffed* by someone?!

I can't believe I'm turned on by this. By *him*. By a fucking *hockey player*.

I've seen the print of him through those sweatpants he wears. Even in black, they do nothing for the imagination. I sincerely hope that he's overcompensating, and that's why he's so bold.

But no, from the print I've seen, he's not overcompensating for anything.

The idea is terrifying and thrilling all at once.

Shaking my head, I quickly head to the bathroom so I can shower the day off. I just need to wash off and get in bed. Sleep it off is all.

I walk to my bedroom, shedding my clothes to throw them in the hamper. As I do; I catch sight of my panties in the floor-length mirror on the wall.

Soaked into the front of my undies is a large wet spot and I groan in annoyance.

Fine. *Fine.* I'll take care of it. If I take care of it, I won't be reacting to him like this.

I'm in a dry spell, that's all. A man is giving me ardent attention and I just happen to be turned on by it.

It's biological, there's nothing *specifically* about Gunnar that is the issue with this situation is all.

Reluctantly, I volley the idea back and forth before groaning loudly and moving to my bed. I haven't done this in a long while, but at this point I'm aching for a release from his teasing. There is no way I would ask him to fix this for me. What an absolutely insane idea.

Psychotic even.

The man wouldn't even be able to contain himself.

I slip the band of my thong from my hips, pressing them down more and more until they reach my knees and I fling it to the floor beside me.

Opening my legs, I slip my fingers into my center.

Fuck.

I can't remember the last time I was this wet.

My fingers circle my clit and my head presses back against the pillow as I feel how slick I am.

The pressure slowly climbs the longer I rub myself and soft pants leak into the surrounding air.

At first, I just think about the way it feels.

Until Gunnar's voice echoes in my head, *"Hard? Soft? Deep? Shallow?"*

How the fuck does one say I want him anyway he'll have me?

Why the fuck do I want that?

I groan once more as I push the thought out of my head and focus on the way it feels.

My free hand trails along my body to grip at my tits, and I tug at a hardened nipple.

The action causes an electric shock to course through me, and my breaths lighten as I scale that summit higher and higher.

Gunnar's face flashes across my mind. His low, lidded eyes and the sight of his lip bit between his teeth causes the summit to approach at an increasing speed. I attempt to push the thought of him away, but then the vision of what his cock would look like arrives. The way it would feel... *God damnit.*

Thick, long, and pulsing. I can't help the way my pussy clenches around nothing as I imagine him 'stuffing' me like he promised to do.

Soon, stars blast violently across my eyelids and a moan releases from my throat as my orgasm barrels through me without warning.

My fingers slow against my clit and my hand falls from my center as I lay there, panting at the ceiling.

This fucking hockey player crept his way into my life and I just fucked myself at the thought of him.

The longer I think about that fact and reality, the angrier I get and it propels me out of bed and into the shower. I scrub my body in a futile attempt to rid my growing attraction to Gunnar away.

It does not work.

Not even a little.

The next morning, I wake up and groan as my alarm blares through my room.

Five a.m., as usual.

I take a little more time getting ready as I realize I have to take Gunnar to the arena.

Eventually, I finally get ready and I open my front door, expecting to see Gunnar there.

And while I am right, he's not dressed for practice. He has a coffee in his hand and a smile on his face that is way too big for this early in the morning.

He's actually in nice jeans and a Seattle Stags hoodie.

My brow furrows as I look at him. "Why aren't you dressed for practice?"

"I texted Coach and told him I needed to borrow the lawyer to buy a new vehicle because mine shit on me."

I look at him with a questioning quirk of my brow. "And... what did he say?"

"He thought it was a good idea for the rookie to have legal advice on a big purchase like this. So, go change. I doubt you wanna look at cars in that getup," he says as he nods at my outfit.

I look at my business attire and sigh.

He's entirely right. There's no way I want to be looking at cars in fucking heels.

I groan as I roll my eyes. "You can come in while I change. But no coming into my room."

Gunnar bites back an excited grin as he ducks under the threshold to come inside.

His head swivels as he looks around, letting a whistle go as he shoves his hands into his pockets. "Nice place," he remarks.

I ignore him as I head to my bedroom to quickly change into some Uggs, a hoodie and some black leggings.

Once I come out, he turns to me and whistles again.

"Sweet as sugar," he says with a playful grin.

My thoughts go back to last night and the act I committed with him on my mind.

Heat rises to my cheeks as I look past him, zeroing in on my smaller backpack and quickly grabbing it. I quickly move some of my essentials from my tote to the backpack, throw it on my back and run like a bat out of hell out of the apartment.

Gunnar follows, shutting my front door behind him to catch up with me. He's quiet as we make our way to the elevators and I try to get my brain off of last night.

"So, where were you trying to go?" I ask.

Gunnar ponders for a moment, his face contorting and twisting as he thinks. "I want to go to a Chevy dealership."

The elevator arrives, filling the hallway with the sound of the beep as the doors open. Gunnar gestures to the car, letting me in first, and I roll my eyes as I walk in. He follows and presses the button for the lobby floor, and I lean against the wall with my arms crossed over my chest as I watch him.

"Okay... And what are you thinking about getting?"

"I have a few thoughts. I have an expendable income from my draft bonus, since I barely spent any of it. I just gave some to my family and bought this apartment."

My brow tenses as I listen to him. "You didn't do *anything* crazy with it? You didn't buy a brand new, state-of-the-art stick or new gear?"

I knew about the truck. But I didn't know he barely spent *any* of it.

Gunnar laughs and the way it fills the small metal box, fills my heart with heated butterflies.

"I didn't find it necessary. I like what I have just fine. Charlotte knows what I like, and she makes sure they're prepped right."

I shouldn't be jealous at the mention of my sister. But for whatever reason... I am. I don't like the way he says her name, and I take a deep breath as I try to focus on the task at hand.

"So, vehicle. You want a car? Another truck? Maybe an SUV?"

The elevator doors slide open as we reach the lobby, and there is silence between us as we continue to the elevator for the parking garage.

Even when we enter the elevator for the garage, he's quiet, worrying his lower lip in thought.

"I'm not sure," he finally murmurs. His gaze slides to me as he looks me up and down in a heated gaze. "I'm sure I'll know when I see it," he says. His lips quirk to one side in a playful grin.

Again, the heat returns in full force and I am eternally

grateful to hear the ring of the elevator as it exits to the parking garage.

I pound the pavement out of the elevator and head straight for my vehicle. Unlocking it, I climb in and start the engine.

Though the heat from his attention fades away as I watch Gunnar. He goes to the driver's side of his old truck and attempts to start it. The engine sputters and clanks for a long moment, grinding and wailing as he attempts a few more times. Eventually, he stops, and I see him sigh. He strokes the steering wheel with a slow, pained sadness.

I don't like the way his sadness stirs something in me. He did say it belonged to his grandpa, so I imagine it held sentimental value to him. Maybe I won't be so mean to him today since he's dealing with this.

He takes another moment, patting the wheel before he gets out of the truck to climb into mine.

Gunnar shoves into the passenger seat of my car and he gives me a soft smile as he buckles his seat belt.

"Ready," he says. But there is no playfulness in his tone and there is not the same twinkle in his eyes.

It feels as if my chest tightens at the sight of him so distraught over this. But I nod and slowly pull out of the spot to drive out of the garage.

Once we make it to the roads, we move along the streets. But Gunnar is still quiet. *Very quiet.*

He stares out the window and watches the world go by in utter silence.

I didn't realize just how much it meant to him. And the longer he stays silent, the longer the weight of his sadness crushes me with it.

"Do you wanna talk about it?" I ask softly as I take a ramp onto a freeway.

Gunnar seems slightly startled as I bring him from his thoughts and he gives me a hollow laugh.

"It's nothing. I wish it would have lasted longer. But I may have to have my dad take it to see what he can do with it."

I'm silent as he speaks and he moves his attention back to the window.

It's quite a while before he finally speaks again.

"I have a lot of memories of that truck," he breathes.

My brow furrows, but I say nothing.

"I told you how my Pa is the reason we all skate. Well, in the winter, he would drive us in that old truck, out to a random lake. We'd have a net, a couple of pucks and sticks in the bed and we'd drive out to wherever he wanted to go that day."

The road seems to blur in my line of sight as I escape into the little portrait of his past that he's painting.

"I remember pulling the net out of the bed to carry it to the ice. I'd push it against the fresh snow on top and Pa would spend a solid amount of time moving the snow from a small area so Gretz, Brooks and I could skate. I was about fifteen at the time, so I had some skating hours under my belt. Gretz and Brooks weren't very old, so it was up to Pa and I to get them squared away."

He shakes his head as he lets out a small laugh. "After skating, we'd go get some hot chocolate to warm up. He taught us all the stuff we know. He's the reason the Hayze brothers are the enforcers we are. Pa told us to never take shit on and off the ice. It's why I always go for what I want."

I suppose if you have memories of something like that, there is no car made that could replace it. My chest aches with the thought of him having to find a new vehicle. Especially after this one has been such a big part of his life, pretty much the entire time.

It feels like a weird compulsion, one I couldn't stop even if

I wanted to. But I reach over, softly grabbing his hand to offer the smallest bit of comfort. The rough callouses of his palm grip against mine as his hand tightens in surprise. His attention is drawn from the window, to look down at my hand.

I glance to him with a small smile and he smiles back as he pats my hand softly.

I don't know why I feel better coming with him on this excursion. Part of me is glad that he's not going through this alone. For someone like him, where it seems as if hockey is his everything, this truck seems to be a big part of that. I can't really imagine the sadness he may be feeling to see it stop working.

Perhaps in his eyes it's the end of an era. And if there is anything I know about hockey players, is that they really hold on tight to the good ones.

He holds my hand as we ride to the dealership in companionable silence.

CHAPTER THIRTEEN
GUNNAR

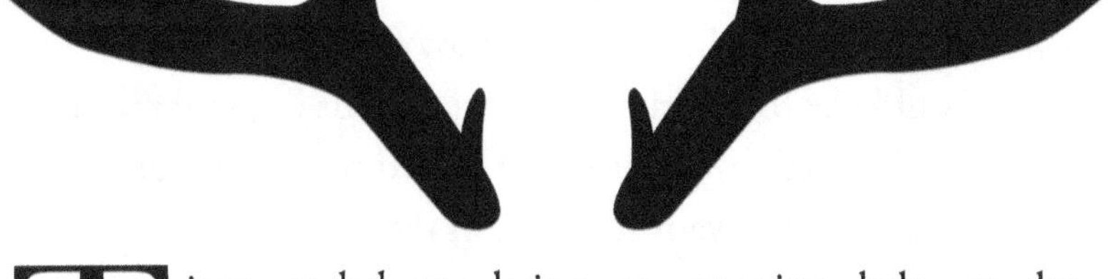

Tiana ended up being an amazing help at the dealership.

Because of her interest in cars and Formula One, she saw the guy was charging way more than was necessary for the vehicle and she talked him down.

She really didn't have to. I had more than enough money to buy one. But she was insistent. Honestly, it was sexy as fuck to have a woman fight on my behalf, and I kinda enjoyed seeing her go into lawyer mode.

It turns out that having a lawyer on your side is, in fact, a very nice thing in the moment.

I ended up going with a bright red Corvette Stingray, with black bow ties and black accessories. Unfortunately for Tiana, it's not a manual. But it was one of the fastest ones on the lot.

As we looked around, I really wasn't sure what I wanted. Pa's truck was everything I needed and more. I didn't need anything fancy and flashy. But when Tiana reacted to the Stingray... I don't know. There was something there that told me that was the one. She tried all she could not to seem excited. But she couldn't hold back.

When I told the dealer that was the vehicle I wanted, she made a loud squeal. An interesting sound, actually. And her hands flexed and tightened with glee. I'd never seen a person react to anything like that. But it was cute. Endearing, even. Perhaps it was a look at what she hides under that brood she keeps over her face.

When I get the keys, I hand them out to her and she gives me the most perplexed look. The car doesn't mean much to me in that sense. But I know for a lead foot like Tiana, that driving this thing is going to be an absolute joy for her.

I would like to be driving Pa's truck. But I've said my good-byes, and I texted my dad that we'll need to meet up and get it taken away. I don't want it sitting in the parking garage, and if need be, I'll pay for a place to store it.

But somehow, Tiana's excitement for this vehicle makes the ache a little less.

She's fun to poke at and I enjoy messing with her, but this... there's something deeply satisfying about seeing her indulge in something she loves.

It's different from attraction, different from infatuation. It's a weird, warm feeling where I want to see more of those smiles from her. I want to feel more of that excitement from her on my behalf.

I get in Tiana's vehicle, extremely thankful to be a man that still knows how to drive a manual transmission. Considering Pa's truck was a manual, this is a piece of cake for me.

Unfortunately, I underestimate Tiana's excitement, as she damn near burns out the tires on her way out of the dealership. She crosses through the roads and does all the fun things I suppose a lead foot would do. She takes as many side streets as she can, trying to wring out her time with my vehicle. I honestly have a hard time keeping up with her because she's faster than I think even she knows.

But I'm happy to give her this time. If she cares this much about cars, I'll let her drive it as often as she wants.

When we arrive back at the apartment, we park the vehicles next to each other. At least beside the truck. Tiana takes a moment to look over the Corvette again, admiring it in silence. There are moments where it seems like her excitement tries to escape her in wiggles and shakes. I laugh every time because it's the most precious thing I've ever seen.

Eventually, she finally walks away from it, handing me the keys with a smile she can't fight even if she tried.

Since we technically have the day off, Tiana takes it as a chance to hide out in her apartment for the rest of the day. I decide not to bother her, if she wants her space, I'll let her have it. She deserves her time to herself, even if I so badly want to spend it with her.

The next two weeks come and go in a blur. Tiana has been parking next to my new vehicle at the arena when I arrive before her. I have even seen her face once or twice in the box during practices. I try to pull out all the best moves I know when she comes around.

And by the next Friday, we have an away game that we win. It sets me up for a thrilling high as I dress for my date with Tiana the day after.

Standing in the bathroom, looking in the mirror, I adjust the lapels of my suit that I bought specifically for this day. A black on black situation with a bright red tie.

Tiana loves black and I imagine she'll also be wearing black. So, I tempt fate to try and match her.

My heart pounds hard in my chest, flooding my body with nerves of pure glee.

Slowly, she's been opening up to me. She's been showing me little bits and pieces of herself. A smile at work. Or letting me walk her to her car at the end of the day. I go to her office every day after practice. Carry her things and sometimes we race to see who gets back to the complex fast.

Tiana almost always wins.

Sometimes I'll ask if she wants to walk outside with me to take Tucker out to the dog park. And she'll accompany me.

The girl knows a lot about stars. She knows so much about the constellations, where their positions are, and she'll point them out as we look out at the sky together, waiting for Tucker to finish. She even knows some of their origins.

And maybe Tucker realizes what's happening, or maybe he's in his own world, but I swear he takes longer outside when Tiana is with us.

But I take every little bit she gives me, cradling them close and showing her I care about them. Whether it's her words at the end of a workday where she gets to blow off her steam, or just a small thing about herself.

I love seeing the way she nervously fidgets when I come to walk her out to our cars. Or the way her eyes light up when she points at Orion's Belt. Or Ursa Major.

A knowledgeable little woman, she makes me feel things I've never felt before. But I feel like I still don't know her as well as I would like to. Which is why I'm excited about tonight. I'm going to crack the shell of that sweet girl wide open and I'm gonna see what she is hiding underneath.

Another deep breath courses through my lungs and I

adjust my hair one last time before taking another look at myself in the mirror.

I nod in approval when I feel like I look good enough and turn to Tucker. He comes to wag his tail at me with a bark and a laugh escapes me as I scratch at his head.

"Big day, today, Tuck! Wish me luck!" I say as I grab the handful of roses on the kitchen island.

Heading for the door, I exit and lock it behind me before I make my way to hers. Another deep and steadying breath comes from me before I knock softly.

It takes a moment, but soon, she answers.

Heat rises all over my skin in a flood of tingles and sparks when I feel my jaw slack as I see her.

Her hair has been perfectly curled in those tight natural curls she has. Every one separated and coiled in touchable ringlets. Her black glasses sit against her heated cheeks as she glances at me with those big green eyes of hers. Her dress is a tight, red number. One that hugs and grips every part of her decadent frame. With a long slit that goes all the way up to her hip to show the expansive tanned skin beneath. Her thighs have strong ridges in them with moisturized, shiny, soft skin. I swear I almost drool as I look at the way the fabric contorts around her curves and I groan as I run my hand through my hair.

I honestly have no words for how she looks. My cock seems to agree as it hardens to near pain in my pants.

Her eyes connect with mine nervously, almost in anticipation. "Do you not like it?" she asks.

I shake my head as I bring myself back to the present. She has me hypnotized.

"Like it? Sweetness, there are no words to describe how absolutely breathtaking you look," I tell her with a sincere smile.

Pink swallows her face, and it makes the little splats of brown freckles on her cheeks brighten.

I hand the bundle of roses out to her and smile. "These are for you," I breathe.

Her eyes roam over the blooms as she takes them from my hands, and she smiles adoringly as her eyes come back to me. "These are gorgeous," she says in a hushed, sweet tone.

"Yes... yes, they surely are," I say as I take another gaze over her.

I feel like my heart has stopped and I can't breathe. She looks stunning. Magnificent. I don't have a thesaurus big enough.

She leans into her house to place the roses on her kitchen island before she comes back and nods to me in readiness. I reach a hand out, where she eyes it for a moment before her shimmering chest rises in a deep breath and she places her delicate hand in mine. Sparks crackle beyond comprehension as our skin touches, and I squeeze her hand as I guide her to the elevator.

When we arrive at the glass garden, Tiana stares out the window at some sculptures that are illuminated through the foliage, lending a magical glow to the darkened leaves in the night.

The actual venue is two areas. A garden with glass sculptures and a large walk through museum area with more glass.

Once we park, I help Tiana out of the vehicle and loop her arm in mine as we walk through the pathway around the garden. Some of the art is twisted and contorted in such a way that it looks like something out of a cartoon. But Tiana lingers on some pieces, tilting her head and observing them in awe.

I wish I could say I knew what a lot of those pieces really looked like. But I was so captured by *her*. The way her eyes twinkled at the glass. The way she rounded the sculptures, trying to look at them from every angle she could before she moved on to the next one.

As we continue moving through the garden, Tiana doesn't say much. She seems to be in her own world, admiring all the glass. And her silence doesn't bother me, not when I get so caught up in watching her.

At some point, we make it inside, where we're greeted by one of the employees. I make sure they have us down, and the woman tells us to enjoy our walk through, and dinner will be ready for us in the glasshouse when we make it down there.

Tiana is so excited that she tugs my hand with full force through the exhibits.

"This one looks like crystals!" she says in excitement as we stop at one sculpture in the front.

All the pieces inside are illuminated by lights, making their colors more vibrant. It lends a nice, dull warmth as we meander through the area.

I will say, it is nice to walk leisurely through here and not have to share the space with any other people. Maybe Tiana is right in that regard.

But her heels tapping against the floor add a soft echo through the space, one that makes me really lean into the fact that it's her and I in this space together.

We walk and admire the pieces through the building for a while until we come to a massive glass house at the end.

The room is cleared out, and you're surrounded by giant glass panes, staring straight out into the stars. But you also get a view of some of the illuminated sculptures that rest in the garden. The only lights inside are present on the massive waving sculpture that rests above our heads. Oranges, reds and yellows, make up a massive display of glass art that looks like giant flowers, and as we walk in, Tiana's completely entranced by it.

Her lips part and her eyes widen as she swirls under the sculpture, looking straight above as if she's never seen anything so magnificent.

But I can't notice all the details in the pieces. Not when I watch her. I don't think there will be anything more magnificent than her.

My hands slip into my pockets, my eyes stuck to this woman I've chased for the past several weeks.

Her guard has slipped tonight. And I've gotten to see a star struck woman that appreciates these things in her vicinity more than you'd think. She's taken her time with all the pieces, looking at them from all angles, absorbing the way they look. And there's something admirable in that. In the way, someone gets so lost in the sight of something so... well crafted.

I suppose I would know.

A lone table with a black tablecloth sits in the middle of the room, directly under the sculpture. With large chairs, empty wine glasses, and glasses of water. But I let Tiana take her time, moving at her pace until she feels as if she is ready to sit down. And when I notice her moving to the table, I move with her, going to pull out her seat.

She sits down with a shy smile, and I scoot her in before I make my way to my seat.

Charlotte mentioned Tiana likes steak and potatoes. A simple girl she is, but I made sure she had it. Of course, with tons of bread.

Tiana's face glows with a feeling of content as she takes another look at the glass walls surrounding us.

"This has been an amazing night so far, Gunnar. I'm honestly impressed," she says with a sweet smile.

A smile crests my cheeks as I lean in against the table. "Well, I do like to keep the promises I make," I say as I take a sip of my water.

More pink creeps across her face as smiles sheepishly at me. "And what promises are you referring to?"

My smile widens as I place my cup down. "The one where I said I'd be so good to you if you gave me the chance."

More and more, her blush grows and she gives me a shy smile as she looks back up at the enormous sculpture over head. Her head tilts as she tries to capture every detail in it she can.

"I wanna know more about you," I tell her.

That brings her attention back to me and her eyes widen as she registers my question. Her head tilts curiously. "What is it you want to know?"

I give her a soft laugh. "Well, if we had all night, I'd ask for everything. But for now, I'll just ask for what's important."

She rolls her eyes with a soft smirk. "Well, ask me a question."

I smile at her challenge. The intense little lawyer has come out to play. After seeing shy Tiana, I kinda missed that fiery girl.

"What made you want to become a lawyer?" I ask as I take another sip.

She thinks, her eyes gazing off as someone comes to fill her glass with wine and bring us a basket of bread.

"I'm sure you know my mother is a lawyer."

The waiter comes to fill my glass, but I bring a hand up to stop them and they nod in acknowledgement as they walk away.

"I do," I say with a small nod. Tamisha Dawn was the one who had done all my paperwork for the Stags.

"Charlotte was always the one that loved hockey. The chaos of the fights. Dad has always been a coach. Minor league, mid, now the pros. I was more like my mother. I like the structure, and to be honest, I enjoy the mundane. It keeps me grounded in a high paced area like this," she explains.

She reaches for some of the bread and tears small pieces from it to press into her mouth.

I watch her intently, because, well; I love hearing her speak. I love her voice and I love the way she commands a room, at least when she's trying to. I suppose you need to be able to do that to represent people in a courtroom. But it seems as if that's just the way she talks.

"I enjoy helping people out of tough situations. Even if they were the ones to get themselves into it. I enjoy problem solving and arguing. That happens to be the best part of it all, if I'm going to be honest," she says with a small giggle.

That tracks.

I smile at her words and her enthusiasm for something like this. It's so sweet that it makes my heart flutter in my chest.

"Why didn't you go more toward the racing realm if you like Formula One so much?" I ask as I peel apart a piece of bread.

Her finger traces the lip of her wineglass as she thinks. Her head rests in her hand, tilting as she watches the liquid ripple against the walls.

"Formula One is more international. I mean, hockey is too. But not as frequent as Formula One. Almost all of their races are overseas and a good majority of their racers are foreign. And I don't know many languages. I don't mind traveling, but I wanted to stay in one place. Plus, I like my space and I can't have that if I'm traveling the world. There's also many more people involved than what I deal with now, and I don't exactly enjoy interacting with people all that much."

Even in her responses, she's methodical. She has an answer for everything, a reason for it all.

I love a woman that can lead. A woman that knows what she wants and isn't afraid to stick it to the ones who think it's not for her. She protects her peace and her energy, something that I think more people shouldn't be afraid to do.

She's herself. And I love that.

"Why are you single? I don't think that's a bad thing, but I am curious," I say as I take another sip of my water.

Her eyes roam the glass structure, looking around as she speaks, "Men are... confusing. The ones I've attracted have never enjoyed that I like time to myself. They called me boring. Or they said I was no fun. I never really cared much. If they didn't want to be around, I didn't have much of an issue not having them around. And after some time, I decided I'd much rather just live my own life and not have to worry about the opinions of others. Not when I'm happy in my space."

My head tilts, and my brows furrows. "What an odd thing. For them, obviously. Not you. A woman needs her space."

Tiana's eyes come back to mine, and a small smile crests on her lips as she nods softly. "I agree," she says.

Our food comes a bit later and we spend the rest of the night eating, drinking and talking. I tell her some of my favorite hockey chirps I've heard on the ice and about some of the best fights I've been in. How it was, growing up with hockey brothers.

I ask her about her likes, her dislikes. Her favorite animal— it's a sloth—and I ask anything and everything I can about her.

By the end, and four glasses of wine, she's incredibly loose. She giggles and laughs at my jokes so much more. My cheeks ache from how much smiling I'm doing in her presence, and I don't even care. If she's the cause, I'll take the pain. Of course, I'm completely sober because I'm driving us. But I'm glad she gets to relax some. Part of me feels like she doesn't really get to do this very often.

When we leave the exhibits, she wobbles out on her heels and she groans as she rips them off. Subsequently reaching her arms up at me to carry her. Of course, I can't resist, so I swing her over my shoulder and she squeals an excited noise as I carry her to my vehicle.

She slumps happily against my shoulder and I gently place her in the passenger seat, buckling her in and waiting for her to get comfy before I get in to drive us to the complex.

Tiana has a sweet smile on her face as she rests in her seat. Her eyes closed, and she makes a gentle humming noise of some kind as I drive through the streets.

Seeing her in my car like this, so lost in her happiness, thrums a happiness *in me*. A calm even. Something primal, in a sense.

I want to see this version of her all the time. This night with her is everything I could have asked for. Getting closer to her and seeing what she has under that shell of hers makes me beam with a sort of pride. That somehow, out of the other men that may have tried, I'm the only one that succeeded.

I'm glad that I've been able to get her to a place where she feels safe enough to open up to me. That's really what it's about. She feels *safe* with me.

When we get to the parking garage, I come around to the passenger side, lifting her out of the car in a cradle hold and carrying her to the elevators. She rests so peacefully, with her head against my chest as I walk her to her door.

"Where are weeeee?" she asks with a slight slur. It's obvious she's a tad inebriated.

"We're at home, sugar," I whisper softly before I bring her inside. And there is something in those words that stirs something warm inside of me. Like a bowl of soup after a day of skating on the lake.

Softly kicking the door closed behind me, I walk to her living room to sit her on the couch. I make sure she's comfortable by grabbing one of the throw blankets she has and wrapping it around her shoulders before I move to the kitchen to get her a glass of water. It takes a bit because I have no idea where her dishes are, but I get it done.

Tiana leans back on the couch, her head slumped to the side before I kneel in front of her with the water.

"Tiana," I whisper to get her attention.

Her head straightens, though wobbly, and she smiles sweetly as she catches sight of me through her glassy, lost eyes. I offer her the water and her hands graze mine as she takes it. She sips it deeply with a contented sigh before she hands it back to me, and I turn around to place it on the coffee table. Turning back to her, I place my hands on the couch beside her knees, giving her a smile, and making sure she's well enough to be at least left alone here.

Her teeth bite softly into her lower lip as she smiles and slowly, she reaches forward to graze her hand against my jaw. Soon, her eyes close and she leans in, a small purse to her lips.

My eyes widen as I realize she's going in for a kiss and I quickly grab her wrist to stop her. Light enough to know I'm not upset, but quick enough for her to know 'not now.'

The movement pulls her out of her stupor, and she stares at me in shock. Her lips part on a small gasp as heat rises to her cheeks.

"Oh... oh my god. I'm so sorry... I thought..." she slurs.

I give her a kind smile as I drag her hand away from my face. Turning it over, I place a small kiss on the top of it.

"I don't kiss intoxicated ladies. Sorry, sweetness. Part of the code."

I'm not sure she understands me, but she gives me a slightly sad look as she nods.

I would love to kiss her right now. More than anything in this world. But I can't. She's had some alcohol, and I had to bring her to her apartment. It's just not the right thing.

"I'll check on you in the morning?" I ask as I come to stroke a thumb over her cheek.

She doesn't connect with my gaze as she nods. "Uhm.. uh sure," she responds quietly.

I smile as I stand, checking her cup again to make sure she has enough water before I take my leave.

As I walk to the door, I glance over my shoulder to see her curled up on the couch with the Seattle Stags blanket wrapped tight around her. Soft breaths leak out of her as she falls asleep against the cushions.

With that, I exit the apartment as quietly as I came.

CHAPTER FOURTEEN
TIANA

Absolute pounding consumes my *entire* skull.

I really shouldn't be hungover after only four glasses of wine. But I am.

A groan rumbles in my throat as the sunlight from my windows blasts against my face and ruins my sleep.

I try to remember bits and pieces of the night. And while they are a tad blurry, there is one specific instance I remember too vividly.

The way Gunnar rejected my kiss.

It hurt. A lot more than I expected it to.

A lot more than any other rejection in the past.

I bury my face into the couch cushions as red, hot embarrassment washes over me. The vision replaying on an annoying loop in my head repeatedly.

I can't believe I tried that. I took a chance on something and was rejected. It's so *dumb*. It's so stupid.

He said he doesn't kiss inebriated girls, which I guess is a considerate thought. But I wasn't so out of my mind that it would have been bad for me to kiss him. I just wanted a taste.

He gave me a night that I couldn't forget. His full undi-vided attention and made it seem like for just those few hours, I was the only thing that mattered. And it made me feel... so fulfilled.

Most men didn't give a shit about what lurks beneath the surface. They made me feel like it was all superficial. But there was not a single moment with Gunnar where it seemed like it was a game or a ruse.

He just wanted to know *me*, see me for what I truly am. And I gave him everything I could, with what little I knew how to give.

Now it feels like maybe I shouldn't have, if he could reject me so easily. How does someone chase that hard and then deny a kiss? It doesn't make sense.

I shake my head at the thoughts and embarrassment before I get up to take a shower.

Prying my dress off of my shoulders, I let it pool on the floor before I step into the running water. I let it wash away the icy feeling of rejection. It doesn't really work, but at least I feel cleaner. And when I come out, I dry myself off and wrap up in a silky black robe. But not so long after, I hear a knock on my front door.

A groan works through me when I remember that Gunnar said he was going to come back and check on me today.

My eyes roll as I huff an annoyed breath and tighten the sash around my waist. I push away my shame from last night, donning a face of stone as I open the door.

Gunnar stands there with a sweet smile and a cup of coffee. A large bottle of water in his other hand.

"Good morning, sweetness," he says softly. As if he's trying to be considerate of me possibly being hungover.

I give him an annoyed look as I survey the little gifts he brought. "Hello."

"How do you feel?" he asks.

"Fine," I respond, deadpan.

Gunnar's brow furrows in confusion as he looks at me. "Is there something wrong?"

I look at him in disdain before I reach out and grab the coffee and water from him.

"Nope. All good."

His frown deepens, and he nods.

"Alright, well. I hope you're feeling better. I have to get back to Tucker," he says, almost sadly.

"Thanks for the coffee," I murmur as I close the door.

Is it rude? Probably.

But, I'm still in shock over the fact he rejected something from me he pined so hard for.

It reminds me of why I stopped dating. Games, games and more *games*.

I work for a hockey team. I do not have time for any more fucking games.

Sure, he told me his intentions. He showed me how attentive he could be. But if he wanted to fuck me so badly, why reject a simple kiss?

It infuriates me and I spend the rest of the day curled up on the couch, sipping the coffee and water that he brought me.

The entire weekend I spend wallowing in my sadness. I really shouldn't let something like this affect me so much. If it was some other guy, it wouldn't. But with it being Gunnar, it sends me into a pit of utter despair.

So when Monday rolls around and I make my way to my

office, I'm almost pissed to see Gunnar standing by my closed office door.

He gives me a shy smile as I approach, and I don't even look at him as I unlock my door and drop my stuff on my desk. Gunnar hesitantly follows in behind me and stands quietly as I unpack my things for the day.

"What do you want, Gunnar?" I murmur as I open up my laptop.

Gunnar has a nervous smile pulling at the corner of his mouth as he rubs the back of his neck.

"Did I do something wrong?" he asks quietly.

I roll my eyes. "No. You're fine. Go to practice."

Glancing up for the merest second, I see his brow furrow in confusion. "Did you enjoy the date?"

"I did," I tell him. Because even though he didn't return my advances, I did enjoy the date. That is the truth.

"Well... Would you like to go on another some time?"

Glancing at him, I give him an incredulous look. "Pass."

He gives me a sad smile as he nods. "I understand. I'll see you around, Tiana," he says as he leaves.

But god damn my stupid heart, I *watch* him leave. I watch the way he crouches down to exit, closing the door as he does, and a loud sigh leaves me. Falling into my chair, I breathe a noise of utter annoyance.

My hands run over my face and my office fills with my loud groan.

He sounded so destroyed and I'd be lying if I said it didn't send a pang of hurt through me.

But he kept to his word. I took him on one date and rejected the other, so he's leaving me alone.

I have to at least enjoy that for the most part... right?

So, why do I feel like this?

Bad...? I feel *bad* that I was so mean to him. I don't feel like he deserved that. He has been so kind to me, albeit horny. But kind, regardless.

I'm upset that he gave up so easily. I thought he wasn't like that.

Maybe I jumped the gun...? Maybe I'm being too harsh. I don't even really know. I feel sad that I won't see Gunnar like I did before.

But this is what I wanted... *isn't it?*...

Isn't it? I try to ask myself.

And when nothing answers, I feel as if this *isn't* what I wanted.

I've been hurt and burned in the past from rejection. Even if those times weren't a big deal, this time *does* feel like a big deal.

I hate to say that I like Gunnar. I liked the date we went on and I like the way he treats me.

He's respectful of my space and my time. He's never once made me feel like a burden, and I never realized how much the others made me feel like one until I met Gunnar. He showed me something I've never seen before. He's kind. He's actually funny sometimes. He's incredibly thoughtful. He's generous. Not to mention, he's stunning. He's good at his job.

Still, how could he reject me?

The warring thoughts in my head damn near consume me, and I try to focus on the work at hand. It's the only thing that will at least be able to keep me from going insane over everything.

This is another reason I don't enjoy dating. I'm so focused on the logistics of everything that I can barely get a grip on the things I should actually be doing.

I shake my head of all the conflicting thoughts and force myself to lock in for the day.

And by god, I fucking do.

CHAPTER FIFTEEN
GUNNAR

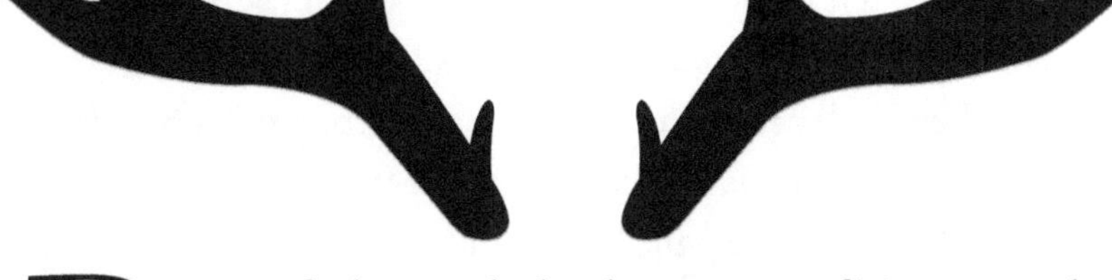

Practice fucking sucked today. Because of Tiana's weird mood toward me, it threw me entirely off kilter.

I don't understand why she's so wishy washy, and I have to say, it stings. She seemed to enjoy herself on the date, and she even said she did enjoy it. So, why is she so upset with me?

It can't be because I didn't kiss her? Surely she understands the circumstance.

It's wrong to engage with an intoxicated woman. It's just bad manners.

The whole time, the boys chirped at me with my lack of awareness. Honestly, I don't blame them, I would've chirped too if I fucked up as badly as I did today.

The day goes by in an absent blur. My mind spent the whole time trying to decipher Tiana's strange moods and wondering what I should do.

I made her a promise. If she went on one date and rejected me, I'd leave her alone. So that's what I'm doing.

I stay out of her way, either leaving before or after her, so we don't run in to each other at the complex or in the halls of the arena. I don't want to push my luck.

Hopefully, I won't have to see much of her. In all honesty, I don't think my heart could take seeing her like I was.

I really enjoyed getting to know her during our date. And I really liked the small routine we had set up in the time we had. There is so much of her that intrigues the fuck out of me. She just so happens to be wrapped in a gorgeously sculpted package. Maybe I'll give her some time to cool down before I talk to her again. I'll leave her alone like I said, but if I really don't have a chance, I want to make sure that rink is closed for good.

When Friday rolls around, the entire group of us have been packed on a tour bus for an away game. It's only in Oregon, so it's not a far drive at all, but color me surprised when I see Tiana climb the bus with the most annoyed expression on her face and her headphones rested around her neck.

I'm confused because there's no reason she should be here. She's the lawyer. When I look around the bus, I notice Charlotte isn't on board. She's the one to make sure we have any bits and bobs for our gear if something happens or doesn't work out.

Tiana can't be filling in for Charlotte, can she?

I watch as Tiana looks over the seats, trying to figure out where to sit. When her eyes land on me, I'm not surprised at the look of disdain on her face. But as she makes her way toward me, my brow furrows, and I realize the only open space is next o me.

My heart stutters in my chest as she approaches. Opening the overhead bin, she shoves a large weekend bag into it and then crashes into the seat next to me.

"Well, howdy, sugar," I say gently. I test the waters, considering we're locked next to each other for the next several hours.

"Hello, Gunnar," she sighs as she throws a blanket over her lap.

"What are you doing here?" I ask as I press my back against the window to get a better look at her.

She's positively cozy in her hoodie and sweatpants. And while I love a dressed up Tiana, there is something so cute about her wrapped in a bunch of thick cotton.

Tiana sighs in annoyance as her head hits the headrest and she stares at the ceiling.

"Charlotte is sick and isn't able to play equipment manager this week. So I had to step in for her."

I get to be in close proximity to Little Miss Business again. This is gonna be a weekend for the books, boys.

As we get to the hotel and everyone gets situated in their rooms, Tiana and I are left at the front desk. With Tiana almost yelling at the poor concierge.

I have yet to get my room because I was stuck on bag duty, while the others started getting their digs. Tiana had to make sure everyone got the shit they needed, so we ended up getting to the front desk together when everything was said and done.

"What do you mean, I have to 'share a room!?' With who!?" she yells.

"I'm sorry, ma'am. It's a big game this week, and all our rooms are booked. The last room available you have to share with one of your teammates," the lady at the front desk says.

"Who is the only player that hasn't gotten a room?" Tiana asks.

The lady looks over a piece of paper beside the desk,

running her finger over it a few times to make sure she gets the right information.

"A... Gunnar Hayze?" she asks curiously.

Tiana's face pales as she looks at the woman.

"You're kidding. This is some kind of prank. Which one of them put you up to it?" she asks.

The woman gives her a confused look. "No one set anything up. That's just how it happened. It's first come, first serve."

Tiana groans and I honestly can't help the rush that runs through me at the idea of sharing a space with her.

I'm sure Tiana isn't happy about it.

"I will pay extra for anything you have. It doesn't matter if it's a fucking broom closet at this point. I'll take it."

The woman sighs and types into her computer for a little longer. I imagine looking for anything, until she turns to Tiana and shakes her head softly.

"I'm sorry, there are zero rooms," she says.

Tiana's head leans back, her gaze stuck on the ceiling above before she takes a deep breath.

"Just give me the damn keys, please," she murmurs.

The woman nods before she prepares the key cards for our room. I have half a mind to keep my mouth shut. I reckon Tiana has a tongue like a knife and I'm not trying to be on the sharp end of it.

Eventually, the woman slides the keycards across the desk and Tiana grabs them from the counter before she stomps off toward the stairs. Her large weekend duffle bag slung over her body as she makes her way to our room. I quickly gather all of my things and follow close behind.

The urge to snatch all her bags consumes me, but I'm not an idiot. I know when I'm not needed. I reckon she'd throw her tongue at me in a bad way if I even attempted to touch her things.

We make it to our room and she throws her things down next to one of the beds in the space before she walks to the bathroom and slams the door.

I take a moment to look around. It's nothing incredibly fancy. A small entryway with the bathroom on the left wall, right when you enter, and a small closet by the door. When you move farther into the room, there's a recess to the left, behind the wall for the bathroom. With two queen beds situated beside each other, and a nightstand in between. On the far back wall is a window, with a desk against the right wall in front of it, and a dresser with a tv beside that.

I take the bed on the far end, placing my bags at the foot of the bed before I pull out some of my night clothes so I can shower when she comes out.

Tiana must really be in a bad mood. I don't think I've ever seen her this mad before.

I hear the shower turn on, and after a while she finally emerges, fully clothed in some light pajamas and throws herself into the empty bed.

Without so much as a single huff, she curls up in the blankets and I don't hear a peep from her the entire night.

CHAPTER SIXTEEN
TIANA

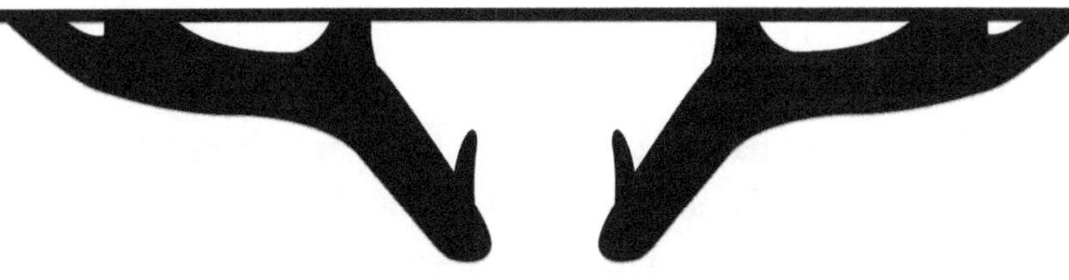

The universe is out to get me. I'm sure of it. I am almost *positive* at this point.

When my dad called, saying I needed to step in for Charlotte for the away game, I damn near threw my phone.

I don't go to away games, that's not my thing. Not to mention, it's my weekend. Those are *so* precious to me, and it's been ripped out from under my nose.

Now, not only do I need to attend the game, I have to *do* stuff for it. I have to take pictures and videos and make sure the equipment is good to go.

Of course, I have the knowledge to do all these things. My dad made sure Charlotte and I were both able to work the rink if we needed to. But that doesn't mean I *want* to fucking do it!

I almost threw my purse at the front desk lady when she said I had to share a room with Gunnar. I felt bad yelling at her, but after this past week, I was just taking out my frustrations on her. The hotel room was the straw on the camel's back and she just happened to be the one to place it. I know it's not her fault, but fuck me.

It doesn't help that I've been mad over the fact that I've missed Gunnar bothering me after practice. Mad because I missed seeing him at the end of the day to walk me out to my car. I hated that I didn't see him at the complex all week.

It's stupid, it's dumb, and it consumed all of my thoughts.

The fact it made me mad, the fact I missed him at all. All of it has been a tornado, and even *that* makes me mad! All of it does!

To make matters worse, I had to sit next to him on the ride here. He didn't say much, and he left me alone to the best of his ability.

But that's what I had asked of him, right? That's what he's supposed to do. I don't know why I should expect him to pine after me. He said he is a man of his word, and boy is he. In the good ways and the bad.

When I fell asleep in bed, I tried so hard not to think about the fact he was naked in the bathroom next to me when he went to shower. Or that he curled up in the second bed and went to sleep without so much as an utterance to me.

Granted, I don't think I would have said anything in response. I have to at least keep up the facade that I'm mad.

The next day, he still says nothing to me. When he goes down to the lobby for breakfast, he does bring me up a cup of coffee and some water and tells me 'good morning.' But that's it. I imagine he's getting in his head about this game.

He's had his headphones on while he jumps around the room. Thank god, because I don't think I have the nerve to deal with him today. Not when I have to work this game.

It's rare that I ever have to do this, but even before Gunnar, I really didn't enjoy having to fill in. I don't particularly enjoy hockey games. I never have. The amount of people, the loud buzzers, the cowbells. It's a sensory nightmare and I abhor it in so many ways. It's why I bring headphones on game day.

But fuck me if the way he doesn't lock in on game day isn't hot as sin. I love the way his brow tenses against his forehead as he bobs his head to his music.

With his eyes closed, he makes random lunges every so often as he loses himself, as if he's trying to picture himself on the ice.

He takes quite a long time stretching, and I try to ignore as much of it as I can. However, it's damn near impossible. With the way his muscles flex in his tank top and shorts. His skin glistens with a faint sheen of sweat as he moves about the hotel room. I pretend to be working on some things from my laptop, and he doesn't even seem to notice the way I almost gawk at him. I keep getting distracted by his massive body.

After a bit, I realize I can't fucking take it. His muscles and the way he is so tuned into his own world... it makes my pulse skyrocket and I decide to go down to the lobby. I need to get at least some of my work done before we have to leave the hotel for the game.

Fuck me, it's so damn loud. I feel like it's louder than I remember. Even through my headphones.

That first home game where I had met Gunnar, I stayed in my office with headphones on so I didn't have to hear the calamity outside of my office door.

I supplied all the men with whatever the fuck it is they need in the locker room. Some may have fucked up mitts or their sticks need to be taped. It's a wonder some of them even got here. I never realized how much they need or end up forgetting. Gunnar didn't seem to need anything from me. He didn't even really acknowledge me because he was so in the zone. Merely had his head down with his hand clasped around that stag pendant on his chain.

But currently, I sit in the box next to my dad, waiting for the game to start.

Soon, the lights dim and the songs for the teams play. The swirling spotlights spin around the arena and the ice. When the announcer goes through all the names of the players, I pay closer attention when Gunnar's name is called and he runs out onto the ice before he skids to a stop and waves to everyone. The crowd loses their mind around us, and it's then I realize how much he really means to this team. I never thought about it before. How many people actually may look up to him or just appreciate him because of how he plays.

It's almost shocking, because I've never been interested in a hockey player. Which means Gunnar is showing me a strange perception of this game I never considered. That discovery is jarring when I consider how long I have been in the hockey world. My whole life and I never peered at this side of the coin. I tell myself that is a severe oversight and that I need to fix that going forward. Not just in hockey, but with everything.

I shake my head at these realizations as I go back to watching him. As the announcer keeps calling names, more and more hockey players have come to the ice, skating and moving around each other. Gunnar, however, is the only thing I can focus on. He moves with such a lethal grace that I'm beginning to see why my dad wanted him so badly. He is so laser focused, it's almost as if the world outside of the rink doesn't exist. In all honesty, I had no idea he was capable of that. But the game *is* everything to him. Here it surely shows.

The lights come back to their normal brightness and the teams line up on their sides of the rink. His mouth guard sits between his teeth, flipping it back and forth as he holds his head and shoulders high.

God, is this what a 'beaut' is?

Before long, the puck drops and I forget all about why the fuck I'm supposed to be there. I'm supposed to be taking pictures for social media and supplying water and shit to the players. But the way Gunnar fucking moves. It's hypnotizing and downright sinful. He shoves his body into these players with such ease, it's like they're knocking into a solid wall. It sends a shiver through my entire body.

I have to be reminded several times by random players I have a job to do when they come up to me for something.

When the game ends and my dad brings us into the locker room for his normal pep talk, I do my absolute damndest not to look at Gunnar. It's fucking impossible with the way he looks right now, though.

Flushed and pink with exertion and from the chill of the rink, sans his jersey and chest protector. His enormous arms are crossed over his broad chest and the sight causes my body to heat. A large set of deer antlers are tattooed on his pecs that I hadn't noticed before. Granted, I hadn't even been slightly interested in him at the time. But now that I've seen what he's capable of, I can't believe I didn't take the chance to look at him when I could. He still sits in his pads and pants and he seems to pay me no mind as he listens. It's almost as if he's just in a world of his own as he breathes slowly.

He leans against the cubbies with his head tipped back and his chain in between his teeth as he listens. Like a sculpture in Italy, his body is carved in such exquisite ridges and bands of muscle. Along with his enormous height, he's also just a big pillar of hard muscle, anyway.

The boys won tonight, with Gunnar even making a few goals himself. But it seems as if it doesn't even affect him. At least not in this moment.

Watching him play was hotter than I thought it could be. It's attractive to watch a man do his job and be good at it.

I don't like that I found it hot. But I have to admit, I may actually be liking it a lot more than I expected.

We make it back to the hotel and luckily, Gunnar had showered in the locker room, so when we get back to our room it doesn't reek of sweaty man.

It is a massive undertaking to stop looking at him when I get out of the bathroom after my shower. Gunnar sits on the bed with a laptop in his lap and his headphones on. Even if he's just relaxing, there is so much more attraction I feel after watching that game tonight.

He looks almost irresistible like this. A pair of black sweatpants, no shirt, and his arm rested behind his head as he lies on a bed that is barely big enough for him.

My teeth sink into my lower lip as I admire him. The long expanse of his bared skin and relaxed posture makes me hotter than the shower did.

And I take my moment where I can.

I sit on my bed, facing him, and I snap in front of him to get his attention.

His brow furrows in confusion as he moves one ear from his headphones and looks at me.

"You were amazing on the ice tonight," I tell him nervously.

He gives me a humble smile and nods. "Thanks, Tiana."

Tiana?

"Tiana?" I ask in confusion.

Gunnar's eyes slide around the room for a moment before he quirks his head in question. "That... is your name, isn't it?"

I roll my eyes. "What happened to sugar?"

Gunnar places the laptop beside him on the bed and removes his headphones as he sits up.

"You said you didn't want me to bother you anymore. So, I'm not. I thought you made that pretty clear."

I cross my arms in annoyance as I glance away. Not annoyance at him. But annoyance because he's right.

"I was just... upset."

His curiosity is piqued, and he comes to sit on the edge of the bed. Planting his feet on the floor, he leans over with his elbows on his knees as his eyes lock onto me. His head dips toward his chest to catch his silver chain in his teeth.

"Go on," he says through the chain.

The silver chain has a silver pendant in the shape of a stag head on it and it dangles against his chest as his tongue swirls around it.

I stare at it for a moment too long before I glance back up at him with a small sigh.

"After our date, you rejected my kiss."

Gunnar gives me a sly smile as he grits the chain between his teeth, speaking through it, "Tiana, there is a lot of willpower that went into that action. But I have a code. I don't kiss intoxicated women."

My eyes roll. "I wasn't that drunk," I remark.

He sits up and crosses his arms against his chest. His large thighs spread wide, damn near taunting me as he bounces one of his legs.

"Maybe not, but you had some alcohol in you and you asked me to carry you. Clearly, you were not fully of sound mind if you were asking for that."

Fuck.

"I just don't understand."

"I don't either, Tiana. You run very hot and cold. And

sometimes, as much as I would like to chase after you, if you tell me to leave you alone, I will. I really didn't want to. But, you are specific about your space and who am I to take that from you?" He shrugs as he explains his reasoning.

That stupid tongue of his still fiddles with the chain in his mouth and it causes my anger—or arousal, I don't even fucking know anymore—to rise.

"So, what? That's just it? You're done?"

His brow arches in curiosity.

"I don't have to be. But you don't make it very clear about what you want."

I growl as I come to a stand in front of him. "What if I want you to kiss me?"

Gunnar's head follows me and his eyes glimmer with challenge. A small smirk rising against the chain in his mouth. "What if you do?"

He's playing a stupid fucking game, and if there is anything the lawyer in me can do, it's fucking winning.

"Then would you?!" I ask as I throw my hands up at him.

Gunnar's smirk widens, his brow quirking in amusement as he stands.

I don't so much as flinch as he takes a step near me.

I crane my head to look at him and his eyes sparkle.

His lips part to drop the chain, the small jingle as it hits his chest is the only thing I hear against the vibrant pounding of my heart in my chest.

His hand wraps around the back of my neck, tangling into the strands of my hair there. His thumb lines my jaw and he uses it to press my head the way he wants, tilting me as he leans in, pressing a deep kiss to my lips.

CHAPTER SEVENTEEN
GUNNAR

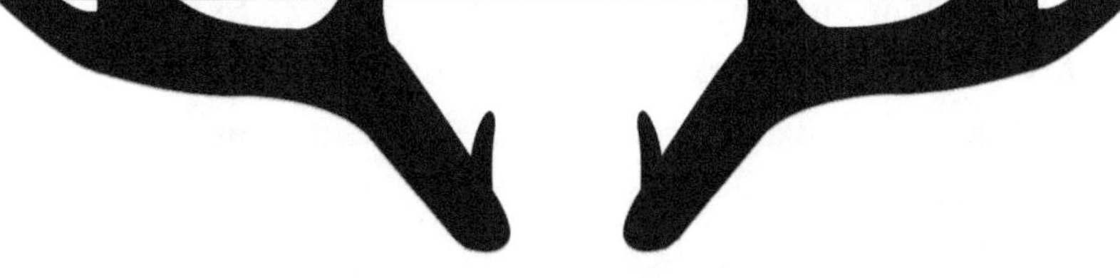

Fucking *finally.*

Little Miss Business stepped up to the center ring and slapped a puck straight into the fucking net.

There is no fucking way I'm gonna stop that. If she has to take time to figure out her wants, that's fine. At least I can't say that I pestered her into doing this.

She has been sending me mixed signals for days. I was just going to leave her alone because it seemed like she was going through her own issues and I wasn't trying to taunt her any more than I needed to.

But now, she wants a taste of hockey player. Who am I to say no to that?

I bring her lips into mine, angling her head just the way I want to taste as much of her as I can. Soft and desperate, she kisses back, with her delicate hands gripping at the sides of my sweatpants as I pull her in deeper. She tastes like everything I imagined.

Sweet as sugar.

Her body melts against mine, becoming delightfully pliant

in my hands and my cock pulses hard against the material of my sweatpants.

A soft moan leaks out of her, but as I press my bulge harder against her, it turns into a small gasp.

"What the fuck is that?" she asks as she pulls away with wide eyes that flick back and forth from my face to the hardened mound in my sweatpants. "That... there's no way?"

I give her a sly, taunting grin. "Scared?" I coo.

Her brow furrows in challenge and she reaches up to wrap her hands around my cheeks and bring me back to her mouth. My tongue slides against her lips as hers meets me in the middle. They dance around each other in a heated tango, volleying between my mouth and hers.

My hands grip hard on her hips, feeling the way they move under the thin fabric of this robe she's wearing. I will say it was hard to ignore the way her body looked in it when she came out of the bathroom. Fresh with that insanely delicious coconut smell.

Even now, it floods my senses as I try to absorb as much of her contact as I can. It causes my pulse to rush through me even harder. The urgency of seeing her naked climbs the longer this silk stays wrapped around her.

Hoisting her up, she wraps her legs around my waist and her arms around my neck. She's so light that my entire body engulfs hers as I hold her against me. Her arms grip tight around my shoulders and she runs her hands through the small curls at the bottom of my flow. As I adjust my hold on her, I bring my hands to grip tight on her ass. It has the perfect amount of give and the feeling of it causes me to swat at one of her ass cheeks, with the loud pop ringing through the room as she squeaks.

I've only ever heard her hardass voice, and the one she used at the dinner. But the noises she's making now give me an idea of how fucking amazing it'll be to be inside of her. That's made even more apparent when she grinds herself on my bare stomach, her pussy slick and hot against my skin.

The sensation is maddening, causing my eyes to roll before I let a small growl go.

I walk her over to my bed, leaning down to place her on the mattress. All the while, I kiss and nip at her lips as she tugs and pulls at my hair. My hands roam over her silky little robe, searching for the tie that keeps it wrapped around her, before I find one end and tug. It unravels under my grasp and slowly, the fabric falls away, baring all of her for me.

Caramel soft skin covers every inch of her and it's gleaming as if she drenched herself in lotion before she came out here. I'm not complaining. It smells just fucking like her and my mouth waters with the urge to devour her.

Rising to my full height, I look down at the delicious display in front of me. I sink a bite into my bottom lip as my dick hardens more and more and I release a low, tortured groan. Running my thumb over my bottom lip, a whistle escapes my lips as I survey the gorgeous bare body in front of me.

Her large tits sit pert on her chest with small brown nipples. Further down, she already glistens with wetness. The flat expanse of her stomach leads right into it and I want to press a kiss to every single inch of her.

Her nipples call my name and I lean in to squeeze her tits. Even with the generous size, my hands swallow them and I grip one with contained strength as I swipe my tongue against one of the hardened peaks.

A breathy gasp leaves her plump lips as her hands bolt to my hair and her delicate fingers thread through the strands.

A grin rises against my lips as I suck her nipple into my mouth, my thumb swiping over the other one. Her hips grind against me, looking for any bit of friction as I taunt and take my time with her. My cock feels like it's about to burst the longer I stay out of her, but fuck me if I'm gonna rush through this. I worked too damn hard to get here. I can tease her a bit longer.

"Gunnar..." she breathes as her head pushes back into the mattress.

One of my hands leaves her tit to run down her ribcage, her stomach, it creeps further south to rest on the bare mound of skin above her core. I take mental notes of every valley and curve that her body is carved out of and the way she melts into my palms. The way her skin feels against my rough hands and the way she shivers beneath my touch... it sears into my soul and imprints something feral deep inside of me.

It's fucking insanity the way it feels to have her under me and my heart beats a song of anticipation in my chest.

She grinds against my hand, beckoning me, and I press a finger into her core. Tiana lets out a gasp as I press into her clit. She's absolutely drenched and I groan into her breast as she coats my fingers.

I press deeper, roaming down to her entrance, where I press my fingers shallowly into her. I'm a big guy, in more ways than one, and I have to see what I'm working with, so I know what to do to get her ready for me.

Her hands go to my shoulders as she takes it. Pressing my fingers in deeper, up to the second knuckle. I switch my angle, using my thumb to slide over her clit as I work in and out of her.

"G-Gunnar...!" she moans.

My lips tilt in a satisfied smile. "I like the way you moan for me, sugar."

Releasing the hand around the tit in my mouth, I press my sweatpants off, letting a relieved breath go as my cock is finally released. I bring a hand up to stroke it, trying to relieve the smallest bit of pressure as I continue shimmying my pants down until I can kick them off behind me.

She glares at me through her tortured breaths before I remove my hand from her core and rise before her. I stroke my cock slowly, waiting for her to catch sight of me before I slip my fingers into my mouth. Making a show of it, they separate against my tongue, and I bore my gaze into hers as I suck her taste from my fingers.

She sits up on her elbows, breathlessly watching me with wide eyes. Those gorgeous green irises volley between my face and the hand that fists my cock.

I take a deep breath as I let her taste sink deep into me, and a grin rises against my face.

"I love being right," I say after I pull my fingers from my mouth in a deliberate *'pop.'*

Her focus splits and her eyes trail up my body, from my cock, to connect her wanton gaze with mine.

Her head tilts in question. "What?" she asks with a pant.

"Sweeter than sin," I whisper as I come back down to kiss her, letting her taste herself on my lips. She moans into me and I reach down again to press my fingers back into her. My pendant and chain dangle around my neck, dragging along her chest as I kiss her.

While I am big in stature, that wasn't spared with my dick, either. Call it overconfidence, but it's the truth. I'm not trying to hurt her with how tight her pussy is. She can barely fit my two fingers in her.

I take a few more moments, pressing my fingers in and out of her. Her moans pitching higher as her pussy tightens around my fingers.

"Gunnar, p-please..." she pants desperately.

I press soft kisses into her parted lips. "Ohhhhh... I

knooow... It's so much, isn't it?" I coo teasingly as I slip a third finger into her.

Another gasp leaves her as I stretch her more. "F-fuck...!"

"There she is. It's alright, you can take it. Just relax. Breathe deep," I whisper.

I grin hard against her lips before I kiss down her jaw. I trail kisses down her pulse point before I nip at her throat, taking soft licks of the skin there.

"You're doing so good for me. Just keep breathing, you're almost there," I whisper softly.

She groans as her head tilts back, her hips writhing against my hand.

"Gunnar, how the fuck am I gonna take you?" she pants.

I kiss at her throat. "It'll fit, sweetness. I promise."

Scooching her up on the bed, I get in between her legs, running the head of my cock through her center. Her eyes roll back as I rub myself into her clit, before I tease her entrance. Taking shallow presses into her to feel the resistance, she releases a throaty moan as I stretch her.

Her wetness covers me in an instant and my mind implodes at the sensation. Until I pause, my head coming back to the moment as I look around for my bags.

Tiana looks up at me in confusion. "What's wrong?"

"Condom," I say with a pant as I begin to retreat.

Tiana stops me, gripping onto my hand. She breathes heavy, watching me with a small bite at her lip and her eyes half-lidded in pleasure.

"I-I have an IUD."

My brow furrows quizzically. "Which means...?"

"Y-you can come in me," she whimpers.

Raw?! Ohhhhh, fuck yes.

I grin as I lean in, branding her neck with heated kisses as my hips take shallow thrusts of just the head into her.

"Are you sure?" I breathe against her skin. Her pussy tightens around me and it takes every bit of restraint I have not to shove every fucking inch into her. I want to feel this tightness all the way to the hilt. *Fuck.*

Tiana nods desperately as her eyes clench shut and I press myself in just a tad more. Her groans fill the room as I wait for her to adjust before I can press in further.

"See? You're doing great, sugar," I praise as I rub my hands down her sides.

My hands take as much time as they can as they move down, feeling every fucking inch of her before I make it to her ass and grip hard. Groaning, I tilt her hips, trying to work myself in deeper.

I, on the other hand, am six seconds from busting in her.

She's just as sweet as I imagined. She fits around me like a custom mitt and more groans crawl from my throat as I push farther and farther in.

Her head tosses back, her skin shimmering with her sweat against her already moisturized skin. My head drops to her shoulder as I take a few deep breaths to steady myself.

"Fucking hell," I growl.

Her hands wrap around my neck and shoulders, pulling my body closer to hers. Her skin lights my insides on fire. I never thought someone's body could feel like this against mine, and I want nothing more than to be a part of it forever.

Focus. Have to focus.

It's so fucking hard to focus with how her pussy feels, but I lift my head to see her eyes clenched in pure pleasure. I bring a hand up to grip her chin, moving her head to face me.

"Eyes on me, pretty girl," I tell her with a soft pant.

Soon, I've worked myself all the way inside of her, letting her walls spasm and clench around me as she relaxes.

Her eyes open and her pupils expand as her lips part in a

small gasp. I share the small space with her, looking deep into her eyes as I inhale every tortured breath she exhales. I watch every twitch of her face as she feels me fill her up entirely.

"There she is. There's a good girl, huh?" I whisper. My hips roll, pulling in and out of her in smooth strokes as our breaths exchange between us. "Suuuch a good girl, taking my cock so well," I tell her as I press small kisses into her parted lips. Her mind is gone with the way I've filled every bit of her.

Tiana pants and struggles to keep eye contact with me as she attempts to decipher the way I feel inside of her. Her green eyes are covered in a haze of lust, and no thoughts live in that pretty little head of hers.

"Care to answer that question for me now, sugar?" I ask as I take slow thrusts in and out.

Her eyes roll, her body writhes as I wrench the pleasure from her.

"W-what question?" she asks with a soft pant.

I nip into her neck, grinning against it. "Hard?" My hips thrust forward in a brutal pound, slamming myself balls deep into her, and she moans out as her body tightens. "Soft?" I roll my thrusts again, taking my sweet time, pulling every inch out and slowly pressing it back in.

Another moan leaves her as I feel her nails press into the muscles in my back. The pain is delicious and I keep going.

"Shallow?" I ask as I pull most of myself out. Pressing just the head in and out of her, I find I may not even be able to take that. She feels too fucking good, and my head tilts back with a loud groan.

Her moans blend with mine, and the harmony of it is intoxicating.

"Deep?" I ask one more time.

This time, she nods mindlessly, her body damn near vibrating in response.

"D-deeper, please," she moans.

"That's what I thought," I say. I move my hands from her ass to her hips, gripping tight on the frame of her before I slide balls deep into her.

Her nails grip harder, her moans ringing in my ears, making my thrusts bury into her. Every stroke deeper than the last.

Her mouth gapes as my thrusts pick up, moving deeper and faster, just like she asked. "F-f..."

"Fuck, you feel so fucking good," I pant.

She nods in mindless agreement, her eyes locked onto mine.

"You take me so fucking well. I told you it'd fit," I whisper.

More speed consume my thrusts, and she tries so hard to keep her eyes on me but they threaten to roll back with every stroke I take. My own eyes are locked onto her tits that jiggle and bounce against her chest.

But soon I wanna see those pretty eyes of hers roll again, giving in entirely to my movements. I lean down to nip at her chin, bringing her focus back to me.

"Ah, ah, ah, eyes open, sugar. Concentrate. I wanna see you take it," I say to keep her looking at me.

Meanwhile, my resolve crumbles, and I have to concentrate on not busting before she's had a chance to come. I move against a part of her insides that threatens to break her, and she moans out as her hands grip tighter into my skin.

"There it is," I murmur to myself as I lean up. I look down at where we're joined. My hands come to grip under her knees, pressing her legs open so I can watch the way her pussy swallows me.

"G-Gunnar!" she moans as her hands scramble to a pillow nearby to cover her face and muffle her moans.

My thrusts bury deeper, pounding hard and precise into that spot that makes her squirm. I rip the pillow from her hands and throw it across the room. Stroke after stroke is harder than the last as I grip tight on her hips, fucking into her with punishing thrusts before I lean down to nip at her earlobe.

"Let them hear the way I fuck the coach's daughter. I want them to hear the way my fucking name sounds coming out of that pretty mouth you've got on you."

Her eyes widen as she registers my words, but the surprise is quickly replaced by the overwhelming pleasure coursing through her.

One of my hands leaves her leg to press into her clit, rubbing it as I continue pounding into her. She writhes under me, her hips bucking and her back bowing.

"That's it, sugar. Come for me," I growl as that tingle in the base of my spine threatens to spill into her.

Her body tenses and I feel her tighten and spasm around my cock in harsh waves. I can barely move with the tightness of her and I gasp out as I come without warning. Stars blast vibrantly against my eyelids as they clench shut and her pussy locks me in place.

"Fuck! Tiana!" I groan as my thrusts halt, her pussy keeping me locked inside of her.

My spine crumbles and I catch myself on my hands as I fall into the bed. They plant on either side of her head, where I try so hard to move inside her, but I can't. My head falls, looking down to where I'm stuck inside of her, and a low growl rumbles out of me as I wait for her orgasm to finish. I've never had someone fucking milk me like this before, and it makes my orgasm last much longer than I expected. My vision wavers as my eyes roll, relishing in the way she grips every fucking inch.

Eventually, her waves slow and I can take a few shallow pumps into her.

"Fucking hell..." I pant as I look down at her.

Tiana's arm covers her face as her chest heaves. Her skin glistens with sweat, and I lean down to lick between the valley of her tits. The taste of her explodes on my tastebuds, lighting my attraction anew and I drag myself out.

I make a tortured noise as I watch the way I spill out of her.

"Goddamn, sweetness," I pant as I look up at her with a grin.

Tiana looks at me between pants and lifts a brow in question.

"I mean, I fit, but it sure was a tight squeeze," I laugh as I collapse on the bed next to her.

"It's been a while," she mumbles.

I give her another laugh as I reach over and pinch her nipple.

"Hey!" she says with a small pant as she swats my hand away.

"What? They're just so nice," I say with a sly grin.

Tiana rolls her eyes as she moves herself with limp bones to rest her head on the pillows. Soon, her body relaxes as she attempts to even out her breaths.

I take the lull to get up and grab a rag to wash her up.

When I come back, she's watching me with a confused look on her face.

Her brow furrows as I come up to her. "What are you doing?"

My face contorts in question. "I'm... cleaning you up?"

"Why?" she asks.

I take a look around the room, almost dumbfounded as to who she may be asking, because I have no idea why she's asking me.

"Why wouldn't I?"

"I've never had a man clean me up before," she murmurs.

My brow raises as a small laugh bubbles out of me. I sit on

the bed, pressing her legs open. She complies, but she seems nervous, so I lean in to press soft kisses to her lips. She lets a small noise go and her body relaxes from where she had tensed and I drag the cloth between her legs, trying to clean her up as much as I can.

"Real men clean up their mess," I whisper as I pull away. I throw the rag on the floor by the dresser before I grip her hip, tugging her into me as I kiss into her neck. "You did so good for me, sugar."

Her skin heats under my lips and I can't help the grin that tugs at them. Kissing up her neck, I come to meet her lips, placing one more kiss there before I pull away. Picking her up, I cradle her in my arms to move her to the clean bed so she has a better place to sleep. She's already drifting to sleep as I help her into the blankets. She pulls them tight around her and my heart squeezes at the way I've made her so relaxed.

"Get some sleep," I whisper before I move over to my bed.

Her eyes are already slowly blinking shut, but that doesn't stop her from speaking. "That was actually incredible," she whispers softly.

I smile as I give a light chuckle and curl up in my blankets. "I know it was."

CHAPTER EIGHTEEN

TIANA

The last thing I remember is curling up in the hotel bed after Gunnar cleaned me up.

Last night was... almost a fever dream. One moment, I'm admiring his body and the next, he's fucking the soul out of me.

Aside from the fact his dick was nearly as big as he is, I've never had a man talk me through sex like that. I had no choice but to submit and honestly...

I loved it.

I don't think I've ever had the chance to give in to a dominant bedroom personality like that, but there was a huge part of me that felt freed by it.

So much of my day-to-day is being a dominant personality. Even if I don't spend a lot of time physically with people, I have to assert some level of dominance in my emails or on the phone. I have to make big decisions regarding other people's futures. That can weigh on you after a time.

The thing is, I just didn't realize the weight until Gunnar

hoisted it from me and gave me a chance to just fucking *breathe.*

To have all your decisions made for you in a small part of the day. Giving up the control and letting someone take the burden of those choices off of you while letting you give in to a release.

It was so incredible. Even if that wasn't his intention.

I hate to say that Gunnar has given me the chance to find a part of myself I didn't know existed. Or maybe it was just being cared for on a level I didn't know I needed.

It was... life-altering... I don't even know how to decipher it all.

Sunlight from the back window bleeds into the room, landing on my face. Slowly, my eyes open and I find Gunnar passed out in the other bed.

Relaxation masks his beautiful face as he sleeps peacefully. Sprawled out on his back, his leg bent at an angle with the other sticking straight out. I'm not sure if he just decided not to put his sweatpants or boxers back on, but the sheets on him are strewn about his groin. It doesn't help that it's the only part that covers him. Or attempts to.

Even if he's completely soft, I can see the outline of his dick clearly under the thin sheet. And my fucking thighs ache at the sight.

This fucking early? Just horny as hell in the hotel room with the brand new rookie after he fucked my brains out the night before? What is this life?

I'm glad he slept in his own bed because he would have crushed me in his sleep. He takes up the entire queen bed.

My eyes gaze over his sculpted frame and I get a good look at the ridges and divots of muscle that make up his exterior. His legs are almost like tree trunks, with massive thighs and toned calves. He looks like he could crush my head between them like a watermelon. But again, my eyes go to the fucking bulge under the sheets.

And I can't stop my mouth from watering as I gawk at him.

Would it be weird if I...?

No, I can't do that. He seems to have his code. Would it be wrong if I... woke him up with...?

No. No, no, no. I can't. That's so wrong.

I shake my head at the thought and lay in the bed watching him.

There is a bit of warmth that eases through my chest. One that almost aches for him. After the date, and after last night, my feelings for him have almost doubled in the time I've spent with him.

Heat crawls over my chest and face as I watch, with my teeth sinking into my lower lip. It sends visions of last night dancing through my skull and I don't have the want to push it away. If anything, I want *more*.

Gunnar stretches wide against the mattress, with his muscles writhing under his skin. The heat that pulses in my cheeks and chest moves through all of me, settling deep in my core. My breaths deepen and I watch him for a moment longer.

His eyes blink open, staring at the ceiling before his head falls to the side to look over at me. His sleepy eyes soften as he realizes I'm awake, and the heat intensifies as he catches me staring.

"Good morning, sweetness," he murmurs. The sleep is thick in his voice, causing it to be handsomely gruff and deeper than normal.

I damn near fan myself at the sound of it.

"Good morning to you," I remark as my eyes flick down to the boner he has under the sheets.

His eyebrow quirks as he glances down at it with a grin.

His hands move behind his head as he adjusts himself on the bed. "You like what you see?"

I laugh at his lame attempt at seduction. "I did until you said that."

The leg that's barely on the bed slides off as he sits up, the sheet sliding across his lap as he comes to place both feet on the floor. He dips his chin to secure his silver chain between his teeth to fiddle with it with his tongue. My chest aches from the way his body moves and contorts in the sunlight, sending my heart into a sporadic rhythm of beats. His elbows rest on his knees as he leans over, watching me like a hungry predator. His cock twitches under the sheets and he stands, letting the fabric fall from his lap.

"How about now?" he asks in a low, taunting purr.

My throat works in a gulp as he walks over to my bed.

He leans down to cradle me and throw me closer to the other side as he lays down in the bed next to me. His arm goes behind his head as he wraps his other hand around his cock, stroking it slowly.

"Don't be shy now. You talk a big game, but when it comes time to play, you get cold feet. We aren't on the ice in here, pretty girl," he says with a low groan. My eyes bounce between the way his tongue swirls against his chain and the hand fisting his cock.

I bite down hard on my lip at his words and his display. The way his voice grinds out of his throat sends the pulsing in my chest straight to my core. My thighs feel entirely way too hot and the urgency creeps in, gripping me by my throat.

He leans over, releasing his chain in his teeth, before nuzzling into my hair and pressing kisses into my neck. All the while, I watch the way he strokes his cock up and down. His hips buck gently, his cock pressing through his hand as he holds it in place and he groans into my skin. Soon, his lips part and his tongue slides against the kisses he laid there. Shocks of pleasure skitter through my limbs as he taunts me further.

"It's nothing even close to the feel of your pussy wrapped around it," he rasps.

Another gulp tugs at my throat as my eyes widen and I blow out a low breath to steady myself.

"You think I can't play?" I ask. Though my voice is less than confident.

The way I crumble under his influence is honestly impressive. I'm not exactly the most experienced in bed, so to have him take the lead and make me his plaything... It's fucking sexy.

He pulls away, taking the hand from behind his head to grip my chin in his fingers. Watching my eyes for a long moment, he scans over my face before landing on my lips and lingering there.

"Do your worst, sweetness," he whispers as his eyes come back up to meet mine. The hazel is vibrantly devious as he continues to pull me into his orbit.

My eyebrow quirks and I lean up from the sheets, gripping them against my chest, as his free hand comes to pull them away.

"Not around here. Those stay out," he says as he nods to my tits. He comes up to pinch at one of my nipples, with the act sending small shoots of pleasure through every bit of my body.

I let him, because there's a small part of me that's perceiving this as care. And fuck me, it feels so fucking good to be cared for after so many years of being so independent.

He tugs at my nipple softly and I breathe deep through the pleasure, trying to remember what the fuck I was supposed to be doing.

Play. Gunnar. Right.

As I move myself to get between his legs, his fingers release my tit to slide up my chest. They linger on my collarbone, my neck, before he brings his hand up to my cheek to stroke a thumb over it.

I watch as he bites into his lower lip, his gaze intently focused on me. My hands wrap around the base of him, leaning his massive cock toward me to swipe my tongue across the head. The taste of his pre-cum covers my tongue and my eyelids flutter as I let a blissful moan go.

I glance up to see his gaze locked on me, watching me carefully as his chest rises and falls in slow movements. His hand caresses my cheek, where I feel his fingers attempt not to twitch as I swirl my tongue around him.

A smirk tugs at my lips as I take the entire head into my mouth. His neck tilts back, his eyes rolling as he presses his head into the pillow. A groan seems to vibrate his body as it leaves his throat and his hand moves to my neck, pressing tight on the sides. His breaths continue to deepen the farther I take him into my mouth.

He releases a deep groan as his hips buck instinctively up at me, forcing him deeper into my throat.

"Fuck Tiana," he groans.

Dragging his cock from my throat, I use the saliva to stroke over him softly.

"Who's sweet now?" I ask as I take long licks up his length.

His head rises from the pillow to give me a sweet grin before he brings his hand back to my face. A thumb rubs lovingly over my cheek, while he holds a soft admiration in his eyes, but his grin contorts into something mischievous.

"Ride it," he purrs.

My eyes widen and I freeze.

Fuck. If I ride him, he'll be in my goddamn throat. But from the other side.

And it seems as if he notices my hesitancy.

"Don't be shy. Sit... on... it," he says with a sharp annunciation to the last of his words.

A small nod is all I can muster as I take a deep breath. I lean up from his cock, still stroking it before moving slowly to position myself on top of him.

I basically have to be all the way up on my knees for him to even press his tip into me. He glances at me through his lashes with a devious gleam in his eyes.

He grips at my hips as I press him slowly into me. My breaths hitch, my eyelids flutter as I feel him stretch me more and more, heat pulsing through every bit of my body.

Slowly, *ever so slowly,* I slide down his length.

His pants and groans swirl against my moans and he takes a chance to pull his chain into his mouth to bite at it.

"That's it. There's a good girl," he grits through the chain as he watches himself bury deeper into me.

I can't fucking *think,* I can barely fucking hear him. The way he fills me wipes any thoughts out of my skull and I have to concentrate on his voice to even listen to his words.

"Gunnar, fuck!" I pant as I lean forward to place my hands against his chest.

"Go slow if it's too much. I'm not in a rush," he breathes.

His hands take soothing strokes up my bare thighs, giving me a moment to ground myself as he fills me more and more.

I nod as I listen to him and I *do* take my sweet fucking time. Not only because he's so thick, but because it feels *insane.* Soon, he's somehow pressed all the way into me and I have to manually breathe through the way he's splitting me in half just to relax around him. As I pant, I feel pressure deep in my lower stomach and I look down. It takes me a second to realize what is happening until it finally clicks.

It's his fucking dick...! This man is in my fucking stomach!

His hand splays against it and he presses into it, causing a mind-numbing sensation to course through me. A moan unlike anything I thought I was capable of leaves my throat. My eyes roll, my head falls back, and I give in to whatever the fuck this sensation is. I've never felt anything like it before.

"There she is," I hear him whisper.

His smooth words are like an anchor to this world and I struggle to keep them in the forefront of my mind because... god *damnit*.

"Gunnar, it's..." I struggle to speak. The only thing I can register is *him*. "Fuck, it's so much," I pant.

"Say the word and I'll take the lead," he says as his hands move to caress my hips.

I nod desperately, because there is no fucking way I can move on top of him.

"Put your legs out," he murmurs as he strokes my thighs.

I look down, unfolding my legs from under me. All the while, his cock moves and twitches inside of me, hitting unknown parts of me I didn't realize he could. He sits up, slipping his arms under my knees so they sit on his forearms. His hands come to grip tight on my ass and he buries his face into the crook of my neck.

"Hold on tight, sugar," he whispers as he presses kisses into my shoulder.

I comply, wrapping my arms around his neck and holding myself against him. The feeling of his skin on mine, his hands gripping me, causes my blood to pour through my body like lava. And it only intensifies as he moves to press himself to his knees, hoisting me up against him. My tits rub against his bare chest, which teases and slides against my nipples. Shocks of pleasure course through the lava in my blood and a tortured moan fills the air as I try to grasp all the feelings.

His lips softly press, and his teeth nip into the skin of my shoulder as he slowly works me up and down his cock. His arms flex and writhe under my legs as they move me.

"Such a good fucking girl. Such a tight pussy," I hear him pant. Though it's gruffer; husky and tortured.

I can hardly believe the ease at which he plunges me onto him, not even a movement of his hips. He just lifts me up and down with bicep curls like I weigh nothing. His groans rumble in his chest as he pushes me deeper onto him. The depth, the stretch, everything about the way he fucks me is mind numbing. All fucking consuming and there is nothing outside of this feeling. I want to experience it forever.

His voice breaks through the sensations. "Lean back," he whispers into my neck.

I pant as I comply, my hands tightening on his shoulders as I lean back, just enough to remove my chest from his.

"Look between us," he adds as he kisses softly into my lips before leaning back.

He pauses in his movements, waiting for me to look down.

As my head drops to look at *us*, I see his cock slick with my wetness and he moves me ever so slowly on him. I watch as he pulls me deeper and deeper onto him. The sight combined with the feeling causes fired pulses of pleasure to pound hard through my veins. I've never had a man make me watch before and it's hotter than I could have ever imagined.

His lips collide with my throat as he licks and nips at it, while his pace picks up. Some strokes are shallow, like he's working the head of himself with me, before pulling me down all the way to the base of him with a heavy slap. He reaches corners of my body that I didn't even know existed, and the feeling is absolutely maddening. Trembles wrack through me at the differing depths and speeds, and my body tightens as I get closer to the edge.

"You gonna come for me, pretty girl? You gonna come all over my cock?" he grits through his teeth as his pace picks up.

I can't even speak, I can barely even hear over the fill of him. I can only nod.

"Tell me. Say it, Tiana," he whispers.

"I-I... fuck. I- " I scramble through my brain to figure out what the fuck he wants me to say, but come up empty.

"Use your words, sugar. I know you can," he says as he slows his thrusts even more.

Leisurely moving me up and down, it's torturously slow, but I feel every single inch that moves in and out of me.

I groan at the overwhelming sensations, at the knot of pleasure at the base of my spine that tingles beyond control.

"I-I'm gonna c-come all over your cock," I pant.

"Yes, you are, pretty girl," he whispers as his movements pick up again.

I lean in to hold on to him for dear life as he holds me in place to thrust into me. His pace and depth causes me to scream out as lightning blasts against my eyelids and my body shudders against him.

"That's it, come for me," I hear him grit through the waves.

"Fuck. G-Gunnar!" I moan again as quake after quake rocks through me.

I lean my head back, letting each wave crash over me again and again and *again*. My hips grind against him, trying to wring out every bit of my orgasm that I can. It's transcendent, this feeling, and I want to be devoured by it.

"There's a good girl. Ride through it, baby, I'm right here. Come all over me," he grits as he kisses my throat.

His lips against my hot skin are a subtle grounding point as my orgasm continues to roll through me.

As it finishes, he sets me down against the pillows. His cock leaves my core and I feel like a puddle of bones as my body shakes.

And I do get a few seconds to breathe. That is a kindness. Until he flips me over onto my stomach.

"Ass up, Tiana, I'm not done with you yet," he pants with a small slap to my ass.

And because my brain is fucking mush, I comply. Lifting my hips just enough, I arch my back for him. He nudges my knees apart, opening me for him to slide his cock into my sensitive core. A shiver wracks through me as I pant through the last throes of my orgasm.

His powerful hands grip at my hips before another punishing swat stings my ass and I feel him work deeper into me. The sticky heat of his hard chest clings to my back as he leans over. With his hands sliding up my body, he takes my arms with them, pulling them to rest on either side of my head. Gripping my wrists tight, he pins them against the mattress.

"I'm going to fill this tight cunt so full of my cum that you won't be able to walk without it dripping out of you," he whispers against the shell of my ear, and the gruff tone is lethally promising. Honestly, it's a wonder he can speak at all because I can't even understand what he's saying.

His tongue glides along my ear before he shoves every single inch into me in one solid stroke. My pussy spasms and clenches around him as I release a loud moan.

He waits for me to adjust before his hand grips harder at one of my wrists.

"Do you understand me, Tiana?" His voice loses the whisper and all that's left is the rough, unfiltered sound of his feral promises.

I nod desperately against the sheets.

"I want to hear you say it," he growls as he retreats all the way to the tip to throw another solid stroke into me.

Another loud moan claws at the walls surrounding us. "I... I wanna be so full of your cum that it drips out of me when I walk," I pant.

Every word he says, and the way he says it, sends a shot of ecstasy through me. It's devilishly addicting, and I never knew something could be so intoxicating.

"Good girl, sugar. There's a good fucking girl, huh?" he teases roughly as he sets a punishing pace.

Every thrust is deeper than the last, sending quake after quake through me as he fucks into my already orgasming pussy. My eyes have rolled all the way back into my head as he wipes every thought from my brain. He lets go of one of my wrists to wrap a hand around my throat. Pressing my head back, he leans over me, licking and kissing me through every single thrust.

I moan into his mouth, pulling away as it becomes too much. My moans get so loud it feels like the walls tremble with them and he presses his chest against my back as his thrusts slow.

"If I knew you were a screamer, I would have fucked you harder last night," he whispers before pressing kisses into my shoulder.

His thrusts pick up again and my body rocks against the mattress as he takes everything he can, all the while his name scrapes out of my throat.

"That's it, sugar. Scream my fucking name. Let the rest know who fills this pretty little cunt," he growls in my ear.

I feel his cock swell and harden inside of me before he groans deeply. Rigid twitches rock against my walls as he slows down and releases every ounce of himself into me.

"God, Gunnar! Fuck!" I moan out as I feel him fill me.

"That's right. Say it. Say my fucking name," he grits through his teeth as his thrusts slow more and more. Eventually, they stop and he holds himself above me, panting as sweat drips from his hairline. I lay in a puddle of mindless ecstasy against the mattress, taking heaving breaths as I try to regain my bearings. I have to fucking remind myself where I am at this point.

Hotel. Away game. Gunnar.

I look back at him through my heavy breathing and give him a weak smile. "Good lord," I murmur.

"I'm sorry. I'm not sure what came over me. I think I blacked out," he laughs breathlessly.

My eyebrow quirks as I look at him. "You mean this isn't a usual occurrence?" I breathe.

Gunnar chuckles again. "Not usually. But you're so docile in bed, I wanna take the chance to throw you around when I can."

Heat runs over my cheeks and chest as I realize he's noticed the freedom I've relinquished to him.

Even if it's just a small thing, it's somewhat... special. He's noted my personality in and out of the bedroom and used it to his advantage. I can't help the small flutters in my stomach from being so... seen?

I'm not being forced out of my comfort zone for his happiness. He's showing me new pieces of myself and then... enforcing them? Making me see who I am and what I can be with the right amount of care.

It's jarring... shocking. Way too many things to think after getting my brains fucked out of me.

His cock softens before he slides out of me and collapses on the bed next to me. His chest heaves as he stares up at the ceiling, and I turn my head against the pillows to watch him.

His profile is delightfully handsome. A powerful jaw, his lips puffy and his skin is damp and pink from his efforts. The sweatiness on his brow soaks the strands of his hair, darkening it more from the already dark brown that it is. It sticks to parts of his skin or is just thrown into disarray from me gripping and tugging at it. I look at the hard carving of his collarbone, his shoulders, and his chest. All of it is sculpted into a well-defined machine of a man but also so inherently organic that I feel a flutter of attraction in my stomach as I look over him.

Not only from his poundings, but just from the sheer look of him.

He's fucking gorgeous.

His head falls to look toward me, noticing my observations, and he gives me an exhausted, sweet smile.

"You really do take me so well, you know that right?" he asks as he rolls onto his side. A hand comes up to cup my cheek, his thumb stroking softly over it as his eyes roam over my face. As if he's observing me the same way I did to him.

Heat swallows my face and ears as I bite my lip. It buzzes with the blood pooled in it from kissing and licking at him.

"I could barely even ride you," I respond nervously.

"Sweetness, I could see my cock bulge out of your stomach," he says with a laugh. But his eyes almost glitter, as if he swells with pride for me.

If there was any chance I could get even redder, now was that chance.

"It was sexy as fuck," he murmurs as his teeth bite into his lip.

His eyes slide down to my lips and he leans in slowly to press a gentle kiss on them. His hand wraps around the back of my neck, pulling me closer to deepen it.

And I give in. Because I've never felt something this full before.

Being cared for. *Seen.*

I never imagined that a hockey player would be the one to show me freedom in this sense. But part of me... isn't complaining.

"Well, I'm glad you think so," I respond quietly as he pulls away.

"I know so," he says with a confident grin.

I roll my eyes as I bat at his chest.

"There she is," he whispers as he catches my hand and pulls me against him.

A giggle falls from me as he holds me, the aftereffects of our sex rolling through me in waves of bliss. I press myself deeper against him, trying to get as much skin to skin contact as I can.

All the while, something stirs within me. Something I don't think I've ever felt before.

Craving... longing?

All for Gunnar.

And now that I've had him, I don't think there is any way I would ever let him go.

CHAPTER NINETEEN
GUNNAR

I don't know if Tiana has any effect on how well practice is going for me recently, but it seems to be the only change and I've been killing it on the ice.

We spent that entire weekend in that hotel room fucking each other. I don't think I've had that much sex in a while. But once I unlocked that little demon in her, she played coy. I could see that taunting glimmer in her eyes. She wanted me to put her in her place, and when I did, she bent to my every touch. But I took real good care of her after it was all said and done.

The team had to come find us because we were taking too long and when they got us, we quickly showered but ended up fucking in there too.

We sat in different seats on the bus back to Seattle, where I looked over at her every so often to find her knocked the fuck out.

It gave me a small sense of pride to know I put her ass to sleep like that.

I'm not sure what made me feel like I could control her the way I did. In all honesty, I'm pretty intuitive when it comes to reading what a woman needs. And she needed to feel... like she wasn't in charge of her world.

Even if it was for a few moments. She wanted to be free but feel safe in her freedom.

Maybe I can read a person's energy, or maybe I'm just fluent in reading her. But she was glowing by the time I finished with her.

After we made it home, Tiana needed some time to herself, so she retreated to her apartment.

After the sex we had, I probably needed some rest too.

From what the boys have said and what I've learned from others about Tiana, she's very particular about her time. I'm not exactly sure why. But it doesn't really bother me. If I know she's here with me, I'll give her all the time she needs. She deserves to feel safe in her own company, and I'm more than happy to give that to her.

The boys have noticed how much more chipper I've been since I've started fucking Tiana. And while I don't think they actually know the reason for my good mood, a man surely doesn't kiss and tell. Not to mention, Tiana wouldn't want her business out in the air.

I may tell Tiana to scream my fucking name when I'm balls deep in her, but that doesn't mean I'm gonna tell them myself.

This morning when I come into the arena, I see Tiana. But she merely gives me a small, shy smile and retreats to her office. When she does, I feel my heart swell beyond measure. I knew I wanted her when I first saw her. But now that I've had her and see a side of her that no one else gets to see...

I shake my head of the thoughts as I make my way to the locker room to get ready for practice before I move quickly out to the rink. I glide onto the ice, taking leisurely presses back and forth around as I wait for the others to join us.

"Good fuckin' game this weekend, boys," Adrian says as he

glides around the ice. He volleys a puck back and forth with his stick.

"Thing of beauty, it was, I reckon." I nod as I skate backwards to watch him. My stick down, waiting for whatever it is he does next.

"Let's see if we can keep up that momentum this weekend too, huh?" Adrian laughs as he slaps the puck toward me and I volley it back and forth on the ice before slamming it into the goal.

Our goalie dives for it and completely misses and I let out a whistle in accomplishment.

"God damnit, Hayze!" I hear our goalie grumble as he stands from his dive. With a gentle shrug and a laugh, we continue to wait for everyone else to show up for practice.

As soon as the day ends, I shower and rush to Tiana's office. The things I need to ask her have to be when the door is closed, because I know she's strict about her timing.

There is an overwhelming rush of giddiness I get when I think about seeing her. Maybe this is what Tucker feels like when I come home. It makes my blood run hot just knowing I get to have a glimpse of her gorgeous face.

As I leave the locker room, I survey the halls, making sure Bubbles isn't anywhere in the area.

I feel like I saw him go to his office after practice and right now all I see are some of the physical therapy assistants and janitors.

When I find the coast to be clear, I sprint down the arena halls and into her office. Quickly, I close and lock the door behind me before I pull the shutters down. I peak through a small slit in them to make sure no one saw me before I turn around to face her.

Tiana's brows furrow in confusion as she looks up from her computer. "Gunnar, what is your issue?" she asks.

I look at her for a long moment, admiring every bit of her.

God, those eyes. Green like emeralds.

Her hair. Perfect little coils of brown and gold.

Her face. The caramel tone with the small freckles dappling her nose and cheeks.

Her work ethic. Her independence. Her fucking brain. God damnit.

Her.

A smile tugs at my lips.

"Come here," I murmur as I shrug my backpack off my shoulders and walk toward her.

Her brow furrows even more, completely surprised by my arrival, and she stands from her chair.

As I come around to meet her, I lean down to cup her face in my hands, pulling her in for a deep kiss. A gentle startled noise vibrates our lips and her hands grab at my hips as she presses herself against me. Her body softens, and she sinks deeper into this moment between us.

I pull away with a breathless smile as I stroke her cheek with my thumb, gazing into emerald green eyes. This little lawyer absolutely rocked my world in every way. Someone that plays by her own rules and doesn't give a shit if it gets in anyone else's way. She goes for whatever she wants and doesn't mind stepping on toes to get it. She sees the world around her and takes in all the things that she can, just because she wants to.

Fuck, I love a woman who can take reins like she does. This is Tiana's world and we're all just living in it.

And holy *fuck*, am I thankful to be living in Tiana's world.

She's unlike anything I've ever experienced and it drives me wild.

She drives me wild.

Tiana smiles softly before she looks questioningly at me. "What is going on?" she asks.

"What are we?"

A look of surprise washes over her as her head shakes with confusion. "What do you mean? We've had sex a few times."

I release a contented sigh as I stroke her cheek, visions of the weekend playing through my thick skull.

"It was more than a few times, but I digress," I whisper with a teasing grin.

She gives me a playful roll of her eyes in response.

"Are we... together? Are we just fucking? Are we exclusive?"

I sincerely hope that we are exclusive. There's no way I could share this little beauty with anyone else. I want her all to myself and I know that dating is scary for her. But fuck, the way I need her is like I need air.

Tiana backs away slowly, and she worries her lower lip with her teeth in thought. Her eyes shy away as a nervous blush rolls over her cheeks.

"I don't know, Gunnar. It's not exactly legal for us to date. And I don't even know if I'm ready for that kind of commitment. Since I'm the go between for the team, there are rules. We can't really... be seen together?"

Fuck, I never thought about what legalities may be in place. That explains at least part of her hesitancy... but...

"What rules?" I ask quietly.

"There are conflicts of interest if you were to get in trouble and I had to represent you. I don't know really what the work around is for something like this."

So she may lose her job... This is riskier than I thought it was going to be.

"Okay... so... we'll take it slow... play it safe," I reiterate softly.

"Slow... yes... safe, especially," she murmurs as her eyes glance away. "But we can't tell anyone anything. I have worked far too hard to lose my job for dick," she says with a quirk of her brow.

"Sugar, I would never want you to lose your job. I know how it feels to throw your all into something," I respond with a reassuring smile.

"Mhm, I'm sure you do," she says with a playful roll of her eyes as she shoves out of my embrace.

I catch her hands and hold them against my chest. I lean in, being enveloped in her amazing beachy scent, and nip at her earlobe.

"I threw all of me into you, didn't I? You didn't seem to mind that."

Her eyes widen as a blush creeps across her cheeks and her teeth tug on that plump lower lip of hers. This shy persona she eases into in my arms is fucking sexy. Especially when I know how she can be around others.

Above all, I'm glad I can give her this comfort and safety to experience this.

"If I recall, you seemed to love it. Especially with the way you screamed when you took every inch of my cock."

Tiana gasps and shoves me away with a playful, shy smile. "Oh, my god! Gunnar!"

"What? You've been on my mind all practice, sweetness. I can't help it," I say with a soft bite to my lower lip as I gaze over her face with lowered eyes.

She rolls her eyes as walks over to her desk. To get a better look at her desktop computer, she bends over, her mouse clicking as she closes out some open programs.

Her round ass strains against the fabric of her tight pencil skirt and I blow a breath out as I back away.

Now that I know what it's actually like to be behind her, it's harder to control myself than when I was just curious.

Her eyes flick to me and she quirks a brow in devious challenge before she bends over lower. Her lower back curves in the most delicious arch and I'm two seconds from fucking her right here.

"Sugar, you're killing me," I groan as I turn to grab my backpack from the ground.

"What? So you can tease me, but I can't tease you?" she laughs as she closes out her computer and stands up straight to pack up her things.

I watch her, noting the things she usually puts into her bag. I can feel my blood pump faster as she gets closer to placing her laptop in, which is the last thing she adds before she closes it. Tiana looks up at me as she finally places it and her arms cross against her chest as she looks at me. She gives me a knowing grin before gesturing to her things and I smile wildly as I grab them from her desk and open the office door for her.

Tiana shakes her head with a roll of her eyes as she walks in front of me, leading me out of her office.

She turns down the hallway, swinging her hips just a little more as I walk behind her before she sends a sexy brief look over her shoulder.

God damnit, I've unleashed a little demon.

"You're going to be the death of me, Tiana Dawn!" I call out to her with a laugh.

"That's what I'm hoping for, Gunnar Hayze!" she throws over her shoulder with a wave as she continues leading me to the exit doors of the arena.

CHAPTER TWENTY

TIANA

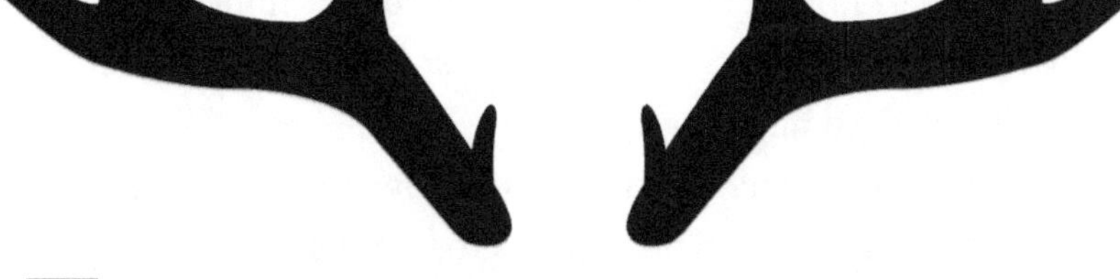

I don't think I have ever felt this way about a man before... felt... thought... hell, *craved* a man like this.

There have been so many nights recently when I wanted to knock on his door just for him to come over.

Sex... cuddling. It doesn't matter, I just really want to be near or with him. It sends confusing signals all over my body, and I don't know how to decipher any of them! I should just give in and let things happen. But I can't. Not when my job stands in the balance. If I grow complacent in our sneaking around, things could get sour *very* quickly.

Gunnar could lose his position on the team he worked so hard for, and I could be out of a license. I want to have my cake and eat it too, but it feels almost impossible without sneaking around.

I have to play it smart and lock into my little lawyer brain to play the game properly.

There's no way we can have my dad finding out about this. Charlotte has had her chance with hockey players, and that was fine because she's the equipment manager. It's not that big of an issue.

But as the legal representative for our team, it's pretty much illegal for me to get into relationships with my clients.

It's a liability. A huge one, all with a number of unsavory consequences.

Part of me doesn't even know if I'm ready for a relationship with this man. I love fucking him. That's for damn sure.

But a *girlfriend.*

I don't know if I'm ready for that sort of thing. That feels like a lot of commitment. That almost feels like a lot of work I don't feel like doing.

Granted, Gunnar has shown me how easy it has been with him. The way he's cared for me before and after he finally got his chance with me.

God, it's honestly so tempting. I want to give in entirely to the idea. Part of me really, *really* does.

But I can't. Not with everything surrounding us.

I shake my head of the thoughts and bring my attention back to the random movie I had put on an hour ago. I had started it but retreated so deep into my head that I forgot I was even watching it.

This is what happens when I'm alone with my thoughts. And what's even worse is I *know* Gunnar is just right on the other side of the wall. He's *right* there.

It's like living with temptation. But I must show restraint. I have to. No man wants a woman who throws herself at them whenever they want. Especially someone like Gunnar, who seems to enjoy the chase.

No, I'll let him come to me. Which I know won't be hard because he already does that.

A groan exits my throat. The frustration in me climbs to a peak, and I feel like I need to talk to someone about this. Luckily, I feel like I can tell Charlotte most of anything. She knows at least some complications with all of this and knows how to be quiet. So I know that she'll be more than happy to help me out.

I pick up my phone and scroll through my contacts to find her number before pressing the call button. The line rings a few times before she answers.

"Helllllooooo?" she singsongs in her normal cheery tone.

"Charlotte," I say sternly.

"Tiana!" she responds.

"I'm having issues."

"Wiiiiiiiith?" she asks.

"Are you busy?"

She's quiet for a moment before her voice comes through the line. "Not right now. Why?"

I sigh. "Do you want to have a sleepover?"

A high-pitched squeal comes through the line, and I have to pull the phone away from my ear to keep my eardrum from bursting.

"YES! YES! YES! I'M GONNA BRING SO MANY SNACKS! GIVE ME AN HOUR!" I hear from the phone held about a foot from my face.

I shake my head with a small laugh. "Okay, I'll see you then."

I hang up the phone and tidy up around my house.

I'm able to get the kitchen and living room squared away. The dishes get done, as well as some general clean up, when I hear a knock at my door.

My brow furrows because there is no way that can be Charlotte. It's not like she lives in the same complex as me.

I pad over to the door, still in some soft fleece pajamas, and open it, peeking around the corner to see who it is.

But Gunnar is there, with an enormous bottle of water and

a little basket of goodies. He wears a simple black Seattle Stags t-shirt and black sweatpants. It's intoxicating how good he can look in something so casual. It seems as if it's all he wears.

But... I love it, honestly.

However, what he's holding ends up grabbing my attention more.

I look at him in confusion as I survey the things in his hands. "What... what the fuck is all this?" I ask.

Gunnar smiles as he presses the basket into my hands. "It's a 'thanks for taking my dick so well' basket."

My jaw drops as I look between the gift in my arms and his grinning face. "You're kidding me."

He laughs as he shoves his hands in his pockets. "Only partially. It's partly a thank you for going on a date with me. Annnnnd, for taking my dick so well. A slapshot, if you will."

My eyes roam over the things inside the basket, realizing some of my favorite candies and chips are in it, with my favorite chocolate bars as well. There is even a small card, and I furrow my brow as I place the basket on the kitchen island. I grab the little envelope and open it to find a thank-you card, with little flowers on the outside and a swirly script font. When I open the card, written in his handwriting is;

"Thank you for giving me a chance, sugar."

Heat swallows my face, and my heart pounds in my chest at this small gesture. I have no idea what the fuck to think about this. The reasoning feels insane. Who gives someone a basket for fucking them?

I glance from the card to watch as he stands in the doorway. He holds a brash sincerity in his eyes that tells me he's actually not kidding about any of this.

Bizarre.

"Where did you even learn how to do this?" I ask as I pull some things out of the basket to place on the counter.

"I do have a mother," he says with a playful grin.

My hands brace against the counter as I look over all the sweet things and the intention behind this gift.

This man gave me a fucking 'thank you' basket for going on a date with him? What even is this? I am so lost.

As if I needed to be more confused about him. He already settled on exclusivity, but part of me can't help but think this is another little trick to get me to be his girlfriend.

My arms cross against my chest as I turn slowly to face him, narrowing my eyes on him in accusation.

"You aren't trying to convince me to be your girlfriend with this, are you?"

Gunnar gives me a confused, incredulous look as his head tilts. "No... No ulterior motives. I just wanted to thank you. Maybe give you some snacks. But that's really it."

I tap my foot as I watch him. He crouches to enter my apartment, enough to lean against my door frame. With his hands shoved into his pockets, his foot crosses one over the other. He dips his chin, flicking out his tongue to secure that chain of his in his mouth. He flicks his head back up, so it rests in the corners of his lips as his tongue curves and swirls around the center.

A heated gaze swirls in the hazel before it darkens, and he takes a sensual look up and down my body.

"You look real good today, sugar, you know that?" he says sensually as the chain continues to shift between his teeth and tongue.

Heat engulfs my face, all the way up to my ears, and some of my defense drops. "I'm just in pajamas," I murmur.

Gunnar's eyebrow quirks as his gaze swipes over me again, his tongue making a deliberate flick with the chain as he thinks.

He shoves his shoulder against the door frame to propel himself from it. As he does, his foot flicks behind him to close the door. His massive body is imposing as he comes near, with his luxurious forest scent swallowing me. His eyes glance down at me as his tongue slides against the silver chain.

I can't help but admit how hot it is.

"Did you miss me, sweetness?" His voice is rough, taunting. Like a deadly male siren. It sends my pulse straight through the roof.

A strong hand tugs at my hip, pulling me into him to mold my body to his. I bite my lip as the heat moves from my face to fill my body, causing sparks to course through my blood.

"It's only been a few days," I murmur nervously.

I glance innocently at him through my lashes, and slowly slide into the persona I've adopted in his arms. The one that lets go of her control and is at the mercy of his. The one that feels like the world outside of them can't touch her because he's got her.

It lights a generous fire within, and I lean into him more.

His tongue drops the chain before he leans down. A nip is felt on my earlobe as his breath grazes over my skin. His hand tightens on my hip as the other comes to press me flat against him.

"I've stroked my cock to the thought of that tight pussy wrapped around me. Every. Fucking. Night." He enunciates the last few words with sharp letters. He drags one hand up my body, lingering against my tit before he brings it up to cup my cheek, tilting my head up to lock his gaze onto mine.

I feel my vision widen at his words, my eyelids expanding as I blow a soft breath out. Shock waves of lust run up through my spine to fall back down and pool in my core.

"I've thought about fucking a baby into that pretty little cu-" he whispers.

I'm pulled from my lust as his words register. My gaze turns crazed as I shove him away and push myself out of his arms, damn near clutching my hands against my chest in shock.

"A WHAT?! What the fuck are you talking about?!" I ask quickly.

I don't want a fucking baby! Is this man fucking insane?! A BABY?! We aren't even close to that sort of thing!

Gunnar laughs. "That's probably my bad. I should have warned you. I, uh... I have a breeding kink." His hand nervously scratches the back of his neck as he glances away.

My jaw drops. "A... a what?"

I'm not super experienced in bed, and as far as I know, I don't have any wild kinks of my own.

Blush creeps across his cheeks, and a shyness washes over his features as he glances away. "This does not feel like a safe space," he grumbles.

I roll my eyes playfully as I sigh. Mentally, I take a deep breath and a small step back to assess the situation. If he has something he wants to explore... or something that he enjoys that's harmless, I can indulge. He has given me space to explore things I didn't know I liked.

Smiling, I close the distance between us to press my body against his as I bring my hands up to cup his face. Slowly, I pull his gaze back to mine, trying to portray some level of safety for him.

"What... is a breeding kink?" I ask sincerely.

He looks at me with a small bite to his lip. "So..." he breathes deeply. "I get turned on by the idea of... getting you pregnant. But without actually getting you pregnant. It's just... a... primal thing that kinda comes up."

My eyes widen more, and a vibrant pulse is set ablaze *low* in my core.

His eyebrow quirks as he watches my face. His eyes roam

over my features, taking note of how this has pierced through me.

"Oh..." he says with a pleased grin.

"Can you tell me more?" I ask breathlessly.

His firm hands wrap tightly around my back, and he pulls me to his chest. His fingers slide down my lower back, to the crest of my ass, then further south to grip my cheeks in his hands. Tiny bites pepper my neck and collarbone when he bends down, making my back bow as he holds me close to him. His cock is hard as stone as he presses it against me.

He breathes against my neck, inhaling my scent before his voice breaks through the haze, smooth and low.

"Well... I like the idea of fucking deep... *deep* into you and filling you so full of me that I know you wouldn't be able to leave this room without it dripping down your thighs."

"Gunnar..." I pant as I reach for his sides. The soft material of his shirt barely grounds me as his words seep deeper into me.

My pulse speeds up, my breath catching in my throat, with my teeth pulling at my lower lip. The soft pressure of his lips against my skin sends lust rushing through every part of my body.

"I enjoy imagining you carrying my baby. The idea that *I* put that baby in you," he whispers. His hips grind harder into me and his rigid cock lets me know how much this turns him on.

"Fuck," I pant as my head tilts back further, letting myself melt into him.

One hand releases my ass, coming to the front to press into the band of my pajama pants. His fingers move slowly as he presses his hand deeper, cupping my pussy before he prods softly into the now damp material. A gasp escapes me, feeling the way he just barely brushes against the spot that begs and pleads for more from him.

He continues speaking as he presses deeper against that wet spot. "That I fucked you so deep that I marked you as mine forever. I staked my claim, and everyone would know the reason you're plump and swollen is because of me. The way you'd look carrying *my* fucking kid. God, Tiana, the way you would fucking glow," he almost growls to himself. He groans as he grinds against me. "I can see it so clearly."

The visions dance in my head, my breath catching and my throat tightening at the way he says it all. The intimacy of the fact that I'm carrying his child. The way he would beam with pride for what he's done. The level of protection he'd have for me...

It's madness. This shouldn't be turning me on at all. But fuck me, it *is*. Plus, it's just... role playing in a sense? I have an IUD, so I'm not getting pregnant anytime soon.

Of course, being hit with it from the side is jarring.

He presses just a bit deeper against the wet spot, softly stroking my clit through the material.

"It's the only thing I've thought about since you let me come in you. The way you felt with my spend filling that perfect pussy of yours."

Another jolt of pleasure runs through my blood, a soft moan coming from me.

The more he teases me in that smooth and sultry tone of his...

"Gunnar..." I moan again.

"Yes, sugar?" he whispers against my skin. His voice is husky, rough, and absolutely tortured. The sound sends a hearty shiver up my spine.

"My sister will be here soon."

"I'll be quick. I just need my fix." His hips roll against me again, and with every grind, I feel him get harder and harder.

"What do you need?" I ask breathlessly.

Every point of contact I make with him sends hot lava through my veins. His chest against mine, his fingers teasing my aching core, his lips on my neck, and his hard cock begging for me.

He pulls his hand out of my pants to lay a harsh sting across my ass before he grips it tight.

"You," he murmurs.

I breathe a tortured moan as my head drops back. The way this man touches me, talks to me, it all makes me melt into a puddle, and I can hardly believe the effect he has on me.

His lips leave my neck as he pulls back, just enough to search my eyes. He pushes the gift basket on the counter away before a feral grin spreads across his face. Both hands go to my hips, and he lifts me onto the kitchen island. As his hands roam my legs, his tongue comes back to leave fiery trails against my skin. The hot muscle sliding along my neck and throat.

My hands grip his shoulders as I give in to the feeling of his touch. His large, rough hands tease the hem of my soft pajama pants before he tugs them off. The cool air hits my center and my legs as he presses himself between them with his knuckle coming back to rub into the wetness.

"Is someone learning something new about herself?" His breath is cool against the wet spots he left on my neck, and something about the wild sound of it undoes me. Gruff and raw, he rasps as he touches me.

I nod as I lean back on my hands, giving him more access. His fingers press into the wet fabric, deep against my clit. A torturous groan crawls out of me, and I pant in frustration. It's so teasing, and I need *more*.

"You like the idea of me filling this little cunt? Marking you? Letting the world know that I claimed you?" he mumbles against my neck as he pushes my panties to the side and slides his fingers up and down through my wetness, just barely grazing my clit.

I groan again, damn near in a growl. "Gunnar..."

He's teasing me, and I'm about to start barking for him.

"You're so fucking wet. You want me to put a baby in you, sugar? I'll be real gentle," he pants as he kisses deeper into my neck.

"Somehow I don't believe that. But I need you to fuck me. Now," I quickly say. The tension in me rises to a peak, and I writhe against his fingers, desperate for more friction, more pressure, *anything*.

"So demanding. I like it," he whispers. He presses one last kiss into my neck before he leans back.

His eyes slide down my body to land on my wet, panty-covered pussy, and his teeth sink into his lower lip. He slides his fingers into his mouth, sucking them clean before one of his hands drifts down to press against his dick through his sweatpants.

He takes another moment, admiring me before he drops to his knees in front of the kitchen island. His lips are soft as he presses them against the skin of my inner thighs. It sends small shock waves skittering through my nerves the closer he gets to my center. His large, rough hands glide up my skin as he looks up at me with a sly grin.

"I told myself that one day I'd be on my knees worshipping you," he murmurs.

My breaths come out as soft pants as I lean back on my elbows, watching him as he hooks a finger into my panties and pulls them to the side. The warmth, the wetness of his mouth, it covers my center before sucking the slickness from me.

A gasp rings through the apartment, and my head falls back as I feel him. My fingers bolt for his scalp, gripping into the soft strands to pull him deeper. I bring my head back up to look down at him. His eyes connect with mine as my hips writhe and grind against his face. I can't look away as I watch him move between my legs. His hands continue to caress the skin of my thighs as he dips his tongue in deeper, parting through the seam to flick against my clit.

My body trembles as he does, and I moan torturously in response.

"Gunnar... Fuck!" I pant. He sucks my clit into his lips, flicking his tongue against it.

Suddenly, one of his hands leaves my thighs to press his fingers into me. He works them in and out as he laps at my clit. The pleasure is insurmountable, and I can only groan as he devours my need. My eyes roll back, and my neck loses its strength. Letting my head fall back, I give in to the way he feasts on me.

He laps at me for a few more moments before I feel his tongue leave my center, and my head rises to look at him, only to find he's come to a stand. His fingers work in and out of me as his thumb glides over my clit, with his eyes focused on the attention he keeps on my core. He presses the band of his sweatpants and boxers down, letting his cock bob free.

Gunnar switches hands, slicking his fingers with a swipe against his tongue before pressing them into me. The one covered in my wetness fists his dick, stroking it and rubbing me on him. There is a calculated precision with the way he goes about pleasuring me. It's a level of experience and confidence that is hotter than I'd like to admit. He knows what he wants, and he knows how to go about getting it.

His head tosses back as he twists his hand around the head of himself. A groan comes from him as I watch him stroke his dick with my wetness. I feel the heat fill my chest, my focus momentarily pulled from his hand in my pussy.

He leans down to press a kiss into my wet center and his

tongue sneaks out of his mouth to swipe at my clit again. A small tremble shocks through me at the tease.

I don't have time to process the small movement before his warm body parts my thighs and I feel him slide the head of his cock through my wet center. He lingers at my clit, rubbing himself against it. My body shakes against him and he pulls my ass just slightly off the counter to press himself into me.

"Fuck, Tiana," he pants as he looks down between us.

He tugs the hem of his shirt up to bite it in between his teeth. In the process, he bares his hard, rippled stomach. The striated muscles under his skin writhe as he slowly presses deeper into me. His eyes linger on where he enters me, taking shallow strokes and watching the way he fills me with a tilt of his head.

"This counter is the perfect height for fucking," I hear him mumble to himself from where he grips his shirt in his teeth.

I can't respond, I can't *think*. There is only Gunnar and the way he fills me.

He takes slow strokes in and out of me, his teeth tighten on his shirt as he groans torturously.

"You feel so *fucking* good," he grits. Though it's muffled by how hard he tightens his teeth against his shirt.

His words send pleasure coursing through me, and I moan out as I hear him. The idea that I'm making him quiver like this is a bit empowering, considering how big he is.

I grind back against his length, anchoring my hands against the counter, and his thrusts halt. He watches as my hips roll against him, his hands clasping behind his back as he presses his hips forward.

"God, sugar, are you trying to make me bust?" he groans as his head leans back.

His chest rises and falls, my sight locked onto the tight muscles in his stomach, his throat. The hard lines and veins pressing against his skin are a visual admiration that only adds to the fact that this gorgeous fucking man is inside of me.

He groans as he leans over my body, gripping my face in his hands to kiss me. Holding me in place, he thrusts into me. I groan as his movements speed up and my body goes limp. I grip his wrists as he holds me up, throwing stroke after punishing stroke into me.

"You wanna be my little cumslut, baby?" he pants against my lips.

My eyes roll at his words. The filth of them breaks me out of this pattern I've known for so long. The chaos of it all makes me feel a level of weightlessness I've never felt before.

"Fuck... yes, I wanna be your little cumslut. Please... fuck, please make me your cumslut," I pant breathlessly in response.

"Good girl, sugar. That's a good girl, you're getting the hang of it," he whispers.

He presses his forehead against mine as his eyes glance down, watching himself move in and out of me.

"I..." My head scrambles for the words. I've never done this before, but I'm trying to satisfy the part of him that wants this. "Put a baby in me. Fuck me until I can't hold any more of you, please..."

"Fucking hell..." he groans as his thrusts turn into rolls. His eyes clench shut as he slows, almost trying to keep himself from coming too quickly.

"I wanna feel the way you fill me... please, I want to you to drip out of me, Mr. Hayze, please," I whimper desperately.

His groan turns into a growl as his thrusts turn chaotic. Feral and deep, he pounds into me, his hands gripping tight on the sides of my neck, his fingers laced behind it as he not only thrusts into me but pulls me onto him.

"Call me that again," he growls.

The pleasure he's sending through my body with each

piston of his hips has my thoughts scrambled, and I can only listen to the sound of his voice. The way it drips with a primal sort of pleasure I've never heard from him, like an animal looking to claim.

"I wanna make you a daddy so fucking bad, Mr. Hayze. Fill me, please, please, please, I need you, please, fuck," I whimper desperately. My voice is begging, light, tortured, *just* for him. I take every thrust he throws into me, over and over, letting him fill me with every inch of him.

His eyes roll as he adjusts one of his hands to wrap around my throat. He kisses sloppily against my lips as he swallows every noise I make.

"Fuck, I needed this, Tiana. This pussy, you, *fuck,*" he growls.

This is a truly primal side of him I don't think I've seen before.

"You feel..." I groan, letting the waves wash over me for just a moment before I bring my head up above water again. "Fuck, Gunnar you feel so fucking good," I pant.

"You like the way it feels to be stretched by my thick cock?" he whispers as he slows his thrusts.

His hips roll into me in languid, precise strokes, and a torturous groan crawls out of me. He holds his face inches from mine, his hand applying pressure to the sides of my neck to force my eyes up.

"Eyes on me, sugar."

My sight has been locked on the way his abs tense and contort as he thrusts into me. The way his cock shines when he drags it in and out, covered in my wetness. But his voice pulls me up, my focus trailing up his body to meet his dark, lust-filled hazel eyes. His gaze is intent, and he tries so hard to keep his focus on me. He pulls out every inch, leaving merely the head inside before he pauses.

"Breathe with me, baby, ready?" he says softly. "In."

Slowly, inch by torturous inch, he pushes into me, taking a deep breath as his pupils blow. And without thought, I do the same, inhaling deeply through the sensation of his press.

He sits himself balls deep, holding himself in as he pulses and twitches his cock against my walls. And I feel every single place he reaches.

"Ready?" he whispers again.

I nod desperately, because every fucking part of him inside of me has my brain in shambles and my pleasure choking the life out of me.

"Out." He slowly pulls out again as we blow out our breaths together. "Good girl, baby. That's my girl," he says.

I groan, the way he goes through all these motions, these methods. It's insanity in the *best* possible way.

"Breathe deep... One more time," he whispers. And I comply.

Inhaling slowly and steadily until my lungs fill. His lips tilt in a devilish grin before he shoves every rigid inch in at once, and every ounce of air I inhaled escapes in a deafening, pleasured scream.

"Thatta girl," he says as he looks down to where he holds himself inside of me, laying a soft slap against my ass.

Soon, his thrusts pick up and his hips piston in and out of me in a steady, dizzying rhythm.

The tension builds more, tightening my spine and snaking around it in a menagerie of sensations everywhere. My pussy flutters and clenches around his thick length as I scale that summit faster and faster.

"God damnit, you're close, you're so fucking close," he whispers as his lips latch on to mine. Our tongues tangle and one of his hands moves down to my pussy to rub into my clit.

"You gonna come for me, pretty girl? You gonna come all over this cock and show me who it belongs to?"

I nod desperately as I give in to the feeling of him and the speed at which I approach the edge.

When a knock sounds at my door. Heart-pounding fear momentarily replaces my lust, but Gunnar doesn't stop. His hips continue to move and his fingers slide faster against my clit.

"G-Gunnar...! Fuck!" I whisper moan, trying so hard to keep my voice down, but he was right. I am a fucking screamer.

"Focus, baby. I need you to come for me. I'm right here. Come for me," he grunts as his thrusts speed up.

I bring my arm up to bite into the skin to keep me from being louder. The tingling in my spine and the sensation of his fingers on my clit, his cock filling me and his gruff voice talking me through every single thrust causes my body to tense in immense pleasure. His hand leaves my neck, coming to toss my arm away so he can replace it with his hand. His other hand leaves my clit to hold the back of my head to steady me as he pounds recklessly into me. My orgasm rolls through every one of my nerves over and over, again and again.

My eyes roll back, my vision blanking as he pistons harder through my climax.

Gunnar hisses out. "Oh! Fuck!" he groans as my pussy locks him in place, clenching in tight waves around his entire length. I feel him spill into me, pumping me full, just like he said he would, with my screams muffled behind his palm.

He gives me a moment to settle before he plants two hands on either side of my hips against the counter, his chest heaving as he takes small thrusts in and out of me. Without him holding me up, the bone-melting pleasure causes me to fall back onto the counter-top, relishing the way the cool marble chills my overheated body.

Another knock sounds at the door.

"Jus'aminute!" I call breathlessly.

Gunnar continues his small strokes as he finishes fucking through his own orgasm and he pants as he gives me a feral little grin.

"That was so perfect, sweetness. You did so fucking well," he says before he leans in to kiss my lips softly. He grips my hips as he slowly retreats, and I feel his cum drip down out of me.

A gasp leaves my lips as he pulls my underwear over my core.

He grips my wrist and pulls me in close. "I told you. I keep my promises, sugar. I want you to remember who marked that pretty little cunt," he whispers.

He kisses me again, slower, deeper. All the while, he nudges a knuckle against the sensitive spot, and I wriggle against him before I slap his chest. It's much harder than I expected, and I pull my hand back with a twinge of pain.

He leans down to grab my pajama pants and helps my legs into them before he pulls me off the counter to tug them the rest of the way up. Quickly, he stuffs his cock into his boxers and pulls his pants back up. He wraps his arm around my back to pull me flush against him.

Some of his words from earlier come to the forefront of my mind, and my curiosity gets the better of me.

"Do you really come to the thought of me every night?" I ask as I look up at him. His eyes are half-lidded in satisfaction and he damn near glows as he bites into his lip.

Gunnar grips my chin in his thumb and forefinger before he presses a kiss to my lips, taking his time.

"Every. Night," he says when he pulls away.

My cheeks heat, and his gaze stays locked on me as the knocking comes again.

I toss my head back in frustration. "One second, Charlotte!" I call through gritted teeth.

"I'm just a knock away, sweetness. I'm at your beck and call whenever you need me. I'll never turn down the chance to see you," he whispers.

My eyes widen, and he leans in to kiss my lips again before he pulls away to open the door.

Charlotte's previously cheery face turns to one of complete surprise as her gaze tracks up Gunnar's body to his face.

"Oh! Gunnar! Hi...?? Is...? I'm sorry, where is Tiana?" she asks curiously.

I peek out from behind his back to give her a nervous smile.
"Oh! Hi Tiana. What is...?"

"Nothing, don't worry about it. He had some uh... a contract with someone he wanted me to look over," I say quickly and begin shoving him out of the door.

Gunnar crouches when he walks out, before he turns and gives a sly smirk to me as he nods his head in goodbye.

"Goodnight, Tiana. Charlotte," he says with a grin before he retreats, and Charlotte steps into my apartment.

"What was that about?" she asks with a perplexed expression.

Before I close the door, I dip my head out to look down the hall. When Gunnar approaches his door, his hand on the knob, he turns to look at me. He gives me a sly grin and a wink as he blows a kiss my way. I smile as I roll my eyes and pop back into my apartment.

As I close the door, I take a deep breath. I'm hoping with everything in me that Charlotte didn't hear any of the things that just happened in here. Even if she's about to find out, I still didn't want her to hear it.

I sigh with a groan. "Did you bring the snacks?"

Charlotte grins as she holds up a few grocery bags, and I lead her to the couch.

CHAPTER TWENTY-ONE
TIANA

Gunnar and I have been leaving the complex together in the mornings. He will come to my door and stand guard, waiting for me with a cup of coffee to walk me to whichever car we take that day. I really can't say that I hate it. It actually helps me out. Being able to just get ready for the day and not have to worry about grabbing or even making my morning pick-me-up, it takes a big amount of stress off of me.

Not only does part of my routine get done for me, it's done when I need it to be done. And I didn't even have to ask for that. It's just something he started doing on his own.

I'm also impressed with his ability to wake up so damn early, just for the sake of getting said coffee. We have moved into this sort of... comfortable routine. He's somehow integrated into my schedule, trying to make it easier on me.

I can't even explain how endearing it is. I'm somewhat appreciative of it.

Men have never wanted to integrate into my life. They've always wanted to come in to disrupt it. I didn't have time to move around my schedule for theirs. In my eyes, they didn't have careers that warranted that level of sacrifice.

But Gunnar... he's made it easy. He's wanted nothing more than to just be a part of my every day.

And I'm starting to love it. I didn't realize how nice it was to have company in my day-to-day.

Some people have gawked, or made fun of us.

We tell them we're just friends and that it's easier to carpool because we live in the same apartment complex.

Technically, we are *just* friends.

We're friends who happen to have really hot sex... but still friends. Though I am warming up to the idea of him possibly being my boyfriend. But the legality of it makes me quiver. And not in a good way.

I don't know if I'm willing to risk my career for him. I certainly wouldn't want him to risk his career for me.

If push comes to shove... I'll figure a way to make it work. I can sneak around until I'm able to get the proper information. I just have to be careful. Very... *very* careful.

Today, my mother told me there is a case coming up soon that she'll need my help with. She hasn't told me anything else, but it makes me a tad anxious considering it's a much bigger case than one I've ever worked on. I think it'll help with my career, but it's still scary. Either way, it's one of those things I need to be prepared for.

Instead of doing the work I need to do, however, I take the time to look up some rules on fraternization.

There are a variety of reasons you shouldn't date your clients. Some, of course, I already know.

Because I represent the team, he technically is my client. Even if I haven't represented him *in* anything yet.

But would I be able to find a workaround for all of this? The thought makes me nervous. It creates a small pit of guilt in my stomach. One that makes it churn with uncertainty and causes my throat to tighten.

What if he does somehow get in trouble and I have to represent him? Everything I will have worked for would technically be a lie. The oath and truths I've been sworn to uphold would be for nothing. Then my integrity as a lawyer would be in question.

And I'll be damned if someone questions that. I've wanted to be a lawyer since I saw how badass my mother was. It was everything I wanted to do.

The complexity of it all is frustrating. I can't directly go to my mother. She'd think something was up. Especially with Charlotte saying I found a 'boyfriend.'

The rest of my day is spent researching, and by the end of it all, I feel like my stomach is in knots. Horrible twisted knots that are struggling to unravel themselves.

It feels like I can't have my cake and eat it too.

As I pack up my stuff for the day, Gunnar's fresh-from-the-shower scent alerts me before his signature little knock on my door frame. My heart beats a little faster when I know I get to see him, and he smiles as I look up at him.

"You ready to go home, sweetness?" he asks softly.

A blush crawls over my cheeks, and the knots in my stomach are slowly unraveled by some of the butterflies that have taken flight there. Besides that blush, I smile as I nod to him, waiting for him to come and grab my things. He does so with vigor and I give a small chuckle at his excitement over such trivial things.

As we walk out of my office and pass the rink, Gunnar stops to look at the ice, sighing softly in content.

My brow furrows at such a reaction. "What?" I ask.

Gunnar looks at me with an enormous grin before looking back out at the ice.

"They just resurfaced the ice, which means it's nice and smooth."

My brow rises. "Why is that such a good thing?"

Gunnar gives me a laugh. "What do you mean, 'why is that such a good thing'? Have you never skated on fresh ice before?"

I shake my head as I give him an incredulous look.

His lips part as he looks at me like I've grown three heads. "You're kidding?"

I shake my head again. "Why would I be kidding?"

"Uhhh, well, your dad is a hockey coach? And Charlotte used to play hockey before she became the equipment manager."

I roll my eyes at him with a small half-smile. "Yes, *that* is Charlotte. I've never really been totally interested in hockey. I mean, my dad tried to teach me when I was really young, but I really couldn't get the hang of it."

Gunnar grins as his face lights up with what I can only imagine is the worst idea ever.

"Stay right here," he tells me.

My brow rises as I watch him run off with my things. Only for him to return a second later.

"Can I have your keys, please?"

My face contorts with unbelievable disdain as I nod to his shoulder, where my tote is slung over it like it's his. His eyes track down to where he grips the handle of my bag against him, giving me a nervous smile.

"Right. Okay, be right back."

Gunnar runs off toward the exit of the arena and I wait.

The only people out and about are the custodians cleaning up for the day. Even the ice surfacer is gone. I know my dad left, because he came by to make sure I got the email from my mother and I told him I did.

I turn to the rink, gazing at the fresh layer of ice that has frozen over.

He is right about one thing. The ice is actually exquisite after it's been resurfaced.

Usually when I've had to see it, it looks as if it's been chopped to shit. Which makes sense, considering the large men that skate on it absolutely wreck it during a game.

Gunnar's thudding steps alert me of his presence and I turn to see him, with two pairs of ice skates. Both are way too big for me, if that's what he plans to do. My bags and his backpack are also gone.

My face contorts in question as he approaches, and I look at the skates in his hands in disbelief.

"There is no singular way I am going to use your nasty, sweaty skates!"

He laughs and hands me the pair that looks a bit more held together. Granted, both of them are pretty fucked up.

"Gunnar, this can not be safe! These are way too big for me!" I groan.

Gunnar laughs again before he leads me to a bench off to the side and presses my shoulders to sit me down.

He kneels in front of me and begins pulling my heels off. The sight is sexier than I could have ever anticipated, and he gazes up at me through his long, dark brown lashes. His gaze heats as he takes my foot in his hands, and my cheeks respond with the same sentiment.

Kissing my ankle, he pulls a pair of socks from inside the skates to pull onto my feet. He takes his time sliding the skate onto my foot and lacing it up.

Before long, I'm wearing a pair of skates that are way too big for me. As I come to a stand on the blades, my ankles and knees wobble like a newborn deer as I try to walk toward the door of the rink.

I truly can't believe I'm doing this. This is madness. But it's kind of sweet that he wants to teach me something like this. I think I can dip into his world for just a little bit. I can give him that. And honestly, I think I need a harmless distraction from all the turmoil I subjected myself to today.

Gunnar quickly puts on his skates and comes over to the door of the rink. He steps onto the ice with such grace that it seems more natural than walking on solid ground for him. It's as if they aren't two different surfaces.

My eyes widen as I watch him move, and he takes a few leisurely strides across the ice. He goes to one end, walking backwards with his hands behind him as he tilts his head back. I swear I see him take a deep breath of relaxation. His eyes closed as he feels the smooth new surface for himself.

Soon, he comes back to the present, taking sight of me from the other end of the rink. A smile tugs at his lips as he races toward me, fast as sin, before he skids to a stop. The scrape of his blades sends slush spraying all over my bare legs, chilling and wetting them instantly.

"Pfft! Gunnar!" I groan as I kick the melting ice from my legs.

I think trying to learn how to ice skate in a pencil skirt is probably a worse idea than trying to skate in his damn skates, but whatever, we're here.

We're doing this.

Gunnar reaches a hand out for me, and I look at it for a moment before I grasp it. Once again, those familiar sparks of his touch run up my arms, lighting my whole body on fire. He reaches for my other hand, holding me steady as I slowly step my way onto the ice.

My knees bend in at the middle, and I feel like my ankles are going to break, but he is right. The ice is extremely smooth.

He crisscrosses his feet behind him as he skates backwards to pull me along. And the fact he hasn't gotten 'the ick' from how I look right now is a mystery in and of itself. But he looks at me with the biggest fucking smile and a level of bright happiness in his eyes that I don't think I've ever seen from him.

I didn't think this simple act would mean so much to him, but I enjoy the fact that I'm able to give him this. Even if it is completely out of my comfort zone.

I find myself more open to ideas when they come from Gunnar. I don't know if it's because maybe I feel a sense of safety with him I've never gotten elsewhere. Or maybe I just want to give back to him being so understanding in my everyday life. He gives me space to be alone, which is something that I crave. He knows not to impede certain places because of how important said space is.

Granted, he's pressed those lines, but he's always been a gentleman and stuck to his word. Regardless of how crazy it may have sounded to come out of his mouth.

I lose myself in my thoughts, and his face as he pulls me along the ice, until he lets go of my hands and I glide along without him.

"Ah! Fuck! Gunnar!!" I call out as I hold my arms out to keep myself level. They spin to keep me steady before I fall back straight on my ass.

I groan in pain as the frozen rink sends shockwaves of pain through me, and he rushes over to help.

"You need to build up your ankle strength, sweetness," he says with a pained smile as he lifts me under my armpits.

He holds me in place as he spins to the front of me and puts his arms out for me to hold so I can regain my bearings.

"Ughhhh, that shit hurts. How the fuck do you even fight on something like this?" I groan as I grip his large forearms. The hard muscles underneath are webbed with thick, pulsing veins, and they send small pulses of lust through me.

I squeeze his arms softly in my fingers to distract myself from the pain in my ass.

He's quiet as he speaks, seeming to notice how I've turned to his muscles. "We can stop if you want. You've done really great so far."

I look up at him, and even though I so badly want to, I've never seen him this happy.

His eyes beam with a brightness so intense that it almost makes my chest hurt. I know hockey is everything and more to him, and it would be like if he came to sit in on a big case of mine.

One I may have been prepping for, and was extremely nervous about.

I can give him this. I can open myself up to his world in this way.

And so I stay.

For the next hour, Gunnar and I skate on that fresh ice together.

I don't fall for the rest of that hour.

CHAPTER TWENTY-TWO

GUNNAR

Tiana did something I never thought she would do in a million years. And I can't help admitting it was the greatest thing ever.

Hockey is my life force. And even if I didn't teach her hockey, I got her to skate. Which is just half of the equation.

After we finish skating, I feel sweaty and have the urge to shower again. I help Tiana off the ice, and we sit on the bench to remove our skates before we make our way to the showers. As we walk to the locker room, I glance around the halls and realize there is no one around. My brow quirks as I turn to her with a grin.

Her brows furrow in question. "What?"

My teeth catch my lower lip as I wrap an arm around her back and grip her chin with my thumb and forefinger. I tilt her head up and to the side to bare her neck for me.

"Sweetness," I whisper into her skin amidst the kisses I press there.

She releases a breathy gasp as she melts into my embrace.

Until she realizes that we're at the arena, and she quickly shoves me away.

"Gunnar! We are in the arena! We can't be seen doing this here. We don't know who could be here lingering." Her eyes look nervously around us to see if there is anyone nearby.

I pretend to glance around with her before I pull her back into my embrace.

"I saw the last custodian leave about thirty minutes ago, and I know your dad left earlier. We're here by ourselves," I whisper as I bring a hand up to twirl one of her brown and gold curls around my finger.

She bites her lip, and her back bends just enough to allow her body to melt into mine.

"Well... what did you have in mind?" she whispers to me as her neck cranes back.

I grin as I lean down, nipping on the skin at her collarbone before I press my lips against the small marks left behind.

"Are you gonna be my cumslut again? You want me to fill up that tight little pussy?" I rasp against her skin.

She nods desperately as she clings to my hoodie.

When I first brought up my kink to her, I hadn't even realized what I had said. It slipped out in the heat of the moment. And honestly, with how Tiana is, I should have been more careful.

But the way she indulged me, even for a few moments, made *me* feel... safe.

I have only ever explored the idea on my own. It's not exactly easy to bring up to just anyone, but Tiana... fuck, I wouldn't mind making dreams reality if she'd let me.

For now, I'm happy just to play make-believe with her.

Even now that she plays the game with me, it heats my body beyond comprehension. I swing her to the locker room doors and lead her inside. Locking the door behind me, I double check it, just in case I may have missed anyone. And gingerly, my hands graze over the lapels of her suit jacket. Opening it, I slowly press it off of her shoulders to let it fall to the floor behind her in a muffled rumple of fabric.

Her moans are sweet and breathy as my hands roam her body. But there's nothing sweet about the way I rip off her blouse. Hooking my fingers into one of the empty spaces between the buttons, I pull hard. The buttons pop from the small stitches, sending a light clatter of the round pieces echoing through the empty locker room.

Her hands scramble along my body to find the hem of my hoodie and bring it above my head. Granted, she can't reach that high, so I crouch just enough for her to pull it off me. She throws it to the side before she desperately tugs at the band of my sweatpants and boxers.

She doesn't pull the band out far enough and it catches on my hardened cock. I bite my lip with a rough groan.

"Needy today, are we?"

She gives me a sultry look in response as she leans her head up to reel me in with those magnificent eyes of hers. Pressing the bands down far enough to bare my cock, she wraps her soft hand around my length to stroke me.

My head falls back as this little lawyer forces me to melt into her palm. The way her fingers change in pressure as she works me up and down has my head spinning, and I can't do anything but pant.

"Sugar, you're gonna fucking kill me here," I groan as my fingers wrap around the back of her neck, lining her jaw with my thumb to control her head.

I press her chin up to me, kissing her deeply as she wraps the other hand around me. One over the other, she pumps my entire length in slow, sensuous strokes. Twisting and gripping in a way that has me bucking into her hands.

I feel like I'll bust if she keeps this shit up and my free hand goes to grip both her wrists.

Her mouth pulls in a grin against mine as I remove her from me, and I pull my pants and boxers the rest of the way off before I kick them to the side.

The silky material of her ripped blouse slides from her skin as I press it off her shoulders. I toss it with the rest of our clothes before my hands graze her arms.

I have no idea what she does to make her skin so soft, but I admire every bit as I trail my hands up to push one strap of her bra off. I press gentle kisses into the skin there as I do the same to the other shoulder. Reaching behind her, I clasp the little hooks and pinch. They fling open, with the band snapping back at me. I pull myself away, just enough to let it fall to the floor in front of us, and make quick work of her skirt.

As I press the band of her skirt down, her tight hips and muscles slide beneath my hands. Tight and luxurious. She wears a black lace thong, and I groan at the sight of her in just that little scrap of fabric. My cock twitches and my pulse rockets through my ears as I admire her.

My lips collide with hers as I wrap my arm around her waist and pull her with me. While my cock presses against the warm skin of her stomach, I move her to one of the benches inside the shower. I reach over to twist the water on, allowing it to heat up. Soon, steam wafts from the heated water, filling the tiled room and fueling our passion higher.

As she goes to remove the thong, her fingers hook through the sides, and I stop her, nipping at her jaw and pulling her hands away.

"Those stay on. I like the way your pussy looks in them."

Her already pink cheeks deepen in color, and she nods with a soft bite to her lip.

As the steam wraps around us, I pull her under the stream

of water, and the heat of it melds our skin together. My lips furiously take every ounce of anything that I can from her.

Her hands go back to my cock and I swat them away. She gives me a slack-jawed look of shock as I grin at her, caressing one of her sides.

"I can have you suck my cock, if that's what you're asking for, sugar?" I tease.

She rolls her eyes before her attention is brought back to my hands on her skin. Her body becomes pliable in my grasp, and I feel the way she melts with the hot water as a catalyst.

My mouth latches onto hers, slipping my tongue around hers. With gentle breaths bleeding between us as the anticipation builds. I trail my hands down further and rub the seam of her pussy through the now drenched fabric.

There is a level of slickness that you can't get from any shower, and a groan rocks through me as I feel how wet she is. Her moans mix with mine as I deepen our kiss, sharing breaths as I continue to tease her clit through the thong.

"Sugar, you are just..." I groan. My finger wraps around one edge of the cloth barrier before I press it to the side. I slip my finger through her wetness, grazing her clit that pulses against my fingertips.

Her nails dig into the skin at my waist as she holds me, and her lips part in a heated gasp. I steal it from her as I press deeper, swirling soft circles into her clit.

Her moans pour from her throat as her body softens more and more, and I swallow every noise she makes. Putting more pressure on her, her legs wobble, and I grip her waist tighter to hold her up.

"You're doing so good stretching around my fingers. You're almost ready for my cock, sugar," I moan against her mouth.

My fingers slide down to tease her entrance. Her pussy clenches around me as I press farther into her, slowly grinding the heel of my hand against her clit. My fingers slide deeper, and her walls tighten even more. Her mouth opening to moan, and I look into her eyes.

"That's it, let me stretch you," I whisper.

I slide my hand up her back, dragging my nails against her skin before I thread my fingers through her hair, gripping a handful at the nape. I tug softly to pull her head back, looking down into her eyes as I pull her body tightly to mine, and I pump my fingers in and out of her.

Fixing my angle, I replace the heel of my hand with my thumb, rubbing it side to side as my fingers pick up their pace. Her gasps and moans get louder, and her body tightens against me. I feel the way her cunt pulses around my fingers and the way her nails dig deeper into my sides, subjecting me to absolutely delicious pain.

"It's right there... Right... fucking there... isn't it, baby?" I whisper.

She gives me a nod, and her eyes roll back as I torment her.

"Answer me, Tiana," I purr in command. I slow my hand inside of her, teasing and moving within her until she finds her words.

"R-right there. Don't stop, p-please," she manages to pant. Her eyes continue to roll back, and I speed up my attentions.

"Ah, ah, eyes on me," I growl, tightening my grip on her hair and pumping in and out of her faster.

Her eyes open, misty with the loss of her thoughts, and she pants against the onslaught of sensation as I work her closer to the edge.

"There's my good girl. Breathe for me baby, you're almost there," I whisper.

Her pupils blow as her lips part on a gasp, her eyes rolling back as she comes apart. Tremors shake through her body, and her moans echo through the shower room as I feel her nails cut into my skin from her grip.

"There she is." I pant into her neck. Her hips buck against my palm as she continues riding it through her orgasm.

"Take what you need, sugar. Use me," I whisper as I lean down to press kisses into her neck and collarbone.

I loosen my hold on her hair to stroke her shoulder. Her skin is hot and slick from the water cascading over her. Tugging her by her waist, I pull her over to the benches.

I sit down, leaning back against the tiled wall that now drips from the accumulation of steam. Turning her away from me, I rub softly over the pert musculature of her ass. Small marks of dark blue and purple are forming under her deep honey skin, and I give it gentle kisses.

I move the kisses to the curve of her lower back before I nip softly above the bruise and swat at her other cheek. The high-pitched sting rings through the locker room and she yelps a sexy little sound as I lean back enough to grip the base of my dick.

Soft pants leave me as I slap my hard cock against her ass, before swiping the head through her center. Her slick core coats me, and any thought I had goes out the window.

There is only Tiana now.

A groan and another slide through her wetness, I position myself at her entrance, slowly pressing into her. Her warm cunt grips the length of me as I slowly pull her down on me.

My head thunks against the tiled wall as my neck loses strength, my hands gripping tight on her hips.

"Gunnar, fuck, I don't know if I can," she pants. But slowly, she eases down more and more.

"Yes, you can, sugar. I've got you," I respond as she continues sliding down my length.

Her pussy wraps around every inch of me, and her gasps of pleasure grow louder the deeper I get into her.

"There you go, baby. Take your time. You're doing so good," I praise as she settles all the way down into my lap.

Tiana pants as she adjusts to me, and I lean forward just enough to wrap my arms around her waist.

My hand presses against the bulge in her stomach, now that I'm deep in her. Her moans echo through the steamy shower room as she takes a soft grind of me.

"Feel that? Feel how deep I am?"

Tiana's head drifts down, and her hand covers mine before she slowly slides up my length. The bulge decreases the further I come out of her.

"That's my good girl. Ride me until I pump you full of my kids," I whisper as I kiss her shoulder.

Her head falls back into the crook of my neck, her back pressing into my chest as she pants.

My hand that rests on her stomach slides up her ribcage, between her tits, to wrap around her neck and press her tighter against me.

Her pulse thrums violently against my fingers as my other hand moves down to rub her clit. I swirl and press against it in time with her movements.

Her gasps and moans get louder as I slide myself off the bench enough to thrust into her while I hold her in place. I feel the tension in her body as I throw deep strokes into her. My cock bulging from her stomach hits my forearm as I continue to work her clit.

The idea that I'm fucking her this deep drives me insane. I bite down on the soft flesh of her shoulder and tighten my grip at the sides of her neck as I ram the full length into her with every thrust.

"Gunnar...! Gunnar, you're so... d-deep," she moans.

The sounds of her pleasure ricochets off the walls and blend in with the sound of the running shower, along with the slapping of our skin.

"I know, baby. I have to be. I need to feel all of you," I moan back. And fuck me, do I ever.

Her hips begin to grind on me as her hand snakes down to grab my balls. She cups and rubs them, making me pause in my thrusts as she rolls her hips more.

"Fucking hell, Tiana," I groan as my back hits the wall.

My hands move to her hips and grip for dear life as she takes control. And the way she rides me sends shock waves of pleasure through me like I've never known. My eyes trail down her spine, where they land on the way her ass ripples when she slams down on me. My own eyes roll back and I can barely hold on to my composure.

"God damnit, Tiana, I'm gonna come if you keep fucking me like this," I groan.

Her hips continue to swirl and she tosses her wet hair over her shoulder as she looks back at me with half-lidded eyelids, her green eyes pumping with desire.

"Good," she purrs as she slowly presses all of me into her, filling her up.

I release a loud groan as I feel her hand grip my wrist, and she brings it back to where I press against her stomach.

Without warning, I explode. Stars against black as I inhale a deep gasp. My rough groan clashes against her silky moans, bouncing around the room, causing an overwhelming flood of sensations as I pulse deep inside of her. My cock twitches and pulses against her walls as I fill her to the fucking brim.

"Tiana, fuck!" I groan as I thrust up gently into her full, slick cunt.

I feel my cum drip out and down my balls as she slows her movements. Her grinds and swirls stop, and she pants as she regains her bearings. Her back expanding and deflating with the heaving of her breaths.

"You took me like a champ, sugar," I pant as I stroke up and down her spine slowly, letting her settle with me still in her. Wrapping my arms around her waist, I press my chest flush to her back, as I take gentle little kisses all over her shoulders.

Her head leans back, giving me more access to her neck, and I pepper kisses up the tender skin there too.

"That... That was so fucking good, Gunnar," she pants with a satiated smile as her body melts against mine in relaxation.

Tiana lays there against me on the shower bench, with my cock in her and we relax in the shower's steam for just a little longer.

CHAPTER TWENTY-THREE

TIANA

My mother must have a death wish for me, because this case is much more intense than I expected. This feels so out of my wheelhouse, and maybe this is just her chance to progress me so that I could one day take her spot. But a lot of this is so incredibly ridiculous.

While I don't mind taking her position one day... I really am having a hard time focusing with my mind so consumed with Gunnar.

And I don't even care that much that he's the reason for it.

Every morning, we leave the apartment together, and he has my coffee for me every time. At night, when we come home from work, I go outside with him to take his dog out to the dog park beside our complex. We sit in the darkness and look at the stars, enjoying the cool air and the way Tucker continuously brings us a tennis ball to toss.

Home from work.

Even that has a strange warmth in thinking about it.

It's simple. It's nice. And it's weird to say that I'm not exactly used to this sort of treatment. Gunnar always seems to make the hard days worth it. He'll tell me about his practice, and he's always welcoming the silence when I'm a little quieter than usual.

There are so many ways that it feels... domestic.

And I never thought about domestication. I'm not a prim and proper housewife.

But I think Gunnar knows that. He would never make me stay home to care for everything because he knows how important my career is to me.

That knowledge just fuels my feelings for him more.

Someone who has taken the parts of me that no one else wanted and cradled them to his chest in acceptance. While also giving me the space to try things at my pace.

I've never had a man so willing to go at my pace. I was always chastised for not going fast enough, for caring too much about my job. For wanting to have my space and knowing the importance of downtime to recuperate.

Gunnar doesn't make me feel bad for any of it. If I tell him I just want to have some time to myself in the apartment, he gives it to me. If I need space, he gives it.

And it's good to feel so accepted when I've been forgotten over those same things.

He is also punctual to a fault. Something I didn't think he could even be, to be completely honest. But every day, he gets done with practice, and then he's at my office door, waiting for me.

People have whistled and hollered at us as we walk out of the arena, but we never hold hands there. He usually just carries my things, and he doesn't even bother me about it. I just let it happen.

And I like it. I like *all* of it.

I have gotten used to Gunnar being a part of my life. And I wondered how I went without a boyfriend for so long. Maybe it's because they aren't as kind, funny, and hot as Gunnar. Or maybe that's what it is. He's assimilated into my life instead of forcing me to roll with his.

He treats me like a queen, and it makes me feel special. I've even taken to going to a few games. But I leave on my own and try not to make myself known.

And he'll look for me when he's waiting to play, or when all the men are stretching out on the ice. He'll give me a look, and then nod down toward the ice like he's going to do that to me later.

And usually, he does.

The sex has been constant. But it's been so good, and I feel as if I can't get enough of him. I know he surely has not been able to get enough of me. Every time I think he has done all conceivable positions with me, he somehow proves me wrong. I don't mind either. After years of being in control of my life, he lets me be free in that space. Leaving me at the mercy of him and his touch.

It's renewing. I love the way he controls me and throws me around. It's become part of our dynamic. I control him out of the bedroom, and he controls me in the bedroom.

I have to stop myself from rubbing my thighs together in this office chair as I stare blankly at the email my mother sent me earlier this morning explaining the case. I've been trying for the past two hours to focus on it, but every time I do, I think of Gunnar's hand around my neck. Or the sound of his voice in my ear right when I'm teetering on the edge of that black abyss he likes to throw me in.

He's a fast learner because he knows what it does for me. A sharp pain shoots through my face as I realize how hard I'm biting my lip, and I shake my head of the thoughts keeping me from my job.

I take a moment to actually look through the document.

A basketball player from the NBA wants to marry their sports trainer.

Fine enough.

The problem here is that it seems as if their pre-nup has slowly started becoming a bit more skewed as he has asked her to sign one.

I think it's fair. He's a pretty big name and has come from nothing to get where he is.

But it makes my heart tick. In a bad way.

The way things can become so skewed so quickly when you're with someone from your team. Of course, this case doesn't have the same legalities as what Gunnar and I are going through. She's their sports trainer. But if something happens to the fallout of them, then they're looking at some big changes for themselves. It's an eerie sort of foreboding having to work on this when my mind is so consumed by the consequences of what would happen if Gunnar and I got caught.

The thought makes my skin prickle with nervous skitters.

I don't know why my mother has me doing this stupid case.

My heart beats a wonky tune as I continue staring at the screen. My vision isn't able to lock onto it. It instead plays visions of a scenario of Gunnar and me falling apart. I lose my job; I lose my license. He gets kicked from a team he's worked his whole life to get to.

Tightness pulls at my throat, and my mouth dries. I reach for my Stanley, taking a sip and swirling the cup around to hear the ice clinking around inside to bring me back to the present. I take a deep breath as I set it down and glance at the screen again.

Slamming my laptop shut; I groan as I run my hands over my face in annoyance.

I... don't wanna lose Gunnar.

That realization is shocking when I think about how adverse I was to the idea of it all in the first place.

Even though I've only known Gunnar for as long as he's been on this team, no man has treated me with more respect or kindness than him.

Not only that, I *trust* him.

I don't trust easily. There is no reason for me to throw my trust out to whoever can grab it. I have too much going for me, and I don't have time to weed through the bullshit.

But somehow Gunnar broke through the walls like a blazing bat out of hell, and he showed me it could all be worth it.

Surely, the sex is.

I sit with my head in my hands for far too long. Long enough that I'm eventually interrupted by Gunnar at my door. His smile is more intense than anything I've ever seen before, but he also has a nervous flush on his face.

I give him a gentle smile before a curious tilt of my head. "What is that face for?"

He looks in the halls before he rushes into my office and closes the door behind him. Clicking the lock into place, he pulls the shutters down on the door's window. As he turns around, his eyes linger on me before he takes large strides toward me, like a man on a mission. His backpack hits the ground with a thud as he shrugs it off of his shoulders and I stand to meet him halfway.

A hand wraps around my jaw, pulling me into his body with a strong grip to my hip as he latches his lips to mine.

I wrap my arms around his waist, leaning into him and giving him all that I can.

He doesn't do this often in the arena. For obvious reasons.

We shouldn't be doing this. Especially after the spinning thoughts. But... fuck, his presence is calming. He's an anchor in the storm of my mind. And for now, I welcome his affection.

His tongue roams my mouth in languished strokes and licks before he pulls away, his thumb grazing my cheek as he looks in my eyes. In return, my pulse flutters uncontrollably before it travels down into my belly.

The bright hazel of his eyes seem to shine with fear, excitement, and nervousness. His tongue flicks out to swipe against his reddened lower lip before his teeth bite into it.

"Will you be my girlfriend?"

My eyes widen as the question hits me like a freight train, and my body tenses.

I haven't been asked anything like this... in...

God, it's been so long that I can barely remember.

I still, my breathing slowing to nothing as I think. I could...

I... maybe? Should I?

I shouldn't. I really, really shouldn't... It's illegal. After the day I've had mulling over everything and fearing over everything, I really shouldn't.

But... I want to be Gunnar's. And I don't think I've ever wanted to be anyone's like this, probably ever.

I want to do the things I wouldn't do before. I want to take the risks. I want to spend the long days and the long nights with him. I want to wake up to him.

I *want* Gunnar.

And I can have him while I figure out my next steps. I can take this risk for Gunnar.

Because I think in the end, Gunnar would take this risk for me.

My eyes come to focus on his, and I search that sea of hazel.

"I have conditions," I respond softly.

His thumb doesn't pause or skip. It moves, ever so smoothly, against my cheek. "I'd expect nothing less, sugar."

My lips tilt in a playful smile. "No PDA at the arena. No holding hands at the arena, and no one knows, for now. We can be seen together, but no touching with other people around."

His smile fades, and I reach up to grab his face, looking him in the eyes.

"Gunnar, if I could be on your arm, out in the open, I would. And I want to, more than anything in this world, do I want to. But this is illegal. I could lose my job, I could lose my license. You could lose the team. Everything. We have to play it safe until I figure out what it is I need to do to make this work legally. In the apartment complex, we can do whatever we want. But in the arena, we can't. You know this."

His eyes dip to my lips as I speak, before they come back up to my eyes. "You're beautiful when you're telling me what to do."

I roll my eyes as I give him a soft smile. "Do you understand?"

"Of course, sugar. I mean, who wouldn't want to be seen with this gorgeous specimen?" he asks with a wide grin before he pulls his arm away from me.

He rolls his sleeve up to flex his massive bicep. He looks at me with a cheeky grin, and I slap at the hardened piece of meat.

It hurts more than I expect, and I have to whip my hand away and shake it.

"Awwww, did small wittle waryer huwt hers wittle hand?" he teases as he pushes out his lower lip and gives me big puppy-dog eyes.

"Shut up! I didn't realize how hard your arm is!" I groan as I move to my desk and start placing my things in my bag to go home for the day.

His smile is handsomely devious as he bends over to pick up his backpack and sling it over his shoulders. "I'll show you how hard something else is later, if you're good."

My cheeks heat as I slip my laptop into my tote.

"Did that turn you on, sugar?" he asks as he glances at me. His body shifts to fix his backpack more securely on his back.

I glance up at him through my lashes, and my teeth sink into my lip. His brow quirks with delight, and he takes a slow step toward my desk to stand in front of it. He towers high above me, and I can't help the way it heats me even more to be under his control in this moment.

He knows how much I love the way he plays with me, and he teases me any chance he can get.

"It did, didn't it?" he asks with a teasing grin. His hands plant into my desk, further asserting his dominance.

But I ignore him, because I enjoy tempting this side of him.

Slowly, I continue packing my things, and he stops me, taking my chin in his fingers to tip my head up. I meet his gaze as my teeth tighten harder on my lip.

"Say it, Tiana. Good girls respond when they're asked something, don't they?" he asks. His eyes glisten with amusement.

I feel the heat rise all the way to my ears as he taunts me, here in the arena, and my eyes glance to the door to make sure the lock is in place. My core pulses and I feel a shock wave of anticipation zing through me.

"The door's locked. No one is coming in. Now, use your words... and say. It." His words are punctuated and sharp as he waits for my answer. His eyes are steady on mine, peering into my soul.

"That did turn me on. So... so much," I breathe.

"Yeah? Why'd it turn you on?" he asks as he leans in, pulling me in to press a soft kiss to my lips.

My eyes flutter and I release a small moan. "Because I wanna be filled by you," I murmur against his lips.

"I can make that happen. Is that really what you want?" he asks.

"P-please..." I whimper as I lean deeper into him. Like a moth to a flame his seduction sucks me in, lovesick as I breathe through the heat of it all.

"Using your words. There's a good girl, sugar. Such an obedient little cumslut, aren't you?" he whispers.

I nod, shrinking before him as my knees weaken from the lust that spears through every ounce of my blood.

God damnit, his voice. The things he says. I feel like I can't breathe with the way my throat tightens at his words. Like he's choking me with just a phrase.

And I adore it. I love that it feels like I need to be kneeling before him and he'll do anything to make me feel good. The way I know if I was on my knees begging, he'd make me scream until I couldn't anymore.

I never expected to be submissive in this way.

But for Gunnar... fuck, for Gunnar I'll crawl if he asked me.

He presses one last kiss to my lips before he releases me and waits for me to finish packing my things. Taking a few steadying breaths, I try to focus on the task instead of the promises he'll fulfill.

Because the man surely keeps them.

Soon, I finish packing my stuff away and I hear a soft click as I zip my bag shut.

Before I even have time to think, I hear the crash of my door opening and my things have disappeared from the desk in a blur of black cotton, and Gunnar's thudding footsteps fade into the distance.

"RACE YOU TO THE CAR!" I hear his voice echo through the halls.

I run around my desk, trying to catch up to him, but these fucking heels! God damnit!

As I exit my office and make my way down the hall, my dad pops out of one of the side doors.

"Tiana." His voice is gruff, and I halt just short of him. I nearly stumble as my heel slips on the slick concrete.

Righting myself, I take a deep breath through the initial startle, with my eyes widening as I stand in wait. "Yes?"

"Come talk to me for a moment," he says as he nods to the door he just popped out of. His hands shove in his pockets as he turns on a heel and heads inside.

It's one of the equipment rooms, and why he chose here to meet me, I have no idea.

But I can't imagine it's for anything good.

My pulse picks up, and my mouth dries as I follow him inside the musty room. All the hockey sticks and extra padding reek of man sweat. It doesn't help that the lights in here are much dimmer than they are in the arena halls.

The shadows cast on my dad's face are inherently harsh as he waits for me to close the door, and I cross my arms against my chest.

"Why have you been hanging out with Gunnar so much?" His voice is tense, and there is not a hint of wiggle room in it.

"He has been having trouble with a few legal issues outside of hockey. Some deed things and personal property stuff. And you know we live right next to each other, so we carpool to the arena because it's easier," I say.

A lawyer has to be able to do two things.

Stretch the truth. And evade it.

"Mmm." He grunts as his eyes narrow on me.

I level him with a glare of my own, attempting to stand my ground. Even though my insides are squirming uncontrollably at the idea of my dad finding out about Gunnar and me.

"He is a rising star, Tiana. And you are the lawyer. If anything is happening between the two of you that goes beyond work, it gets cut off and shut down immediately. Are we clear?"

I stare at him, hoping no minor facial twitches are happening to have him allude to anything, and I nod.

"Strictly business," I respond tersely.

"Strictly. Business," he repeats.

Though his face tells me he doesn't believe me.

CHAPTER TWENTY-FOUR

GUNNAR

Tiana has been more reclusive lately.

My little lawyer, who had previously let some of her guard down, has slowly begun retreating inward.

And it breaks my heart. Even as we make our way out of the parking garage, after a long day at work, she's quiet. More so than usual. Usually, she's telling me about her day or some of the stuff she's had to work on. And even if she's completely silent some days, this time is different. There is an unsettled energy she seems to have. I felt it in the car on the way here, as well.

As we make our way through the lobby, I reach for her hand, tangling my fingers between hers.

"What's on your mind, sugar?" I ask softly, trying to coax something out of her.

Tiana doesn't look at me; she merely leans into my body and walks at a strange angle as we keep heading toward the elevator hall.

"The day you asked me out, my dad found me and asked if there was anything up with us."

My heart pounds viciously, and I feel the pulses every-where. My steps halt and I look down at her, and she glances up at me through her sad lashes.

"Why didn't you say anything?" I whisper as I take her face in my hands.

Tiana loosens, putting the weight of her head on me as her green eyes shimmer with sadness and guilt.

"I was scared. My mom gave me this case, which has also just really put me on edge. I'm so used to holding everything in that I didn't think to share it with you. I didn't want my dad's paranoia and this case to mess up how nice everything has been."

I give her a gentle smile. "Tiana..." I sigh softly.

This sweet woman didn't want to dampen my mood, so she took the brunt of the fear all on her own. It's genuinely sweet coming from her. She would have thrown it at me as soon as he spoke to her if she weren't in this with me. So the fact that she did... makes my heart swell. But it also hurts. I would have eased at least a little of the burden off of her.

She doesn't deserve to carry that kind of pressure on her own. Not when it's something we should carry together.

"I'm sorry. I should have said something, but we've been having such a good time," she murmurs as her eyes track down my throat, zoning out on my chest.

Pulling her head closer, I rest it against me as I stroke her curls gently. Her arms wrap around my back, and she relaxes in my grasp.

"You don't have to do this alone, Tiana. I'll always make sure of that. We're in this little charade together, you know," I remind her.

She doesn't say anything, she merely nods against my chest before looking up at me with a little spark of hope in her eyes.

I give her a reassuring grin as I lean down to kiss her. She moans softly into my lips as her hands grip my sweatshirt.

The sound rolls through me in tumultuous waves of lust. It sends my pulse straight to my cock and I think of just the thing to cheer her up. Granted, I have no idea how she'll respond. But it's worth a shot.

"Come with me, baby," I whisper before I press another kiss to her lips.

Her eyes are questioning as I take her hand and lead her to our elevator.

When we enter the doors, they slowly close behind us, and a beep sounds as it ascends. I pull her bag from her shoulder and place it gently on the floor before I knock my backpack off and turn to face her.

Her wide eyes are curious, yet full of concern, before I grab her cheeks, bringing her close and kissing her with all the of intent I can offer. A soft moan melds between our lips, and she melts into me.

"Gunnar, we can't do this here," she whispers against my lips.

I grin and stroke her cheek ever so gently, before I turn around and slam my fist on the emergency stop button. The elevator trembles and a loud siren blares through the small box as it comes to a halt.

Tiana's eyes brighten in shock as she looks at me like I'm insane. "Gunnar! What the hell are you doing?!"

"I have an emergency," I say with a devious grin.

I pull her body back into mine, holding her against me as I devour her mouth. Her soft noises vibrate between our lips as I roll my hips against her. The ache is incessant, and any amount of friction I can get from her is one I welcome.

It doesn't help that I just *need* her. I need her to know that I'm in this with her.

I reach down, slipping my hand up the hem of her tight black skirt. Trailing up her inner thigh, she gasps when my fingers make it to her pussy.

"Sweetness? Did you forget your underwear this morning?" I ask as I dip my fingers into her bare cunt.

She gasps as I graze her clit, stroking through her wetness softly. Her eyes drop halfway, and she takes stuttered breaths as I press deeper.

"You're so fucking wet. I can't believe I do this to you."

Her teeth bite hard into her lip, attempting to quiet her moans and gasps. I wrap my arm around her back, holding her in place as I press two fingers through her entrance. Her walls tighten as I pump them in and out of her.

"G-Gunnar," she pants as her eyes haze with the pleasure coursing through her. Her neck loosens as her head falls back.

"It's alright, baby, I've got you," I whisper. I pepper little kisses over the muscles in her neck and chest, letting her fall apart. Her little sounds and whimpers drive me to insanity, causing me to lose my control with every one and I decide I need to taste her.

I remove my fingers, sucking them clean before I drop to my knees in front of her.

The sudden movement snaps her out of her stupor, but before she says anything, I slide her skirt up around her waist. Pulling one leg up, I throw it over my shoulder, resting it there before I grip the other one, and do the same. I press her against the mirrored wall so she's steady and then my mouth is on her, lapping from her entrance to her clit over and over before I suck and swirl my tongue around it. A small thunk sounds off in the small space as her head tips back against the mirrored wall.

Delicate fingers thread through the strands of my hair with urgent need as she pulls me in deeper. My eyes track up her body, and I watch as her mouth parts on a silent gasp. The sight of her coming undone makes me work harder, swirling my tongue around her clit and sucking it deeper before my tongue flicks against it.

The skin of her soft thighs meshes with my hand as I stroke the top of them, while the other presses back into her. I pump my fingers in and out of her, with her muscles tightening as she gets closer and closer. Tremors rock through her, making her legs shake around my ears the more I lap at her. Her thighs tighten and loosen around my head, and it's so fucking sexy the way she trembles.

I groan into her as my dick hardens to near pain. Even in my sweatpants, that much blood in one place is going to hurt.

Her cunt clenches around my fingers, her orgasm closing in quickly, and I keep pace. Hooking my fingers into the soft spot on her inner wall, I press, begging her to fall apart. She pulls her arm up to her mouth, biting down on the skin to silence her screams, and soon, her body rocks against me in violent shakes as she barrels over the edge. A grin pulls at my lips as I lick and suck her through every bit of her release.

The muscles in her legs tremble around my head, her hips grinding against my face, riding out her orgasm against me. When she stills, I release one of her legs, slowly placing her foot on the floor, before I peel the other from me.

I make sure she's not wobbly before I come to a stand. Threading my fingers through the curls at the nape of her neck, I take control of my feisty girl, just the way she likes.

I tighten my grip, forcing her head back to look at me, before I lean in to kiss her deeply. With the taste of her fresh on my tongue, I slip it into her mouth, letting her taste herself.

A grin rises on my lips as I realize I have her under my control; my sweet girl has lost her inhibitions. I spin her around, keeping my hand on the back of her neck as I use my other hand to pull her right leg up against the metal handrail in the elevator.

"Grip the bar, Tiana," I tell her with a soft kiss to her shoulder.

She nods submissively as she attempts to catch her breath and her hands wrap around the golden pole, gripping tightly as her eyelids flutter.

Her long leg stretches out along the length of the handrail, and I can see the long expanse of beautiful honey skin that covers her calves and thighs.

The sight of her bent and pliable for me sends my heart racing, and I can't fucking take it any longer. Quickly, I pull my dick from my sweatpants, lining myself up at her entrance before slowly pressing in.

Her neck cranes against my grip, and I hold her in place as I advance further. Her eyelids clench, and her chest expands as she registers the stretch of my cock.

"Fuck... Fuck, Gunnar... you feel so fucking good," she pants.

Sliding my hand, I bring it to the front of her neck, pressing into the thrumming pulse on either side of her throat.

"God, do you fucking ever, baby," I pant softly. My lips press into the crook of her neck, letting her scent drag me under. "I've never had pussy like this... do you know how good you have to feel for me to take you balls deep in an elevator?" I whisper with a tortured chuckle.

The whites of her eyes are bright in the mirror as they roll back, and I press in deeper. Taking small thrusts in and out of her as I reach the halfway mark, I tease her just enough to pleasure her.

Her face in this mirror is intoxicating. The small sliver of skin that peeks through the top of her unbuttoned blouse shimmers with sweat, as the small pockets of space in the hollows of her collarbone appear with every calculated breath she takes. The relaxation that washes over her face while my hand decorates her pretty throat. It causes my thrusts to delve deeper, slower, and I take my sweet fucking time feeling every single bit of her.

It's like she was fucking made for me. And soon, I can't take it. I need to feel all of her.

Her eyelids clench shut as I pick up pace, and I tighten my hand around her neck.

"Eyes open, sugar," I grit.

Her lashes flutter as she opens her eyes, and the lustful haze over them attempts to focus on us in the mirror. The lost gaze tracks around us, from my hand on her throat, to the other gripping her hip, to the way I lean over her and gaze back at her with my own desire.

"This pussy is fucking mine. *You* are fucking mine. Do you understand me?" I grunt with every thrust I take into her.

She pants and nods, but I tighten my hold on her throat as I press in balls deep, holding myself there.

"Words, sugar. Use your words. I wanna hear you."

Her teeth catch her bottom lip as she attempts to concentrate on my voice.

She's struggling. Aw...

Good.

"I-I'm yours, Gunnar. This pussy is yours," she pants.

"There's my good girl, Titi. You know how much I love hearing that voice of yours when my cock is buried in you."

Her moans get louder, higher-pitched, as I pick my pace back up.

A loud beep echoes in the elevator, and the intercom crackles as a man's voice comes through.

Halting entirely, with my cock held deep inside her, I wait; only for a few moments. Before I start my thrusts again, slow, precise. My gaze floats to the ceiling as a voice fills the space.

"The emergency button was pressed. Is everything alright in there?" the voice asks.

I glance at Tiana's face in the mirror. While she's temporarily pulled out of her pleasure, I reach down, stroking her clit with calculated thrusts into her.

"Tell them you're fine, Tiana," I whisper lowly.

She pants quietly, trying to register everything happening all at once, and she struggles to find the words.

I press into her clit, making her quake in my arms.

"Tell. Them," I say again. My thrusts move deeper, pulling every inch out to the tip before slowly pressing every fucking inch back in.

"W-We're good! J-Just... fuck." She bites her lip as she tries not to groan. Her eyes roll, and all she can muster are pants and groans of frustration as she attempts to follow my directions.

"What?" the man asks through the speakers.

"Come on, Tiana. Be a good fucking girl, and tell the nice man that you're fine," I whisper as I press balls deep into her, rubbing over her clit quicker.

She groans again, angrier. "We're good! Jus'anaccident!" she manages to get out.

"Okay. We'll start the elevator up again," the man says, and the elevator begins its slow crawl up.

"There's my good girl. You listen so well, baby," I say as I nip into the skin of her jaw, turning her head toward me.

She groans once more in response, but I pick up my thrusts, rocking into her faster. The prospect of the doors opening to me, balls deep in my girlfriend in the elevator of our apartment complex, sends my adrenaline soaring through the roof.

Soon, the anticipation builds to a peak, and that knot of

pleasure in my spine slithers through my entire body. My hand tightens on her throat as I thrust one last time into her, filling her full of my cum with a rough groan.

The elevator beeps in my consciousness, bringing me to the present. I pump the rest deep into her, groaning when I have to reluctantly pull myself out and tug her skirt down.

My chest heaves with breaths as I stuff my dick back in my sweatpants and I twirl her body from the mirrored wall to face the door.

Her eyes are a haze, and her body wobbles as I move her around. I grab my backpack and throw it on my back before I take her bag in my hand, wrapping my other arm around her shoulders.

Her breaths are deep as she attempts to regain herself, and the doors slide open.

"What the fuck..." I hear her murmur, and I lean over to press a kiss to her forehead.

An older couple stands outside, unaware of the things that took place here. With a wide grin and a nod at the couple coming in, I guide Tiana out the doors and down the hall.

All the while whistling a tune as I walk us to her apartment.

CHAPTER TWENTY-FIVE

TIANA

After a long week–and an even longer home game–Gunnar and I spent that Friday night in our separate apartments. Honestly, as much as I love spending time with Gunnar, I still enjoy my alone time. It almost makes me feel like if we got married, I would love for us to keep our apartments. I think we make more than enough to supply the two. Plus, if we wanted to be in a place where we wanted Tucker to leave us alone, we could have one of the entire apartments to oursel-

Fuck, am I really... really thinking about marrying him?

I've never been this smitten over a man before in my *life*. Not one where I think about marrying him of my own free will!

I shake my head as I focus on the spurting sound of coffee coming out of my Keurig, waiting for it to fill up my mug. As it finishes, I go to my fridge to get the creamer. But as I pour it in, my mind swirls, the same way the cream does in the dark liquid. More than it should, with so many things. The idea of what life could be with Gunnar.

I wrap my soft fleece robe tighter around me before I take a soothing sip of my coffee. I let the warmth of the mug settle in my hands as I tip my head back with a groan.

There is so much to consider. The ethics, the legality, and it feels like the tension grows day by day, making me more nervous as time passes.

And really, how long do I really have?

I don't want to be without Gunnar. He's become a handler of sorts. When things get off kilter or they become too off the rails, he brings me back to the present.

I sigh as I take another sip of my drink before a knock comes at my door.

Of course, I already know who it is, and my heart pitter-patters a little unsteadily as a smile crests my lips.

Placing the mug down, I go to open the door to see Gunnar standing there, sans his shirt. With some Seattle Stag sweatpants sitting low on his hips. His hands grip the top of the door frame as he leans in. The action pulls his entire body taut. It accentuates the veins that web and run under his skin, over his abs and along his entire frame. It etches out the deep V that carves his hips, highlighting the rigidness he's built of.

My pulse quickens as my gaze takes all of him in before roaming down much lower, following that line of hair that runs into the band of his sweatpants. Something that is much more sinful than it should.

"Morning, sugar," he says with a sweet smile.

His hair is wildly disheveled, as if he just woke up, and it sends a hearty, lusty pang through me.

He's so damn attractive. I can't even believe this man is as smitten with me as I am with him.

I smile back at him, nipping at my lip. "Hello."

His eyebrow raises at my nervousness. "I wanna take you

on a little trip. It's not long and I know you'll like it," he says with a devious grin as he leans into the door frame.

I quirk an eyebrow at him and what he may be concocting.

"What are your intentions here, Mr. Hayze?" I ask skeptically, as I cross my arms against my chest and pin him with a playful glare.

He grins as his arms drop lazily beside him and he bends to come inside. "First off, be careful when you call me that," he says.

There is a familiar feeling that grips me by my throat when he comes this close, teasing me. Or at least when I feel the anticipation of it. It's... fun. *Stimulating.*

I adore it with Gunnar.

He wraps an arm around my waist, pulling me taut against him, and I press my hands to his chest. My eyes gaze up at him like a lovesick puppy, grinning when his hand comes up to grip my chin in his fingers, tilting my head up at his.

His smile is sweet and possessive as he leans down to press his lips to mine softly.

"It turns me on..." He pauses, stroking a thumb over the skin. "Second, I have many intentions, sugar. But this is merely a short trip, and then we'll go get some snacks so we can have a little sleepover. Your place or mine, it doesn't matter. I just wanna spend the night with you," he says.

Wow, he seems to have this all planned out.

Then again... he usually does.

"Do any of these plans have anything to do with sex?" I ask with a grin.

He gives me a shy smirk. "They never have to, baby. But I would never mind if they did," he says sweetly.

He dips lower, leaning in to press a soft kiss to my neck. "Never feel you're obligated to fuck me just because, sugar. I love having sex with you, but I never do any sweet things with the expectation of sex," he whispers.

His breath skates across the small bit of wetness left behind from his kiss, causing small shivers to crawl over my skin as the tension grows between us.

My cheeks heat as I sink deeper into his embrace. "Do you know how hard it is to believe that when you do shit like that?" I giggle.

He kisses up my neck, my throat, my jaw, pressing just a bit harder when he gets to my lips.

"Honestly, that's fair. I think that's why I had to remind you," he returns, and I feel his lips quirk in a playful grin against my lips.

"We can go do your little plan. I wanna spend the night at your house though," I say with a nip at his lip.

"Yes, ma'am," he whispers.

I breathe a soft moan into his mouth before I pull away.

His gaze is heated enough that I can see the admiration he holds for me. It sends my insides fluttering, because the feeling of being adored is... unfamiliar.

Have I gone this long in my life without realizing all I wanted was to be seen and accepted?

I push the thought away for now... too many emotions to sort through when I can just appreciate the man I have in front of me.

Playfully, I roll my eyes as I shove him. "Go get some clothes on. I have to get ready."

He nods. "I'll be waiting for ya', sugar," he says.

I smile with another amused eye roll before I close the door and rush to get ready for the day.

After I finish getting ready, Gunnar is at my door. He wears one of his favorite combos. His black hoodie with a hockey jersey over it, while dark jeans cover his lower half. He wears Air Force Ones with the tongues sticking out over the hem of his jeans.

The longer I admire him, the longer a vibrant pulse moves through my whole body. I truly can't believe how attractive he is.

He seems to notice because he grins and ducks across the threshold to get closer to me.

Using a hooked finger, he presses my chin up to gaze at me. He leans down, pressing a soft little kiss against my lips.

"Like what you see?" he whispers.

"You're insufferable," I whisper back.

He nips at my lower lip. "Only for you."

I roll my eyes before I kiss him a little longer. Reaching my hand down, I thread my fingers into his free hand, gripping in between his roughened calluses.

"So, because I know you like to drive, I loaded the directions onto my phone so they'll pop up when you're driving us," he says.

I give him a small, playful gasp. "In the Vette?" I ask with a bite to my lip.

He nods with an amused smile as his other hand holds up his keys. A squeal of glee rings out of my throat to echo in the halls, as my hands flex and flap with excitement before I lean up on my tippy toes to kiss him on his cheek.

I run inside to grab my backpack, throwing it on my shoulders. When a thought arises.

"Piggy-back?" I ask as I grin up at him.

Gunnar smiles, giving me a soft chuckle before he turns to squat down in front of me.

A giggle escapes me as I jump onto his back, wrapping

my arms tight around his neck. His arms are so long he merely reaches behind him to hold my ass in his hands. I squeal as he squeezes it before I slap at his chest. He rises from his squat with a laugh before he makes his way to the elevators.

It's interesting to see everything from this height. I think I'd get air sickness if I were this tall all the time.

Eventually, we make it down to the parking garage, where he drops me by the driver's side door of the Vette before he opens it for me. A shy smile plasters my face, and I nod sheepishly in thanks as I climb in and he shuts the door. Then, rounding the front, he moves to the passenger seat to shove himself in.

I can't get over how comfortable he always looks in that seat, and it causes my heart to flutter in my chest.

When I press the ignition, the small screen in the middle of the dashboard lights up with directions to our first destination.

My brow furrows as I look at it, and I shoot a sly look at him from the corner of my eye. Shifting into gear, I move out of the parking garage, following the directions on the screen.

After so long down the road, his hand drifts to my thigh, gripping and rubbing it softly, mindlessly. As if it's more of a comfort for him more than it is for me.

The feeling of his hand swallowing my leg causes blood to rush through me, and I take a harder grip on the steering wheel as my pulse whooshes through my ears.

"You seem so happy being a passenger prince," I breathe.

He lets out a small laugh. "Well, usually in my 'gentlemanly code book,' I would drive the woman everywhere. But you are so happy to do it yourself that I feel like your happiness trumps my need to be a gentleman."

Heat rises on my cheeks as he explains his reasoning. He has always talked about this gentlemanly code book of his.

Though I've never seen a physical version of it, he sure seems to stick by it.

"Where did this little code book of yours come from? Does it exist in actual book form?" I ask as I turn onto another street.

"It was just things I felt were necessary to treat a lady well. My mom always put an emphasis on raising good boys who will be good to their wives or partners. She always said 'I'll be damned if you give them hell,'" he says with a soft laugh and a shake of his head.

My lips smirk in thought. "And are you going to teach this codebook to your children?"

"*Our* children. But yes, of course. We're not raising any foolhardy hooligans."

My jaw nearly drops at the confidence he thinks we'll be having children together.

"You seem pretty sure on that front," I say through a soft breath of shock.

He hmphs. "I am almost one-hundred percent sure on that front, actually," he says.

I glance at him from the corner of my eye to see him throw his hands back behind his head and watch me with one of the smuggest grins I think I've ever seen from him.

I turn my attention back to the road, our destination closing in quicker than I had expected.

"What makes you think I want kids?" I ask.

"You surely seemed eager the other night when I pumped that fake baby into you."

Now my jaw drops as I look over at him. "Sir, YOU said it was something that turned you on and you wanted to explore!"

He laughs. "And *I* am very appreciative of you indulging in my fantasies, but considering how soaked you were, I would place bets on the fact that you would be up for the task."

While I never really thought about kids too in-depth, yeah,

thinking about having his was something I never thought would make me feel the way it did.

"And what makes you so sure *you* want to have babies with *me*?" I ask.

"Because I don't think there is a single woman on this planet that I would let have the pleasure of doing such a thing," he says with a small shrug.

I have pulled us into a small parking garage somewhere in downtown Seattle. But as the rumbling of the car engine dies when I turn it off, the shock of his words settles deeper.

I glance at him. Wondering how this thought of life with him, the same one that had me in such a tizzy this morning, is something he's thought about.

Something he wants... with *me.*

"You... what?" I ask softly.

He doesn't want to have kids with anyone else? I mean, yeah, we're dating, so he would say that anyway. But it's not the words he says, it's *how* he's saying them.

With the confidence and conviction of everything in the entire world. He says it all as if there is no wiggle room for any other possibilty.

As if this is the only thing he's thought about since he met me.

"Why would you want me to be the one to be the mother of your children?" I ask, quietly, nervously.

I don't know what to make of it all. Confused? Excited? I... I'm not sure.

"Why wouldn't I?" he asks in confusion.

He brings his hand up to my cheek, stroking it softly with his thumb.

"I just don't think I've ever had a man tell me they wanted to marry me... hell, date me for too long, let alone have kids with me," I whisper.

His hazel eyes are the perfect mix of curiosity and sadness. "Then they were idiots. You are incredibly smart. You're logical, you're gorgeous. You are strict and disciplined with all that you do, but you are also up to trying things if they are worth your while."

My throat tightens as my eyes burn, while my heart is a violent drum in my ears as it pounds deep in my chest.

I've never had a man feel this way about me. And in all honesty, it never mattered what they thought about me. Maybe I just didn't care enough about them as well, for the instance to not have any effect on me.

But there is something about the way he says all of those words. The way it feels like he means every bit of what he says.

There is no doubt in his tone about it. And with that realization, I nip my lip, intending to hold back the small tears that threaten to escape.

"You are so much more than I think you know, Tiana. And I was smitten with you from the moment you walked into that locker room. I needed you in every way that I could, and that's why I was so hellbent on seeing you. I needed to have at least one moment alone with you. And I'm so glad I did."

"Gunnar," I murmur in response as that small tear escapes from my tearline.

He smiles as he watches it fall down my cheek before he wipes it away with his thumb.

"I mean it, Tiana. There was no way I wasn't gonna give you a shot. I needed to meet you."

I take a deep breath as I nod. I don't know how to respond to this sort of thing. I don't even know how to perceive all of this right now. It's so many thoughts, emotions, and feelings all at once that it feels impossible to process in this small point in time.

"Thank you." Is all I can murmur in response.

"Thank *you*, Sugar," he whispers.

Before my heart threatens to burst, I take a deep breath and shake my head to rid myself of the feelings threatening to pour out of me. Quickly, I hand him the keys before I reach back to grab my small backpack.

He gets out of the car and quickly makes his way to the driver's side door to open it for me. I smile at him as he extends a hand out to help me and pulls me up.

Keeping my fingers interlaced with his, we walk to the exit of the parking garage, where he leads us onto the street. He stays on the side of the sidewalk where the cars are closest, and I take a look at our surroundings.

It seems as if we're going to one of the small mom-and-pop shops that still exist downtown.

My brow furrows, and he continues leading me in companionable silence until we approach an unfamiliar storefront. The front is comprised of large windows, with a hand-drawn name gilded in large swirling letters.

"Plot Twist."

My confusion deepens as I look over it. Around the name of the store are hundreds of pages, torn out of books and placed all over the window. They're covering it to where you can't see the interior of the store.

He turns to it, opening the door for me. When you walk in, there are two levels, with dozens of rows of books. An old library aesthetic, the shelves are wooden, lining the store in a wonderful maze of books of all genres.

My jaw gapes as I look around the shop. He knows I like to spend my quiet nights reading, even if I don't expressly talk much about it. It's sweet that he has noticed such a thing.

I rarely go to bookstores because I don't enjoy being around other people. I don't even really enjoy shopping, in general. I would much rather buy all my books online.

Even my groceries I like to order for pickup. Any excuse I have to not talk to human beings is one I relish in.

But experiencing this little store with Gunnar... my heart threatens to implode.

"Gunnar, this is amazing," I murmur as we ease further into the store.

He follows behind me as I tug his hand along.

"Well, there's one more thing."

I turn to him with a confused tilt of my brow.

"I'm giving you a two-thousand-dollar spending limit on whatever you want in here," he says with a smile.

My jaw drops, gaping like a dead fish as I stare at him.

He smiles. "Sugar, you can't suck my cock here. It's uncouth," he whispers.

My brow contorts wildly from the whiplash of this experience. His use of a word that... advanced? Pulls me out of my stupor. Now, not only am I dealing with his gift, but I'm also dealing with the fact that he has a weirdly advanced vocabulary.

"Two things?" I ask gently.

"Shoot," he responds as he looks at some books on the shelves. He steps ahead of me, leading me through the rows as he shoves his hands in his pockets.

I follow behind him. "One, how the fuck do you know what uncouth means?"

He laughs softly as he glances over his shoulder at me. "That's the thing you're stuck on?"

I roll my eyes as I wait for his answer.

He pauses to pick up a random book, flicking through the pages and not glancing my way. "I did have to go to college to get drafted, sugar. I know some big words."

I scoff with a cross of my arms against my chest as I pin him with a glare. "Two, what do you mean I have a 'two-thousand-dollar spending limit?'"

He smiles as he places the book back down and stuffs his hands back in his pockets, perusing the other titles.

"I see your little books in your apartment and when you've grabbed a new one because you finished the first one. I think it's nice to have a well-read woman," he says with a shrug.

My cheeks heat. "Gunnar, most of them are romances."

He turns to me, his gaze darkening with lustful intent. His fingers grip my chin, tilting my head up, while my hands come to grip his sides. Soon, he leans down to press a small kiss to the pulse point in my neck. "I'm aware, sugar."

My eyes widen, and a shock jolts through my spine at the roughness of his whisper as it grazes my neck. My throat tightens as I seemingly hold my breath.

Fuck. He knows how to make me nervous.

"You mean I can get anything I want?" I ask with a nervous bite to my lip to contain my excitement.

"On one condition," he whispers.

"Which is?"

"You reenact one of your favorite scenes with me," he says as he presses one last kiss to my neck before he rises. His thumb strokes over where he holds my chin, grinning at me. "Is it a deal, Ms. Dawn?"

"So you did have intentions of getting me into your bed," I say with a fold of my arms.

"I never said it had to be tonight. I thought you were supposed to know the meaning of loopholes. That's your whole job, isn't it?"

My jaw gapes, and he runs his thumb over my lower lip. "Not here, sugar."

I roll my eyes as I push hard into his chest. He laughs as he stumbles and catches himself to smooth walk out of it. He runs a hand through his hair and pins me with a mischievous grin.

I look over all the books and the spines. My excitement

winds tight around my spine, tightening my limbs. I resist the urge to squeal with joy as my hands flex and tighten. There are so many new books I've been wanting to get. But with work, I've been so busy that I haven't had the time to order any of the new ones that keep coming out.

I've always loved the way so many books look in one place. On shelves, either neat or in disarray. Piles of them. Old, new. It doesn't matter. I've always loved the way books look.

This little shop seems to have all the ones I've been looking for. And maybe if they don't have any I'm looking for, I can ask them to order it?

I feel like a kid in a candy store.

And while I rarely want a man to pay for my things, who is gonna turn down a shopping spree like this?

Hurriedly, I grab all the books I've been eyeing for months and stacking them in Gunnar's arms.

One by one, the stack grows and begins to tower above his face.

I have him put down the ones he has so the cashier can begin ringing them up. The rush of going through and picking all these books I've been eyeing spurs me through the store like a little bat out of hell.

When I can't find a few of the titles I've been looking for, I halt my search in the store to ask the cashier if they can order them for me and have them shipped to my apartment. Luckily for me, I can.

My excitement grows, and I get lost in all the books I'm itching to read or to just have.

As the cashier finishes scanning everything, she looks at the screen. "That will be..." She presses a few buttons. "$3,569.38."

My lips part in shock, and my mind runs. Looking over the books, I try to figure out which ones I should put back. But soon the keycard reader beeps, and I look over just as Gunnar slips his wallet back in his pocket.

"Gunnar!" I groan.

His brow furrows. "You think I didn't know you'd go over? I may be a goon, but I'm not stupid," he says with a grin.

"But you gave me two thousand! You did *not* have to do that!"

"Sugar, I promise. It's not a dent," he says as he leans down. "Now shut that pretty little mouth before I stuff something in it to keep you quiet."

I inhale a small gasp, sucking my lips in with it to press them together. Not because he told me to, but because he's so bold with his words in public that I'm taken aback. I don't know why I didn't expect him to tease me. He's always done stuff like this.

"'Atta girl. Now go grab the Vette so I can bring these books out," he says as he holds the keys up beside my head.

I glare at him for a moment before I glance at the keys and snatch them from his hand. "You... are insufferable," I grit playfully.

"Only for you, baby," he says before he presses a peck to my lips.

The lady has completely ignored us as she scrounges up some boxes to put my books in.

I rush out of the shop, making my way back to the parking garage. All the while, my heart pounds. There is so much happening between us. Things I've never experienced, things I didn't know I enjoyed.

Gunnar has shown me this whole new world of relationships and what can be done with someone. Someone who treats you like a princess out in the world, but shows you how much you mean to him in the bedroom.

He has always put in maximum effort with everything he does, and I don't think I've ever had a man go this far for me.

It feels like everything I had in the past couldn't even be described as the bare minimum.

Wow, the bar is in fucking Hell.

A small rush runs through me. I got so many books... and I get to play with them all and put them all away!

Do I feel bad that I went over the budget? I mean, of course.

But I don't think he would have let me put back the books even if I tried.

He wanted to treat me, but I think I need to treat him somehow...

I think I know exactly what I can do, too.

CHAPTER TWENTY-SIX

GUNNAR

These books are much heavier than I expected them to be.

It can count as exercise for the weekend. We're supposed to keep working out or doing something of note during the weekend, so I can just tell Coach I did some heavy lifting.

Especially since I'm going to have to bring these upstairs to Tiana's apartment.

When all the books are loaded up and we've gotten back into the car, I turn to look at Tiana with a breathless grin and she watches me with a gratefulness in her eyes that squeezes my heart.

I'm sweaty from bringing the boxes to the car, so I bring my hoodie-jersey combo up to wipe the sweat from my face, feeling the cool air from the AC brush over my damp abs as I do.

As I press my hoodie back down, I look over at Tiana, whose eyes have now glazed over.

My brow furrows. "Are you alright, sugar?"

She clears her throat, nodding furiously as she glances away. "Yeah... yep. Uhm. Honestly, I just can't get over the way your body looks sometimes," she says with a shy bite to her lip.

A seductive bite to my lip accompanies my grin as I lean over the center console to thread my fingers through her hair at the nape of her neck, pulling her close for a deep kiss. I tilt her head, commanding the kiss and deepening it before I pull away.

"The feeling is mutual," I whisper against her lips.

She grins as she presses one last peck to my lips and turns on the car. Her eyes glance over her shoulder to check the street she parked on so she can pull out. But I stop her, gripping her thigh softly.

"One last thing," I say quickly.

She turns to me with a tilt of her head and a questioning expression.

"There are a few things we can do next," I offer. "We can go home. I'll bring all the books up to your apartment, and you can organize them while I go get the snacks for tonight. Or... we go get the snacks now and go home."

She bites her lip in thought as her face tightens nervously. Her head tilts as her face contorts in a 'Sorry?' type glance.

I laugh. "You wanna do the first one, don't you?" I ask with a smile.

She nods sheepishly.

I shake my head playfully as I chuckle. "Sugar, why do you think I offered the choice? I know how much you like your alone time. Especially with your books."

Tiana smiles before she leans in to throw her arms around my neck in a crushing hug. Her body extends over the center console to get as close to me as she can.

A soft sigh leaves her, before words leak from her lips. "I love you," she murmurs.

My eyes widen, and Tiana's body goes eerily rigid.

I'm shocked. Not because I don't feel the same way. But because she's the first one to say it.

My heart beats like a thousand wild stallions in my chest, and I wrap my arms around her, tightening my grip as I stroke up and down her spine.

"I love you too, sugar."

It took me some time to get all the books upstairs to Tiana's apartment, but as I brought them in, there was nothing I wouldn't pay to see the smile and joy on her face.

She goes through all her books, one by one, looking over the bindings and the pages. And when I bring the last of the books up, I linger there... watching her for a moment too long. All the while, a warm, bone-deep feeling settles in my chest.

One that I don't think I could ever push away.

She sits, surrounded by her new books, quietly looking over and through each one. Organizing each one into neat piles or stacking them beside each other. She flips through the paperbacks and admires the hardcovers. She's lost in this tower of hers, while I get lost in the vision that forms around her.

Bookcases as tall as the vaulted wooden ceiling, with a ladder along them. In a room, in a house that I had built just for her. Something I put so much thought and effort into making perfect just for *her*.

Our house.

Fuck.

I run a hand over my face at the thought. At the reality of the things I'm telling myself.

I haven't been with her for long. Hell, I've barely known

her just as long. But I meant what I said earlier. There is no woman that could ever measure up to her.

I want to know every bit of her. I want to know how she takes her coffee in the morning when she makes it at home, and I wanna know her routine for bedtime. I wanna know how she winds down at night, and I want to know... *everything*.

A soft, adoring smile tugs hard at my lips as the visions dance in this thick skull of mine.

"I'll be back, sugar. Text me what you want," I tell her. My voice comes out softer, love-sick.

She waves a hand over her shoulder as she looks over her books, and I shake my head with a small chuckle.

Walking down to the parking garage and back to the Vette, I think... and I think... and I *think*.

The thing I'm about to do on top of getting these snacks... It's dumb. One of the dumbest things I think I'll ever do. But I'd be a fool not to do it. To at least give it a fair shot.

When it comes to Tiana, I will always give it a chance. She deserves that more than anything.

I shake my head with a deep breath, gripping hard at the steering wheel as I pull out of the parking garage and make my way to the store.

When I get there and inside, I peruse the aisles for a long while, grabbing some things that I know Tiana likes and just taking my time. I want to give her as much time as I can for her to spend with her books, since I know she'll probably be reluctant to pull away from them, so I try to waste time for her sake.

I'm man enough to admit that I'm also trying to talk myself up for the next task I want to embark on.

I can't get my mind off it, not since I saw her surrounded by the books I bought just for her.

There's no reason I should be scared of this part. But I am

because there is a large chance it won't go the way I would like it to.

Tiana is skittish. She always has been. And I don't want to push her into a place she may not thrive in.

But I will the fear away, and think of the game plan as I load the snacks into the Vette and head to my next destination.

The buildings change as I make it to the more expensive area of downtown Seattle. A higher-end section of town has a jewelry shop that I have seen on a few occasions. I don't come down here often, but I've always noticed it when I've had to come through this area. It's hard to miss it because it is extravagant, even from the outside.

I pull into the parking lot and stare at the large glass doors on its front. They taunt me. They call me a pussy for lingering in my car for so long, but I take a deep breath and throw the driver's side door open to climb out and head to the entrance.

I am probably vastly underdressed for this sort of endeavor, but I don't think it matters. At least to me, it doesn't. Looks and money are not mutually exclusive entities.

An older woman stands at one of the large glass cases that surround the entire perimeter of the shop. The lights in here are almost blindingly bright. She has her dark brown and graying hair in a bun on the top of her head, with a pair of glasses hanging from a chain around her neck.

"Hello! What brings you in today?" she asks kindly.

I linger on some of the different bracelets and necklaces in one case before I slowly make my way to her case. Perhaps I'm lingering on them so my heart doesn't explode when I look at the rings she guards in her section.

Eventually, I'm able to bring my gaze from the case below to her with a nervous smile and a rub at my neck.

"I'm uh... I'm looking for an engagement ring."

Her brow quirks as she steps back, looking me up and down before she gives me an incredulous look.

"Are you sure you're in the right place, sir? Some of these pieces go for hundreds of thousands of dollars."

I blink, almost dumbfounded, before my eyebrow arches in confusion as I stare down at her.

"I am aware. Why do you think I'm here?" I ask.

Her eyebrows rise as she shrugs and shakes her head. "I just wasn't sure. You don't exactly... exude the energy of someone who would be in here looking for something like this," she asks as she gestures wildly over my body.

My brow rises as I watch her, almost in shock at her boldness.

"I'm here because I want to find an invaluable ring for the woman I'm in love with, because I'm going to ask her to marry me." I pause as my eyes glance away. "Eventually," I murmur.

"And you can afford a ring like that?" she asks.

My brows furrow in disbelief, looking at her for a long moment before sighing and rolling my eyes. I fish my phone out of my pocket and swipe through a few home pages before I find my banking app. I open my account and turn the phone around for her to see it.

She pulls the glasses from around her neck to place on her face, leaning in to look at my phone.

Her face pales, and her eyes widen before they flick up to me in shock. I give her a knowing tilt of my head as I eye her with a smile.

She gulps nervously and pulls her glasses off her face.

"Right this way, sir," she murmurs.

A grin slides along my lips as I pocket my phone and follow her down the line of cases.

CHAPTER TWENTY-SEVEN

TIANA

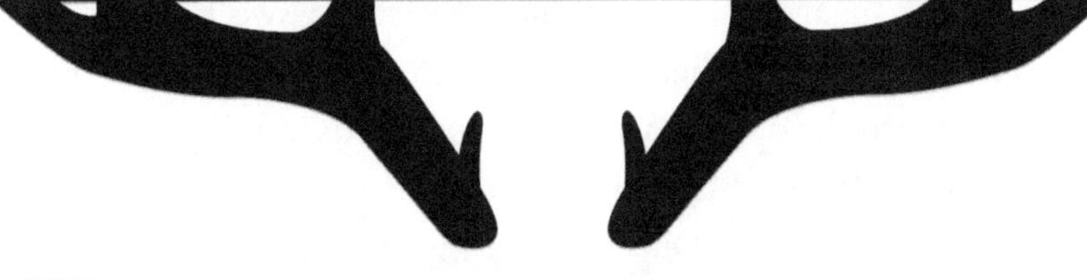

It feels like Gunnar has taken entirely too long to return. I moved the books to a corner of my apartment for later organization, and he still isn't back.

I sit on the couch, flipping through the pages of one of my new books as I wait for him.

All the while, I feel a pang deep in my chest.

Is this what longing feels like? Because... I... I miss him?

I'm excited for him to come back, and I'm excited to spend the night with him. It's somewhat incredible that we haven't had a sleepover like this yet. You would think with how close we live to each other, that we would trade off every other night. But I really just like to have my bed to myself, to be honest. As much as I enjoy time with Gunnar, he's massive. I feel like he would crush me on accident.

But tonight... I get to spend the night in his arms, and I get to wake up next to him.

The idea makes me a tad bit giddy.

Impatience gets the better of me as I wait for him to return, before a knock comes at my door. It catches me off guard because I imagine if it were Gunnar, he would just come in.

But my brow raises, and I place the bookmark back in my book before I stand. I had changed into a silky little black robe with matching shorts and a tank top set underneath while I was waiting. Not knowing if it is Gunnar, I tighten the sash around my waist to cover myself as I go to answer the door.

Padding over to the door, I open it to find Gunnar standing there with a grin.

"Hey sugar. You ready?" he asks with a sweet smile. His arms are above his head, gripping the top of my door and leaning into the open space like an enormous monkey.

He's removed his hoodie-jersey and is back in his simple black sweats. I can't help the way my eyes sweep over him in admiration of his physicality. I'm not sure if he does this on purpose. This method of grabbing hold of the door to lean in. Because it makes all of his muscles taut and his veins bulge throughout his entire body. The ones over his hardened stomach are thin and webbed, leading right into the band of his sweatpants. The ones along his forearms and biceps are thicker. Eventually, my eyes finally make their way to his face, where I see him give me an adoring smile. As if he watched me admire him and merely waited for me to finish.

I can tell by the look on his face that he was doing just that, and I feel a slight tinge of embarrassment. As heat covers my chest and my face, I give him a nervous half smile.

"It's alright, sugar. I do the same," he says with a sly grin.

I roll my eyes as I jump up to wrap myself around his body. The scent of his clean, piney cologne floods me, and a rush of joy surges through me. He makes a startled *oof* as his hands release the door frame to come and grab my ass.

"I missed you," I say as I press soft kisses to his neck. I inhale deeply against his skin, letting him seep into my veins.

He chuckles as he moves a hand from my ass to stroke my back.

"You missed me, huh? I reckon I missed you more."

I giggle against his skin. "I've been waiting for you to get home."

And saying those words out loud... fuck me, they bring about a feeling I've never felt before. One where a future throws visions through my head. And I don't push them away... Not when he makes me feel like this.

"That's surprising," he says with a laugh as he leans into my apartment to close the door.

He replaces the hand on my ass to carry me down the hall to his apartment.

"What took you so long?" I ask as I inhale him again. Every breath is like a little release to my nervous system. It unlocks it, letting it settle in his presence. Peace, unlike anything I've ever known, eases through me the longer I smell him.

"I just wanted to give you some extra time with your books. I had to make a few stops for gas," he says as he opens the door to his apartment.

Tucker doesn't greet us when we enter, but I hear him barking from somewhere in the apartment. Even if it is muffled.

"Where is Tucker?" I ask as I lean away from him to look around.

"I put him in one of the extra rooms so he wouldn't clamber all over us. I wanted to take you straight to the room. It's where I put all the snacks," he says with a cheeky grin.

I giggle as I swat at his chest. "Well, onward!" I shout as I point at the back hallway.

He laughs in response before he takes a harsh swat against one of my ass cheeks. The sting of his palm sends a heat through me as I yelp. Something about being manhandled like this just spurs me up. And *quick.*

His steps carry us to his bedroom, and it hits me then that I've never seen it.

The glow of the massive TV is the only bright light in the room. The lamps in the corner of the room are dimmed. And as the day slowly turns to dusk, the oranges, pinks, and purples coming from the window on the back wall lend a soft calm alongside the other sources of light. Long, black curtains are tied back to allow what little sunlight is left in, and the city greets us from below. A massive, king-sized bed rests on the wall right beside the door, with the TV mounted on the wall directly in front of it.

Neatly decorated with a satin black bedspread, he slowly sets me down on the bed next to all the snacks he's got in the middle. Though, the bright red pillow cases are what really catch my attention. My head tilts curiously at them.

"Why do you have such nice sheets?" I ask as I stroke a hand over them.

Glancing over at the snacks, I take a little inventory of what was brought. Some of my favorite chips, candies, and drinks are all ready for us and it makes my heart sing. I'm very particular about my food and I don't really enjoy much. If there isn't stuff around that I know I like, there is a level of panic I start feeling without it.

And someway, somehow, Gunnar has made sure that I always have something safe to indulge in.

I've never had someone see me like this and my heart squeezes at his observation skills.

My hands flap excitedly as my neck tenses with happiness, and Gunnar laughs as he cradles me, throwing me further onto the bed, before sitting down on the bed beside me.

"Well, aside from the fact that I like to have nice things to sleep on? I bought the pillow cases recently. I've always been so enamored with your hair that I wanted to make sure my pillows didn't do anything to mess it up."

My brow furrows. "What?"

"I did some research, and silk pillow cases are best for hair. So I bought some for when you come over."

My heart threatens to burst, and my hands go over my chest to keep it from coming out.

"Gunnar…" I murmur with a soft smile. "You didn't."

"I did. I had to make sure you were comfortable here," he says as he leans over to grip my chin in his hands. He pulls me toward him, pressing a soft kiss to my lips before he pulls away to push my hair behind my ear. "I got this for you, too," he says as he leans over to his nightstand.

My head spins as I watch him pull a swatch of black silk fabric out of one drawer, and he holds it out for me.

"3B, right? I know the type of material for bonnets doesn't matter, but I got some hair products for you. They're in my bathroom."

I take it from him, looking over it. "You bought me a bonnet?… And… My hair type? You researched my hair type?" I whisper.

Part of me feels as if I'm thinking it, but I know I'm saying it out loud because I am so in shock I don't know how I could have stopped my mouth otherwise.

"I really… *really* like your hair. I just don't want my pillows to be a reason for them to get messed up. My hands are a different matter entirely. But at least that's for good reason." His eyes are warm and so… so fucking sincere.

I feel like my chest tightens and my throat constricts. I can't believe he paid that much attention to my hair in that way.

"How did you… even…?"

"I stayed up researching one night because I just want this

place to be comfortable for you in any way I can make it," he says softly. His eyes glow with sincerity, admiration... All the things, and I can't believe I've gone this long in my life without knowing what that kind of look felt like.

Perhaps it's because I didn't really care to look at my ex's faces. I never felt comfortable enough with them to look them in the eyes this way. As I don't particularly enjoy eye contact, but I usually do it for the kindness of others.

But there is something about the way Gunnar brings me calm and safety. Where it feels like a gaze into his eyes is peace. It's happiness. And I've never had that feeling before.

I throw my arms around his neck, hugging him tightly because it's the only response I can muster. I don't know how to express the way I feel about all of this. It's so much all at once, and I feel like a hug tells him everything he needs to know.

He's always done things I never knew men could even do, and it's the reason I'm so smitten with this feral little hockey player.

Leaning back, I take his face in my hands, looking over his sweet hazel eyes.

He smiles. "You're a fuckin' beaut, Tiana," he says softly. His eyes flick down to my lips before they come back up to meet my eyes.

A laugh bubbles out of me as I shove his chest. "There's the Gunnar I know."

He wraps an arm around my waist, pulling me to the pillows as he grasps the side of my head and pulls my face to his lips in to lay a bunch of thick, wet kisses against my cheeks. I screech out playfully as I try to fight out of his grip.

"Stop! You're getting your wet drool all over me!" I shriek playfully.

He laughs before he settles down, his hand resting on my back.

"What did you wanna watch?" he asks as he makes soft circles where his hand rests.

My mind works, because I don't really watch a lot of movies, to be honest. I might put one on if I'm really bored, but it's very rare I sit and watch a movie of my own volition. And I really just want to lay here with him sharing the space.

"I'm happy with whatever you want to watch," I say as I snuggle into the crook of his arm. I rest my head on his shoulder, swirling a finger along the lines of black ink on his chest and along the rigid lines of his abs.

He reaches over to the nightstand for the remote and scrolls through some movies he has.

"I wanna watch Goon," he says with a grin.

I shake my head with a smile. "Of course you do."

"Whaaaat? What do you expect?" he asks with a teasing grin.

I glance at the TV, watching as he goes through the movies and picks the one he wants.

Soon, it starts, and he wraps his arm around me, pulling me close and leaning his head on top of mine.

As the opening credits begin, I snuggle closer, and his arm tightens around me, with his hand resting on my back, swirling mindless circles into my spine.

I don't think I've ever had the chance to just lie with him like this. Just spending time like this. Enjoying the sound of our breathing, enjoying the moment together.

The feeling is oddly... domestic. Which is nothing I ever dreamed of.

But just the idea of coming home from our jobs to rest in bed, watching a movie.

It's nice. Even after all the time I've spent alone.

I think this might be better than time by myself.

A little over halfway into the movie, a thought comes to mind, and I look over his slowly rising chest.

Gunnar has had his chain in his mouth the entire movie so far, and I've heard the way it's clicked and clacked against his teeth. But I don't mind. It's soothing in a way, because it's so distinctly him.

"Gunnar?" I ask quietly as I glance up at him.

"Hm?" he responds as he keeps his focus on the movie.

"How did you find out you have a breeding kink?" I ask.

It's something that I've wanted to ask for a while, and honestly, the thought just now came to me. I don't think there's a better time to ask than now, to be fair.

I watch him, waiting for a reaction, and he glances down at me with a sly quirk to his brow. All the while, I feel the way his heart picks up from where I lay against his chest. His lips pull in the corners, against the chain, as he gives me a soft grin. The hand that has mindlessly rubbed my back continues... though now it's calculated, not as smooth, as if he's anticipating something.

His tongue flicks out, dropping the chain against his chest.

"I'm not sure," he starts. The circles change directions. They move differently now, as he thinks. "I've always wanted a wife. And I guess I liked the idea of being able to get her pregnant. It sounds weird. But it's something that tickles the animal part of my brain."

My breaths work deeper into my lungs as I think about the fact that I would be the one to do something so... big for him. That *he'd* be the one to put a baby in me.

And I can't help but admit that I see what he's saying.

I think if anyone else would have approached me about this, I wouldn't have been able to see their side of it.

But with Gunnar. Oh, I see it.

I certainly feel it.

"Have you ever tried it with anyone else?" I ask.

He chuckles, his chest moving my head as he does. "No sugar. I've never wanted to try it with anyone other than you."

Heat builds along my body. My chest, my face, and slowly, my eyes glance toward the band of his pants. A rigid mound has grown there, pulsing and twitching under the fabric of his sweatpants.

I feel the heat collect in my core, and my pulse ratchets up as I nip down on my lip.

Fuck.

"So... when you have imagined it... what do you see?" I ask. Dragging a soft finger down the middle of his abs, I tease the line of hair leading into his sweats.

His chest rises with a deep breath, and I feel his hand tighten against my back.

"Well..." he says with a shaky breath.

Slipping into the band of his sweatpants, I let my hand graze the hardened planes of his lower stomach, seeking out his rigid length and wrapping my hand around him. He throbs in my palm, hardening even more at my touch.

He lets out a low groan as he shifts against the bed, his hand slowly moving down to grip one of my ass cheeks.

"I imagine filling you... propping your hips up after so it stays in, and I know it takes." His voice deepens, turning husky and tortured.

The heat in my core rises, growing slicker with every word.

"I imagine rubbing and kissing your stomach, taking pride in knowing *I* put that fucking baby in there," he breathes.

I release him to pull my hand from his sweats and press the band down to let his cock free. His groans get louder, and I glance up to watch him. Though his gaze is locked on the way my hand wraps around him, stroking up and down slowly.

"What else?" I whisper as I press kisses into the skin of his chest. My eyes glance back down to watch as pre-cum pools at the tip.

"I imagine holding your swollen stomach while you're on your si-" he pauses with a groan and a pant when I run my thumb over the head of him. His head tilts back when I slide the pre-cum over his tip before I bring it to my mouth, my eyes locked on him as I do.

As he tilts his head back down to watch me, his pupils blow and he gazes with rapt attention. I lick him from my thumb before moving it back to his cock, stroking him up and down again.

"Go on," I whisper as I press more kisses into his chest.

He bites down on his lip, leaning his head back again, his eyes lowered to stay on me as he continues. "I'd stuff my cock into that pregnant pussy and knock you up twice," he teases.

My breath catches. He's catching onto my game, and he's ratcheting up his own plays.

His hand comes over, rubbing a thumb softly over my nipple through the thin material of my robe.

"I like knowing I'm pumping my cock deep into the mother of my children. The one who can take it all from me. That *I'm* the only one that gets to fill that sweet little cunt," he says as he leans over, nudging my chin up with his head so he can gain access to my neck.

I hiss a breath when he strokes his tongue across my skin, causing my nipples to tighten as he turns the tables within a split second. The shocks of lust spear through me to soak my center more.

He turns just enough to force me back into the pillows. His hand moves down to press my legs open, his fingers grazing over my rapidly heating core before it glides back up my body. Smoothing his hand over the material, he looks for the tie of my robe, tugging on one end when he finds it. He lets the sash fall from my waist and pushes the loose panels from my middle. The tank top I'm wearing is just a silky crop top, so when the robe falls, cool air brushes over my stomach at the same time his hand does. He rubs it for a moment as his licks and kisses move up my neck and jaw to land on my lips. He's slow as he presses his tongue between my lips, seeking my tongue.

He moves his hand further north, lingering at my tit as he presses it under my top, forcing the fabric up to bare my chest. He grips it, running a thumb over a hardened, sensitive nipple. A moan bleeds into the way our tongues tangle between our lips, his touch sending heated sparks through my blood and straight to my already aching core. Soon, he lets go, moving up higher to press the fabric of my robe from my shoulders, his movements slow and precise.

I shrug out of it, letting it fall from that shoulder, and he strokes his hand over the skin there before his hand roams back down. It slips into the silky shorts to rest on the skin right above my pussy. I bite my lip, stroking and working his cock as I pull away from his lips, leaning my head back.

I feel him move, his lips hot against my throat as he runs a finger down the wet seam of my pussy. His tortured breaths against my throat are hot, begging as his hips buck softly into my hands.

"I like knowing *I'm* the one who makes you this fucking wet," he says before he presses his fingers into me.

I gasp and the hand holding my ass spears to the back of my neck, threading his fingers into my hair and holding it tight to tilt my head back farther as he nips at my throat. My hands abandon his cock as he takes control of me.

A predator catches his prey in *her* trap. And fuck *me* if it doesn't spur my passion higher.

"You thought you could lead this time, didn't you?" he whispers against my neck.

I nod feebly as he works his fingers in and out of me, his thumb rubbing over my clit.

"You thought wrong, pretty girl," he adds. He presses a third finger in, stretching me and preparing me to take him. The prep is well needed, and I'm so glad that he takes his time with this part.

"Get on your side," he says, his voice low and raspy.

I turn in his arms, giving him my back, and he releases the hand on the back of my neck. He removes his hand from my core to take the rest of my robe off, pressing kisses into the skin of my shoulder. Before moving his hand down to slowly push my shorts down.

When he gets them off, he grips my ass, pulling my thighs apart just enough to press his cock between them.

His length rubs against the wet, sensitive outside of my core. Just barely brushing against my clit. The teasing is maddening. It causes me to pant and groan in frustration, damn near whimpering for more. My hips roll as I work for friction, work him *any* amount closer to my clit.

"Such a needy little cumslut, aren't you, baby?" he whispers against my neck before he kisses it.

I nod desperately, because right now I surely am. I need all of him.

Now.

His hand leaves my ass and his chest leaves my back as he leans away. Soon, his cock slides from between my thighs to heavily slap against one of my ass cheeks. His breaths slow as he presses the head back between my thighs, but instead of through them, he slips the head of himself into me. I groan and pant as he stretches me, my head tilting back as I press myself into his body. His girth fills me, and I sigh a breath of pleasured relief as he advances more and more.

"So tight, sugar. So fucking tight," he grits as he kisses into my bared neck.

He seats himself balls deep in me, his hand coming around my front to grasp my tit.

His hips move, pushing in and out of me, and my moans consume the room as his length consumes *me.*

"There's my good girl. You feel so *fucking* good, baby," he groans.

His movements are slow, precise. Pillaging every bit of me in sensuous strokes. The heat at my back from his body and the brush of his skin there sends my thoughts fleeing. The sensations bringing me deep under.

His hand releases my tit to move between them, resting there to grip the front of my throat. His fingers put pressure on the pulse points on either side of my neck, causing my head to lighten in breathless euphoria.

"I like the idea of coming home after a long day on the ice and fucking you into submission after you spend a whole day yelling at people... I like knowing *I* have a leash on that fire inside of you," he growls in my ear. With every slow stroke, he sits himself balls deep.

"Gunnar," I pant breathlessly.

My head leans back, resting in the crook of his neck. His other arm is under me, wrapped around my ribcage, and he brings his hand up to pinch and tug at my nipple as he continues his thrusts. His lips branding my skin with every press.

"I've got you, baby. I'm gonna take such good fucking care

of you..." he murmurs. His groans mixing with his heavy breaths.

Again, my brain tries to scramble for what would sound good at this moment. He has more experience with talking like this, but I want to please him the way he pleases me. I want to satisfy his cravings the way he satisfies mine.

"I want to be filled with you. *Fuck,* I want to make you a daddy," I pant. And the idea. Fuck, it's hotter than I imagined. The way he'd hold me and kiss me, the overall protectiveness he'd have of me.

"God damnit, Ti, you're playing with fire," he rasps desperately against my neck. But he meets me shot for shot. "You're going to be such a beautiful mother, baby. So fucking sexy and so fucking *mine*," he growls as his thrusts pick up. I feel the nip of his teeth against my shoulder. His hand tightening on my neck and on my nipple.

My moans grow louder, filling the room with the increased speed of his thrusts. "Fuck, Gunnar, fuck!"

"Take it. Take every fucking inch of me. I know you can. I've *seen* you take this cock," he growls again.

My hips roll against his thrusts, meeting him with every bit of me.

I let him fill me, I let him and everything he *is* consume me.

The hand on my throat comes higher to grip my chin, turning my head toward him. His eyes are burning with passion as he looks into mine.

His lips latch onto mine, his thrusts slowing to rolls as he moves his hand on my tit down to my core, rubbing and stroking at my clit.

"You're such a good fucking girl, aren't you, baby? My perfect little cumslut, taking my cock so fucking well, don't you?" he moans into my mouth.

My eyes roll, my pleasure climbing with every thrust and pet he makes of my clit.

"You're gonna be such a perfect wife. You're gonna take my cock every fucking night, aren't you? Let me fill you like this every night?"

I nod desperately. Not just for the play of it all... But because fuck, I *do* want that. And the way he takes all of me, thrusting every inch of himself into me and telling me how he'll come home every night just to fuck me. The stimulation of his touch, his words, the way he fucking *feels*. I need it all. I need all of *him*.

And I need it *forever*.

"Good girl, Titi... There's my good girl..." he groans into my mouth as he slows his thrusts down more, but he keeps speed on my clit, throwing me to that edge faster than I expected.

My body tightens, my moans getting louder as he throws stroke after torturous stroke into me.

"Come for me. Lock me in that cunt, I need to feel you come," he grunts until he slams a few more strokes into me.

His hand tightens on my throat, my pulse throbbing against it, and my breaths lighten more and more as the haziness rushes through my head. His other hand freezing against my clit as his strokes slow and I feel him fill every bit of me. I come with him, his hand releasing, and the blood pumping rapidly through my head as my orgasm rocks through my body. It causes an overwhelming feeling of ecstasy to flood my brain all at once. Shudders roll throughout me as the pleasure crashes over me in wave after wave after wave.

"Fuck... fuckfuckfuckfuckfuck," he pants and groans quietly against my lips as he takes smaller thrusts into me, wringing out his orgasm.

My body goes limp in his arms, my chest heaving as I relax

against the warmth of his body and the sticky sweatiness of him. He does the same, panting and easing his grip on me before I glance over at him.

His head tilts, and he grins through his heavy breaths. He says nothing as he wraps a hand around my jaw, pulling himself toward me to press kisses on my lips. His lips are gentle and soft against mine as he rubs a thumb over my cheek.

"You're my good girl, Titi... You're going to be such a pretty wife," he whispers.

The idea of him saying this to me, actually meaning it, and it not being a game... it scares me. It terrifies me.

But... since meeting Gunnar, I don't mind doing the scary things with him.

"I love you so damn much, Tiana Dawn." His voice is soft, almost desperate as he presses more kisses against my lips.

And it's the desperation in my soul. For him, for us, for... *this*. That has me saying it back.

"I love you too, Gunnar Hayze."

CHAPTER TWENTY-EIGHT
GUNNAR

The weekend with Tiana goes by in a blissful blur. After our tryst, we laid in my bed. I played with her beautiful ringlets. They were frizzy and a mess from what we had done. But I admired them all the same.

We talked... for a while. About the future. About kids. About... life.

I don't know what shifted. Maybe it was me. Maybe it was her.

But I wondered what our kids would look like with her curls. With her eyes. If they looked like her, or if they would look like me.

We agreed they would have to ice skate in some capacity. I don't think our families would allow anything else. And begrudgingly, Tiana agreed. If only so she wouldn't have to hear the gripes from her father.

We treated it like a game. No concrete things or plans. Just for fun.

But even if we called it that, it didn't feel like it. Not with the way I wished so badly it could be a reality.

Eventually, we slept. I held her close all night. I let her weight settle in my arms, and I held her like she wouldn't be there in the morning.

But waking up to her, seeing her in my bed, either asleep or awake. Relaxing in my arms or sleeping between our movies. It didn't matter. I enjoyed being with her.

Because I am so desperately and utterly in love with Tiana Dawn.

I may have been in love with her from the moment I saw her. It's hard to say. But I would give up everything to spend my life with her. Even the game... if I really needed to.

It would suck. But I think not having Tiana in my life would suck exponentially more.

Her ferocity, her silent passion. Her ability to put her boundaries in place and not let anyone interfere with her life. I suppose, except for me. Her beauty, her grace. Her work ethic and everything she does to make sure her life moves at the exact pace she wants it to. She's the most incredible woman I've ever met.

And I'm more sure than ever that I want to make her my wife. I want to ask Bubbles for her hand. But there's no way I can do that right now. So, I have to come up with a plan.

So that's what I do for the rest of the week. During practice, and during my showers after practice. Every second, my mind works, thinking of how I can make this happen. And I quietly gauge what I can do.

On Friday, before we prepare for the game, I shower as usual, and go to Tiana's office.

She's still working on something at her computer when I enter. Her eyes intently focused on the screen as she looks over her work. But the focus drops when I walk through the door, giving the frame my signature knock.

Her smile rises to her eyes as her teeth catch her lip, and a blush stretches across her cheeks. That blush that highlights her freckles and sends a soft bit of steam against the bottom of her glasses. That smile that makes her green eyes glow.

A lot is going on in the halls, with it being a home game tonight. Vendors and ice managers are setting up the rink for tonight. So I imagine no one is going to care about us in here.

I approach her, reaching a hand out to grasp hers and pull her from her chair. She follows with ease, leaning into my body and wrapping her arms tight around my waist as she looks up at me with an adoring smile.

"You know," she starts as she breathes in a heavy sigh of my shirt. "I love the way you've integrated into my schedule instead of throwing it off its path," she says.

I take her chin in my hand, tilting her head up. "I know routine is important to you, sugar, and I'd never want to ruin that for you. I only want to be a part of it." I don't know if she realizes the implication in those words. But it doesn't matter.

One day she will.

I brought my backpack with me, because I was going to keep it in her office while I played. But I also have something I want to give her.

"I have something for you," I whisper softly before I give her gentle kiss.

She makes a soft moan as she leans in, pressing deeper against me until I rub a thumb softly over her chin before I pull away to shrug off my backpack. It hits the floor with a thud and I crouch down to open it, pulling out a bundle of fabric.

I glance up at her with a smile and she gives me a confused look as I come to a stand.

Neatly folded with "HAYZE" in bright white letters sitting front and center, I hold the gift out to her.

Her head tilts as she takes the bundle of fabric and shakes it out, looking over it. A gasp leaves her parted lips, and it seems as if her eyes glaze over as she looks at me over the fabric she holds.

"Your jersey...? You gave me a jersey?" she asks quietly.

"Of course, baby. I want everyone to know which player you belong to," I say with a playful grin as I come back to her.

She holds it to her chest, leaning in to me to look up at me with adoration. "I love it, Gunnar," she whispers.

Her green eyes glow; *she* seems to glow. The way she is around me now is something I think I have dreamed of at one point. And I've worked so damn hard to get here. I played her games. She played mine. And we ended up in a stalemate of hearts. Twined into one another.

I lean in to press a kiss to her lips, stroking her cheek softly, before a loud crash echoes through the room.

Startled, we both turn to the door, and my eyes widen before they roll in disdain as I take sight of who has opened it.

Bubbles... God fucking damnit...

His brows clench in fury, his eyes rabid as he slams the door shut behind him. "Tiana," he growls.

"Dad, I-" she tries to say, but he stops her.

"And you, Hayze," he says as he points a thick finger at me.

I say nothing. I merely fold my arms over my chest since I have it in my right mind to know when I've been caught. Especially for something I know we weren't supposed to do.

"How many times... did I warn the both of you?" he asks.

Neither of us speaks.

"You both have dishonored not only this team, but this family. Tiana, what in the hell would your mother say?" he warns low and serious.

"Dad, Gunnar is-"

"I don't give a shit, you knew the consequences," Bubbles says.

But I step in front of Tiana, hiding her behind me.

"If you have a problem with this, blame me. Tiana never wanted any of this. If there is anyone who needs to be reamed, it's me, Coach. Tiana was just a subject of my pestering."

"She's a grown woman making grown woman decisions, knowing damn well what it means for her career!" Bubbles yells as he shoves a finger in my chest.

I glance at his finger. Allowing him the poke because I know we're in the wrong here. I'll let him have that.

My eyes follow his finger up to his eyes and I lower my voice. "She is. And she wouldn't have made those decisions if I hadn't asked her to. Either way, don't blame her. Bench me for the next six games or whatever punishment you wanna give me. Suicides on the ice for three hours. I don't give a fuck. She is not to blame here," I say as I level him with a sober gaze.

His eyes volley around my face before he fixes them on Tiana behind me. Soon, they come back to me, fury pulsing in them. "Out, Hayze."

I watch him for a long moment, my gaze narrowing on him. "I'll move. But I'm not leaving this room."

His lip lifts in a sneer. "Move."

I step to the side, letting Tiana stand before him. Her face has turned into a mask of angered annoyance as she crosses her arms over her chest, my jersey flung along her arms.

"You're moving out of your apartment and into the house. You'll be put in the firm with your mother until we figure out how to clean up this god forsaken mess you've made of yourself," Bubbles growls at her. I watch as his eyes flick down to the jersey before they go back up to her face.

"You shouldn't have any damn say in the people I date," she says defiantly.

The image of that stony little lawyer from that day in the locker room comes into view, and my heart pounds.

"Tiana, you are well and fully aware of your position here and what it could mean for your job," he says.

Tiana lifts a brow, rolling her eyes as her black heel taps impatiently against the ground. "Yes, I *am* aware. And I took that chance because I love Gunnar."

Bubbles' lips part as he looks between us. "You're in love with him?"

Tiana nods affirmatively. And I can't help how much faster my heart moves in my chest at the admission. She's told it to me before, and it was a lot then. But to hear her say it out loud to her dad, of all people. That's a new beast entirely.

"The punishment stands. You'll have to see what your Mother has to say about all of this," he says.

"Fine. But I *will* find a fucking loophole. The way I always do. And I'm going to be with Gunnar at the end of it all," she says.

Her dad merely glares. "Leave."

Tiana moves back to her desk, shoving everything in her bag before she trots out of the office, slamming the door behind her.

Her father turns to me, glaring daggers into my soul.

I stand my ground, folding my arms over my chest as I glare back at him. He may be my coach, but he shouldn't have talked to my girl like that.

"You didn't have to do that to her."

"I did. If she ruined her career for a player, her mother would never forgive her."

"And you would?" I ask lowly.

"I would. But only if it was legal, Gunnar."

I roll my eyes. "What about her happiness? Does it mean nothing to you?"

"It does. But obviously, her happiness can't be her own

fucking client! I know how much her career means to her. And she would never forgive herself."

"It seems she already has."

His eyes narrow as he watches me, as if trying to calculate everything. "We talked about this. About what would happen."

"And I took the risk. Because I'm so madly in love with your daughter that I'd fucking drop my stick *right now* just to be with her."

His brow furrows. "You'd throw away the pros...? For Tiana?" I swear his eyes turn glassy.

My brow rises in confusion. "Why wouldn't I? She's incredible. I..." I pause, sighing as I run a hand through my hair.

Why the fuck would I say this to him here? Now?

But it's an effort. And I'm nothing if not a man of my word and a man of maximum effort.

I reach a hand into my pocket, fishing out the small black velvet box I keep on me.

Why? I don't know. Maybe for moments like this, where I need to plead to keep the woman I love in my life.

I hold it out to him before I flick open the lid. A silver band features a large emerald-cut diamond in the center, surrounded by smaller diamonds that extend down the band.

He looks at it, his eyes widening before they glance up at me. "Marriage, Gunnar? You love her so much, you would marry her?"

I nod as I flick the box closed, and it echoes through the small room with a sharp click before I shove it back in my pocket.

"I would do anything to have that woman in my life for good. She is everything I've ever needed. I love her rigidity, her dedication, her drive, her interests, her brain. I love that she loves her space. And I love that she is *her*. She knows what she wants, and she doesn't let anyone stand in her way. She's gentle, she's kind. She's sweet." My heart beats a little harder on the last one.

My sugar.

I smile. "She's everything to me, Dawn. And she deserves to be happy in her comfort. She's worked hard enough to secure at least that for herself."

Coach watches me for a long moment, his eyes moving about my face as he absorbs the weight of my words. He lets a long sigh go, as if he was holding his breath, before he claps a thick hand on my shoulder.

"If Tiana can figure out the legality of it all..." he breathes deep as he drops his head in defeat, his pause seeming much longer than it should be. "I'll give you my blessing."

My brow quirks as I look down at him.

"But until then... You guys can't be together. Or even near each other. Tiana can *not* lose her license. And I can't lose a defender like you."

I narrow my eyes on him. All of this is horseshit. It's stupid.

But I get it. I don't want to.

But I do.

I nod tersely before my arms come to cross over my chest. "Fine."

"Tiana will figure it out. If there is anything about her, she'll find her way to get what she wants. She probably won't be able to sleep until she does. That's just how she is."

"Not helping, Bubbles," I growl.

He shakes his head before he takes another slap on my shoulder. Releasing me, he shoves his hands in his pockets before he heads for the door and leaves. With the quiet click of the door, it tells me I'm in Tiana's office without her.

I linger there. Just a few more moments. Looking at the place she sat and sighing before I turn to leave the office, and get ready for tonight's game.

CHAPTER TWENTY-NINE
TIANA

Stomping out to my car is easy. Facing my dad was easy. He doesn't scare me. It's annoying having to go through this. But whatever, I should have known my time was limited.

But the hard part, the painful part, is climbing into my car. Throwing my things down in the passenger seat and gripping the steering wheel as the tears heat and beat against my clenched eyelids. This part... this does hurt.

The one man I've ever truly given a singular fuck about, and my dad had to ruin it.

I knew the precautions. I knew the risks. I knew what could happen. But it didn't matter. Not when Gunnar made me feel as if I could be loved as I am.

I've never had a man go with my flow the way Gunnar has. He broke me out of my shell while allowing me to be in my own space and grow the way *I* wanted to. No man has ever embraced me for *me*.

Not once did he ever ask me to change. He never asked why

I had a routine or chastised me for it. He never once nagged about how I like to be alone, or that I need time to myself.

He took it all in stride. He took *me* in stride.

The tears burn all the way down my skin, to land in small puddles in my lap as my head rests against the horn of my steering wheel. My fingers ache from where they grip it.

I have never cried over a man. Not even the ones that dumped me. I didn't understand why they were so upset with the way I liked to live my life. In my head, if they didn't want to be in my life, then fine. I didn't need the annoyance.

Losing Gunnar is the closest thing to heartbreak I've ever felt, and it's so painful. I didn't think it could feel like this.

How am I going to go about my routine without him? Having to be back in a new place and go to a new location for work all at once? It makes my throat tight and my chest vibrate unsteadily. Nausea rolls through my stomach. My heart pounds in my chest over the idea of having to change everything about my day so quickly and without warning.

And I wish so badly that Gunnar could be here to tell me it'll be alright. At least to be the small light in this storm. I don't know when I'm going to see him again, which only causes my nausea to escalate. I don't know how I'm going to talk to my mom *or* my dad. Considering he was the one who pushed us apart.

I suppose I can't blame him entirely. I knew what we were doing was wrong. But he's the one that dropped that straw on the camel's back. So for now, he's who I'm mad at.

Through it all, though, I'll figure out how we can be together. Gunnar is not getting out of my grasp, just like he didn't let me go. He's part of my life, whether or not he wants to be. And luckily for me, he does.

So, I have to try. Not only because I deeply want to, but because I know Gunnar wouldn't give up on me. Or on us.

My fear and panic shift, turning to anger that fuels me as I turn on my car. My mind runs with the ideas and ways I can work around this as I speed to my apartment. It's the only thing I can work with, and the only thing making it easier for me to grab my things. The faster I can move my things to my parents' house, the faster I can hole myself up in my room and find a solution.

Gunnar will be at the game tonight, so I can pack up the things I need and head to my parents' house.

I'll comply. Do whatever the fuck needs to be done, and I'm going to get Gunnar back.

So that's what I do. I go to my apartment, linger for just a moment when I walk past Gunnar's door, before I go into mine.

I grab a large Seattle Stags duffle bag and shove as much stuff into it as I can. Different clothes, books, and other bits and pieces I'll need. I know it's temporary.

I can use this moment to my advantage. If I'm going to be working at the big firm, I can look more at some of the documentation there to figure out how to work around this.

Sure, I can get the case done that my mom wants me to. But I'll be damned if I don't find a legal way out of this.

I *could* stand up to my parents and tell them I'm going to date Gunnar, anyway. But I'm taking the petty route.

Defiant compliance.

Because not only am I going to show them it'll be fine, I'm going to prove *factually* it'll be fine.

I'll miss Gunnar. I'll miss seeing his face in the mornings and riding with him to the arena. Hell, I'll miss the arena. Because he was there and because of my small cave, I had all to myself.

But I tell myself it won't be for long.

I quickly change out of my clothes, throwing on a simple

black hoodie and sweatpants before I make my way to my vehicle. Turning on the car, I rev the engine. I let the rumbling of it and the growl that echoes in the garage take my nervous thoughts away. I let it seep into my blood, into my veins, and fill me with just enough power to fuel my hope. And when I feel as if my car has done enough of the heavy lifting for my mood, I speed out of the parking garage.

I swerve through the roads and streets of downtown Seattle, making for the outskirts and heading straight for my parents' mansion in Tacoma. They wanted to be a suitable distance away from the arena. So the drive there is longer than it would be to get to the stadium.

Eventually, I reach their house. A large modern cabin made of massive logs in the middle of the forest. Neither of their cars is in the long, rounded driveway. Though there could be one or two in the garage.

I know my dad is at the stadium, especially since today is game day. But I have no idea where my mom is. I'm sincerely hoping she's at the firm because I do not want to talk to her right now.

Staring at the exterior of the house, I sigh. My eyes roam over it, trying not to be angry at it. At all of this. But it's hard. There's a flood of emotions running through me, and part of me feels like when I walk through that door, it'll all come crashing down. Reality will pull me under, and I won't have Gunnar there to tug me from its depths.

With a heavy breath of courage, I pull my duffle bag and backpack from the car before I get out. I walk up the large driveway, coming up the wooden steps to the emerald green door on the house's front.

Pressing the code into the number pad on the door handle, I wait for the beep to tell me it's unlocked. When the mechanism clicks, I press open the large green door and walk in.

Slowly, as quietly as physically possible, in case my mom is here.

The foyer is a large open room with a chandelier made of deer antlers hanging right in the middle. The inside walls look similar to the exterior, considering they are logs. Like a massive rustic homestead.

If the rustic homestead was made of money.

My parents had built this house once Dad started coaching the Seattle Stags. That's been for quite a long time. Which means I do have a room here, even if I don't know what they've done with it since I've moved out.

I stop in the foyer, seeing if I can hear any kind of movement coming from anywhere. It's eerily silent, and I move through the house, looking around to make sure I'm in the clear. I walk through the foyer, to the back corridor that leads to the living room on the east side of the house.

No one is there.

Then I move through the small hallway behind it, taking myself to the kitchen.

No one is there either.

I inhale a deep breath, going through the kitchen and back out to the foyer to take the carpeted stairs to my bedroom on the second floor.

The hallway is lined with doors; offices, bedrooms, and bathrooms. It's also dismally dark because none of the lights are on, and there aren't any windows in this area. But my parents' room is on the west end of the house, so I shouldn't run into anyone on this side. I peek into some of the open doors, passing my dad's home office.

My eyes gaze around the open doors, and I think the coast is clear until I slam into a wall of distinct Chanel perfume and jingling bracelets.

I startle as I back up to see my mother standing in front of me, her arms crossed over her chest with her face contorted in... anger? Disappointment? I'm not sure how to read it.

"Tiana Raye Dawn," she says lowly.

She's in a black pantsuit, and it seems as if she's just had her hair silk-pressed. She must have a big case coming up because it seems as if she's either just come back from the office or is going in.

I glare at her. "What are you doing here?" I ask in annoyance.

"Aside from the fact that this is my house? I was fixing up your bedroom," she responds. "This is beyond the dumbest thing you have ever done," she adds.

"Oh, so everyone is happy for me to get a boyfriend until it's a fucking hockey player?" I ask with a roll of my eyes.

"YES! Yes, Tiana, exactly! Do you know the kind of mess you could have gotten yourself into if he did something stupid and you had to clean up *his* mess?! Do you know how that looks not only on yourself but the firm!?" she shouts as she gestures to the surrounding air.

My stomach drops.

Fuck. I didn't think about the consequences of the firm... I've never had a man distract me like this.

But I stand my ground. At least externally. I'll deal with the mess of the firm later. For now, I have to at least prove something of his worth to her.

"You could have had any man in the world. And you choose the brand new rookie on the team you represent? What on earth has gotten into you?" she asks with a shake of her head and a sigh.

She brings her hand up to pinch between her eyebrows. Her French-tipped nails rubbing into her forehead.

Running my hands over my face slowly, I breathe a deep sigh.

I get her frustration. I do. The paperwork involved in something like this, if things blew up, would be a nightmare. And to an extent, I have to think about that. I have to think about the blowback on the firm if something went awry during all of this. She is one hundred percent right.

But I... love Gunnar. And I have to think about keeping him, too.

I give her a small look of remorse. "I love him, mom. He's the only man who has ever given me a sliver of time to learn how I work. He's always gone at my pace. He's attentive. He's sweet. He's funny... He's..." I sigh.

My stomach twists, and my throat feels as if it dries. I've never been one to admit my emotions or feelings for anything or anyone. I've never really wanted to, or felt those things, to say them like this.

But Gunnar... I can't let them think it was just a fling. That it was just fun. If I have any hope of convincing them we should be allowed to be together, I have to be honest. And that means admitting things I never have before.

Her head tilts as her brow furrows, peering at me. "You love him?" she asks.

I nod. "He is the kindest man I've ever met. When he took me on our first date, he asked Charlotte for my schedule so he could make sure he worked around it properly. He didn't want to impose on my space. And even after our date, when I had asked for a kiss, he denied me because I had some wine to drink."

She looks at me incredulously, her heeled foot tapping against the carpet in the hallway as she thinks. "It still stands, Tiana. He is a rookie. You represent him. Surely you know you can't have a relationship like this with your clients."

"I..." A sigh escapes me before I groan in frustration, my

nerves and emotions ratcheting higher the longer she corners me. "I know that! I... know. But he..." I pause.

Not because of her. Not because of this. But because I've never said this out loud before.

"He's worth the risk. I wouldn't have taken it if he weren't."

My mother is silent as her eyes volley between mine, and she sighs. Almost defeatedly.

"I have to go to the office. I have to get started on that case..." she mumbles.

She walks past me, and I inhale a deep breath, pushing the stirring emotions away. The anger, the sadness, the panic, the confusion, the guilt. All of it becomes too much, and I feel like I need to hide away. I have no idea what any of that could mean in the grand scheme of things. But it's done.

All I can do now is wait for the blowout to settle and work toward an ethical path forward for Gunnar and me. That calms some of my nerves.

What's done is done... what's done... is done.

That small mantra is what I tell myself to keep from falling apart as I walk down the hall.

As I move to the door of my old bedroom, I hear my mom's voice echo from the stairwell.

"This is not over yet, Tiana Raye Dawn!"

I roll my eyes and press the door open. Everything is just how I had left it, except with some new sheets. My bed is along the back wall in front of the large window. My dresser is on the left wall beside my bed.

Sighing, I drop my bags on the ground in a heap and kick the door closed behind me. Everything feels heavier than it ever has as I trudge toward the bed and collapse on it face-first.

As I do, the weight gives way, and it crushes me in the process.

I won't get to see Gunnar for a while... I won't get to hear any of his jokes or the warmth in my stomach from his teasing. I won't get to ride to work with him in the mornings, and I won't get to walk to my apartment with him. I won't get to take Tucker outside with him at night and point out the stars. I won't get to smell his clean, piney scent after a long day, the one that lets me know it's time to go home, that calm is on the horizon.

A gasp courses through me as I try to keep my head above water. The threat of my job, the threat of never seeing Gunnar, and having to move out of my apartment for good. I'll lose my freedom and my space. I'll have to find a new firm to work for. I'll never be allowed at the arena again.

And as all of those thoughts spin and whirl in my head, I feel as if my breaths thin. My heart pounds, and fear washes over me at the intensity of the changes.

How will I manage it? Will I be able to stay calm through it all? What if I don't like my new job? What if I can't be a lawyer at all?

Heat takes over every inch of my skin, causing an uncomfortable sensation everywhere that burns behind my eyelids, and I fold in on myself. I reach up to grasp the pillow at the headboard and hold it to my chest as I sob into it. My body shakes like bugs are all over my skin.

And in an attempt to keep myself from panicking, I grip the pillow with all my might, rocking myself into calm as I pretend, for just a moment, that it's the big, silly goon I fell in love with. And I let it take my sadness and tears away.

The same way I know Gunnar would.

CHAPTER THIRTY
GUNNAR

"**S**tupid fucking cunt," I growl as I check the opposing team's right wing into the boards. The jackass flounders on the ice, and I don't take a second to look back at him. There's no joy I'm taking in this.

No. This is all pure grit and frustration.

I was entirely silent in the locker room today when we were getting ready, and I could hardly look Bubbles in the eye when he was addressing us. I sat utterly silent with my head down, chewing on my chain. The game is everything to me. It always has been.

And I thought it always would be. Until I met Tiana.

Now that she's gone and I don't know when I'll see her again, I can barely concentrate on this thing I've devoted my entire life to.

The game is fun. It gives me purpose, and it gives me life. But fuck, Tiana makes me *happy*. She felt like the other half of me, the part that gave me a sense of structure and rigidity.

I'm usually a go-with-the-flow kind of guy. Skating by with the wind in my hair. But there was peace in the schedule and routine that Tiana and I had set up. There was a certain expectation, and I was happy to follow those expectations, because Tiana was there at the helm.

She had even come to a few of my games, including the away ones. And even amongst the thousands of screaming fans, there was only one I cared to see.

That was my sweet girl up in the stands. I would always look for her.

Even now, I look out at the stands to see if I can spot her. Maybe she snuck in after she left and came to watch.

But she's not here. She's not in any of her usual seats behind the box. I've tried the entire game, and I've missed a few checks or passes of the puck.

And honestly, I don't give a shit. I can't.

During a change-out of players, I take a better look at the arena, trying to spot that perfect head of curly gold and brown hair.

When I can't find her, I go back to watching the game. My hands grip my stick so hard over my knees that I feel like it may snap in half. The boys don't even look at me, and they say nothing to me.

Honestly, I don't blame them. I don't know if they know about Tiana and me. Maybe they can just see how I'm doing. I'm not my usual self. Or maybe they heard the fallout when Tiana stormed out of her office earlier.

The game goes by, and we lost. Part of me can't find it within me to care. Maybe losing was my fault, maybe it wasn't. But I shower, forgoing Coach's little spiel and heading straight to Tiana's office.

Even if she isn't there, it's become part of my routine.

Game... practice... shower... *Tiana.*

As I open her office door, the scent of her perfume swallows me. My hand clutches harder on the straps of my backpack as I look at her chair. Wishing so, so badly, that she was sitting in it, waiting for me.

My soul aches to see her, and I pull out my phone. I know I shouldn't talk to her, especially so soon. But Bubbles isn't going to go through my phone.

I take a picture of her empty chair and send it to her.

Wish you were here, sweetness.

I stare at the open text for a while... waiting.

The picture changes from 'delivered' to 'read', and my heart pounds a little in my chest as the three little bubbles pop up.

Only a few seconds later, her message comes through.

For Tiana, I'll take that.

A small smile graces my lips as I leave her office, closing the door behind me with a soft click.

As I shove the phone back into my pocket, I see Bubbles standing by the arena doors, looking down at his phone. I ignore him, heading for the doors, when his voice sounds from behind me.

"I'm sorry, Gunnar," he calls after me.

I pause, not facing him, and wait for him to speak.

"I didn't know how much Tiana meant to you. And I didn't know how much you meant to her."

I turn just enough to see him from the corner of my eye.

"Tiana has never cared enough about a man to actually disregard her job like this. She's always been independent, and she's never been one to give a man this kind of attention."

"Get to the point, Bubbles," I murmur with a sigh.

He steps closer, coming to stand beside me. "I wouldn't have done this if it were legal, and I want you to know I don't hold any hard feelings."

I give him an incredulous look as I furrow my brow. "*You* don't hold any hard feelings? What about Tiana? What about her feelings?" I ask in annoyance.

"I want to figure this out so you guys can be together. If there were anyone I could pick on the team to date any of my daughters, it would be you or Banks. I know about the truck. It's a very admirable action."

I glance at him from the corner of my eye before I glance toward the doors. He's trying to suck up to me. But I don't care. If he were truly sorry, he would let Tiana and me be together.

"I've never been one for materials," I murmur.

He smirks with a small scoff as he shakes his head. Bringing a hand up, he grips hard on my shoulder.

"I'll try to figure something out. Because Tiana deserves happiness. And I think you two deserve each other."

I look at his hand on my shoulder before I glance back at him. "Thanks."

He sighs as he gives me a small shake and then lets go, walking past me to head out the doors.

I linger there for a moment, waiting until he gets into his truck to drive off before I head outside to climb into my car.

The other players are climbing into their cars. The night, pitch black, swallows the forest around the arena. It reminds me of the first night I walked Tiana out of the arena. The first night I met her. Another game night.

The air wasn't as cold as it is now. With fall turning, frost coats surfaces, and the air puffs out of my mouth in thick flurries of white steam.

She was hesitant to even be near me. And in hindsight, I don't blame her.

I laid it on thick. But there was something deep inside of me that tugged me to her. She was all I could think about during my shower, and I needed to get a second alone with her.

I needed to talk to her. I don't know why. But she was mine. I knew it from the moment I saw her. And not having her here beside me right now, it hurts.

I'm not even upset we lost the game. I'm not upset that it may be my fault.

I'm just upset that I don't have my girl driving me home in the Vette I bought just for her enjoyment.

I climb into the car, rubbing the leather of the steering wheel before pulling out of the parking lot to head back to the apartment complex.

CHAPTER THIRTY-ONE

TIANA

This is dumb.

It's sweet. But it's dumb.

I have no idea why I'm doing this now, when I should have done it so much earlier. Perhaps I'm doing it now to give myself some semblance of hope. Maybe to give me some more strength through the storm.

As a lawyer with only an apartment and a car note to my name, with no kids, I have a large expendable income.

How did I choose to spend that income this weekend?

By fixing Gunnar's truck.

It took me some time to find a body shop good enough that could get it done, and do what I needed done on a vehicle this old. But I found one. I was also able to find out where Gunnar's family lives.

All of that information is public record, so I just needed to find it. Luckily for me, I am a woman on a mission. And nothing will stop me from going about that mission in the best way I know how.

Of course, I can't do it on my own. Not with the things I

need to ask and me not knowing these people. I also have a feeling these people have no idea who I am, either.

So now I sit. In the driveway of a pleasant house in the suburbs. The front has a tall fence around the property, and when you enter the open gate, there is a driveway that sits right in front of the house, and to the right of the house is a detached garage with a few cars parked in front of it.

I pulled up a few minutes ago and have just been waiting for the other part of my plan to come into play.

When it finally does, alerted only by the sound of a roaring diesel engine.

Adrian Banks, the team's captain, parks his massive black pickup truck in the driveway beside my vehicle and cuts off the engine.

I take a deep breath, willing all the nerves away. At least the ones that the breaths *can* take away. The lingering ones, however, settle deep in my stomach.

I don't like talking to people, in general, I merely like defending things. There's a difference between my job and actually having to interact with people on a personal level. And it's not lost on me that this is my... ex-...?

No... no, not ex. He's still my boyfriend. Yes. Semantics be damned, he's my boyfriend.

My *boyfriend's* parents' house. It merely makes my nerves that much more heightened. I reach quickly for my Stanley, taking a long draw from the straw to push away some of the nausea before I get out of my car.

Adrian has already left his vehicle and come around to meet me at mine.

Adrian has been on the team for a long while and is the only African-American on it. I like to think my mother was adamant about having him on their team when drafts were coming around. She was one of the first African-American sports lawyers to start her firm, and she was eager to sign Adrian on as the first African-American on their team.

He's a pretty calm personality in general. He doesn't say much, and he does a good job of keeping any of the new guys on the straight and narrow.

How Gunnar got out of his grip on that first game to run to my office? I'm not sure.

Maybe he was just worn out from first-season game jitters. But I've asked him to come help me with this next part. I figured it would be strange for me to show up at their house on my own with no other member of the team. I'm not the face of the Stags by any means.

Adrian walks up to me in tight Wrangler jeans, a button-up flannel, and a black cowboy hat. His Ariat boots tap against the pavement as he does. From my understanding, his family owns a ranch somewhere in the Midwest. I guess he grew up on a farm, riding horses and wrangling cattle. Every time I've seen him outside of the arena, he's wearing the same sort of get-up.

He tips his hat as he approaches. "Miss Dawn," he says lowly. His voice is deep, thickened by a southern twang.

"Thanks for coming. But you can't tell Gunnar about this. It's a surprise I have planned for him, and it has to seem like it's an idea from the team," I plead a tad more desperately than I should. My nerves leak into my voice, and I can feel the jitters roam through my limbs. It causes a vibrating sensation all the way to the tips of my fingers.

"Understood, ma'am," he says.

"You know you don't have t- You know what? Nevermind. Are you ready?" I ask, with a deep breath. The intensity of what I'm about to do has my mind scrambled and everything feels as if it's moving entirely too fast, even if it isn't.

Adrian nods as he slips his hands into his pockets.

We both make the climb up the wooden steps, standing on

the small landing at the top. But my heart pounds like a drum in my ears as I look over the door.

Just do it. Knock on the fucking door.

I lift my hand, lingering there for a moment before I finally rap against it once... twice.

A middle-aged woman with long brown hair answers the door after a few moments. A warm smile sweeps across her lips as she tilts her head curiously.

I take a deep breath and give her the sweetest smile I can muster. "Hi, I'm Tiana Daw-"

His mom beams an enormous smile as she registers who is at her door.

"Adrian! What brings you here?" she asks.

Adrian presses a kind smile to his face as he tips his hat in hello.

"Afternoon, Mrs. Hayze, a pleasure to see you again," he says with a tad more inflection than I've ever heard. "Our lawyer for the Stags here needed to accompany me on an endeavor we're working toward for Gunnar."

"Oh? Is he in trouble?" she asks with a soft chuckle.

Adrian laughs, and it's rich. One, because I've never seen him laugh. And two, just the mere sound of it.

"No ma'am, we just want to do a kindness for him. We heard his Granpappy's truck stopped working recently, and the team wanted to get it squared away for him as a gift."

His mom holds a shaky hand to her chest as her lips part on a small gasp. Her eyes glass over as she takes in his words. "Daddy's truck? They wanna fix it up?"

'Daddy?' God damnit. The grandpa is HER dad? What have I done to myself?

The new information hits me like a freight train, and I feel bile rise in the back of my throat. Every instinct within is urging me to run. But all I can do is tense up like a statue as Adrian continues to talk.

If I fuck this up, I have a feeling I would actually lose Gunnar's heart.

"That's correct, ma'am. He's done well as a rookie, and he deserves to see it brought back to glory. I know the meaning of a truck like that," Adrian says with a sympathetic smile.

Gunnar's mom glances at the detached garage beside the house as a tear slips from her eye to run down her cheek, and she sniffles softly.

"You guys would do that for him?" she asks quietly.

Adrian nods. "We would be honored," he says kindly.

She sniffles again as she nods and takes a steadying breath. "Let me... uhm..." she pauses, watching the garage for a long moment as a tear runs down her cheek. "Let me go get the keys," she finishes. Though much quieter this time. She nods to the both of us before she enters the house again and closes the door.

I release the breath I was apparently holding, and double over.

"Christ, that was horrifying." I gulp massive breaths of air as I try to get my heart rate back down.

"You represent people in a courtroom, but talking to Gunnar's mother was the straw on the donkey's back?" I hear Adrian ask.

My eyes slide over to see him glancing at me, and I come back to a stand. Brushing my suit jacket and skirt off, I glance at him.

"Spare me, Banks. You're saying you wouldn't be scared if you had to talk to your girlfriend's parents?"

"Nope. Don't need to be. I know my girlfriend's parents quite well, actually," he says.

My brow furrows as I turn to him. "You have a girlfriend?"

"Sure do. You may know her," he says with a nod.

"Who would I possibly know th-" My words halt. The realization washing over me. "No...?"

A small smirk tilts on Adrian's lips as he glances at me from the side of his eye, where he faces the door.

"Since when!?" I ask as I throw my hands out.

All these things happening at once, *all* the time, is making my head spin, and I feel as if I need to hide under my blankets where no one can talk to me for several weeks.

"A gentleman doesn't kiss and tell. I'm sure you know," he says with a confident nod.

The weight of his admission slowly fades away as the words come out of his mouth, sounding more like Gunnar than I expected, and I groan.

"Miss him, huh?" Adrian asks quietly.

"Yeah..." I respond with a soft sigh. My heart settles beside the nausea, causing my anxious nerves to take a deep dive into sadness.

"He's been pretty aloof since the fallout. Doesn't say much to anyone in the locker room."

I groan in annoyance, knowing our fallout is the reason.

"He hasn't even really been playing as well as he could be," he adds.

"Not helping, Adrian," I grumble in response.

I see his hands go up in surrender before he shoves them back into his pockets. "I'm not here to sugarcoat things."

Sugar.

"UGH!" I groan as I throw my head back.

Soon, the door squeaks open. I quickly right myself and don the sweetest smile I can. Even though I am crumbling into nothing over this entire situation.

Gunnar's mom smiles sadly at Adrian, holding out a set of

old keys. Her eyes are red and puffy, as if she had taken her time because she was crying.

"Is everything alright, Mrs. Hayze?" I ask softly.

She nods graciously. "Oh, yes, of course. I just... I can't wait to see it restored. I grew up in that truck too, ya know. It would be nice to see it look the way it did way back when," she says as she gazes off at the detached garage.

A smile tugs at my lips as I realize just how important this is, not just for Gunnar, but for his whole family. It makes the need to do this so much more. But my nerves become that much more.

I can *not* fuck this up.

"We'll take wonderful care of it, ma'am. Scout's honor," Adrian says as he holds up three fingers.

I resist the urge to groan as Adrian once again shows another piece of Gunnar to me, and choose instead to smile even wider.

"I know you will," she responds softly as she hands the keys to Adrian.

She presses them into his hands, folding his fingers over them and cradling his hand before patting it softly. As if she needs to know he's holding it tight. Merely for her sake.

I don't blame her.

"And if you could keep this a secret from Gunnar, that would be very much appreciated," Adrian says with a small nod and a wink.

Gunnar's mom nods. "Yes, yes, of course! I can do that," she says.

"Have a blessed day, Mrs. Hayze," Adrian says with a tip of his hat. His mom nods in goodbye before she closes the door.

I take another heaving breath and begin walking down the steps.

Adrian tosses me the keys as he meets me at the bottom, and I catch them before gazing off at the garage.

"So, what's your plan now?" he asks.

With my eyes stuck on the garage, I respond, "A tow truck is coming. I've found a good restoration company in the area, and they'll take it there."

"It's gonna be a pretty penny to get her fixed up," Adrian says.

"I'm aware. But Gunnar deserves it," I respond.

It's silent for a moment, and I look back at Adrian.

"He sure does, Ms. Dawn," he says with a sweet smile.

I roll my eyes with a playful smile. "Get outta here. I appreciate the help."

"All in a day's work, ma'am," he says. He tips his cowboy hat in goodbye before he walks to his truck to swing the door wide open.

As his foot plants on the running board to haul himself in, his head crests the top of the truck and I call out to him, "Be nice to my sister!"

"Can do!" he responds with a wave before he climbs in. The engine roars as he turns on the ignition, and he pulls out of the driveway to leave. I watch his truck disappear, then turn back to the garage, looking over it with a heavy sigh.

"I'm going to get this fucking truck up and working," I tell myself out loud.

Come hell or high fucking water.

CHAPTER THIRTY-TWO

GUNNAR

It feels like the more time I spend at the rink, the angrier I get knowing Tiana isn't here.

I still go to visit her office, and every time I want to rage in it.

I've hurt a few of my teammates with the checks I've laid into them.

Yeah, I feel bad. But I feel even worse with her being gone.

I text her all of my thoughts. Dumb. Smart. It doesn't matter.

I think the other day I told her I was having a smoothie at the cafe down the street from our complex.

Usually, she reads them and reacts to them in some way. A heart or a thumbs up.

I'm not sure what things are happening behind the scenes on her end.

I don't find her lack of words to be a lack of love. I don't know why, but I feel like she still holds a spot for me in her heart. Maybe it's the way mine beats for her that has me living these delusions of grandeur... but I hold on to the idea that hers beats the same for me.

I've spent all of practice merely chewing on my mouth guard. I listen when they call for me to do something. But a lot of it feels... useless. What's the point of being a hotshot hockey player if I can't have my girl on my arm? At my games, cheering me on?

It shouldn't feel like this. The game is everything. But... Tiana. *Fuck,* Tiana means more. And I never thought a woman could replace the game for me.

By the time practice finishes, I feel as if I've had enough. I don't want to seek out Bubbles. He's the last person I want to talk to... but here we fucking go.

I have to find him. I have words for him.

I shower, grabbing all my things before I wander the halls in search of the man himself.

It feels like it takes forever. But eventually, I find him.

Standing by the front door to the arena.

I take a deep breath, mulling over the words I want to ask him. But I just have to go for it. Same as I did for Tiana.

"How much longer until she's back?" I murmur as I approach him.

He startles, almost dropping his phone, and looks at me, gripping his chest. "Jesus, Hayze, you scared the shit out of me," he says with a deep inhale. He shakes his head, letting the words soak in. "What now?"

I groan as I roll my eyes. "When. Is. Tiana. Coming. Back?" I ask again, slower.

"I..." he pauses before he runs a hand over his bald head. "I don't know. Tiana has been buried in this case Tamisha has her working on. And she hasn't brought up anything..." he says, his voice trails away as he thinks.

"What will it take to get her back in that damn office?" I ask.

"Gunnar, I don't know! You know the logistics of these things!" he responds.

My anger rises, and my patience snaps. "No, Bubbles! I fucking don't! Do you think I'd be asking you if I knew?!" I yell as I throw my hands out. I grit my breaths through my teeth as I glare at him.

He merely raises an eyebrow as he watches me, and I growl in annoyance as I realize I'm making a fool out of myself. Loosening myself up, I back down, the merest amount, and move my hands to grip onto my shoulder straps.

"You good now, Big Hoss?" he asks.

"Get. To. The. Fucking. Point," I grit as I reel my composure back in.

Bubbles rubs the space between his eyes as he pockets his phone and groans. "Do you understand the reason you aren't allowed to be together?"

"Ethics. Morals. Illegal. She represents me technically. It'd be a conflict of interest," I respond.

"YES! Precisely! Exactly! And what would happen if you fucked up somewhere outside of the rink and she needed to represent you?"

I roll my eyes, glancing away. "She'd lose her job," I mumble.

"And do you want Tiana to lose something she cares so deeply about?"

"Obviously, I don't! But this shit is killing me! I feel like my world means nothing without her. I haven't been able to function! We did everything together, and she's been ripped from me. I've never had a woman twist the game for me like this. How the hell am I supposed to cope with *that*?" I sigh.

Bubbles is silent for a long moment, his gaze volleying

between my eyes, as if he's searching for something. Until he sighs, rubbing a hand over his face.

"I get it, Gunnar. I do. But... There's nothing *I* can do about it. You can go to the firm and see if there's anything that can be done. I don't know how you'll gain an audience with Tamisha. She's usually busy and I barely get to see her at home. But I guess you could try to ask her."

My brow rises as I listen to him. "I could have gone to the firm this whole time?"

"I don't see why not. I just don't go there often because I'm here."

My mind works, trying to figure out how I can fix this mess, speed up the process, fuck, anything at this point. I know Tiana is doing her part. Even if she hasn't said anything, I just know she is, but if there is any way that I can help...

"I gotta go," I murmur as I walk away from him. I quickly exit the doors of the arena, damn near running to the Vette. It's at this moment that I am sincerely grateful I got this fast car. Of course, I have to be careful; it's a big target for cops. But I have to try at least one *last* thing from my end.

As I get into the Vette and toss my backpack into the passenger seat, I throw the car into gear and speed my way to the firm.

The road blurs as I try with all my might to imagine my game plan. I have none. And in all honesty, I never do. Tiana would have a plan. But Tiana's not here, so I have to do what I do best.

Slap the absolute fuck out of it and hope I land in the net.

Over and over as I twist through the streets, the small idea I've come up with runs through my head. My chain I've pulled into my teeth gives me a small grounding point as the words work on a loop.

Gain an audience with Mrs. Dawn. Get her to give Tiana her job back. Gain an audience with Mrs. Dawn.

It's the only thing I can do without breaking any rules.

Soon, I arrive at the firm, parking in the massive parking lot. Jumping out, I slam the door shut, running through the rows of cars, all the while looking for Tiana's BMW. As I run like my ass is on fire, I don't see it and decide to say 'fuck it', running straight for the front doors.

I notice the people in the lobby looking at me like a crazed person as I sprint past the front desk. Maybe because I am.

I know where Mrs. Dawn's office is, so I head straight for the elevators, taking the first car to her floor.

Because this is her firm, she's at the very top, and the building is rather large. They are a massive firm for several huge sports teams, and I'm so thankful at this moment that I know exactly where to go. I may accidentally check someone if I had to find her office through other means.

When I exit the elevator to the top floor, it opens directly to a large sitting area with her assistant's desk sitting to the right side when you walk in.

The waiting room is huge, with Mrs. Dawn's door sitting smack dab in the middle at the very back.

I brace against the frame of the elevator door, my chest heaving as I catch my breath from the run here. Trudging up to the desk, I plant my hands against its surface, my head hung as I continue gulping breaths. My hands go to my hips as I swing my head back, licking the sweat from my lips as I glance down briefly at the bewildered assistant.

A skinny woman, with blonde hair and shocking blue eyes. Can't be much older than twenty-one. I give her a kind smile through my exertion, and she eyes me for a long moment, almost as if she's waiting for me to speak.

"Can... I help... you?" she asks slowly.

My breaths continue to even out, and I nod, gulping another breath of air. "Yes. I believe you can. I need an audience with Tamisha Dawn. Now."

Her brow raises as she looks at me. "Do you have an appointment?"

I shake my head, taking a small lap around the area before I come back to the desk.

"Nope. Need to talk to her. NOW," I say again. My tongue messes with my lower lip as I try to be kind about it. I may be in a rush, but I'm not an asshole.

She looks at me, almost in fear, before she leans over to her phone to press a button on it. "Mrs. Dawn? There is a...?"

"Gunnar Hayze," I whisper to her with a click of my tongue and a wink.

"Gunnar Hayze...? Here to see you," she says. She lets the button go, and it takes a second for a noise to come back.

"Send him in," Mrs. Dawn says from the other end.

Her assistant looks wildly confused, and she extends her hand toward the door.

"Thank you so much," I mouth to her as I walk to the office door.

I knock once, waiting for what feels like ages before a voice calls from behind it.

"Come in."

Opening the door, I look inside, hoping to see Tiana.

Of course, she's not here. But a guy can dream.

I stifle the annoyed groan I want to make as I enter, closing the door behind me and smiling at Mrs. Dawn. My hair sticks to my forehead in sweaty clumps, and I press it back as I grin nervously at her.

God damnit, I just raced here from the fucking arena to beg for my girl back. I *am* a lovesick little fool. But I'll run hundreds of miles for Tiana. Every day, if I ever needed to.

"Figured I'd be seeing you soon," she says with a sigh as she stands from behind her desk.

She wears a pitch black pantsuit, with a menagerie of jingling bracelets. The room is heavy with the scent of her perfume. Smells similar to something my mom would wear. Maybe not exactly, but something... middle-aged woman, I reckon, is the best way to put it.

She comes around the desk to lean against the front of it, crossing her legs, one over the other, and her arms over her chest.

"What can I do to speed up this process of getting Tiana back to the arena?" I ask.

She deadpans, staring directly into my soul. "Are you aware of the things that could have happened?"

I groan.

This shit again.

"Yes, Bubbles already gave me the rundown. He's why I'm here."

Her brow furrows as her head tilts in question. "Bubbles?"

"We call Coach Dawn, Bubbles," I murmur.

She tries to hide her amusement at the nickname, but she tamps it down. "So, you're aware of the issues?"

"I am. What do I have to do to get her to the arena?"

Is this what all these lawyers do? Why can't I just get an answer? Why does it have to be a question for a question?

Mrs. Dawn rolls her eyes, coming to pinch the skin between her brows. "Is there a reason you need Tiana back at the rink so badly? We have a replacement coming. I'm sure I can take care of whatever legal troubles you have until then."

I groan again, losing my patience. "Because I love her! Okay?! I *love* Tiana. I love her mind. I love her structure. I love the way she takes her time to appreciate the world she lives in and guards her space. I love that she is herself. I love that she is

Tiana. Is that what you wanted to hear? I'm in love with your daughter and the rink has been a fucking nightmare without her!"

Her brow raises. Watching me like I'm a curious little critter, and her tongue fiddles with her lower lip in thought.

"I really didn't think I'd ever see the day, to be honest," she says with a deep sigh.

My brow furrows in confusion. "What?"

She shakes her head with a small smile as she presses off the desk.

"Tiana has never been one for relationships, one. Two, Tiana has never been one for hockey players. As long as her dad has been in the hockey world, she's never dated a *single* one. She's almost refused to. And yet, somehow, *you* got through her little walls. *You* tore them down," she says. She kicks one leg in front of the other as she walks back behind her desk, watching each foot, as if she's still thinking, with her arms crossed behind her back.

"I worked extremely hard to get into that fortress she's made. I saw her, and I knew I needed her," I murmur.

She glances at me with a small smirk. "That's how my husband describes it," she says softly.

"I've never wanted anything more in my life. Not the pros, hell, not even the fucking Stanley cup. I just... want *her.*"

Mrs. Dawn comes around her desk, leaning against the top of her office chair, where she finally looks up at me. She watches me for a long moment, a smile running along her face.

"I'll see what I can do, Gunnar. But it's going to be a lot of paperwork," she says as she leans back up, spinning her chair so she can sit down in it.

What? Just like that? That's all it took?

My head spins with how... easy this was? There has to be another catch to it.

"You mean you can fix this?" I ask softly.

She rolls her eyes, scooting up to her desk to type something into her computer.

"Of course I can fix this. You think I sit here and look pretty? Obviously, but I also am relatively good at my job," she says with a smile.

"Why didn't you just fix it before?"

"You think I'm just going to take one side of the story? Tiana can say the things she wants. Hell, you could have come first. It didn't matter. But I needed to know where *both* your heads were at before I even attempted anything," she says with a shrug.

"You god damned lawyers," I say with a small shake of my head.

"You're in love with one. Better get used to it," she says with a shrug.

I smile, nodding softly. "Keep me updated, will ya, Suds?" I tease.

She rolls her eyes. "No."

"Sorry... better get used to it," I say with a grin.

As she releases a loud groan in annoyance, I take my leave. Damn near skipping my happy ass out of the firm.

CHAPTER THIRTY-THREE
TIANA

I did not miss being in this fucking building at all. When I finished law school, I had to be my mom's assistant for a long while before I could have my own office. Once my dad got set up with the Stags, I ended up moving to the arena.

I was hesitant at first because I couldn't believe I had gotten roped into another hockey situation but I came to love it. No one had to come in to talk to me, and I got all of my cases through email. I rarely had to talk face-to-face with someone unless there were court dates involved.

But just that small bit is everything for me. I hate communicating face-to-face with people.

For a little hermit like me, my office in the arena was my little spot of paradise. None of the hockey players really bothered me for anything other than their legal troubles.

That is, before Gunnar.

The thought sends an ache through my heart as my elbows hit the edge of my desk in annoyance. I bring my hands up to brush them over my face. Alongside trying to figure out how to get Gunnar and I back together, this case my mom has me working on is an unneeded pain in the ass.

An entire nightmare. I don't even know why she has me working on this. I imagine there are hundreds of other attorneys in this building who are better suited for this.

Essentially, the player is having his fiancée sign a prenup.

Fine, whatever.

However, things have gotten more complicated, pertaining to what she wants in the prenup.

I am representing the player, and he wants to cover his ass. I've been trying to set up the contract and the things they want to protect for themselves, but it's become messy.

That's not my fucking problem people, you're getting married, please just kiss and get your shit squared away outside of court.

The player keeps wanting things added to the prenup, more protections for himself and fewer protections for her. Kind of a dick move, if you ask me. But whatever, I'm hoping I don't have to work on this case for much longer.

I go through some of the personal emails on my phone, when I come across an update on Gunnar's truck. My heart pounds violently in my chest as I open the email to see status pictures. The interior has been coming along perfectly, and they said they're starting on some of the body work soon.

When they had asked what I wanted done to it, all I said was to repair it all to its former glory. Whatever the original was, get it there. I tried to find pictures of the truck from the year it came out so they could replicate it to the best of their ability.

They said that was easy enough. Of course, stuff like this takes time. But it also gives *me* time to get the situation with Gunnar figured out. I would much rather get it done sooner rather than later. At least so when we come back together, I have a gift for him.

He's always done such sweet and amazing things for me. I'm hoping this lives up to his efforts.

Gunnar's been sending me messages every day. And I want so badly to respond to them. But there's not much I can say in response. If, for some reason, this escalates, where I would need to be prosecuted, my messages could be evidence. I have to show that I wasn't perpetrating the situation. My job is more in jeopardy of my responses than his would be.

So I have to play it safe. I so horribly wish I could text him back and tell him I miss him. That I love him. I wish I could even tell him why I can't text back. I think that's the most annoying part of it all.

I get lost in the daydream of being able to just talk to him, when a knock sounds on my small cubicle wall, startling me. Looking up, I see my mother with a smug smile spread across her face.

I roll my eyes as I go back to pretending to work on my computer.

"What is it?" I murmur in annoyance.

"You see the things they sent you to fix?" she asks.

"Yes," I respond tersely.

"Fussy ones, aren't they?"

I groan as I stop typing to look at her. "What do you want?"

"Gunnar came to see me yesterday," she says as she crosses her arms over her chest. She leans against the wall, watching my reaction.

I don't know her angle. I don't know what she's expecting of me.

But I can't help the way my eyes widen. The way it feels as if my breath halts in my throat at the mention of him.

He was here? And I didn't get to see him?

"I don't really remember him being so tenacious at his signing. You must have him in a tizzy," she says.

"What did he say?" I ask quietly.

"Ah, ya know. I'm sure you know how your man can be," she remarks with a wave of her hand.

I fight the urge to smile, because I *do* know exactly how he is. "Yes..." I murmur.

"I'll make you a deal," she says.

My brow raises as I look up at her. "What?"

"I'll take this case off your hands if you can figure out the solution to you and Gunnar being together, and then present it to me in a mock trial, where Gunnar is your client," she says.

My head tilts at her skeptically, and my brow furrows at the request. This all feels... *strange.*

"So, I figure out a solution and I get to have Gunnar back, legally? I get my position at the arena back, and I get this case taken off my hands?" I ask as I cross my arms over my chest.

She nods. "Yup."

"What's in it for you?" I ask.

She smiles. "Nothing. You learn a lesson, my daughter doesn't lose her job, and I don't need to have Gunnar scaring my assistant and showing up at my office unannounced."

"Mmm..." I murmur. Looking up, I measure her expression for a long moment, while also weighing the terms.

Mock trial... Gunnar and the arena. And I get the case taken off my hands. I don't know why, but this all seems too easy. But fuck it, I'll play her game. She wants to play chess. I'll move the knight.

"Fine. But can you take over the case for me to find a solution?"

She shrugs. "Alright. But if you don't find a solution, you

stay here. I put a new attorney in your arena office, and you have to take full control over this case."

My mind runs with the things I have to do. At least I can get rid of this case for the time being. But my mother has always done things like this. Ever since I told her I wanted to be a lawyer. She's put me in precarious situations through law school. Legal ones, of course, but ones that strengthened me. At the moment, I hated them. Just like I hate this idea.

But at the end of the day, it all comes down to what I really want. Something I can actually fight for. The other things she had me do were just to strengthen me as a lawyer. *That* was my reward, *that* was my prize for whatever it was she threw at me.

Now, the stakes are higher. I get to work for a reward that I would give everything for.

Devious, it is. Truly. But I have to hand it to her.

She knows how to work out a plea deal.

I groan as I glare at her, my eyes narrowing, my heart pounding as I give in to her demands.

"Fine," I grit through my teeth.

"Pleasure doing business with you, Tiana," she says with a smile as she turns to leave.

CHAPTER THIRTY-FOUR
GUNNAR

The chain in my teeth is the only thing giving me even an ounce of composure.

It's a risk doing this. Shit, it was a risk when we were doing it before. But now that we've been caught, it's an even *bigger* risk.

Her mom said she was figuring something out. But I can't wait any longer. I *need* to see Tiana. Even if it's just for a few moments.

I'm going insane without her face or her presence. It aches knowing her apartment is *right* there, and she's not even in it.

Should I have sent that text?

No, probably not. But I couldn't resist. I've never been able to control myself when it comes to Tiana.

Luckily, it seems as if she feels the same.

I've asked her to come to the apartment, but worded it as if the landlord had stopped by and needed her for something. She said she would be on her way.

And ever since, I've been pacing. Back and forth, waiting

for that knock on my door. My heart and my soul beating in tandem at the thought of seeing her again.

Smelling her. Fuck, just holding her.

Until it finally comes.

The sound of it reverberates through the silent apartment and straight into my soul, leaving me halting in my tracks as I look at the door. My blood rushes through me in nervousness... excitement. *So* many feelings.

Inhaling a deep breath, I look over my body, sliding my black sweatpants down lower on my hips as I go to answer the door. She's always stared there when I've met her with no shirt on. Even now, I've forgone my shirt. As I release the chain from my teeth, it hits my bare chest, letting me know it's go time.

As I pull it open, Tiana stands there, with a pink blush across her cheeks and a nervous smile tugging on her lips. She wears a pair of tight black leggings, some furry Ugg boots and *fuck...*

My jaw drops as I look over her. Hair pulled into a messy bun at the top of her head, her glasses sitting low on her nose, but the best part is she's wearing *my* fucking jersey. Of course, because of my size, it absolutely swallows her and it's so fucking cute the way she looks in it.

I groan as I catch sight of her, and it takes everything in me to keep my strength in check as I grip her hand and tug her into the apartment. Pulling her in close, I hold her to me as I spin and kick the door shut behind me.

My hands wrap around her cheeks, pulling her in as I lean down to capture her with a deep kiss. Sparks set off between us. And every second I spend connected to her lips feels like sunbeams threading through my veins.

She lets a relieved sigh go through our kiss as her hands grip the band of my sweatpants on either side of my hips. Soft and so warm are her lips, and it's a level of familiarity I've been begging for.

"Fuck, baby, I missed you," I whisper against her lips.

She responds with a soft moan, and I pull away momentarily to rub a thumb over her lower lip that has plumped a little from our kiss. The blush on her cheeks deepens as she gives me a sweet smile.

"I missed you, too, Gunnar," she says softly.

"Turn around, let me see you," I whisper as I take her hand. Holding it above her head, I let her spin slowly with a shy little smile. As she gives me her back, I catch sight of my name on it.

And the fact that it's not just my name, but it's *my* jersey on *my* girl. I can't help the way it makes my dick harden.

As she gets around to face me, I kiss her again. Wrapping a hand around her face, I slide it along her jaw to tangle my fingers in the hair at her nape, as my other hand grips tight at her hip, pulling her flush to my body. And I hold her so fucking tight because I know the moment she walks out that door, I have no idea when I'll see her again.

Her hands come to hold my face, kissing me back with just as much longing and fervor.

It warms my soul to know she missed me just as much. She may not say it, but I can read my girl. I've learned the way her body speaks to me, and right now, it's *screaming*. The way she melts into my hands and moves with every movement I make. The way I can feel her energy flood from her in waves of relief.

I pull away, stroking a thumb over her cheek as I look into those green eyes I've missed so much.

"How have you been? Are you doing okay?" I whisper.

She nods softly before resting her head against my chest. And I take a moment to run my hand against the her neck, letting her relax into me.

"My mom... she offered me a deal," she says with a small sigh.

My brow rises, and my heart beats a rhythm of doom.

Did her mom offer something that would pull us apart for good? Why would her mom say one thing to me but something different to Tiana?

The thoughts begin to run away from me, but I silence myself and my mind, waiting for Tiana to respond.

"If I can find a solution for us to be together, I get my position back at the arena, and I can have you. But I have to present it to her at a mock trial where you're my client." I feel the way her fingers fiddle with the band of my sweatpants from where she holds them.

My face contorts in confusion as I pull her away just enough to look at her, blinking in disbelief. "What?"

"I know. It's... strange. But I think it's my mom's way of teaching me a lesson somehow. She said the blowback could have looked bad for the firm if something were to happen. And that's fair, I just..." She sighs as she leans back into me.

So she *is* working on a solution. I knew it. But whatever she needs, I'll be there for her.

"I'm sorry. Tell me how to help," I breathe as I take soothing strokes of her neck.

Tiana looks up at me with a sweet smile, resting her chin against my chest as I hold the back of her head in my palm. My other hand grips tighter on her hip, as if at any moment she could no longer be in my grasp.

"It's alright. I'm just glad you asked me to come see you. I've missed you so much," she says as she wraps her arms around my back. Her eyes close in relaxation as she turns to rest her head back against my chest, inhaling deep breaths. It's as if she's finally allowing herself the freedom to breathe after everything that has happened.

"I don't enjoy being back at my parents. I can't text too much back, in case it may be used against me if things go sideways. I wanted to tell you, but it's been difficult. I just need you to know I'm working on it," she says with a small, hopeful smile.

A soft grin pulls at my lips. "I knew you were, baby. I never doubted you for a minute," I whisper as I lean down to kiss her again.

Her lips send jolt after jolt of lust-laden fire through my blood, and my need rises the longer I hold her against me.

"You look good as fuck with my name on your back, sugar," I murmur against her lips.

She pulls away, nipping at her lip, and her cheeks turn a brighter pink as she shies away from me.

"You think so?" Her eyes glance up at me innocently.

"I know so," I whisper as I kiss her again.

I can't stop... fucking... touching her!

I've craved her in so many ways, and soon my control snaps without warning in her presence.

Moving my hands down to her hips, I pick her up, grasping her ass in my hands as her legs instinctively wrap around my waist.

"Fuck, baby..." I whisper as the weight of her body settles in my arms. Her perfume, her body, all of her. It melds into my body, and I need... her. *Fuck*. I need her. "Can I taste you?" I rasp desperately.

My tongue slides through my lips, teasing hers, and she slips her tongue around mine, grinding her hips against me as a moan leaks from her.

She pulls away, breathlessly watching me. Her eyes bright with excitement as she realizes my question.

"Aren't you already?" she asks.

"No," I respond with a grin as my eyes rove up and down her body.

She grins and her eyes flick to the back corridor, where my bedroom is, before they come back to me.

I take that as my sign and haul ass straight to my room, my arm wrapped around her back as I enter and slam the door behind me.

Placing her feet on the floor, our hands, lips and tongues collide. She desperately tries to rid me of my sweatpants while I press off her leggings and try to pry her boots off with my feet. She beats me to the chase, ridding me of my sweatpants before I can get her undressed.

Before I even have a chance to think, her hands wrap around my aching cock, stroking me up and down with glorious pressure.

"Fuck..." I groan as my head falls back and my steps falter as I sink into her touch. The feel of her hands around me is a familiar reprieve. One I didn't realize I missed so much.

I buck into her grip, my hand coming to stroke a thumb over a hardened nipple through the thick jersey material. Her body moves, her nipple leaving my fingers, and I glance down to see my girl on her knees. A pink tongue awaits me before she slaps it with my cock.

"Fuck Ti," I pant. The feeling of her tongue against me is one I'd pay millions of dollars to have for the rest of my life.

She moans a soft noise before she wraps her lips around the head, slowly swallowing as much of me as she can. Her mouth tightens around my length, and I bring my hands to the back of her head. Gently, I press, forcing more into her mouth, and she complies. She glances up at me as she takes more and more of me down her throat. And I have to lean my head back to look away or I'll fill her throat full of my fuckin' kids.

"There you go, Titi. There's my good girl," I groan as my head tilts forward to look down at her.

Her eyes are bright and devious as they glance up through her long lashes, and she gives a sly quirk of her brow. As if she knows exactly what she's doing to me.

Her tongue slides along the underside of me, and the only thing giving me an ounce of composure is the way the hair in her bun feels under my fingertips. But the way her lips look wrapped around my cock and the way her eyes water the deeper I go in her throat, *that* nearly undoes me. I hear–and feel–the way she suctions around me and I can't take it anymore.

My jaw drops, and my thoughts flay at the way she feels and looks with my cock in her throat.

I quickly pull out of her mouth, my cock webbed and strung with her saliva as it exits her mouth and twitches.

"God damn," I pant as I look down at her with a small quirk to my smile.

Her smile is achingly seductive and playful. With her lower lip, shiny and plump from sucking me, caught in her teeth before her jaw opens again to reveal that pink tongue. She drags it along the underside of me once more, causing my eyes to roll, and I take a heaving breath. Reaching down, I pull her up by her armpits and toss her on the bed.

She weighs next to nothing, so tossing her is easy. Once she lands, she moves herself, scooting closer to the pillows at the top of the bed. I tug off her leggings that are still stuck to her feet, and she leans up to pull the jersey off, but I stop her.

"Nah, I'm fucking you in *my* jersey," I tell her as I kneel on the bed in front of her.

Her brows rise, and she nods. That lip of hers still caught between her teeth as she leans back on the bed, opening her legs for me. Her pussy gleams with her wetness and I fist my cock as

I lean down, burying my face in between her legs. My eyes roll at the taste she covers my tongue with. I've missed it so *fucking* much.

I lick from her entrance, all the way up to her clit, humming into her as I flick my tongue against it. My moans vibrate through her as I continue stroking my cock and with the combination of my grip and the taste of her on my lips, it's enough to drive a man absolutely wild.

Her moans pour through the room, and I glance up to watch her knead her tits through the jersey. With her delicate fingers pinching her nipples as she grinds against my face. I press two fingers into her, letting her relax around them as my pace picks up on my cock.

I want to ram every fucking inch into her and feel her wrapped around me. But I wanna taste this perfect cunt before I take her. She grinds harder, her hips bucking and her body trembling as I work her into a frenzy.

"Gunnar... Gunnar fuck, *please* I need you," she pants desperately.

I take one last suck at her clit before I lean up, licking her wetness from my lips as I keep my pace on her core with my fingers. Though I add my thumb to her clit, making her writhe in frustration against me.

"I know, baby, but I've gotta stretch you first. It's been too long," I whisper when I lean down to kiss her. Adding another finger, I work them in to the third knuckle, pulling all the way out before slowly pressing back in. My thumb speeds up on her clit as my hand tightens around my cock. Her gasps are so fucking tortured, practically begging for me as I get her wetter and wetter with every press of my fingers.

"You want it to feel good, don't you?" I ask with a pant.

She nods, mindlessly, desperately, and my pendant taps at her chin as I hover over her.

"Bite it," I rasp as I continue to prep her.

Her eyes open, lust covering them before her tongue flicks out to grab the stag, biting it between her teeth.

"Use it to ground yourself," I add, watching her lathe her tongue over the bottom, her eyes closing as her hips grind and move in time with my hand. She wants me inside her, but I'm a man of my word.

"You're almost there. Breathe for me," I say as I talk her through it, kissing softly into her lips.

Soon, her lips lose function, and I move my kisses to her throat. Slowly down, I press kisses into the skin of her chest before I let go of my cock, moving my hand up to press the jersey above her tits. I kiss between them, taking one of her nipples into my mouth, and swirling my tongue against it before I nip at it.

Her wetness coats my hand, her body relaxing around my fingers, and I switch hands. Using the one covered in her slick, I wrap it around my cock, stroking from root to tip to feel every bit of her that I can.

I'm not trying to let any of her go to waste.

Pressing my hips deeper in between her legs, I let go of her tit from my mouth with a gentle 'pop' and lean up. I drag my cock through her core, and it moves with ease, considering I already have her all over me. Lingering at her clit, I rub the head against it before I press my cock down to her entrance. Soon, I'm feeling that resistance I've come to know and love from my Tiana.

My head tosses back as I fall deeper into her. My groans clawing from my throat as I just fucking descend into the way she feels.

And my God, the way she *feels*.

Even with the number of nights I've imagined her as my hand, nothing will ever top *her*.

I look down at her, inhaling sharp breaths as I take in the sight below me. Her soft honeyed legs bent, waiting for me, and her tits on display for me as the fabric of my jersey bunches around her neck. I lean back down to pull her nipple back into my mouth to lathe my tongue against it, her moans climbing with every flick.

I push deeper, glancing up at her to see the way her eyes roll, the way her breaths suck in sharply when I stretch her. Her tits press more into my face as her back bows, and her skin meets mine as our bodies collide, pressing closer together. Inch by inch, I keep pushing myself in, watching until the sensation grips me by my throat and my own eyes clench shut.

"Fucking hell, I've missed this pussy so much, baby," I pant as I press into her more.

She can't respond with words, not with the way she moans out for me. Not with the way my cock has wrenched her of tangible thought. I let go of her tits, leaning over her to brace my hand on the mattress beside her head. My other hand comes up to caress her cheek softly as I take slow, controlled strokes in and out of her. With every thrust, my pendant taps her chin or grazes against her chest, a subtle reminder of the way I've chosen her.

I know my girl knows how much I love to control her. But fuck, it's been so long, I want to take my time. I want to show her how much I love her in the best way she understands. I roll into her, grinding and sliding in a smooth rhythm. Her hands come up to grip my shoulders, holding onto anything that will keep her on this earth.

"Gunnar... Gunnar fuck... fuckfuckfuck," she pants.

As her head tilts farther back, she bares more of her neck, and I take soft kisses against it.

"You're doing so good for me, Ti. You stretch so perfectly around my cock," I pant against her skin.

With the way her scent envelops all of me, and the way I grind into her, it sends my heart rate through the roof. The tension between us is suffocating, and I'm enjoying the way she takes my breath away.

"Look at me, baby," I whisper as I pull myself from her skin.

I hold her cheek as I gaze at her. Her clenched eyelids flutter open, and they connect with mine, sending a thrill through me. We exchange breaths, pants, moans in the small space between us.

"You gonna be my good girl and carry my baby for me? You gonna let me fill this pretty little cunt?" I whisper.

She nods, her breath shallow as she feels the way I pull every inch out and slowly roll every inch back in.

"Thatta girl. You're gonna be such a beautiful mother, baby," I tell her.

And fuck if I wish the way I was telling her this was real. I'd put a fucking baby in her right now if I could. Games be damned. I'm trying to make this woman a mother.

Her arms wrap around my neck, her nails digging into the skin on my back as her hips roll against mine. She pulls me flush against her and meets me thrust for thrust.

"That's it, mama, show me who it belongs to," I whisper as I kiss into the crook of her neck. My tongue swirls and laps against the skin there, letting the taste of her flood me, seep into all of me.

"Gunnar..." she moans out. My hand moves down to grip one of her tits, my chest tilting off of her just enough to bare it for me, and I slide a thumb over a nipple.

"I can't wait to see how big these get..." I groan to her. My hand roams down further, pressing into her stomach, where I bulge through it with every thrust. "And fuck, I can't wait to see you swell... I won't be able to keep my fucking hands off of you..." I grit through my teeth.

She holds me in place, pulling me close to her, where her lips meet my ear.

"I had my IUD removed," she whispers. Soft kisses pepper the small space of skin below my ear, and it takes me a second to register what she said against the way her lips feel.

As her words finally make sense, it sends a shock through me, and I pull back, looking down at her in confused concern. My thrusts halt, my cock buried balls deep in her, and I breathe slowly in shock. "

"Are... are you sure?" I ask softly.

A baby... I... Fuck, I *do* want that. And I only really want that with Tiana.

There's no other woman I've felt this way about, no other woman I've wanted to do this with.

No other woman I've wanted to carry my babies.

Only Tiana.

But does *she* really want that? I don't want her to do this just because of our circumstances. I want her to want this. Not just because *I* want it. I'd never put a baby in her she didn't want.

She nods sheepishly, her teeth biting into her lower lip and her eyes rolling as she tries to speak with my cock held inside of her.

"I-I have a career. You..." she pauses to pant. "Y-you have a c-career... Oh fuck," she breathes as her eyes clench shut, taking deep breaths to get herself on track.

I have to admit, it's hot as fuck trying to watch her process her thoughts this way.

"W-We're in good places in our lives. I... I want you forever, Gunnar," she finishes.

My eyes widen, trying to grasp the thing she's *really* asking me to do. "Tiana... what if you can't find a solution? And we aren't able to be together?" I whisper.

"I-I'm finding a solution. I don't let things like this win," she says with a smile. "If you want it, I-I want it. I'm serious."

She's confident. So fucking confident. At least as much as she can be while she tries to handle me and saying these things aloud.

"We don't have to do this right now. Don't feel like you have to do this to keep me. I'll be here for as long as you'll have me, Ti. Baby or not, I'm here for the long haul. I know how important your job is to you."

She smiles at me, writhing her hips and letting a small gasp go. "It's not to keep you. I know you're here for the long haul," she responds.

She licks across my neck, sending shivers through me as she works her hips against me.

"And don't you want to see your pregnant girlfriend at the rink?" Her words are silky, sultry. She tempts me like the sexy little demon she is. Her arms wrap around my neck, pulling me close so I make contact with every fucking inch of her heated, smooth skin.

"Don't you wanna come off the ice after a long day to see me thick with your baby when I come out of my office?"

My eyes roll at her words, my cock twitching inside of her as I let out a tortured groan. She learned how to play my game, and she's using it against me.

Damn well, if I might add.

I can hardly breathe with the words she's telling me. The things she's admitting to me right now. Even with everything that is going on. I'm beside myself, and my mind works through her sexual torture to conjure words.

"I... if it happens, baby... fuck." My words pause as I groan, her pussy clenching around me, and I take the smallest movement in her. "God damn you," I chuckle as I try with all my might to come back on track. "It-it happens. I'm here for whatever happens," I pant.

"Wouldn't it be nice to mark me? Walking around the arena, and everyone knows that the baby I'm carrying is Gunnar Hayze's?" Her hips move under me, grinding and writhing against my length.

She grins, tempting me further with my weakness. I lean down to kiss her, my thrusts picking up again. And the idea of actually doing this... instead of it being a game.

"You little fucking demon," I groan with a grin. But with the truths she admitted, I can't help how deep and hard my thrusts turn.

I pound into her recklessly, claiming every bit of her with a pound deeper than the last. And she meets me with every fucking one, taking every inch of me like it was fucking made for her.

"Tiny little demon. So good at taking my cock. I'll have to give you every fucking bit of it over and over again, won't I?" I whisper in her ear before I nip at her earlobe. "Is this how you want me, Tiana? Deep enough to taste?"

Leaning up, I pull out, looking down at the beautiful fucking mess I've wrought of my girl and her cunt, a grin spreading on my face as I grab her hips, pressing once.

"On your stomach," I say with a grin as I sit back on my feet, watching her.

Her chest heaves, and her grin widens before she complies. She flips over and I lean over her, sliding my wet cock between the top of her ass cheeks as I press a hand into the bed beside her to steady myself. Moving my other hand down, I press my cock back into her, and eer head falls back with a groan of pleasure.

"God, you really are a fucking vision when you've got me

balls deep," I say as I wrap an arm around her waist, hauling her against my chest as I bring her back up with me.

I nip at her neck, kissing it once before I come up to lick against the shell of her ear. "Grab the headboard," I pant as I press kisses into the skin below her ear.

Letting my arm loose from her waist, she leans forward enough to wrap her fingers around the top of the headboard. Her back arches, and I swat one of her ass cheeks as I take a few smooth strokes into her. Her moans fill the air, her head falling back as I pump into her.

I catch sight of my name on her back. Bright white, realizing it'll be *her* name one day. One day sooner than I expected.

I grip the back of her neck, rolling thrust after thrust into her as I bend over her. Gripping one of her hips in my hand, I lean in to bite and lick at her jaw. "Tiana Hayze... That sounds real fucking good, doesn't it, sugar?"

She nods desperately. "Yes...*fuck*. Yes, it does," she moans.

I slide my hand from the back of her neck to the front, gripping under her chin to press her head back and look into her eyes, watching her take every inch of me just like she was made to.

"Are you going to be my perfect little wife, baby?"

She nods again, her eyes meeting mine with a hazy, submissive lust.

"Fuck yes you are..." I grunt as I thrust deeper into her, holding it in before ramming another long stroke in. More and more, I feel that tangle in my spine, the one that grips me by my throat and lays siege to my soul at her will.

"Perfect fucking wife," I say as I thrust hard into her, holding myself in. I press my chest against her back. Shifting my grip, I line her jaw with my thumb and press two of my fingers into her mouth. She swirls her tongue around them as she pants, her eyes rolling, and I use my other hand to wrap around her waist, moving further down to rub at her clit. I pull out slowly, slamming into her again. Her lips close around my fingers, sucking them as a grounding point.

"Perfect fucking pussy," I grunt again.

Her cunt tightens around me, molding me to her as she gets closer and closer.

"My perfect girl, aren't you, sugar?" I groan once more as I feel her contract around me, locking me in place.

Her moans are muffled against my fingers as my cock twitches against her walls, filling her with every bit that I can. She grinds back against me through her orgasm, her pussy clenching and fluttering around me as I release more and more into her. A groan leaving me as I feel how much I've pumped into her.

My arms slump to the sides of her, planting into the bed with my head falling to her back as heaving breaths press in and out of me, and I attempt to regain a hold on my surroundings. I press languished kisses into the white fabric on the jersey, waiting for her to finish before I can move small strokes in and out of her.

Tiana's arms grip for dear life against the headboard, her head slumped as she holds herself up through her heavy breaths. I look up and offer an exasperated chuckle.

Slowly, I reach up to pick each one of her fingers from the tight grasp she has on the headboard and let her fall to the pillows. She crashes into them with nary a strength to her bones, and I let out another soft laugh before I wrap an arm around her waist. I pull her into my chest and roll us onto our sides.

I nuzzle my head into her neck, my cock still pressed in her as I hold her against me.

I may have known it before. Maybe I always have. But if anything, today solidified it for me more than ever.

I'm going to make Tiana Dawn my wife. I never want to be without this fiery little woman ever. Not tomorrow. Not next year. I *always* want to be here in this space with her.

This woman has had me wrapped around her finger since the moment I met her. Whether or not she tried to, she did. And I will cling for dear fucking life.

Her breaths settle, and there is silence for a little bit before she begins to move, as if she's leaving. And I clutch my arm tighter around her, holding her there, before I sigh.

The sound is sadder than I expect it to be. I should have been more careful with this part. I knew this time had to end before she left. But fuck... I can't say goodbye yet.

"Stay a little longer...? Please?" I whisper to her.

She says nothing. She merely cuddles closer to me, wiggling her butt against me as she relaxes in my arms.

CHAPTER THIRTY-FIVE

TIANA

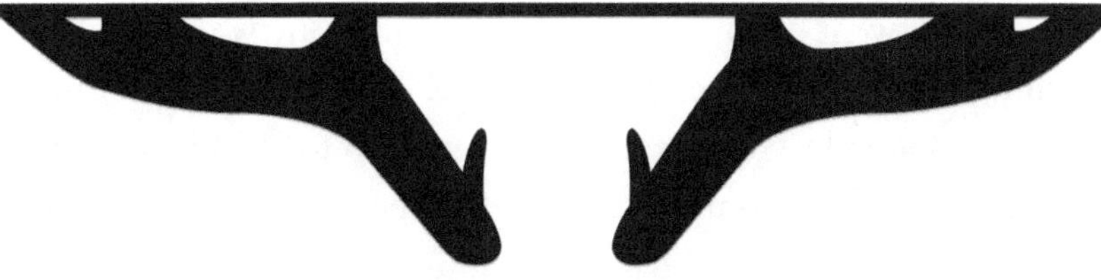

The shop I've chosen in downtown Seattle is rather nice. A pretty new building with a graffiti logo, it's a customs shop that specializes in restorations and other car modifications.

I drive a BMW and I love F1. Yeah, I'm going to know how to pick out a body shop.

Getting the call this morning had my heart racing. Especially after the fear I had when we took the truck from Gunnar's family.

I had no idea how important this truck was to them, and I'm hoping with everything in me, this shop did it justice. At least enough for them to be happy with it.

My hands shook the entire drive here, with my throat threatening to close as the nerves and panic began to filter in.

And when I pull into the parking lot, I take a deep breath as I grip the steering wheel, my eyes roaming over the closed metal garage doors. All I'm doing now is waiting for Adrian to come and help me with this next part.

I have to bring the truck to the Hayze residence to show

them, and then take it to where I plan to store it. Which means he has to follow me and bring me back here to get my vehicle at the end of it all.

As I sit and wait for Adrian to show up, my mind throws flashbacks through my head of yesterday. Possibly to calm my nerves.

Even then, I was scared to meet up with Gunnar. Just because I don't know what things my dad has set up, as far as keeping tabs on us.

But I went because I *needed* to see him. I knew what he was implying with his message. And fuck, I wanted it. I wanted *him*. I wanted to feel his strength; I wanted to feel his comfort. Especially after I found out he had gone to see my mom. I had to make sure he knew I hadn't given up on us.

Yesterday gave me so much more hope for the future. I didn't know in the moment if I had truly planned to tell him I had my IUD removed. And part of its removal was maybe a bit of Gunnar rubbing off on me. Impulsive? One hundred percent.

Do I regret it? No... not even a little. Not even after yesterday.

And as I sit and wait, those flashbacks shift. Into him on top of me. His fingers against my cheek... inside of me. How deep he's always able to go. God and the sound of his voice when he talks me through it all.

I've never had a man so vocal before. Hell, I didn't even know what a breeding kink was before Gunnar. He's opened my eyes to so many things. Things I never knew I liked. Being controlled, being submissive, taking everything he throws at me. Releasing the mental strain of having to control it all. It feels like a freedom I've never experienced.

And I needed it. Especially with so many things out of my control, so many things where I wouldn't know the outcome and the thought of nonsense that could make my world crumble in my head.

Even if it wasn't crumbling around me.

I know the outcome when I'm with Gunnar, and there's a level of safety in that. A level of comfort knowing that no matter where he is, no matter where I am, I'm taken care of. That, at the end of the day, I'm loved and I'm cherished.

And I never knew that I could be loved this way. I had been tossed aside and thought of as too much. Too hard. Too rigid. Too stuck up. I never cared, though. At least, not until Gunnar showed me how well someone could be treated. The rest were just not worth it to care about their opinion.

But I never had to change myself to be with Gunnar, and I've never tried to change Gunnar to be with me. Over time, he just sort of... grew on me. And now there is no way I can let him go.

Case in point, paying tens of thousands of dollars to fix up his truck. And I'd do it over and over again.

I am nervous to see his face when I finally get to show it to him. But I have to wait until we can finally be together again. Whenever that will be.

I'm hoping with everything in me that I'm on the right track as far as my research, because I think I'm getting close to a solution. I have to be, because being without Gunnar is pure torture.

For now, I'm going to pick up the truck, situate it properly, and go back to figuring out what I need to do to get Gunnar and me back together.

I stare at the big metal doors for a long moment before, eventually, the loud sound of a diesel engine pulls me from my thoughts. Looking over my shoulder, I see Adrian's big black truck pulling in beside me. I wave at him through the window, and he nods in hello as he parks. He climbs out of the truck, and I climb out of my car, coming around the front to meet him.

"So what is it you need from me, Ms. Dawn?" he asks in his gruff southern accent as he shoves his hands in his pockets.

"We're going to take the truck to the Hayze house. You'll follow me in your truck. We'll show them the truck, then I'll drive it to the parking garage. You'll follow behind so that you can bring me back here and I can grab my vehicle."

He nods once. "Sounds like a plan to me."

"Great," I murmur.

I take a deep breath as I walk toward the small door beside the large garage ones, pulling it open to be greeted by the smell of engine. Oil, gas, paint. Essentially carcinogens.

But I *love* the smell of a garage.

Approaching the small desk that sits right inside the door, a man in long blue overalls looks over some paperwork. Probably in his late forties, with a long, graying beard and splotches of oil on his face.

"Howdy, you lookin' for somethin'?" he asks as he looks up at us.

"Yes, hi, I brought in a vintage Chevrolet Silverado to be restored, and I heard it was ready for pickup?" I ask with a small smile.

"Blue?" he asks.

"Yes, sir," I respond.

"Yeah, let me bring it around front," he says as he looks at the wall of keys next to the desk.

I nod in response before I look at Adrian. He gives a small nod to the door so I can exit, his arm extending above my head to press the door open from behind me.

Quickly walking to my car, I gather all my things so I can abandon it here until I'm able to come back for it.

Adrian goes to lean against his truck with his hands in his

pockets, and I take a seat against the front of my car, letting the residual heat from the engine warm my butt.

My arms cross over my chest, where I tuck my hands into my armpits. It's much cooler today as fall turns as we slink deeper into the year. But I think there will be a bit more warmth to be had once we're able to show Gunnar's family the truck.

One can hope... at least.

It's silent between Adrian and me for a long while as we wait for the truck to come around, which has my mind moving.

"Why do you have a dually?" I ask as I look over his vehicle. I noticed it before, but I never had the chance to ask.

Because what in God's name does he need with a truck this powerful?

He gives me a small quirk of a smile as he glances at me. "I got horses here, Miss Dawn."

My brow furrows as I look at him. "Horses? For what?"

He nods down to his waist, where a large metal belt buckle sits front and center. As I connect eyes with it, he brings a hand from his pocket to tap on it.

"Barrel racin'. Brought a stallion up from home, bought a little filly when I got here. Plan on breedin' 'em at some point so I can have a little herd of my own." He seems to nod at that. Proudly.

"Barrel racing? I thought you wrangled cattle," I say with a quirk of my brow.

He looks at me before he looks around us, as if he's searching for something and my brow furrows in confusion as I watch him.

"Don't appear to be any cattle here in the city," he says with a small grin.

I roll my eyes. "So you have horses here?"

"Sure do. Fast ones. Out of season, I'm barrel racin'," he says.

"Can't seem to stay still, can you?" I ask.

"No ma'am. When you're raised to wake up at four a.m. every morning to make sure the troughs are watered and the horses are tacked for the day, you don't have much time to stay still," he says with a small shrug.

I fall silent for a long moment, realizing how much of these hockey players' lives exist outside of hockey.

It's... interesting, to be honest. And I also get to learn more about the man dating my sister.

And because of the awkward silence from me retreating to my thoughts, the next words spill out of me.

"Are you fucking my sister?"

Adrian seems startled by my question, looking at me as if I've grown two heads. "A gentleman doesn't kiss and tell, Miss Dawn."

I groan with a roll of my eyes. "Charlotte will tell me," I grumble.

He crosses his arms over his chest with a chuckle. "I imagine she would. But again. A gentleman doesn't kiss and tell."

My brow furrows as I look at him. "Do you and Gunnar share gentleman tips or something? Where is this 'properness for ladies' textbook you all are reading?"

His lip quirks at the edge in a half-smirk. "Most men don't really have the gall nor gumption to treat a lady proper. It doesn't take much. Respect her space, make her smile, keep a good roof over her head and her belly full. In all the way she wants." He punctuates the last part with a small tip of his hat and a smile.

I roll my eyes. "What if I can pay for my own room and

board? Does this impede your caveman brain from 'treating a lady proper?'"

Adrian laughs, his arms jumping where he holds them against his chest as he shakes his head. "Miss Dawn, it appears you really haven't met a proper man before, have you?"

I look at him in confusion. "What is that supposed to mean?"

"A real man is not gonna be intimidated by the fact his lady keeps the roof over his head. He's gonna cheer her on. He's not gonna be hurt by you needing your space. He's not gonna be hurt by boundaries. Hell, a proper person wouldn't. But a man needs to know where the line is with his lady if he's going to keep her. And if that line is that she needs to be the one to put the roof over their heads, then so be it. If she needs to be the breadwinner, he'll eat the bread. If she needs anything, he'll provide it. Even if it isn't in monetary value."

My jaw gapes as I look at him, trying to figure out where all of this was hiding.

Adrian doesn't say much. And this is probably the most I've heard him talk... ever, I think. And with Adrian's words, I realize then who Gunnar is. Who he *really* is.

A real man. He comes off childish, a little impulsive. But at the end of the day, he is a man. Not a man who claims he's a man because he feels as if he's the big guy on campus.

He's a real man.

He's not intimidated by my job. He's not threatened by the fact I drive him around. He doesn't care if I make more money than him, even if I don't.

Aside from following me around in the beginning, he's never... done anything to make me feel as if I wasn't safe with him. Outside of the bedroom, he knows I'm in charge. I call the shots, and he's fine with letting the world know that he's on my leash. But in private, when the world falls away, and it's just us, he makes it known that he's caring for me at the end of it all. That no matter what, I'm safe with him.

And with the realization of it all, my heart aches. That we're apart for this time.

I never thought I would love a man this way. Let alone a hockey player.

Gunnar, however... he changed everything. With that thought becoming even more tangible when the old engine roars as it comes from the back of the body shop.

I step forward, waiting for the vehicle to come to a stop, and for the man to come out before I approach entirely.

As he cuts the engine off, he climbs out and tosses the keys to me.

"Here you are, little lady. You paid and did all the paperwork, so you're good to go," he says with a grin.

Catching the keys, I clutch them tight in my palm as I look over the truck. The exterior is completely redone, with the rust and bits of wear taken care of. I step closer, opening the driver's side door and leaning in to get a better look at the interior. It's been brought back to life. The seats have been reupholstered with new leather, the dashboard redone, and everything shines and gleams as if it just popped off the showroom floor.

I shut the driver's door, walking around the exterior to make sure all the pieces I pointed out originally were taken care of. I even had them fix up the bed to be a bit more durable.

The man pops the hood, and I come around to the front to check out the engine. A shiny brand-new V8 engine is inside, with chrome-plated pipes and fittings. My heart beats wildly in my chest as I look over the completely redone engine, and I almost bite my lip in glee.

There is something about all chrome on an engine block that gets my heart racing.

Gunnar is going to love this, and I can't wait to bring him

this kind of joy. The fear feels like a memory as my focus shifts to how well this restoration went. Taking a few more steps around the truck, I see the brand-new tires and wheels I picked out. I didn't want to go with anything ostentatious. This isn't "Pimp my Ride", I just needed to get it looking back to how it was before. So I tried to choose something that would closely match the original.

All of it looks straight out of a magazine, and my heart continues to swell with emotion. Until it bursts. I look at the man with a glassy smile, and I throw my arms around him in a hug. He freezes in his spot before he presses one light tap on my back in return.

"I'm so sorry. You just have no idea how much this means to me," I tell him in a cracked voice as I pull away and wipe an escaped tear from my eye.

The man laughs. "It's alright. It's not the first time that has happened."

I nod with a small sniffle, and he smiles as he pushes his hands in his pockets.

"I have to leave my car here while I take this back to where it belongs. Am I able to do that?" I ask.

He nods. "Yeah, absolutely. I'll make sure no one touches it while you're gone."

"Thanks," I say with a soft sigh.

As the man closes the hood, he gives me another nod and retreats into the building.

I turn to Adrian with a smile, to see him admiring the truck from a distance.

"They did a great job on it," he remarks.

"You think Gunnar is going to like it?" I ask.

He nods with a smile. "I don't think he'll be able to love anything more."

Something about the way he says that makes me feel a lot

better about this situation. And with it, I get a small air of confidence as I take one last look at the truck.

I turn my head, nodding softly at him with a small smile. "Ready?"

"Lead the way, Miss Dawn," he says.

Once we make it back to the Hayze Residence, I take a deep breath. It clicks now that I'm bringing this vehicle to his family to see. The truck that Gunnar's mom, his brothers, and Gunnar grew up in. The sight of the truck helped push the fear away. But now that I'm here in front of their house, my nerves come back in full force. They roll through my limbs, all the way to my fingers.

What if they didn't do it properly, and it doesn't look like it used to? What if I ruined this precious family heirloom, and there's no way they would ever accept me into their family? I don't know what I would do if his family didn't like me. Gunnar's family means everything to him.

Sure, it looks good to me, but that doesn't mean they'll feel the same way. I didn't grow up in this truck like the family did.

My thoughts have run into the distance, carrying me on its back. Into a future of what feels like doom and peril. Until a soft knock on the window startles me, and I turn to see Adrian looking at me with a confused expression.

I take a few gasping breaths through my initial spook, and the anxiety compounds into one. My heart beats so hard and fast in my chest that nausea creeps in with it, rising to the back of my throat.

Adrian opens the door for me, furrowing his brow. "Everything alright?"

I take a deep breath, nodding. "You don't happen to have any water, by chance, do you?" I ask quietly.

My eyes disconnect from him, locking onto the front door of their house. Which has now become the subject of my fear, in favor of fearing his family. Anything to keep at least some thoughts to a minimum.

I hear the thick clack of his cowboy boots against the driveway as he retreats to his truck. I was so in my head; I didn't even hear his roaring diesel engine as he approached.

Inhaling a huge gulp of air, I push myself out of the truck and take a few jumps up and down. I try to rid myself of the nerves as I shake out my arms and legs. Some of the frazzled emotions slowly disperse as I try with every ounce of power I have to force them out.

Adrian comes back over to me with a bottle of water and hands it to me.

I nod in thanks as I take it and quickly sip some to calm my nerves. "Sorry," I murmur as I continue staring off at the front door.

"No need to be sorry. A good truck is precious. But you did well, Miss Dawn," he says.

"Are you sure?" I whisper.

I can't help the visions of them yelling at me that go through my head.

But Adrian's voice is like a shot of whiskey. It calms my nerves just enough.

"I couldn't be more sure. I've seen a lot of trucks in my life. Old and new. I don't think they could have done any better on an old square body like that."

I look at him skeptically, and he gives me a small smile.

"How did you know what was wrong?" I ask softly.

"Well, when I rolled up, you were white knuckling the steering wheel and gazing out at nothing. I reckoned you were scared to show them. Considering how scared you were to talk to his mother the first time," he says with a shrug.

I sigh softly, groaning at the way these damn players can read me. I need to make a note to myself that I need to be more mysterious, because the way these men can read me is not fair.

"Okay... I think I'm ready. But I need you to do the talking. I don't know if I can do it without gagging," I murmur.

He nods. "Understood, Miss Dawn."

I lead the way up the steps to their house, taking another deep breath before I knock on the front door.

A few moments pass, and a teenager answers the door. He's damn near as tall as Adrian and is almost the spitting image of Gunnar. He's just not as big and bulky as him. Maybe Gunnar, if he wasn't a pro hockey player. But he's holding a massive bowl of cereal.

"Yoho, Adrian! What's up, man?" the kid says as he sticks the spoon in his hand into his mouth to give Adrian a dap.

My brows furrow in confusion as I watch them, following every movement they make, damn near in shock.

Adrian goes along with it, smiling as he returns it, and the two bring the dap into their chests to slap each other on the back before pulling apart.

"Good to see you, Brooks. Your mother home? Or father?" he asks.

He slips the spoon from his mouth with a nod. "Oh yeah, they're in the living room, one sec," he says before he closes the door.

I take a deep breath, letting some of the panic reside.

"You know his brothers?" I ask.

"I'm part of the reason Gunnar is on the team. He's a year or so younger than me, but we played D1 together for a time. Great kid. Even greater man," Adrian says as he glances at me with a small smile.

My brow furrows. I didn't know they knew each other before the Stags. I guess that makes sense, considering the way they seem to think.

"How long have you two known each other?" I ask.

"A bit. We hung out more in college, but once I made pros, things got a little different. I always knew I'd work him in one day. He deserved it. He worked harder than anyone else on that rink, and he never took anyone's bullying," he says with a nod.

"You were part of how he got to the Stags?" I ask.

I still sort of remember when Adrian was drafted. It was a few years back. But it was a huge deal, considering.

"When he was up for the draft, I was in Bubbles' ear, telling him to grab Gunnar before anyone else could. I knew how he worked, and I knew how we worked together. It would be good for the team no matter how it was looked at." Adrian shrugs.

My brows jump in surprise as my head tilts. "Fair enough," I murmur.

Soon, the door opens again, with Gunnar's mom front and center. Gunnar's dad stands behind her.

Or I suppose looms would be a better word.

If I thought Gunnar was big, his father is a behemoth. I can see where these boys get their size from.

Part of me sweats at the thought. Am I going to have to carry one of these big ass babies myself?

Christ, what have I done?

Focus, damn you. Truck now. Babies later.

My head cranes to look up at him, resisting the urge to look scared. Though I imagine at this vantage point, I probably do.

"Adrian! Has the truck come back?" Gunnar's mom asks with a hopeful smile. Her voice holds so much excitement, though there is a hint of sadness in it. She clasps her hands in front of her chest with a sparkle of childlike wonder in her eyes as she asks the question.

Soon, my heart flutters with the deed I've done.

Fear. Happiness. *Excitement*. Grateful to be in a position in life where I can do this for them.

Adrian nods once before he steps to the side. I follow his lead, stepping aside to give them all a wide berth for a better view of the truck.

Gunnar's mother gasps, her eyes glassing over as she brings her hands over her mouth. She quickly wraps her fuzzy robe tighter around her body as she goes down the front steps and straight to the truck. Her sobs echo through the silent suburb as she throws her arms around the hood and places her forehead against it. Her shoulders shake, and the rest of the Hayze men follow. Walking down the steps, they come up to surround Gunnar's mom. Gunnar's dad places an arm around her shoulders, comforting her as the brothers take the other side of her, rubbing her back and looking over the truck.

My chest tightens, with my heart squeezing in pain as I watch. My emotions run higher, as if feeling the family's, and a tear rolls down my cheek as I zone out on the scene before me.

"The bigger one is Gretz. The smaller one is Brooks," Adrian says in a low voice. His smoky bourbon smell telling me he's leaned closer.

My only response is to nod as I continue to watch the family.

His mother continues to sob against the hood of the truck. Her fingers clutch the hood with all its might, as if hoping it could repair some part of her that had broken over it.

Since this was her dad's truck, it would make sense that this would hold so much meaning to her. I love my dad. Even though he triggered the fallout for Gunnar and me, I would still be devastated to lose him.

More tears pool in my eyes until they spill over, running down my face in a gentle river. Of sympathy, of happiness that I could do this for them.

Adrian continues, "Their grandaddy was a big part of their family. He died before Gunnar made it to the pros. Went to all of his college games, was always the loudest in the stands. After every game, Gunnar didn't look for Coach. Didn't look for his daddy or his momma. He went straight for his grandpa. When he died, he promised his grandaddy would be there, one way or another. This truck was his one way."

My heart clenches tighter, my breaths turning shaky as I listen. I stifle the small sob that threatens to break in my throat.

"Buck. Buck Davis. Great hockey player back in the day," Adrian whispers.

I feel as if I'd heard that name once upon a time. Perhaps in passing, while growing up.

But soon, everything begins to make sense. The giant deer antlers on his chest, the stag pendant he wears.

"The Stags..." I murmur.

"That's right," Adrian responds.

"He... he did all of this for his grandpa?" I ask. Though my voice comes out softer than I expected.

"Always has. He said he gave them everything. And so he made sure to keep his memory and contribution alive for as long as he could. When he was drafted, yeah, I had a small hand in that. But I don't think Gunnar would have accepted a pick from any other team. He's always had The Stags on his top. All he ever talked about in college. So, I know it hurt him for that truck to stop working, but he pushed on. You helped, I know that," he says softly.

His hand grips my shoulder, rocking me in comfort. "You did a real good thing, Miss Dawn. Not only for Gunnar, but for his family."

I nod softly as I wipe the river of tears from my face, sniffling deeply.

"Yep... Yep, I guess I did," I say to tamp down the menagerie of emotions flooding through me.

I shake my head of the thoughts, trying to steel my spine as the family turns around to walk back in our direction.

The mom's face is red and puffy, her chest taking sharp, ragged breaths as she wipes tears away and approaches Adrian. She wraps her arms around him to hug him tightly, and he returns it.

I am sincerely glad this is done in the name of the Stags because I don't think I could emotionally handle a hug from his mom right now. I don't break down often, but I imagine right now would be one of those times.

"Thank you... Thank you so much, Adrian," I hear her murmur against him.

He pats her back a few times. "All in a day's work, Mrs. Hayze," he says softly.

She wears a mask of grief and happiness all at once, and I can't imagine what she may be feeling. Especially if she grew up in this truck herself.

"Where will you take it?" she asks as she wraps her hands around herself, stroking her arms softly. Her gaze returns to the truck, watching it for a moment longer before she looks back up at Adrian.

"The plan is to unveil it to him in a few weeks. We're going to keep it stored under a cover in the parking garage of his complex. I don't think he'll realize it's there until we bring him to it."

She nods softly, taking another deep breath as she wipes a stray tear away. "The boys will help load up the tarp. Thank you both, once again," she says before she locks eyes with me.

Her smile is sincere, and I can see how much this restoration meant to her. And I can see the thanks in her eyes before she turns away to head back inside with soft sniffles.

The two boys smile at us before they lead us to the garage. They rifle through the inside after they get the doors open, looking for the tarp used to cover it.

Eventually, they find it and fold it before they hand it to us, supplying us with some bungee cords before they send us on our way.

We throw the tarp and bungee cords into the back seat of Adrian's truck before I lead us out of their driveway to my apartment complex.

On the way to the complex, Adrian calls me. He said he called Gunnar to make sure he was hanging out inside the complex and not coming or going.

I still make sure to park the truck in a place Gunnar never goes near. The parking structure is enormous, so there are a lot of places he'd never venture around. And even if he did, we're covering it with the tarp.

As the bar for the structure lifts and I mosey into the garage, a familiar pang settles in my stomach.

My actual home is here. I'm still paying for my lease, even if I don't live here right now, and it brings me back to those days after work with Gunnar.

Where we went to work and came home together. The mornings together that were calm, quiet. The way he lowered his voice because he knew I didn't like too much noise that early. Small questions, slow movements. The way he just *knew* me, how I was, and he worked with it. He went with it.

After work, where we talk to each other about our day, the feeling of ending the day with him.

And I miss it so fucking much.

But I know that soon I'll be able to have it back, and I truly can't wait until I do.

When I park the truck, I get out, with Adrian merely parking in front of it.

He jumps out of his truck and goes to grab the tarp and bungee cords, handing them to me as he unfolds the tarp. Throwing it over the truck, I watch as it slowly becomes hidden in this little corner of the parking garage.

He offers a hand to me, and one by one, I hand him a bungee cord. Pinning the tarp in place all around before he steps back to check his handiwork.

Adrian looks to me with a ready nod, and I return it before I climb–quite literally, his truck has a massive lift on it–into the passenger seat of his truck.

I put on my seat belt and take one last look at the truck before Adrian drives off, and he takes me back to my car in silence.

CHAPTER THIRTY-SIX

GUNNAR

Tonight is a home game.

My mind is whirling with a number of different emotions.

Excitement for the game. Spurred only by the fact I got to see Tiana. A bit of relief because she told me she was working on things behind the scenes and that everything wasn't for naught.

Of course, there's some horniness there because I keep playing that day over and over in my head.

Overall, I missed *her*. And that surely didn't stop when she had left a few hours later.

But it gave me a bit more hope for us and our future. Especially since she confirmed what I had already known.

Granted, I have no idea what Mrs. Tamisha's angle is with this mock trial. It seems like a lot of backwards fuckery for no reason. But as long as it ends with Tiana as my wife, I don't give a shit.

I'll play whatever game they want me to play, and I'll be a good boy for it. I know I can be.

The thoughts fade away as the Seattle Stags' entrance song plays, and one by one, they announce each of us.

The last few games I've played were honestly... uh... dismal.

But with the prospect of Tiana and me finally being able to be together, there's a much harder push in my skates today. One that is fueled purely by the fact I'm a day, an hour, a minute, a second closer to having my girl permanently in my arms.

It shows even more when I speed out onto the rink and the crowd cheers as our teams circle the rink with the swirling spotlights.

I skate past a few of my teammates, bumping mitts with them as the rush of the game seeps into me the way it used to. The way it felt when Tiana was just down the hall.

Is it silly? Maybe.

But I'm a romantic, I think, at heart.

At least for Tiana.

Soon, the lights come back on, and the lot of us stretch on the ice as we prep for the game. The announcements are going over the loudspeaker, and the cheers of fans are drowning everything out.

And just once, I look out at the crowd.

I look for those brown ringlets with the golden streaks. The ones that make my heart pound and my breath catch.

When I see them. Right behind the box. Right behind *our* box.

She's wearing the jersey I gave her, which she can easily write off as a jersey she bought or got from somewhere.

But my heart nearly implodes at the sight.

We lock eyes, and a smile rises against my cheeks. One that threatens to break my face. My chest swells with the pride of seeing her here, repping my name on her back. And I don't give a shit about the consequences when I blow a kiss to her, for everyone to see. Not when she's here and so close to the rink with the most hopeful look in her eyes.

I watch as she smiles, shying away as her hand comes up to grasp the air, as if she's catching what I tossed her way.

I'm done hiding. We're getting it squared away. We're figuring it out. I can show my girl I love her. At least just this once.

She deserves that.

Especially if she came out to this game to show me she loves me.

The buzzer goes off, and I turn my attention to the center rink, watching as Adrian faces off with the other captain to shake hands and wait for the puck drop.

From there, the stands fade away. My adrenaline pumps, my heart throbbing against the tunnel vision, narrowing my line of sight. I feel a rush of excitement I haven't felt in several games. The clarity of the rink comes into focus as I lean over against my stick, watching the puck.

Puck drop is always the fun part. The start of the game. The lead foot on a pedal, just waiting to go from zero to sixty.

Until all at once, it does.

As if my body is attuned to the sight and sound of the puck, I move. Without thought, without consequence. Hard glides against the ice, watching as Adrian secures the puck, slapping it to our left wing.

Crowder secures it, beelining for the other team's side before he's checked and flounders on the ice. Their captain nabs it to press back toward our side.

I race for their captain, trying to get the puck from him before Leroy, our other defender, reaches him first. A hip check into their captain sends him off course, and the puck is back in our possession, moving back to the other team's goal.

Leroy passes it to Banks as one of the opposing players makes for him. With Leroy ducking out of his trajectory.

Banks is able to secure it, volleying it back and forth as he looks for his next pass. While he's looking around the ice, another player comes around back, swiping it out from under him.

Now it's my turn. I race for the opponent, damn near running on the ice before I hit him with a hard shoulder check. His body flips over mine as I barrel through him. All the while, I swipe the puck from him. My eyes roam the rink, trying to spot the closest player.

Leroy is close, so I slap it straight for him when I connect eyes. One of their defenders attempts to check me, but they don't know I'm riding on a high and meet him where he is. Which causes him to fall like a sack of potatoes onto the ice.

When I bring my attention back to the puck, Leroy has it as another player comes straight for him.

He passes the puck to Adrian across the rink. And while Leroy distracts the other players, Adrian slaps it straight for their goal.

Their tendy must not be on his game today because Banks makes it easy, and the buzzer fills the stadium. Along with the sounds of cowbells and cheering Stag's fans.

"WOOOOOOO!" Banks glides along the ice, one foot in front of the other, as he grips his hands by his side in pride.

"Good fucking shit, Banks!!" I call to him, and he gives me his gentlemanly nod with a wide grin.

I shake my head before we start up again. The puck is moving, and the rest of us are following it.

We won, and I hit the winning goal.

It's a spectacular feeling. The rush of it all. Hell, the *enjoyment* of it all.

I forgot how good it felt to be clobbered by the weight of your team right as the buzzer blares, and I'm the one who got us there. My hair is ruffled over and over again by wet and icy mitts as we walk off the rink to head back to the locker room.

I slump in front of my cubby, exhausted, with a wide grin on my face. There is a difference in this win. A palpable difference that I feel throughout my entire body.

And I know it's because Tiana was there. Hell, I may have even won it for her. Her presence was so much more needed than I expected it to be. I throw my helmet into the bottom of my cubby before I remove my jersey, slowly working off my chest protector and shoulder pads, neck guard and elbow pads to throw in my cubby. My skin is sweaty from the game and the melting ice in the locker room, so I use my jersey to wipe the residual sweat from my face.

I come down from the high slowly, crossing my arms over my chest as I lean my head back and take deep breaths to settle the excitement.

Bubbles soon comes in, his voice loud against his deafening claps.

"Absolutely fuckin' beautiful work out there," he starts. "You guys are looking real nice for the end of the season, and I can see you guys taking the Cup this year. Not that we didn't last year, but I can see us holding that bastard again if you guys keep playing like this. Hayze, just a thing of beauty, great work, bud," he says.

I smile at him and nod in thanks, saluting him with two fingers as I keep my eyes closed, still trying to come back to center.

This part is some of what I do to bring myself down. I like

to sit and breathe through the end of the game while I listen to Coach go over his congratulations.

I dip my chin to swipe up my chain in my teeth, tilting my head side to side and shaking out my arms before I open my eyes. Removing my gear, unlacing my skates, and removing what I can. When I feel it. *Her.*

Tiana.

My head shoots up, gazing at the door to see my girl there. A nervous smile and soft blush on her face as she walks into the room with Charlotte. Of course, Charlotte titters with excitement. But as always, the only one in the room that really matters to me is Tiana.

I keep my composure, my tongue sliding back and forth along the chain as I glance up at her. With my teeth tightening as I grin against it.

She glances back with a playful smirk as she pretends not to notice me, her eyes moving back to her dad to listen to the end of his speech.

Why is she in here? Who knows, maybe she can use the excuse of being the Coach's daughter and is just accompanying him.

Soon, Bubbles quits speaking, and the girls follow him out. Not before I send a small air kiss Tiana's way.

She returns it with a playful eye roll, catching it as she leaves.

My eagerness gets the best of me, and my efforts to get undressed increase. I try to place all my gear back in my cubby as quickly as I can before showering so I can meet Tiana outside.

I know she's waiting for me by the door. I can just feel it.

Throwing my backpack over my shoulder, I ruffle my wet hair and shake any of the excess water out of it as I head straight out of the locker room. My heart continues racing as I loop through the tunnels to the exit doors.

I make the turn toward the doors, past Tiana's office, where a smile crests my lips at the sight.

She'll be in there soon.

And as I take the last hallway to the doors, there she is, scrolling through her phone.

I watch her from a distance, taking in this candid moment of her. The way my name looks on her back in this fucking arena. The way she nibbles on the side of her finger as she scrolls through her phone. Her foot, crossed one over the other as she stands in wait.

Over and over as I watch her, I'm reminded of how this fiery lawyer captured me by the balls. Even if she didn't mean to.

As if she can sense me, her head shoots up, causing her curls to whirl and bounce as she looks around. Her eyes and face soften in a lovesick, adoring look as her gaze lands on me.

I contain the urge to run for her. To scoop her into my arms and hug her tight. It's so fucking hard, but I take slow steps toward her, gripping the straps on my backpack for dear life as I approach her.

Tiana smiles at me, hope twinkling in her eyes.

Fuck, the way I want to grab her chin. The way I want to kiss those perfect lips of hers. This is a fresh torture I didn't know I could endure.

"Thing of beauty out there, Hayze," she says softly. There is a playfulness in her tone, in her face. As if I've rubbed off on her enough for her to speak my language.

I smile at her. "Yeah, you were," I murmur back.

Blush crawls against her cheeks. Those freckles of hers highlighted as a hint of steam collects at the bottom of her glasses.

Her hands clasp her phone in front of her, and she twists back and forth nervously. "So... you need to be at my dad's this Sunday," she says.

My brow furrows as I watch her.

"The mock trial," she reminds me.

My eyes widen, and I feel my breath lighten.

Fuck... Fuck it's *happening.* She's figured it out.

I take a deep breath, nodding softly. "Do... I need to wear anything specific?" I ask cautiously.

Tiana laughs, and the sound rings through every bit of my soul, easing a bit of my nerves over all of this.

"No, no, just wear whatever you'd like. It's just at the house," she responds.

My body relaxes more, allowing a small smile to stretch my lips as I step closer into her space. I can't touch her, I can't hug her. But fuck, I'm going to get as close as I can without breaching rules.

"Who is the judge?" I ask.

Tiana sighs with an amused smile. "Charlotte."

I grin at her, nodding in response. "This is going to be fun," I say.

She rolls her eyes playfully before she shakes her head. Her gaze meets the doors beside us before it comes back to mine.

"Walk me to my car?" she asks.

My heart flutters in my chest, my blood running through me in electrified currents.

"I'd love nothing more, sugar," I whisper.

CHAPTER THIRTY-SEVEN

TIANA

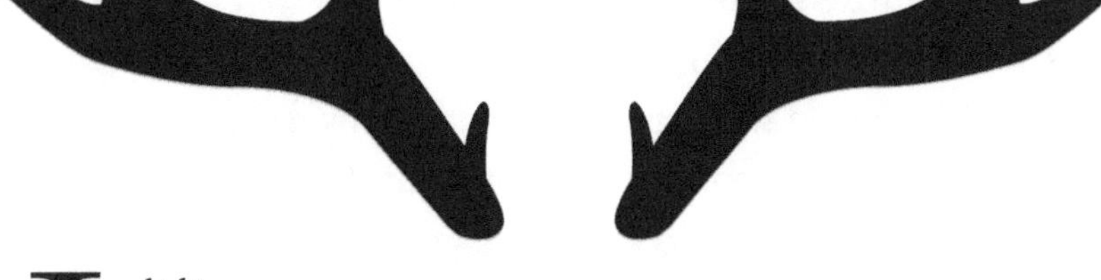

I *did* it.

I figured it all out.

That's why I went to the game on Friday. I needed to tell Gunnar. I was so close to the end that it would be fine for me to be seen there.

After I had figured out my plan, I sat with my parents during dinner one night and told them I'd figured it out, that I was ready for the mock trial. I remember the slightly surprised looks on their faces as they realized how fast I had come to the solution.

It was all so simple; I don't know why I didn't think of it sooner. But I remember the rush of giddiness I felt to look down at my research and look my plan in the eye.

That was after I was done being mad at myself for being so dumb and not seeing it before hand.

I fear I could have saved myself a large amount of strife and heartache.

But I suppose this is a learning experience. At least I got to see what it would feel like to be without Gunnar.

Hell. It was hell.

And now; I pace in the foyer, waiting for Gunnar to arrive.

I need to provide counsel to him before this, so he knows what I need from him. Gunnar is a loose cannon. That much is sure.

And with the prospect of representing a loose cannon, he has the potential to say incriminating things, unraveling the carefully laid plans before me. I worry he may not take this seriously, because it's just a little fake trial in the house.

But I have to give this the best shot that we can. I have to take this seriously, even if he doesn't.

Chewing on the edges of my fingers, my feet pad back and forth against the floor nervously as I wait. Along with my fuzzy socks, I'm wearing his jersey and a pair of black leggings.

Eventually, my steps turn into slides, as I find the sliding helps relieve some of the nervous energy coursing through me.

I feel as if I've been running over my plan repeatedly with no reprieve since I figured out the solution. But I have to. My relationship, and technically my job, rely on this.

I'll lose my cushy little office in the arena, where no one bothers me, and I already know all my clients. If I'm placed back at the firm, not only do I get the case of whoever they throw at me, but I lose my little cave.

And god *damnit*, I really like my little cave!

I lose myself in my pacing, nibbling between the sides of my fingers and my lips. Until the knock comes and my steps freeze, holding me in place as my heart pounds in my chest like a war drum.

It's showtime... fuck *me*, it's showtime.

I take a deep breath, staring at the door as if it's the problem here. Squaring my shoulders, I approach the door, pulling it open to see Gunnar. He's proud, and with a small hint of relief on his face at the sight of me. A softening of his hazel eyes and an adoring gaze held within them.

I look him over, only to find that we apparently had the same idea today. He wears black sweatpants and, of course, one of his jerseys. However, it obviously fits him miles better than it fits me.

A smile tugs at my face as I jump up to wrap my arms and legs tightly around him in a crushing hug. That piney forest scent floods my soul, it calms it, and for the first time since I last saw him, I feel safe.

As if all the worries I had about my job and our relationship have melted away. Warmed enough to melt only because his presence deemed it.

And I like it that way.

When I saw him in the locker room after the game yesterday, I wanted nothing more than to sit on his lap and tell him what a good game he had. How much I missed him, and that I loved watching him play. As long as I've been in the hockey world, I've never cared about the game. Gave even less of a fuck about the players until I needed to represent them.

Gunnar changed every bit of that. At least when it comes to him. I'll go to all the games he wants me to.

His muscular arms wrap around my back, holding me tight to his body while his chest expands in a deep inhale as he buries his face in the crook of my neck. Slowly, he carries me into the house, his hands moving to grip tight on my ass. His foot flicks behind him to close the door, and I loosen my legs from his hips to come back to the floor.

I look up at his handsome face, smiling so wide I'm worried my cheeks will break. Wrapping my hands around his jaw, I pull him in for a kiss, tilting my head and angling myself to taste all of him. He makes a startled noise before his hands come to grab softly at my hips, and he pulls me into him. I've missed the feeling of his body against mine. I've also missed the way his cock hardens against me like this.

He releases a low groan between us as he loses himself and grinds against me. Coming back to the present, I quickly pull away, inhaling a deep breath as I bite my lip.

"Enough of that," I murmur as I glance down at the large bulge in his sweatpants. Heat floods my body at the sight, and I try to inhale another deep breath to push the lust away.

"I'm sorry, sugar. I really missed you," he whispers as he brings a hand up to stroke a thumb across my cheek. His other hand grips my wrist, pressing my hand to the bulge. My fingers flare against his rigid length through the fabric, indulging the moment. Getting a feel of how hard he is, I make a tortured noise, wishing that *this* is what he was here for.

Unfortunately, that's *not* what he's here for.

I preen into his touch and grind the heel of my palm against him before I shove out of his grasp.

"Okay, enough games! We have to focus here," I tell him. Though, I suppose at this point it's more for myself than him, because I'm three seconds from jumping him if he keeps this up.

He looks down at me with a playful grin and nods once. He shoves his hands into his pockets. Probably in an attempt to keep them off of me.

"Follow my lead, don't say anything horrifically incriminating, and please, for the love of God, let me do all the talking unless they directly ask questions," I say sternly.

A glimmer shines in his eyes as he watches me. His lip catches in his teeth as he looks over me with a heated gaze.

"This is really sexy," he whispers as he steps closer to me.

"Gunnar!" I groan as I toss my head back.

"Sorry! I'm just so used to telling you what to do, I forgot how hot it is to be ordered around by you," he says with a grin. His hand attempts to grab my waist, and I swat it away again.

"Focus, damn you!" I groan.

He straightens, rising to his full height, and puffing out his chest as he gives me a salute. "Yes, ma'am!"

I groan as I pinch between my eyebrows. "We are so fucked," I sigh.

Gunnar laughs before he presses a massive hand to the top of my head, ruffling my hair. "Calm down, we've got this in the bag," he says as he walks past me to find the others.

"Somehow, I do not believe that," I groan as I follow him.

Gunnar and I have to spend time in the kitchen before we're called to the living room.

For what? Don't know.

I have no idea what my parents' plans are. They merely said I had to wait for Gunnar to get here, and then wait for them to call us back.

Though I can't complain, as it gives me more time to look over some of the evidence I brought with me. But when they finally call us in, and I take a look at what they've done to the space, I realize that I severely miscalculated my mother's intent with all of this.

The living room, usually a large chamber with a fireplace on the far wall and some couches in it, has now been stripped of its seating. Only to be replaced with three separate tables.

For some godforsaken reason, one desk is large, with an armchair directly beside it, taking space in front of the fireplace. Two smaller tables are in front of the larger desk. With the one on the left having two empty chairs, and the other with both of my parents sitting, waiting for us.

Freezing within the arched threshold of the room, my brow furrows as my eyes volley around the room, trying desperately to understand what the fuck this is.

In wholehearted honesty, I have no idea what I was expecting as far as the environment when it came to this mock trial. I don't think I pictured it. I was just hoping to plead my case.

Unfortunately for me, it seems my mother is upping the ante. In return, my annoyance grows.

Gunnar goes to sit in one chair at the empty desk, and I pass behind him to sit beside him, placing my small folder down. I glance at my mother, who has a smirk pulling at the corner of her mouth.

As if things couldn't get any worse, Adrian walks in from the archway we just came from, coming up to stand beside the desk at the front. He's wearing... a police uniform? But it's obviously a costume.

I look at him in confusion before I glance at Gunnar, and he shrugs.

"All rise! For the honorable Judge Charlotte!" he calls to us.

My mind whirls with this infernal situation. This feels like one giant prank at this point, and I'm struggling to hold it together internally, but I rise anyway. Gunnar and my parents do the same, just as Charlotte—God bless her soul—comes in wearing a black fluffy robe and an abhorrent white judge's wig. It looks so atrocious that you could have sworn she won it from a rabid critter in an alley fight.

"Jesus Christ," I grumble as I run my hands over my face.

"You may all be seated," Charlotte says with a slightly more airy tone to her voice, as she takes a seat on top of the table.

My eyes float to the top of my head in disbelief. "You're not even going to sit in a chair?" I ask.

"The table is right here. Why do I need a chair?" she asks with a confused tilt of her head.

I bring my hands up to rub my temples, closing my eyes and taking a deep breath before I sit back down in my chair. Everyone else follows suit.

Adrian approaches the table with some papers, handing them to Charlotte. She takes them, tapping them on the table before blowing Adrian a kiss.

My eyes roll, and I swear I can feel a migraine forming behind them.

Charlotte looks over the papers, her gaze running along whatever the fuck is on them.

"Mommy, you are here as the prosecutor?" she asks as she looks up at our mother.

For some reason, our mother is in a pantsuit, as if this is as real as a court case to her.

She stands, adjusting the lapels on her jacket. "Yes, Your Honor," she says sternly.

"Tiana, you're the defendant?" she asks as she looks at me.

I groan as I come to a stand. "That is correct..." I pause, trying to grasp the ridiculousness of this. "Your Honor," I grumble.

"Mommy? Would you like to start with your opening statement?" she asks.

My brow furrows. "Who in the hell are we doing this for? There's not even a jury," I ask as I gesture around the room with only the six of us in here.

"Overruled. Mommy?" Charlotte says as she looks back at our mom.

My mother sends me a sly side eye. "It's a bench trial, Tiana. Stay on your game," she murmurs to me before she looks to Charlotte with a sweet smile as she rounds her table. "Your Honor, may I approach the bench?" she asks as she gestures to the table Charlotte sits on.

Charlotte looks over the paper briefly before she nods. "You may proceed."

My mother comes to stand at the front of the room, facing the four of us. "What is law if not ethics incarnate?"

I groan again.

Son of a bitch, you've got to be kidding me.

"As lawyers, we take an oath to our clients. That we will proceed in our methods with sincerity and ethics. Let the record show that Ms. Tiana Dawn has breached her oath. Acting without plausible ethics and fraternizing with her client. She was given a duty to provide counsel to her clients, *not* physical comfort."

My mother looks to the rest of us. "My question to you, the court, is why Ms. Dawn should continue to represent her client while keeping her position at the arena? Surely the ethics of such an instance are in question."

I grind the heels of my hands into my eyes, resisting the urge to groan as I listen to this.

There is no reason for any of this. I would rather have written a damn paper at this point. Pressing my hands into the table, I look up at Charlotte with an annoyed tilt of my head.

"Thank you, Mommy," Charlotte says, and my mother nods in thanks before she takes her seat. "Defendant? Your opening statement?"

I roll my eyes as I press myself to a stand and come around the table to stand before the rest of them, pacing as I begin to speak, "There are many things in this life we will find important. Family. Career. Love. Money. We could control the reins for our entire lives. But come upon a fork in the road. Or a branch causes us to find a way around. What do we do when that branch leads us to a utopia? Or when the side of the fork we choose leads to a city of gold? Are we to walk away from the things that find us when we least expect them? The things that give us comfort from the storm, or provides warmth in a place of cold? I am here to prove that I can not only live in my city of gold, but I can find the warmth in the cold as well."

My mother's brow raises as she leans over to my father, whispering something in his ear, and he nods in response.

As I finish my little speech, I quit my pacing, looking to the three in front of me, before I hear a sniffle from behind me, where Charlotte sits.

I turn to see her wiping snot from her nose and eyes as her voice cracks. "You may be seated," she whispers.

My eyes float to my forehead in annoyed disbelief as I walk back to the table to take my seat.

It's silent for a moment as Charlotte looks over her papers. Her eyes narrowing as they slide back and forth along the sheet before she looks up at our mom. "Mommy? Would you like to present your opening argument?"

"Your Honor, I would like to admit Exhibit A into evidence," my mom says as she stands with a few papers from her folder.

"Exhibit A is admitted," Charlotte says.

Our mother comes over, setting papers on my desk before she moves to the front, placing those papers on Charlotte's desk as well.

"Over the past several weeks, there has been talk. Question. About 'the lawyer' and 'the rookie'. Now, I imagine these words are not said merely as rumor. There must be something there for the team to be so up in arms about it," my mother says.

I deadpan as I watch her before I glance down at the papers. They're pictures. Taken through Snapchat from some players to each other that somehow made its way into my parents' possession.

They aren't anything horrific. Merely us walking side by side from the arena, with some random captions.

"Gunnar and Tiana, sitting in a tree. K-I-S-S-I-N-G!"

Real original but whatever.

"My client had seen the two in question on several occasions. As well as some photographs taken by some of the players. Whether it be in proximity or just merely too close for comfort, that would be defined by legal standards."

I stand, gesturing to our mom. "Your Honor, improper character evidence, a few pictures can not confirm the rumor of intimate contact."

"Sustained. Mommy?" Charlotte says as she looks at my mother.

My mother sends a sly look over to me, and I sit back in my seat. "Your Honor, I would like to call Gunnar Hayze to the stand."

My eyes widen, and I look over to Gunnar, who has his arms crossed over his chest and looks as if he's been pulled from a trance. His tongue freezes against his chain in his mouth, with his lips parted as he comes back to the present. His eyes scan for a moment as the chain falls from his lips.

"Proceed," Charlotte says.

I loop my hands over my head, pulling it onto the table with a loud groan as I hear Gunnar stand from his chair.

Gunnar moves around the table to sit in the leather armchair beside Charlotte's table, wiggling and expanding within it to get comfortable. His hands rest on his thighs as he shifts his hips forward, and I hate in this moment that this man is so fucking attractive.

Aside from this entire experience being one of my worst nightmares, it has me realizing that I don't think I could actually represent him in court if he looked like that.

"Sir, will you state and spell your name for the court, please?" Charlotte asks.

Gunnar's brow furrows, and he looks around. "Uh... Gunnar Hayze... Your Honor...?"

Charlotte eyes him, raising her eyebrows as she tilts her head and rolls her hand in a 'go on' gesture.

Gunnar sighs. "G-U-N-N-A-R... H-A-Y-Z-E..."

"Thanks," Charlotte whispers with a smile.

My mother steps forward, gesturing to the pictures beside Charlotte. "Mr. Hayze, do you recognize any of these pictures?"

Gunnar's brow raises, and he sends a look to me before I roll my eyes with a sigh, nodding.

He looks down at the pictures on the table. "I do."

"And what were you doing with Ms. Dawn in these pictures?"

"I walk Tiana out to her car when it's dark out because it's wrong to let a lady walk around in the night by herself."

"Sweet of you," my mother says.

Gunnar smiles at that, though shyly, before he nods.

"Now, were you aware when you originally met Ms. Dawn that she was your legal counsel?"

He pauses, looking at me for a moment before he looks at my mother. "Yes."

"And when you first made contact with Ms. Dawn, was the instance to request legal counsel?"

"No, ma'am," he murmurs as his cheeks turn ruddy.

"Let the record reflect that Gunnar Hayze's initial private contact with Tiana Dawn was not for legal counsel," my mother says as she continues pacing the floor. "Mr. Hayze, were you aware that you could not initiate personal relations with Tiana Dawn?"

Gunnar's brow furrows for a moment, and he searches the floor. "No, ma'am," he says.

My mother stops pacing and looks at him before she turns to her desk and grabs more papers. "Your Honor, I would like to admit Exhibit B into evidence, please," she says.

"Exhibit B is admitted," Charlotte responds.

My mother places the paper on the table beside Charlotte's leg before she hands me another set of papers.

I take a moment to look over them, my eyes roaming the words before I suck my lips into my mouth to keep myself from groaning.

"Mr. Hayze, do you recognize this paper?"

Gunnar looks over it for a moment. "Uhm. Yes, I signed this during my in-processing," he says.

God. Fucking. Damnit.

This is why I like to be there during in-processing. These idiots don't read the goddamn FINE PRINT! It's one thing my mother has always instilled in me with these contracts and legalities.

Always. Read. The. Fine. PRINT!

"And do you see anything on that paper that states 'refrain from forming personal relationships with all legal counsel'?"

I watch as Gunnar's throat bobs.

"Yes..."

"So you either did not read the document in its entirety or you knew and didn't care," my mother says.

"I..." he sighs. "I was a new rookie playing for my favorite team. The last thing I wanted to do was sign papers for something," he grumbles.

"Objection, Your Honor, relevancy," I growl as I come to a stand.

"Overruled. Mommy?" Charlotte says.

I groan in annoyance as I sit back down in my chair, tapping furiously against it as the sound somehow calms some of my anger.

"Do you admit you didn't read the document in its entirety?" my mother asks.

"Yes, ma'am," Gunnar says.

"Mr. Hayze, do you admit that you and Tiana spent a bit more time alone than you should have?" my mother says.

Gunnar is silent for a long moment, trying to decide how to answer the question. "We live beside each other, and we work with each other. I don't think that was something that could have been avoided."

"And what about the trip to Portland? From my understanding, you two were placed together, were you not?"

Gunnar's brow furrows. "Well, yeah, but I didn't set that up. We were placed there because we were the last ones inside, and the lady at the front desk said there were no more rooms available."

"Who is to say you didn't call ahead and make sure that you two would be roomed together?"

"Tiana came on the bus at the last minute. When would I have had time to do that?"

"That's a fair point, Mr. Hayze. So, let's say you didn't plan this. That the two of you were placed together by happenstance. Why didn't you seek a different room with a different player and allow Tiana the space to herself? Surely if you really wanted to leave her alone, you could have."

Gunnar's brow quirks as he watches her, before his eyes flick to me. I give him a small nod, and his gaze returns to her.

"It was the middle of the night. I had just finished unloading all the bags from the bus. Tiana and I were the last ones inside. Tiana was already mad at me... about some other events," he murmurs as he glances away. "So, I wasn't trying to rile her up any more than that situation already was. In all honesty, the thought didn't cross my mind. I was just trying to get us up to the room."

"Mr. Hayze, did you purposely make sure you stayed behind so that you could get that last room with Tiana?"

"No," Gunnar responds. "It was one of our first away games. I wasn't used to the process of it all with this team."

My mother turns to look at him, her arms clasped behind her back as she stands still for a long moment. I can't see her face, considering she's turned away from me. But soon she speaks, "No further questions, Your Honor."

She turns around, narrowing her eyes on me before she goes to sit in her chair at the table.

"Defendant?" Charlotte asks.

I stand, taking a deep breath as I come to the front of the tables. "Mr. Hayze, when you first approached me, do you remember my words at all?"

Gunnar roams his gaze over me for a moment. It heats before I glare at him, and he clears his throat. "You said not to come and bother you unless I am in legal trouble."

"Let the record show, I had informed Mr. Hayze of my duty to the team at the first meeting," I say to the others. "And when you had asked me on a date? What was my response?"

"You had said no... several times," he responds. Though his face shows a hint of embarrassment.

It spears my heart on its point, and I want nothing more than to grip his cheeks and kiss him. However, I can't, so I give him a knowing smile in return.

"At what point did I accept your terms?" I ask.

"You said you would go on one date, and if you didn't like it, I had to leave you alone."

I pace more, watching the way my fuzzy socks track along the floor. "And after the date, what happened?"

"Uhm... You were a bit more inebriated than you expected, and when you went in for a kiss, I rejected it," he says, his voice soft.

"Let the record show, Mr. Hayze rejected my request for physical contact," I say.

As I come back to pace in the other direction, I glance at my mother. She has an... interesting... smirk on her face.

I've never had to be on this side of the "court" with my mother. But there is a reason she owns her firm. I attempt to hold my own, not showing a hint of weakness.

"Mr. Hayze, when Charlotte was absent for the away game to Portland. Where was I put on that trip?" I ask.

"They put you in the room with me," he answers.

"And who set that up?"

I glance at Gunnar, who appears to take more time to answer the question than I expected.

"I honestly am not sure. You were mad at me. Barely even speaking to me. You had to step in for Charlotte, and all I know is that you had to be put in the same room as me," he says thoughtfully.

"And what was my reaction in that instance?" I ask.

"You were... livid. To say the least. I thought you were going to rip the lady's head off when she told you we were put in the same room together."

"Who put you on bag duty that night?"

Gunnar's eyes float to the top of his head, as if trying to remember the events before we were placed in the room together. "Coach Dawn. He said I was the biggest, and the newest, so I got stuck on bitch duty."

My eyes glance at my mother, gauging her reaction. Unfortunately for me, it's as hard as stone.

I take a deep breath. "Did anything happen in the hotel room the first night?"

"Nope. You didn't even talk to me. And I didn't talk to you," he says. But his gaze floats up and down my body for a moment before I widen my eyes at him to stop.

My steps halt against the wood, and I glance at him before glancing at Charlotte.

"No further questions, Your Honor," I say with a small smile.

Gunnar stands, going back to our table, but not without giving a dap to Adrian as he walks past him.

I roll my eyes as I glance at them. "Really?"

"What? He's my friend," Gunnar murmurs as he sits down.

I groan, rubbing the space between my eyes. "Your Honor, I would like to call Richard Dawn to the stand," I ask.

My mother's brow rises. My father's face contorts in surprise at my request, but he waits for Charlotte.

"Proceed," she says with a small nod.

My father stands, coming around to sit in the leather armchair.

"Daddy? Can you state and spell your name for the court?" Charlotte asks.

My dad's brow furrows in confusion as he leans around me to get a better look at my mother. "Tamisha, do I have t-"

"Do. It. Richard," my mother grits through her teeth.

He sighs as he straightens back up in his chair. "R-I-C-H-A-R-D D-A-W-N."

Gunnar raises his hand. "Your Honor? Objection, lying under oath," he says.

I turn to look at him incredulously. "The fuck are you doing?" I whisper.

"What? He spelled his name wrong," Gunnar says with a shrug.

"What the fuck are you on about?" I whisper as I come back to the table to plant my hands against it and level my gaze with him.

Gunnar leans around me to look at Charlotte. "I believe the correct spelling is, B-U-B-B-L-E-S."

I hear a small snicker from my mother, and my eyes float to the top of my head in annoyance as my arms slack at my sides. My head rocks back in defeat to glare at the wooden logs of the ceiling.

"This is Hell. I think this may actually be what hell is. What have I done? I've been good, why? What did I do to deserve this? I don't understand," I murmur in annoyance as I run my hands over my face.

"Charlotte, just keep going. Ignore the goon," I say as I turn around to face my father and Charlotte.

Charlotte's brows raise, and she nods, merely following my directions. "Uhm... Uh... Proceed...? I guess?"

Wow, there is... wow, I may actually lose it.

I take a deep breath, blowing it out with an annoyed groan.

"Your Honor," I grit through my teeth as I begin my pacing again. I move back to my table, opening the small folder and pulling out a sheet of paper. But not before I send a glare at Gunnar for going off book.

He gives me a nervous grin, and my nostrils flare at him in warning before he holds his hands up in surrender.

I glare at him one last time before I turn around to face Charlotte. "Your Honor, I would like to admit Exhibit C into evidence."

"Exhibit C is admitted," Charlotte says.

I nod before I place one sheet on my mom's table, and I see her brow raise before she looks down at it.

Moving to Charlotte, I place the paper on the table beside her. With all my fingertips, I press into it, spinning it around against the surface so it faces my dad. "Richard Dawn, could you tell me what this paper is?"

My dad is silent for a long moment as he looks over it, and I watch as his throat bobs and his brow furrows in annoyance.

"This is the list of the rooms secured for The Stags during the time of the Portland game."

"Right, and I see here that Gunnar and I were placed in the same room."

"That's... correct," he says slowly.

"And how was it I came to end up in Gunnar Hayze's room that night?" I ask.

My dad thinks for a moment, and it looks as if he is choosing his words incredibly carefully.

"We have an agreement with that hotel in particular. First come, first served."

I nod as I listen to him. "And with me being the equipment manager for that night, while also putting Gunnar on bag duty, did it not occur to you what would happen if we were the last ones to secure our rooms?"

"It was not high on the list of things I was concerned about, no," he says.

"No? So, instead of rooming me with you, you left me with the new rookie? Even after hearing the way he gawked at me after the night of the first game?"

My father grits his jaw as he glances at my mother before his eyes come back to me. "You have never liked hockey players," he says through his tightened jaw. "My thought was that if you and Gunnar are to be together in a room, nothing would come of it because of your history."

"Can you tell me why I wasn't able to room with you? I know Charlotte does when she's on away games."

My dad hesitates, glaring at me for a long moment. "Because I got a room with a single king bed," he grumbles.

"I'm sorry?" I say, tempting him to speak louder.

"Because I made sure I secured a room with a single king bed," he says, though a bit louder.

"Let the record show that Mr. Hayze and I were forced to be in proximity together due to Mr. Dawn's negligence," I say as I turn to everyone else.

My mom's brow raises as her arms cross over her chest. I note the nervous jump of her leg under her table, but choose to ignore it. At least externally.

I look to him with a small smile. "Bit of an oversight, don't you think?"

"Your Honor, objection! Relevancy!" my mother calls as she comes to a stand.

"Sustained. Tiana?" Charlotte responds.

"I'm getting there," I grit lowly. I take a deep breath, shifting gears to get to my point. "And when you realized the outcome of your actions, what did you do?" I ask.

He deadpans at me, his jaw ticking. "I had to make sure I hadn't caused something that needed to be undone..." he grits.

A small hush runs over the room, all but Charlotte's low, "Ooooo" at the idea that this may be some sort of juicy gossip.

"Charlotte?!" I groan.

"Sorry!" she says with a wince.

"And Mr. Dawn, why did you think something was going on between Mr. Hayze and me?" I ask.

"You were seen together more often after the game. I would see him run to your office. He'd walk you to your car. And even after some point, you both rode in and out together," he says.

"Surely you knew our circumstances, did you not? You knew that not only did we live in the same complex, we were in fact neighbors. Wouldn't it make sense for us to carpool?" I ask.

His eyes narrow on me. "To an extent, it makes sense. But there was no reason for it to be every day. It wasn't anything that looked friendly. It seemed as if you guys lived together."

"Would you rather my client be rude and aggressive to your daughter? That surely doesn't seem right."

My father stares deadpan at me, not responding.

"What's the matter? Cat got your tongue?" I ask with a grin.

"It just escalated beyond my control to something that was becoming concerning."

"Concerning in what way, Mr. Dawn?" I ask. My hands clasp behind my back as I pace the floor in front of him, waiting for his answer.

"That my daughter, the representative for the team, was dating the brand new rookie. A rising star on the team who shouldn't have been distracted, and a lawyer whose position on this team could have been compromised by such a thing."

My brow raises as I look back at my dad. "Well. That surely didn't stop you from nabbing the king bed and leaving your lawyer with the rookie in Portland," I say with a shrug.

My dad has nothing to say to that.

I grin as I turn to Gunnar and my mom. "Let the record show that Mr. Dawn was in fact aware of the circumstance Mr. Hayze and I were placed in."

"That doesn't mean you should go back on your duties and risk the integrity of the team and your career," my dad says.

I turn around to tilt my head in amusement. "I believe that bird flew when you took the king bed for yourself at the away game in Portland."

He grits and I grin in response.

"No further questions, Your Honor," I say as I go to take my seat at the table.

After my mother questions our father for the cross-examination, she questions Adrian, for what feels like forever. My patience frays, and it seems as if her questions with Adrian go off base. Questioning other aspects of his life. But Charlotte indulges and stops nothing because it is her boyfriend, of course, so it merely happens.

I drone out the noise for long enough before I stand, slapping my hands against the table in annoyance.

I don't know if this is her version of psychological warfare. But I'm *tired.*

"Enough! I don't know what sick games you're playing at, but I'm over this!" I yell as I point at her.

My mom turns to me with a quirk of her brow as she crosses her arms against her chest. The sound of her bracelets hitting one another makes me see red. But she says nothing.

"I'm in love with Gunnar. Gunnar is in love with me. But we *both* love our careers. They mean everything to us. That being said, my solution is to hand him off as a client to a different attorney in the firm. I will still be the legal liaison for the Stags, IN the arena. Not in the firm. He'll no longer be my client; therefore, there would be no conflict of interest if he were to get into trouble. The only thing that needs to be done is for you to approve it and sort out the paperwork for his change of status. Is that what you wanted to hear? Is that the solution we have gone around in circles dancing about!?" I yell. My breath huffs from between my clenched teeth as I glare at her.

But her position stays still, steady. Until a grin rises on her lips and she nods once. "Granted."

My brow furrows in wild confusion, throwing me off guard. "W-... what?" I murmur.

"Granted. I imagine you've already found your replacement that will take over Gunnar?"

I freeze, shell-shocked. The wood of the table under my fingertips is the only thing I can register against the insanity of everything.

I'm almost unable to comprehend how... easy...? That was.

"What... what is the catch?" I ask.

It feels like a trick. Maybe a punishment for speaking out of turn and losing my temper in what would essentially be a trial.

But this isn't a trial.

This is me having to own up to my mistakes and needing to realize how easily things can fall apart in front of me if I'm not careful. And that thought has stuck with me through this entire trial, through this entire situation. Because I shouldn't have fallen for Gunnar. But I did. And I can't take that back.

All I can do is move forward and fix it.

"No catch. You figured it out. Congratulations," my mom says with a smile.

"Why... why didn't you just do this beforehand?" I murmur.

"You grew complacent in your duties. You work for an enormous firm that represents clients all over the world. One that would have its reputation crumble if something like this were to get out. You are the lead attorney's daughter. The daughter of a coach to a team we represent. I had to make an example of you for the others in other sectors. Your case will be used, without names, of course, for training any new hires that take on other teams."

My jaw drops and I gawk at her, my eyes dropping to roam across the floor.

"You, Gunnar, and the attorney of your choosing will meet at my office on Monday. We'll start the paperwork, and you can return to the arena on Tuesday."

My mom walks past me, clapping a hand on my shoulder, and soon my father follows close behind her.

"Boys! Put the furniture back, please! Charlotte will show you where it goes!" My mother calls from down the hall as she ascends the stairs to the west wing of the house.

I hear the tables move around me as I slump into my seat, pulling my hands over my face in a myriad of emotions. A roller coaster that has gone up and down for what feels like weeks... has finally ended.

Shock. Elation. Confusion. Happiness?

All of them swirl around. Mixing in my head like a stew of annoyance. And all I can do is sit in this chair wondering what in the entire fuck just happened.

But... I... I did it. I do not want to do 'it' again. But I did it.

I got Gunnar and my job back.

And it doesn't entirely click until the sound of the tables stops and the piney scent of Gunnar engulfs me as he kneels in front of me. He places his hands on my knees, stroking them slowly.

"You did it, sugar," he whispers.

I don't know if he's keeping his voice low because he's merely watching me react to this. But I appreciate the calm, regardless.

My head lifts from where I'd lost my gaze on the floor, and I meet his eyes. His hand comes up to hold my cheek in his palm, stroking a thumb over the skin.

All of this was horrible. Losing Gunnar for that time, being back in my parents' house and the firm. Just trying to figure the logistics out for the case my mom wanted me to work on, and this one.

Truly a punishment in every sense of the word.

My thoughts come back to the real purpose, though. The one in front of me. The one with the shaggy brown hair and the bright hazel eyes that gaze at me with such pride that my heart threatens to burst.

All of that sucked... more than it needed to.

But this. Him. His safety. His acceptance.

That makes *all* of this worth it.

"I did it," I whisper in response.

CHAPTER THIRTY-EIGHT

GUNNAR

Monday went off without a hitch. My new legal counsel is some squirrely chap with a bad hair-cut. Doesn't matter. I reckon he'll be fine.

What *really* matters is that I have my arm around my girl's shoulders as I walk her down the street. I scheduled a small room for us at the fancy restaurant I decided to take us to.

Even if it was a mock trial that got us back together, I'm treating it as a win for her. And with a win comes a celly. So we're celebrating not only her victory but also us being able to come back together.

Tiana leans into me as we walk, her hands in front of her, where she holds her small clutch. The sound of her heels tap against the sidewalk, while her perfume wraps both of us in its brilliance. I take a peek at the sweet girl under my arm, admiring the way her curls are wound just right. The way this red dress looks wrapped around her body. Tight in all the right places, low cut in the other good ones.

And as if she senses me looking at her, her head rises and her gaze meets mine, where she gives me a sweet, loving smile. I return it, leaning down to press a kiss to her forehead as we continue making our way to the restaurant.

I don't know how much Tiana likes restaurants like this. I know she doesn't exactly like loud noises or people much. But I wanted to treat her for doing so well on the case. I have to admit, it was hotter than I expected it to be to watch her do her actual job.

This whole time, I haven't had the chance to see this thing she's devoted her life to. She sees me do my job all the time. But, I never got to see her in court, but I'm so glad I did.

I got to see her get shit done and that hardass I fell for in the first place. I love a woman who goes for what she wants... And I'm so lucky that Tiana wants *me*.

It's been nice to be seen out and about together, without the threat of our jobs looming. After the initial shock of her win wore off, she needed a long nap. We went to her room in her parents' house and laid in her bed for a long while. She snuggled into me, wrapped in my arms, and slept for as long as she needed.

It was nice to just... be there with her. For her.

She always seems to calm down in my presence. So I let her. I let her have those moments of peace that she's worked so hard for, and I stay there with her for whatever it is she needs. Even if it's space, or silence, or just company.

After she woke up, I helped her move her things back to her apartment. And the past few days since she's returned to the arena, I've been able to kiss her. To touch her in person. No worrying about the door being locked. No worrying about people seeing us holding hands when we walk out to the parking lot.

It's so nice. Much nicer than sneaking around.

Soon, the lights of the restaurant come into view, and as we approach the doors, I lean a hand over her head to hold the door for her.

I chose an expensive steakhouse in downtown Seattle. Considering I know she's simple for the most part. Meat and potatoes. Just as she liked in the glass garden.

I feel bad that it is rather rowdy tonight, but I made sure to get a private table somewhere in the back, where it was quieter. Where I could have a nice meal and a private audience with her.

We move to the podium at the front of the restaurant, telling the hostess my name, and she looks over her tablet before smiling at us.

"Right this way," she says kindly and leads us to the back. I go in front, taking Tiana's hand and moving through the tables as we follow the hostess.

When a rather enormous bloke with fiery red hair pops out from a table we pass and I'm caught entirely off guard. He wears a neat black suit, and he juts his hand out to me in excitement.

"Wow, Gunnar Hayze, I can't believe I get to see you here!" he says.

My brow rises as I'm caught off guard.

I think it's one of the first times I've ever been recognized in public.

"I've been watching all your games since you joined the team. You've done an amazing job!" he says.

His green eyes twinkle in a childlike excitement, and I glance at Tiana. She gives me a small smile and nods.

"Hey, thanks, man. I appreciate that," I say as I grip his outstretched hand.

I feel something in the palm of it, and when I pull my hand back to look at it, it's a business card.

"Dean Enterprises?" I ask as I look over the card, flipping it back and forth.

"I'm a pilot for a massive aircraft manufacturer in the area. If you ever want a jet or a plane to get you somewhere overseas, skip the airports. I can hook you up," he says with a small wink.

My brows jump in surprise, and I shrug. "Thanks, I uh... I appreciate that. Can I get your name?"

"Axel Bridger," he says with another nod.

I look down at his table to see him on his own date. A smaller woman, tanned skin, long brown hair, and brown eyes. She seems nervous as hell, as if she's not able to believe this guy's actions. She also appears to have... something in her ear? Strange, but surely none of my business.

I return my gaze to him and smile. "Thanks, I'll reach out when I get the chance," I say as I nod to him and his date. "Have a good dinner," I whisper.

He nods in goodbye, giving one to Tiana as well, before he sits back at the table, and the hostess continues leading us back. She continues moving us through the tables until we get to a private room. Red curtains seem to be everywhere, and the entire place is dimly lit with only the orange warmth from some candles on the tables.

She pulls a curtain back for us to enter, and there is but a single table with two high-backed chairs and a burgundy tablecloth with two menus standing at attention in the middle.

When we approach the tables, I pull out Tiana's chair. Placing a hand on her lower back for just a single second of contact with her bare skin, I guide her to the chair, letting her sit in it before pushing it in. She scoots with it, placing her clutch on the table before she sets her elbows on it. I lean down, wrapping a hand under her chin and tilting her head back so I can kiss her.

A small noise blends between us, and I feel her hands come up to grab my face, deepening the kiss before I pull away, lingering for a moment before I press a kiss to her forehead. A blush glows across her cheeks as I move to sit down in my chair. When I scoot up to the table, she offers a delicate hand across the surface, and a smile spreads across my face as I take it, turning it over to press a kiss to the top of it. I stroke a thumb over the skin there, gazing back at her.

"I have a surprise for you when we get back to the complex," she says with a shy smile.

My head tilts, and I smile with curiosity. "Oh?" I tease seductively.

She rolls her eyes playfully. "Not that kind of surprise, but I wouldn't be opposed," she says with a small nip to her bottom lip, and her eyes roam heatedly over me.

I have chosen a pressed black suit for tonight. With a black button-up shirt and a red tie in a double Windsor knot, and, of course, a small stag pinned into one lapel.

Her eyes linger on the pin, almost hopefully, before her eyes flick up to me.

"I know you wouldn't, sugar. And I'm looking forward to whatever it is you have in store for me. I'm just glad to have you back on the other side of the wall," I say.

"Me too. I really, *really* missed my apartment. I did not like being back with my parents. Not that they bothered me, but my apartment is my space, and it didn't feel like *my* space at my parents," she says with a sigh. Her finger swirls around the lip of her glass as she watches the liquid within ripple.

"I figured that's why you went straight there after work," I tell her as I take a sip of my wine glass full of water.

"I'm sorry. I know you wanted to hang out, but I needed to recuperate. I'm glad you get to sleep over tonight, though."

I smile at that, though seductively. "Me too," I respond with a grin.

"Is Tucker going to be okay?" she asks, almost nervously.

My head tilts in surprise. "Someone worried about lil Tuck?" I ask with a chuckle.

"Maybe... I don't know! It makes me sad to know he's over there by himself," she says as she pushes out her lower lip.

I smile as I bring a hand up to run my thumb over it. So soft and warm, I can't wait to *really* feel them again.

Fuckin' *everywhere.*

"He'll be fine, sugar. But if it so pleases m'lady, you can come with me to take him to the dog park when we get home," I say.

Her cheeks tint more, her eyes holding a twinkle in them. "I love the way you say that," she whispers.

"Home?" I ask.

She nods. "Yes." Her voice is soft, contemplative. Hopeful and so full of longing that I can taste it on her words.

I smile lovingly. "Me too, baby," I whisper.

Because I know what she means.

A future is what it tastes like. A future with Tiana. With her strength, her heart. With *her.* One day, when home isn't just our apartments next to each other. But a custom-built library. A custom-built garage. A massive bed for us. Rooms for the kids.

All of it. Beside her. *For* her.

This woman, who would have never given me the time of day. Who was so uninterested in my existence. This woman who now wants to be my wife. Hell, who *I* want to be my wife.

My Tiana Dawn.

We spent the dinner talking, enjoying each other's presence, the company of one another. It was nice. Intimate in a way that wasn't overtly sexual.

Sometimes it's fun when you get to pick each other's brains and reconnect. Learn how this person you love thinks, the things that drive their day forward, even on the cold ones. The things that get them out of the cold. The things that make them warm. The small bits and pieces of themselves that make up the bigger picture.

Eventually, we finish dinner, and when we leave, Tiana wants to drive us back to the complex. The entire way, I hold her hand, tracing a thumb over the top of it as I lean my head back against the headrest to relax. I feel the way she weaves along the roads. Until I hear the beep of the entry arm of the garage.

However, the deeper we get into the garage, the more I realize these turns feel different from the way we usually go, and my brows furrow as I open my eyes to see where we are.

Looking around the dark structure, I try to figure out where we're going. She's never come over here before, so I'm a bit more confused as she crawls through the aisles. The cars get sparser the further in we go. Until she stops in front of something covered in a massive tarp. My brow furrows as I try to make sense of it in the dark, and I wonder if this is her surprise.

She puts the car in park and looks at me with a small nervous smile that she bites in her teeth.

"I hope you love it," she says softly as she glances at the tarped thing.

"Sugar, I'd love it if it were a statue made of dirt," I respond before I lean over the gearshift to kiss her.

She leans into it, her hand reaching for mine to grip tightly before she pulls away and takes a deep breath. Looking over the tarped thing one last time, she exits the car.

I follow suit, and watch as she approaches it. She bends over, looking around for something under it.

I see her carefully peel a bungee cord from what sounds like metal, and detaching it from the small metal ring in the tarp. She does the same with a few other bungees and slowly lifts the tarp back.

In the dark, it's hard to tell what it is, but I watch it for a long moment.

Until I realize what it is.

"Pa's truck," I murmur.

It's been completely redone. Brought back to its former glory. Even when I was a kid, it wasn't this nice, and my heart pounds in my chest as I try to make sense of this. Why it's here, why she knows it's here, and why it's... fixed?

I look at Tiana with a small gape to my jaw, and my brow furrowed. She stands beside it nervously, clasping her hands in front of her.

"After you bought me the books, I knew I had to do something for you," she says softly.

Tears well in my eyes as I approach it, tugging on the handle to find it locked. I look to Tiana, who quickly walks back to the Vette to grab what I assume are the keys. She comes back over, her heels tapping against the pavement as she comes near and hands the keys to me. I smile at her and press a kiss to her forehead before I use the keys to open the driver's side door and look inside. Even the interior has been completely reupholstered, and it...

"Baby," I whisper as I turn to her. I lean out of the truck to grab hold of her face, kissing her deeply before I pull away and lean into the truck to turn on the engine.

It roars to life with a sound I've never heard from it before. Like a beast awakening from a long sleep.

My eyes light up as the headlights beam on, shining a light on my girl from where it sits.

My girl, she fixed up my truck... an heirloom I was worried would never see the light of day again. I had no idea she did this. My parents haven't said anything about it, and I know it was kept there after my dad had it towed.

She kept a piece of my family and my heart going.

If I thought I couldn't love her anymore.

I turn off the engine, stuffing the keys in my pocket before I turn and quickly step up to her. Grabbing her hand, I pull her in close, gripping her face and kissing her as if she is my only source of oxygen.

And it feels like she is, because right now, she is the only thing giving me life. The kiss I give her is deep, hard, portraying the way my heart squeezes to near pain in my chest.

This thing she's done not only for me, but for my family. She not only revived this thing the Hayze family and I value so much, but she also gave it a facelift. She made it live another few years. And the reality of that has my soul screaming for her in every way that I can have her.

I pull away, rubbing a thumb over her plump lower lip and looking in her eyes as I breathe softly through the excitement and happiness of it all.

"I need you to get us to your apartment. Now," I murmur to her.

And it's not a request. It's a demand.

I need her every way but loose at this point.

Her lips quirk into a knowing, innocent smile. That one she uses when she pretends as if she doesn't know what's happening next. Where she knows she's tempting me, and I grin back.

Picking her up, she squeals in delight as I throw her over my shoulder and shove her in the passenger seat. A giggle echoes through the garage as I slam the door and damn near sprint to the driver's side to get in.

I throw the car into drive; the tires squealing as I speed like a bat out of hell to the other end of the garage to park. I shut off the car, running back over to grab her out and throw her over my shoulder again.

I don't even take the elevator this time. In my suit and dress shoes, and Tiana on my shoulder, I climb the stairs up to our floor two at a time. And while most would think this would be a workout—and to an extent it is—I am currently being driven by pure horniness, and the fact I get to be inside of my girl.

When I reach our floor, I sprint to her apartment, reaching into my pocket to pull out her keys and unlock the door. When I get in, I kick the door shut behind me and head to her room.

A tall four-poster bed with black posts and bright white sheets sits against the window on the back wall of the room, with a dresser on the wall right when you walk in the door.

I forgo the need to look too closely because I have other matters to attend to. All I really need to know is where the bed is. The rest can wait.

I take massive steps into her room to close the distance between us and the bed, before wrapping my hands around her waist to tug her off my shoulder and throw her onto the bed. She settles against it with a gentle "*oof*", catching herself on her elbows, before she looks up at me with wanton, dark eyes that heat rapidly with desire.

I loosen my tie, pulling it down enough before I unbutton my suit jacket and shrug out of it. It crumples to the floor, and in a soft scrape of fabric and leather, I kick off my dress shoes.

Tiana kicks off her heels and they clatter to the floor below before she moves to get onto her knees, helping me with my pants. As I unbutton each of the buttons on my dress shirt, I feel her delicate fingers against my belt, undoing it with a clink that causes my cock to harden to near pain and my breaths to come quicker.

As her hands work my pants down, she leaves my boxer briefs on, cupping and grinding her hand against my bulge as I work the collar of my shirt up. Her other hand comes up, helping to loosen the tie on my neck even more, enough for it to come undone. When a wicked thought works through my horny little skull.

A grin rises on my face, and I catch the tie before it falls to the ground. Quickly shrugging out of my shirt, it falls off my shoulders to land with the rest of my clothes.

Her hand roams the skin of my chest as the other rubs against my cock and the sensation makes my thoughts flee. I feel like she never gets a chance to touch my skin like this, and I relish in this moment, where it feels as if her touch is like strikes of lightning.

I throw the tie onto the bed, moving my hands to her shoulders and pressing the straps of her dress off. My lips meet hers in a messy, deep kiss, with my tongue gliding and tangling between our mouths as I continue working her dress off her body.

A low groan vibrates our lips as the pressure at my cock increases, my hands working the dress off of her more and more until it's a pool of fabric on the floor.

I palm her tit, pinching and twisting her nipple as I press her deeper onto the bed until she's on her back.

Of course, Tiana knows just what I like and went sans panties tonight. Reaching my other hand down, I stroke my fingers through the wetness pooled there, my groan deepening as I feel her.

I rub against her clit, stroking it, and her hips buck against my hand.

"There you go. My perfect little cumslut. Already begging for my cock," I murmur against her lips.

I feel her nod, and I open my eyes to watch her face. Watch the way she gives in to every touch I give her.

I use the hand on her tit to pull down the band of my boxers, pushing them down my legs until I kick them behind me. With my cock finally free, I grip it, stroking it before running the head through her slit. Her breath catches, a gasp ringing through the room, and I steal it from her.

"There's my pretty girl. Did you miss this?" I tell her.

I press the head into her, feeling that resistance I've come to know and absolutely fucking love. My head falls as I continue to press inch by inch into her. I watch the way her pussy swallows every inch of me, the way her body takes me like she was made just for me.

"I forgot how good you looked wrapped around my cock, baby," I whisper as I lean in to kiss her.

Her legs rest on my hips, pulling me in deeper. "I need all of it, please," she pants against my lips.

"Don't worry, sugar, you'll get all of it," I respond.

I take a few shallow strokes, enjoying the way she grips me. Kissing down her chin, her jaw, I land on her neck to suck and nip the skin, letting her calming beachy scent flow through my veins, through my *blood*. I let the realization sink in that this is really my fucking girl now.

All mine. No sneaking, no secrets, all fucking *mine*.

The heat of her skin against mine is branding, claiming me in its grasp as her arms come around my shoulders, holding me close to her body while I move in and out of her slowly.

Her hips move under me, pulling me in until I'm pressed balls deep into her, and I hold myself there, letting her relax around me. I grin as I twitch my cock inside of her, reminding her how much I fill her.

"Gunnar," she moans as her eyes roll in her head.

"God, you look so fucking beautiful with my cock inside of you," I pant. I bring a hand up, gripping her chin. "You're my pretty girl, aren't you, Titi?"

She nods, her lip caught in her teeth as her eyes clench shut, and she takes deep, steadying breaths as her cunt continues to relax.

"I get this pussy all to my fucking self... I get to fuck you whenever I want," I whisper.

"Fuck... fuck yes," she pants, her body tensing under me as her hips buck and writhe.

My eyes roam over her. The way her tits bounce with every thrust I push into her. The way her stomach bulges when I'm buried balls deep. She's a fucking vision in tanned honey skin.

"Eyes here, baby," I groan as I look back up at her.

Her eyes flutter, trying to focus on my face. They attempt to roll, to close. But I slip my thumb into her mouth, bringing her back to focus. I bring my other hand under her ass, shifting her hips to hit deeper.

Her full lips wrap around it, her moans turning to whimpers as her eyes roll.

"That's it, pretend it's my cock," I pant as I speed up my thrusts. Her tongue swirls around my thumb as I pound deep into her, making her take every inch, just like she asked for.

Her tongue slides and lathes around my thumb, with every fucking movement sending phantom memories to my dick as I pound into her. I take a few more thrusts into her before I pull out, kissing her as I move to come beside her. My hand creeps between her legs to stroke her clit. Her pussy throbs against my fingertips, with the heat of it begging for more from me. Her legs open wide, urging me in, while my other hand comes around her back, deftly searching the bed for the tie.

When I find it, a grin widens on my lips. I move my body

up on the bed, lying back on the pillows, before I whistle for her. I put my hand behind my head, where the tie is in a ball of fabric in my palm and my other hand wrapped around my cock, stroking it while it's still covered in her.

I always love feeling the way my hand slides against me when it's covered in her wetness. It's a level of pleasure you can't get anywhere else. At least in the self-pleasuring department.

She turns around at my whistle, looking at me with lust-hazed confusion.

"Sit on it," I tell her as I nod down at my cock, echoing that second time we had sex in the hotel. But as she comes to sit on me, I shake my head. "Turn around," I say with a grin.

She bites into her lower lip, nodding softly before she turns around, hovering herself above me before slowly pressing me into her. I let out a low groan, holding my cock in place until she's taken enough length to ride me on her own.

I lean up, causing my cock to press deeper into her, and I leave the tie by my side while I hold her waist, stroking the soft skin there. Trailing my hands around her front, I search for her wrists to pull them behind her as I lick and nip at the skin of her neck.

"You're going to be such a good girl for me, aren't you, Titi?" I rasp against her skin.

She nods, moaning as my cock stretches her with every inch she takes.

"Yes... I'll be your good girl," she pants desperately.

"But even good girls need to be restrained, don't they?" I ask.

"Y-yes," she pants.

I reach for the tie, using it to wrap around her wrists and tie her hands behind her back.

"I need you to lift your hips for me, sugar... just enough.

Because I've got some work to do. Can you be a good cumslut and hold still for me?"

She nods, my hips rolling slowly into her, making her head fall back against my shoulder. "Y-Yes, Mr. Hayze," she says breathlessly.

"Remember what I said about calling me that?" I ask with a grin as I press kisses into the soft skin of her neck.

She shakes her head. Even though I know she remembers, she just can't think with every inch of me inside of her.

"It turns me on," I add as I come up to pinch her nipple.

Her moans snake through the room as she grinds her hips and leans back into my body.

I let her back meld into my chest, giving her a moment to take what she wants before I pillage every bit of her.

"That's it, pretty girl. Use me. It's all yours. Take what you need," I pant.

My focus shifts, locking in on where she grinds and pulses around me, my own eyes rolling as I lose myself to her.

I lean back, removing my skin from hers in a reprieve of sorts. As I lay back on the bed, I look at the gorgeous expanse of her deep honey skin. Her plump ass as she grinds and rides me, the way the red silk of my tie contrasts against her skin.

I groan at the sight, bucking up as I grip onto the middle of the tie between her hands.

"Lean forward, sugar," I rasp.

Her upper body tilts, pulling her hands behind her, and her ass lifts. Just enough for me to take control.

And apparently for me to see more of myself enter her.

Not what I was intending, but it is exactly what I wanted.

With one hand gripping the "reins" and the other gripping her hip, I hold her in place to thrust up into her. Her ass ripples as I do, shoving every solid inch into her over and over. Her moans consume the air; needy, breathy, high, low, groans, and whimpers.

She doesn't know how to process the way I take from her, and I like it that way. I like knowing I'm making her so delirious with pleasure that she can't speak, that she has no idea where she even is.

Soon, I lean up, wrapping the hand on her hip around her stomach and pressing myself onto my knees until she's bent over and pressed into the bed.

I take a few smooth strokes into her as her face buries into the mattress.

Holding tight to her hands tied behind her back, I lean over her side to gently kiss her loose, parted lips.

"Are you okay, baby?" I ask softly.

I may love controlling her, but I still want to make sure she's comfortable.

"Y-yes," she pants softly.

"I'm not hurting you, am I?" I ask again. My thrusts slow, just enough for her to catch her breath, and she shakes her head softly.

"If I'm going too rough, I want you to say 'puck', alright, baby? That's the safe word," I whisper as I press more kisses into her lips. My free hand comes to stroke softly against her ass.

"Bit late for that, isn't it?" she jokes breathlessly.

"Well... better late than never," I say with a grin.

I see her eyes roll playfully, and I take the chance while I have it. Leaning up, I swat one of her ass cheeks, gripping hard at the tie, I thrust into her again. Throwing every bit into her as her screams seemingly morph the warm air around us. My groans blend with it, the loss of thought coming along as I give in to her, wrapped around me. The same way she has wrapped herself around my heart and squeezed with every bit of herself.

The thought that one day she'll be my fucking wife. That I'm going to make this incredible woman a mother to my kids.

That pleasurable tangle snakes rapidly up my spine, choking me as it reaches the top, and I come without warning, spilling into her in rigid, hard twitches. My back bows over her, bracing myself against the bed as I take small thrusts into her to fill her as much as I can.

My head falls to her back as I pant just for a few moments before I loosen the tie around her wrists and let her arms fall to her sides. Slowly, I pull my cock from her, watching the way I drip between her thighs. A grin rises against my face as I shove my fingers into her, pushing it all back in.

She lies against the mattress, panting, before I wrap an arm around her waist to haul her against me.

The sweaty press of her skin against mine has my cock hardening in an instant.

Which is good... because she's not done with me.

I kiss her neck, lick softly at it as I press her hair to the side.

"Are you alright, my love?" I ask softly. I stroke a hand over her stomach, feeling the way her breaths move through her.

"Y-yes... why?" she pants softly as her head leans back against my shoulder.

I grind my hardening cock against her back, groaning as I look down at her body that glistens with sweat.

"I want you to use me, sugar. Use me any way you want to get you off," I whisper.

I see her glance at me as she pants, a grin rising on her lips before she moves out of my arms to lie back on the bed.

Her legs open, beckoning me, and I get in between them, awaiting her next instruction. All the while, I appreciate every fucking dip and curve on her, just like I got to the first time I was in her. Except this time, her cunt is plump and aching, dripping with herself and me.

I resist the urge to fist my cock as I hear her voice break through my gawking.

"Rub yourself on my clit," she pants. Her hands come up, pressing her luscious tits together to squeeze and pinch at her nipples.

I watch, positioning the underside of my cock between the lips of her pussy as I grab under her knees. Opening her wide, I slide myself back and forth in our combined releases.

My eyes roll, my groans filling the room as I feel the way I glide so easily against her.

"F-Faster," she moans, her head tilting back as her back bows.

My focus comes back to her, and I watch with rapt curiosity as my glides pick up. She grinds against my cock, using me as her plaything and losing herself to the feeling of me against her.

"T-tits, suck my tits, please," she adds and I comply, leaning down as I thrust to press both of her tits in my hands. Enough to where I can bring both of her nipples into my mouth to bite and lick at.

A groan rumbles from her throat as her hands grip my hair, her hips writhing harder against me, chasing that high.

"Th-the fuck," she moans as her hands grip harder on my hair, her words catching. "The head, use the head."

My brow rises at her request. I love the way she's taking control of me. *Fuck,* I love it.

I let go of one of her tits, keeping one in my mouth as I move my fingers to pinch and mess with the other.

I use my other hand to grip my cock, rubbing it quickly up and down over her clit. She writhes as her moans turn into gasps and I let her tit free from my mouth as I come up to kiss her.

"Come for me, baby. I wanna feel you fall apart," I whisper against her lips, speeding up my movements against her clit.

Her eyes roll, her back arching off the bed. Her hands move to my shoulders, gripping tightly as her eyes come back to mine.

"That's it, baby. Fall apart, come for me," I tell her.

A high-pitched moan rings through the room, and I feel the beginning spasms of her orgasm before I press my cock to her entrance, shoving every inch into her, sliding in and out as slowly as I can to give her something to release around.

I watch her face, the way she looks when she descends into that ocean of bliss. And I dive under with her, holding her there until she's able to come up for air, gasping. I latch onto her mouth, stealing every breath she makes, moving my hips slowly to help her ride through the last waves of it.

"There's a good girl, use me. Take everything you need," I groan against her lips.

Her waves slow, her back going limp as she brings an arm over her face, and her chest heaves in deep breaths. I hold my cock in her, stroking a hand down the center of her chest to help her come down easy.

I grin, leaning down to press soft and assuring kisses into the skin of her chest.

"You did so well, baby. I'm so proud of you," I whisper.

Yeah, for taking my cock. She should know that.

But I don't think she knows the underlying bits and pieces at this moment. She doesn't need to. I just need her to hear those words. She deserves them.

I'm so proud of her for just *being her*. For fighting for what her heart wants. Even if it wasn't for me she fought for, I'm so proud of her. For always chasing the things that make her heart beat. That fuel, that rampant fire she keeps hidden behind that stony facade. The one I brought down brick by brick and replaced behind me when I made it to the other side.

Slowly, she let me in. And I made sure I didn't disturb anything on the way in.

And I knew from the moment I met her she was going to be everything I needed and more. Maybe in the moment, I didn't know she was going to be my wife.

But I know now. With every fiber of my being, with every single beat of my heart, with every single breath I take.

This woman will be my wife.

And I'm so *fucking* proud of her...

I smile down at her as she removes her arm from her eyes. I lean over her, gripping her face in my hands as I press my lips into hers, running a hand over her coiling tresses. Her eyes glow in satisfaction; *she* glows.

"I love you so fucking much, Tiana Dawn."

Her smile is sweet, considering, as her hand strokes through my hair. Her exhausted, satisfied eyes roaming over my face before landing on my eyes.

"I love *you* so fucking much, Gunnar Hayze."

CHAPTER THIRTY-NINE

TIANA

I know when the day has ended. I can feel it. *Smell it.*

And it's always that piney scent that wafts into my office.

Like a peaceful end to my day, that scent has been a calm for me. One I wasn't expecting. One I didn't want to be a calming thing for me in the beginning.

But I fought for it, for this. I fought tooth and nail for it.

And I am so glad I did. Because nothing beats that grin I get to see on Gunnar's face when he presses open my office door, ducking when he enters, with his backpack slung over his shoulders. He rises inside the threshold, smiling at me, waiting for me to finish putting my stuff in my bag. I move slowly, relishing in this routine we've been allowed to exist in. Without consequences and repercussions.

I remember the small beginnings. When I groaned at seeing him here, wondering why this massive goon was in my office. Why was he so infatuated with me? Why was he here?

No one ever was. I didn't realize anyone ever would be. But

it turns out, Gunnar always just wanted... me. Not someone he thought I could be, not an idea of what he wanted. He wanted *me*, in every bit of who I am, just for that.

Because I am *me*.

My boundaries, my light, my dark, my need for space, and my dislike for people and circumstances beyond my control. He took all those pieces of me, held them in his palm, and kept them safe.

He's shown me that I am capable of being loved as I am.

And in return, I showed him love for who he is.

As I place my laptop in my bag and zip it shut, I gesture to it, waiting for him to come in and grab it. But when he steps closer to grab it, his smile is sweet and filled with admiration. As he wraps his hand around the handle of my bag, he leans in, pressing a deep kiss against my lips.

"How was your day, sugar?" he whispers.

I smile. Because of the mundaneness of it all. The sheer care in just those few words. They fill me with love. With a warmth I didn't think I would ever get to experience at the hands of another.

"Better, now that I get to go home with you," I respond.

He smiles, pressing another kiss to my lips before he rises and nods to the door. I come around my desk, getting in front of him to lead him out before I lock my office door behind him.

I get ahead of him, leading the way and swinging my hips a little more as my heels clack against the polished cement of the arena.

I look over my shoulder, seeing the way his gaze heats as he unabashedly watches me.

"You're playing with fire, Titi," he calls to me. His voice deeper and huskier in a sultry warning.

"I'm trying to get burned, Mr. Hayze!" I call over my shoulder as I walk us out to our vehicle.

Today we took the truck. We've been taking it since it got fixed up, and honestly, I've let him drive it. It'd be rude of me to keep the driving all to myself when I spent so much money getting it fixed up.

It's not as smooth a ride as the Vette, the BMW... or Gunnar. But it's Gunnar's, and that's all that really matters to me.

He opens the passenger door for me, helping me into it so I can settle into the seat and relax.

He puts our stuff in the back seat and moves to the driver's side, while I close my eyes, feeling exceptionally tired after a long day.

I hear the door close with a shake of the vehicle, and there's silence for a moment before I feel Gunnar's hand against my cheek.

"Tired, baby?" he asks softly.

There is always a level of concern in that tone when he's worried about my well-being, and it always warms my insides beyond comprehension.

I nod into his hold, nuzzling into it as he strokes my cheek with his thumb.

"Let's get you home," I hear him murmur.

Soon, the world turns black, and the sound of the engine lulls me into a peaceful sleep.

It lulls me so deeply that I wake up in Gunnar's arms on the couch of his apartment. The large window on the back wall shows the darkness of the night, and I groan sleepily as I look around. Gunnar's shirtless and has placed me on top of him, his head leaning back in relaxation as he rests quietly under me.

He moves his head slowly, tilting it as he looks down at me. A warm smile spreads across his lips as his hand comes up, curling one of my ringlets around his finger, and he glances at it before bringing the hand to my cheek. He rubs his thumb against it.

And soon, his eyes land on me, becoming contemplative, considering.

As my head rests against his chest, I feel the way his heart speeds up, the way it beats just a bit harder.

"You're my pretty girl, Tiana," he says softly.

I feel heat creep against my cheeks, and I preen into his touch as his hand moves under my chin, rubbing his thumb over it.

He's silent for a long moment, watching me. "Will you be my wife?" he asks.

My brow furrows as I lean up, looking at him with a tilt of my head. He's silent for a long moment before I let a small laugh go.

"This is a joke, right?" I ask softly, quietly... almost dumbfoundedly.

He leans up, adjusting himself on the end of the couch as he smiles at me. He reaches into the pockets of his sweats, pulling a velvet box from it. Holding it out to me, he flicks it open to reveal a gorgeous diamond engagement ring within.

My hands come over my mouth, my eyes filling with tears as he slides from the couch to the floor, getting on a knee before me.

"Right?" I whisper.

"No joke, sugar," he responds.

Once upon a time, this would have terrified me. Even the prospect of it being a joke would have terrified me. *Men* terrified me. Relationships. *Love.*

But Gunnar. Not only did he show me love, he showed me what a real man should do. The way he cares for me in and out of the bedroom. His devotion, loyalty. His punctuality. His acceptance.

Handsome as sin. Kind as a saint.

There is no better man in this world for me than Gunnar. There is no man who will love me like Gunnar will. Of that, I'm certain.

And I look into his eyes, his determined hazel eyes.

"Tiana Dawn... I knew from the moment I saw you, I needed you. I needed to know who you were. And I found a headstrong woman. One who defended her peace, defended herself, and the things she cared for. I found a soft underbelly, willing to open up her heart and soul to the right person. I found someone so breathtakingly beautiful. So smart, so independent. So unrelenting in her life. So... *her.* So uniquely herself that she didn't care what anyone else thought. And I knew I needed you. Not just now, not just tomorrow. I needed you forever. I wanted that determination in my future. I wanted it in our kids, in our lives. I craved it. And even now, I crave *you.* Addicted to you and everything you are, like a bad drug. And I would overdose on Tiana Dawn again and again if it means I can hold you. If I can see those beautiful curls, hear that beautiful voice, and see that determined spirit guide the day before her..." He shakes his head as he puts himself back on track. "I love you. I love everything about you. I love what life has been with you, and I love what life will be with you."

Tears beat against my eyelids. His words spearing through my soul, wrapping my heart and soul in a gentle, heated caress.

One that dares not let go. Not even a little. And I wouldn't let it.

Not for anything in this world.

"Will you marry me, Tiana Dawn? Will you be my wife?" he asks.

It's almost a whisper. But it's true, it's real.

And a gasp parts my lips.

WHAT'S NEXT
FOR AURORA?
UPCOMING PROJECTS

October **2025:** ***Check or Treat;*** *a Halloween inspired continuation of Gunnar and Tiana's story*

December **2025:** ***Merry Checkmas;*** *a Christmas inspired continuation of Gunnar and Tiana's story*

Spring **2026: AGOLAB 2:** *the second installment in "A Gown of Leather and Bone" dark romantic fantasy series*

Late **Spring/Early Summer 2026:** *TBD Title the fourth installment of Gunnar and Tiana's story*

ACKNOWLEDGMENTS

Holy shit guys.

We fucking made it. Can you believe this shit?

If you're reading this, wow, THANK YOU.

This book has just choked me, beat me, and wrenched the life from my soul. But I had fun.

LMAO RIGHT?

Anyway.

I have to thank you first, the reader.

For reading this chaotic, smut-filled journey of mine. I wanted to write this for fun. I wanted to play around with some character personalities that I've never played with before.

I had a few tropes and methods that I wanted to experiment with in this book. I wanted to write something low stakes, not only for the story, but for myself. So I'm just really taking a lot of low-stakes risks with this book and seeing what happens.

And for you to go on this experiment with me means the world. It's kind of a nonsensical story. But I'm glad you read it and made it this far anyway.

For whatever reason, some of the things I posted on Threads just absolutely exploded beyond anything I thought was possible. You guys seemed to like the disclaimer, and if I did my job properly, hopefully you're reading this now.

Thank you so much for being here, for picking up this

book. For loving it, for hating it, it doesn't matter. Thank you for being here. It means everything to me.

To my friend Ana, thank you for always hyping me up and listening to me yammer on and on and on about this book. You have always been that voice that picks me up when I want so badly to quit. I'm so thankful to have met you, and I appreciate all the help you've given with me on this book. I love you so much, bestie!

To my BETA Readers; AAron, Emma, Gina, Isis and Marissa, thank y'all so much for reading this damn book so many times.

To AAron; she has always done so, so much for my books, and her tenacity to read my work. I can't tell you how appreciative I am of her. She is always so willing to read anything I throw at her. She will have read it ten times over, and she'll say, "I'll take an eleventh." I am absolutely bewildered by it because I go crazy reading my own work so many times. But she's always there to help, and I'm so thankful for her. She's an incredible friend, an incredible hype woman, and I just can not gush enough about her.

To Isis; LMAO BABY I LOVE YOU. I'm so glad you enjoyed the horny bits just as much as I did. You're so funny and I am obsessed with you. I love all your memes and when we get to kiki over stupid movie quotes. Thank you for reading this and obsessing over Gunnar with me. YOU'RE DUH GOAT BB.

To Emma; I've only met you recently, but I'm obsessed with you and the company you keep with me. You are always there and willing to listen to me yap, and I am so thankful for your presence. You are a wonderful friend, and I hope to have you around for a long while because of the energy, the vibes? Immaculate, need it.

To Gina; you were so willing to help and gave such amazing

feedback in such a quick time, and I appreciate your input and help so much! Thank you for taking the time to go through and read this for me and just being here. I appreciate you!

To Marissa; thank you so much for your input on Seattle and for helping me craft something a bit more believable. And for always pushing me when I was struggling on some days. I appreciate your grit and keeping me steady on days where I just don't want to do the things. I'm so glad I met you and I hope I can know you for a long while!

To Jahnè; Thank you so much for your input on some of the more legal/lawyer aspects on this. I don't think I would have been able to do this as well as I could without you and I appreciate your time and effort and I will always hold on to those voice memos because they were so funny and the absolute best. I always love that it's so easy to pick up a conversation with you. You're an amazing human being and you always do so sosososo much work all the time, and I'm so lucky to be your friend. LOVE YOU POOKIE!

I can't thank you guys enough for being here. For helping me, for indulging my chaos and just being here for me.

This book has been an entire ride and I can't believe this book is actually done. I was lowkey worried it never would be.

Thanks for sticking around and I hope you stay for more!

ABOUT THE AUTHOR

While Aurora is merely an alias, the face behind the name has enjoyed writing and reading for as long as she can remember.

An army wife and a lifelong Alaskan, she has spent her life baking, cooking, and reading. Her lifelong passions.

Being an army wife means keeping busy with hobbies, which has resulted in a menagerie of different pastimes.

She has tried her hand at drawing, makeup, reading, weightlifting, CrossFit, cross-stitch, diamond art, video games, content creation (TikTok, YouTube, Twitch), and now being an author. Her motivation changing day by day as she gets struck by whatever idea sucked her in.

When she's not writing, she's spending time with her husband, 2 kids, 3 cats, and 2 dogs.

instagram.com/author.aurorasteinhart
threads.com/@author.aurorasteinhart
tiktok.com/@author_aurora_steinhart

For more updates and sneak
peeks
be sure to scan the QR code
for links to my socials!

ALSO BY AURORA STEINHART

<u>Elevated Ambitions</u>

Book One in

The "Up in the Air" Series

A contemporary billionaire romance

where SHE is the billionaire.

<u>Hunted By Fate</u>

Book One in

"A Gown of Leather and Bone"

A dark, romantic fantasy ft. a succubus general and a human hunter on a mission to save their world from the terrors outside of their wards.